THE GUILT PILL

Also by Saumya Dave

Well-Behaved Indian Women
What a Happy Family

THE GUILT PILL

SAUMYA DAVE

PARK
ROW
BOOKS

PARK
ROW
BOOKS™

Recycling programs
for this product may
not exist in your area.

ISBN-13: 978-0-7783-6834-2
ISBN-13: 978-0-7783-8770-1 (International Trade Paperback Edition)

The Guilt Pill

Park Row Books
22 Adelaide St. West, 41st Floor
Toronto, Ontario M5H 4E3, Canada
ParkRowBooks.com

Printed in U.S.A.

To S&S, my two babies:
one who inspired the story and
one who helped shape it to completion

NBC NEW YORK

Breaking News: CEO of Tech Start-Up Gone Missing

Published July 27, 2019, 3:46 PM EDT

A missing person report was filed earlier this morning with the NYPD for thirty-three-year-old Maya Patel, founder and CEO of the eco-friendly toiletry company Medini. She was last spotted at her home in Tribeca the evening of July 26. According to deputies, she left her keys behind but seems to have taken her cell phone and wallet.

An inside source from Medini reveals that, in recent weeks, Patel has seemed particularly "emotional" and "upset."

"She's definitely been stressed. And to be fair, what founder isn't, right?" the source states. "But nobody thought things were *this* bad for her."

Colleagues were alarmed when Patel missed an important meeting and could not be reached by phone. "It's not like her to just leave without telling anyone," Josh Kaplan, Medini's COO, told *New York News*.

Patel's husband, Dev Mehta, did not respond to a request for comment.

Maya Patel is five foot three with dark brown eyes and was last seen wearing a red pantsuit.

This is an ongoing investigation.

MAY

before

1

MONTHS LATER, THIS IS THE MOMENT Maya returns to when she tries to pinpoint when it all started.

Her quickening heart rate. Her skin stiff from layers of foundation, powder, and blush. The blur of colors surrounding her, from the burnt-orange couch she will be on in seconds, to the buttery-yellow camera lights, to her emerald-green wrap dress—the first real piece of clothing she's put on in weeks.

Carol, one of the production assistants, gently pats Maya on the shoulder. "You're on in ten."

"Great! Let's do this!"

She can feel the sweat pooling at her hairline, threatening to mess up her concealer. She has to get it together. There's too much riding on this.

All around her, people walk with purpose, clutching clipboards and yelling instructions into headphones. It's jarring to be in the real world again, one that isn't primarily made of burp cloths, onesies, and white-noise machines.

Though a part of her relishes the brief respite from her post-baby life, another part wants to immediately take a cab home to her newborn, Shaan. This is the longest she's ever been away from him.

Before she has the chance to go down *that* rabbit hole, Carol approaches her again, a sheepish look on her face. "I gotta tell ya, my sister loves your Instagram! She also works in tech and always sends me your posts. In fact, she sent me one from just this morning and was freaking out that I was going to meet you!"

Carol tilts the phone toward Maya to show her the photo in question, which now has over fifty thousand likes. She posted it just a couple hours ago. In the picture, Maya's wearing a terry cloth robe, one hand on selfie-duty, the other holding a cup of coffee. Shaan is asleep on her chest, his fists tiny and tight like they were in her ultrasounds. The picture's caption: T minus two hours until my Today show interview!

Maya physically restrains herself from cringing at her own post. "That's so nice of her! Please tell your sister she made my day!"

She makes a show of taking her own phone out. "You also just reminded me to turn this off before I go on, so thank you." Just as she's about to put it on airplane mode, it chirps with an incoming text from her best friend, Alaina.

Alaina: So excited for you! We have it recording on the DVR. The kids are bragging about you to everyone.

Maya: Aw, you are the best. Hope I make you all proud.

Alaina: You already have. And don't worry. You'll prove those assholes wrong.

"Five minutes!" Carol announces. "You ready?"

"Ready," Maya lies.

She has no choice but to be ready. It doesn't matter that she's slept six hours in total over the last two days. It doesn't matter that she's wearing mesh underwear, her breasts are sore, and all she wants to do is crawl into bed for a decade. What matters is that the next thirty minutes could help her reclaim some semblance of functionality in her disaster of a life.

On a screen behind the set, Maya watches the commercials airing before her segment: ads for organic tampons, a nontoxic household cleaner, a dietary supplement helping postpartum mothers "bounce back from that baby fat!" and a female deodorant that's somehow supposed to be effective *and* empowering.

A series of products, each geared toward women, with the promise that *this* will be the one to get their lives back on track.

Yes, because nothing says "empowered woman" like female deodorant! Maya thinks to herself. *Also I'm wearing that one right now, and it's not doing shit.*

Carol makes a "go" signal and whispers, "This is it!"

Maya clenches her fists. It's happening. It's *really* happening.

She walks toward the set and tries to ignore the tightening in her stomach. She puts on her best and brightest smile and repeats one of the affirmations from her daily intentions journal: *I can do this.*

Her all-time favorite host, Taylor Rutherford, welcomes Maya onstage, extending a toned arm toward the couch where she'll be sitting.

Great to have you, Taylor mouths.

Great to be here, Maya mouths back. This doesn't feel real. She's done dozens of press interviews, but the *Today* show? That's on a whole different level.

Her eyes nervously shift to the audience, where she finds her favorite person smiling up at her from the first row: Dev. He's wearing the navy blue sweater and gray chinos Maya picked out for him in a boutique during their babymoon in Cape Cod.

Seeing Dev calms her down and makes her feel brave.

I can do this. I can do this. I can do this.

One of the cameramen gives Taylor a thumbs-up and she starts introducing their segment.

"We're continuing with our Women Who Made It Happen series, with a special focus this week on motherhood to celebrate Mother's Day."

She pauses for applause from the audience.

"Our next guest, Maya Patel, is the founder and CEO of her on-the-rise sustainable toiletry company, Medini, which is taking care of your beauty needs *and* the environment. Now, Medini's products are constantly selling out on their website. And as of last year, you can head over to ten Whole Foods stores in New Jersey to check them out for yourselves and buy them in person."

The giant screen behind them plays a reel of one of the shelves in Whole Foods, now occupied by some of Medini's hottest products: bamboo toothbrushes, shampoo bars, toothpaste powder, and wooden combs. This company milestone should fill Maya with pride, but all she feels is a sense of dread.

She nervously glances back at the audience, where concentrated faces are zoned in on the screen behind her. She blinks multiple times, as if waking up from a disorienting nap.

"Ladies and gentlemen, Maya Patel!" Taylor announces, and the room fills with applause and soft cheers.

It's showtime.

Maya flashes a large grin to Taylor, then back toward the crowd.

"We're so thrilled to have you with us here today!" Taylor flips her blond curls over to one shoulder. There's a slight Southern drawl to her voice, even though she's lived in New York City for decades now. Maya wonders if she plays it up for the cameras.

"I couldn't be more excited to be here." Maya briefly puts

her hand over her now deflated belly, a gesture that's become second nature to her since early pregnancy.

"Now, tell me. What's Medini's origin story?"

Maya smiles. "Well, I initially got the idea after years of working in my family's motel, which is also where my brother and I grew up. Between the four of us, we cleaned the rooms, managed the front desk, did the billing, everything. While I was cleaning, I started noticing the shocking number of unused toiletries that piled up after a long day's work, and how even if they were only partially used, we still had to dispose of them. I spent hours upon hours of my free time researching what goes into making more sustainable products. Eventually, I quit my consulting job and transformed this little passion project into a full-fledged business. And the rest is history."

There are other parts of her story, honest parts, that were excised thanks to her publicist, Beth. *Always give them a feel-good story*, Beth first advised her years ago. *It's all about the story for founders. You have to make it inspiring, compelling. And omit anything that deviates from that.* It didn't take long for Maya to learn how to publicly inflate Medini's success just enough so that she wasn't technically lying, but she definitely wasn't telling the whole truth.

And this rule also applied to her upbringing. People want to be moved by her "rags to riches" story, but nobody wants to hear about how she spent her holiday breaks scrubbing toilets and cleaning up other people's vomit.

Taylor claps her hands. "Fantastic products that are good for the environment. What a win!" She then announces that everyone will be going home with a bag of Medini products, and a flurry of cheers passes through the audience.

"You truly are the epitome of the American dream. Your family must be so proud."

Maya lets out a nervous laugh. "My family's the reason any of this is possible. My parents worked so hard so my brother and I could have a better life. Medini is really just a testament to everything they've built."

Taylor leans in closer, prompting Maya to elaborate.

Here goes some revised family history.

She mentions that her parents immigrated from India before she was born, leaving behind everyone and everything they knew. She speaks to their pride in ensuring every guest enjoys their stay, their fulfillment in having something that's truly their own. And she throws in the friendships they've made with other local business owners for good measure.

But wait, there's more! Maya imagines saying to the audience. *Their retirement gets pushed off year after year, they never take time off, and they haven't seen their families back in India for God knows how long. They've missed out on countless weddings, baby showers, Diwali celebrations... The list goes on. Turns out that all that time taking care of other people's families came at the cost of their own. Isn't that so* inspirational*?*

Maya does a double take when Taylor actually responds with "So inspirational." The audience murmurs in agreement.

"And resilient. *So* resilient," Taylor adds.

Resilient. There's that familiar word again.

"Who were, and are, your biggest inspirations as a founder?" Taylor asks.

Maya's face starts to hurt from smiling. "My parents, of course. Aside from them, there are so many female founders I admire for their grit and determination, for the way they created something that wasn't there before. Such as Stephanie Fine of Power Bar or Easel's founder, Diana Plank, or the cofounders of Limitless, Liz Anderson and Anita Johnson."

Maya watches Taylor's expression shift ever so slightly. *Shit.* The final names on that list were not Beth-approved. She should have thought twice before mentioning cofounders who had a falling out.

But Taylor doesn't skip a beat. "Now, with this being our

Mother's Day series, we can't forget to mention that you're a new *mom*!" The screen plays a slideshow of images from Maya's maternity photo shoot. In them, she's wearing a black turtleneck dress and laughing at something off camera, her manicured hand resting delicately on top of her bump. The fifty-year-old German photographer had called her look "Steve Jobs maternity chic." The photographer's assistant even blew a tiny fan so that in every photo, Maya's hair looked like it was caught in a light breeze.

You are a fertile goddess! the photographer had yelled as the camera winked at her again and again. *You are powerful! You are an energetic force!*

Maya didn't feel like any of those things at the time. Not in the slightest.

"Your son is..." Taylor trails off and Maya chimes in with "Four weeks old."

The audience gives a collective *awww* and Taylor claps her hands together. "Oh, I remember those early days. So magical, right?"

Maya strains a smile. "Totally. I've been treasuring every moment."

"Well, that's just wonderful."

Maya feels like she's playing a parody of herself when she hears herself say "It really has been *so* wonderful."

"And isn't your boy just precious?!" Taylor squeals as she gestures behind her to the screen, which now displays a picture of Shaan in a white onesie covered with baby elephants, a matching hat atop his small head. The outfit was a gift from a boutique baby clothing company, alongside a note from the company's founder: *Feel free to share your bundle of joy's pictures and tag us.* Real subtle.

She makes the rookie mistake of staring at the picture of Shaan for a second too long. The sight of his full, pink cheeks and tiny feet makes her breasts twitch.

No, no, no, she commands her body. *Do not fill up with milk.*

Panic seizes her. If she leaks milk through her bra and dress, there's no coming back from that. She can already envision the memes and Twitter threads.

She takes a deep breath as Taylor says something else about the Women Who Made It Happen series. When Maya looks back up at the audience, some people are staring directly at her and smiling. Well, not quite at *her,* but at her glossy, blown-out hair, her bold red lips, her nude pumps. They don't see how little control she has over her body in this moment. In *every* moment.

"And we have your husband with us in the audience!" The camera turns to face the front row. "How proud is he?"

Dev nods enthusiastically from his seat, confirming that he is, in fact, so proud. He flashes the camera a Crest-commercial-worthy grin.

Maya smiles. "He's been so supportive every step of the way. My hope is that young girls and women everywhere can see that with the right people around you, you can fulfill your biggest dreams—personally and professionally!"

Cheers erupt from the audience, and Maya knows that what she just said was perfect PR material. *You're welcome, Beth.*

Taylor stands up, making a sweeping gesture toward Maya. "Maya Patel, everyone!"

The cheers grow louder, the entire audience rising to their feet. Maya reminds herself to keep smiling as she waves goodbye. The cameraman announces a break for commercial and she's directed back to her dressing room. As soon as she takes her phone off airplane mode, it immediately vibrates with a flood of texts and Instagram notifications.

And then she sees it. The name appears in her direct messages like any other.

Maya! I just caught your Today show interview and you were fantastic!

Her heart races, but before reading the rest, she puts her phone away to find Dev.

When she emerges from backstage, Dev runs toward her and kisses her. "You were amazing!"

"I can't believe that just happened," Maya says, still in a daze.

They're interrupted by a group of women who ask to take a selfie with her. As she prepares to flash her brightest smile, Maya exhales her first sigh of relief that morning.

At least it all went smoothly.

At least no one knows the full story.

DAILY TECH PODCAST

KYLE: Welcome to *Daily Tech with Karina & Kyle*, your number-one podcast for anything and everything tech-related. We're going to jump right in. So by now, many of us have heard that Maya Patel is MIA. I've gotta say, we've covered a lot on our show here, but this is something else.

KARINA: Totally. We hope she's okay. I've heard that many new moms daydream about running away. Do you think it's possible she just needed some "me" time?

KYLE: Let's hope so.

KARINA: Now, our listeners know I love an origin story, especially when it involves two of the most renowned #girlbosses in tech. Let's go back to how Maya Patel and Liz Anderson allegedly first met.

KYLE: It was after that *Today* show interview, right? After Maya referenced Anita Johnson as one of her biggest inspirations, no less? You all know we're tired of the female founder takedown pieces, and nobody loves a good comeback story more than me. But c'mon! You can't just casually mention Liz Anderson and Anita Johnson in the same breath anymore.

KARINA: I'm talking about Liz here, *not* Anita. And what you're referring to are rumors, anyway. So many of us have been guilty of being caught up in the *story* instead of the actual work, you know what I mean? You can say what you want about either of them, but *both* women are tech luminaries, like it or not.

KYLE: Yeah, well, my gut says there's much more to the story here.

2

THEY TAKE THE SCENIC ROUTE OUT OF the studio, passing the gold Prometheus statue that overlooks the skating rink where Maya once witnessed three simultaneous marriage proposals.

Dev successfully locates their Uber, and once they're on their way back to their apartment, Maya turns her phone to face him. "You'll never believe who I just heard from."

He peers at the message.

Liz Anderson: Maya! I just caught your *Today* show interview and you were fantastic! It took me back to when I was on the show with a little one at home. My brain was total mush when I tried to speak but you were so eloquent. And thank you for the shout-out.

"Seriously? *The* Liz Anderson?"

"*The* Liz Anderson," Maya confirms. The same Liz Anderson who's been on multiple lists for *Forbes*, raised hundreds of millions in funding, and regularly rubs shoulders with A-list celebrities. (Rumor has it, she's vacationed with Gwyneth Paltrow.) Liz got her start after cofounding a women-focused mood tracking app, Limitless, and has since reemerged on the tech scene with Women Rise, her popular brand of vitamins and supplements for women. According to the company's website, it "helps women become their best selves."

She types back a response before she can second-guess herself:

Maya Patel: That's too kind. Thank you so much! I've been a fan of your work for a long time, so that means a lot coming from you.

"Wow, I knew your segment was going to get amazing reach. It's all over social media!" Dev says, scrolling through Twitter.

"Really?" Maya says, peering over his shoulder to see for herself. "That's great! Tiffany said the marketing team is already seeing a bump in online orders."

Dev playfully elbows her. "See? You're showing the board they had nothing to worry about."

Maya gives him a tentative look. "You really think so?"

"I do. I really do." Dev squeezes her shoulder. "I'm so proud of you, honey."

She leans against him in gratitude and lets out a long, satisfied exhale.

"Who else have you heard from?" Dev asks.

"I'll check in with Beth to see if she's heard anything specific on her end. But so far, cousins, some family back in India, friends, a couple start-ups, and lots of supportive messages from my followers."

Followers.

Maya never wanted to be an influencer, or anything close to one.

But when she first tried to get funding for Medini, multiple investors hinted that they liked founders whose "online platform reflected their brand's values." Translation: they like *female* founders who are pretty and have a strong online presence. Social media has never been Maya's forte, and she'd spend *hours* obsessing over what content customers would want to see on their feed. She tried professional headshots, press interviews, aesthetic photos of her products, and even sweet date nights with Dev. None of that made a difference, and her follower count remained low.

But then she uploaded *the* picture. The one of her in a teal maternity dress and spiked heels, one hand clutching her silver laptop, the other on her baby bump. The caption: This is what a CEO and founder looks like. The hashtag: #pregnantandpowerful.

She posted the picture in response to the countless unsolicited comments she received from investors, family members, and even complete strangers when she announced her pregnancy. *Does this mean you're stepping down from Medini?* they'd ask. *Are you sure you've really thought this through? How are you going to manage everything?*

The post was reshared hundreds of thousands of times, and the hashtag alone was used almost a million times that week. Maya knew there was an untapped audience there. So she began documenting everything from her prenatal appointments to her third-trimester insomnia to a day in the life of a pregnant CEO. At first she felt silly. She didn't belong in this "momfluencer" space ruled by white, fit, affluent women. But within weeks of the post going viral, *Shape* magazine interviewed Maya about her skin care regimen. A rental clothing company asked if she'd model their spring line. Podcast interviewers started flooding her inbox. And before she could blink, she had amassed *one million* followers. One million eyes on her at all times. No pressure.

Her phone buzzes again.

Liz Anderson: Having a newborn while running a company is no joke. So, I understand if you're too busy, but I'm around if you ever want to chat or grab a coffee. Your segment really resonated with me and I'm always looking to meet other female founders!

Maya first types out REALLY?! then catches herself.

Maya Patel: That would be great! I'd love to hear more. How's next week?

Liz Anderson: Next week works! I'll send over some dates and times. And in the meantime, I'm going to boost some of Medini's products on WOMEN RISE's socials. Sometimes a little goes a long way! Oh and feel free to bring your little one to our coffee date. Finding child care is such a hassle.

Maya Patel: Wow. Thank you—for the social boost and inviting Shaan along. That's so kind of you.

"We're meeting for coffee next week!" Maya exclaims.

Dev kisses her forehead. "Of course you are. I'm not surprised in the slightest that she reached out to *you*. You're amazing."

She leans back in her seat, basking in the excitement of the day. It's the first time in weeks she's felt like herself, her *old* self. Nobody told her becoming a mother would make her feel like a foreigner in her own body. In her own life. It's refreshing to know that the pre-baby Maya is still in there somewhere.

When the Uber pulls up to their apartment building, they thank the driver and take quick, purposeful steps into the sun-filled lobby.

Tom, their doorman, tips his black hat and smiles at them. "Great job this morning, Maya!"

"Thanks, Tom!" She feels like she's walking on air.

"When do you have to be back in the office?" she asks Dev once they're in the elevator. "I'll take a quick power nap if you can watch Shaan. My mom has to be at the motel in an hour and she's already running late." Maya craves sleep so often that sometimes the word *sleep* drums in her mind until it loses all its meaning. *Sleep. Sleep. Sleep.*

Dev looks down at his watch. "I'm so sorry, I wish I could stay but I moved my meetings to the late morning so I could make it to your interview." He gives her a brief run-through of his day ahead at Bainbridge, a real estate investment fund that was started by people who graduated several years before him at Wharton. Typically, Maya loves hearing about his work. But right now, all she can do is focus on the dread growing inside of her. Dread for the hours ahead, nonstop loops of pumping, feeding, changing, cleaning. Dread for not knowing when she will next leave their apartment.

"My last meeting's at six. It's technically a working dinner, so it's in our conference room, and we're just ordering Joe's and beer. I'll work from home after that." A glint of concern passes over Dev's clean-shaven face as he adds "I promise I'll be home as soon I can."

"I know you will." She tries to ignore the tiny seed of resentment burrowing its way into her as she pictures her well-rested husband sitting in a grandiose conference room, laughing with his colleagues over pizza and alcohol. Why doesn't *his* life have to change that much?

Dev wraps his arms tightly around her as they linger in their apartment doorway. She sinks into him, relishing the feel of his light sweater on her cheek, his signature woodsy scent. When they step inside, her eyes fall on the blown-up *New Yorker* cover hanging on the wall next to them. In it, a man and woman are dancing on a subway platform. Dev surprised Maya with it on her birthday two years ago, alongside a card dedicated to his "New York love."

He gently pulls back from the embrace and kicks off his dark blue loafers. "I've been worried about you. You seem so tense lately. Stressed."

Maya pauses from slipping out of her heels—even though

they're practically suffocating her feet by now—and raises an eyebrow at him. "Is that something new?"

"This seems…different. Even Alaina texted me this morning to make sure you get some rest."

"She did?"

Dev nods. "We're all just trying to look out for you, honey. Can't you take a breather from work today? You're still on maternity leave, you know. Plus, I think the *Today* show interview sends a *pretty* clear reminder to your investors that you're more than capable of running the company, even when you're not physically at the office. So they can get the hell over themselves." He pauses. "I really think we need to look into getting you some help around here."

"I know you think we need that," she starts. "But it's com—"

"Damn it! Not again." His eyes lower to an alert on his phone. He types at a rapid speed, pauses, then types again.

A minute passes before he looks back up from his phone, rubbing that spot on his forehead where his headaches always originate. "Sorry, honey. What were you saying?"

"Nothing." She puts on her brightest smile. "You should get going. I'm totally fine. I'm going to see if our little guy will actually latch to my boob later today. It was a disaster before I left this morning. But my mom said she gave him a bottle about an hour ago."

Maya hasn't been able to breastfeed Shaan for more than a minute at a time since birth. He either instantly starts screaming or falls right asleep. A lactation consultant urged her to "keep working at it, and if you absolutely *must*, give him pumped milk through a bottle." She said the last part with a shred of horror. Like it was just one step above her baby starving.

Dev gently rubs her shoulder. "I'm sure he will."

"We can do it!" she says, raising a fist in the air. The gesture is meant to look triumphant but falls flat. "And after that, I'll just do a quick check-in with the office to see how everything's going…"

Dev laughs, shaking his head. "So, no, you're not taking it easy today."

She flashes him a sheepish smile. "Come on. You know I can't just *not* work."

Work is all Maya's known. She used to refer to Medini as her baby until she got pregnant. Then it just got too confusing. And weird.

As much as she appreciates Dev's concern, he doesn't really understand what it's like to create everything you have on your own, to not be handed anything because of connections or money. To feel like it could all be taken away from you with a single wrong move.

Josh, Medini's COO, reassured her he'd hold down the fort while she was on maternity leave. But she's not about to leave Medini in *someone else's* hands, even if just for a few months. She can't. Not when the odds have been stacked against her from the start.

At a shareholder meeting last year, some of her investors argued that women with children "lose their hunger for work." One of them even had the audacity to say he's reluctant to help kick-start female-founded companies because "who knows when they'll just have kids?" They all love the optics of funding female CEOs, but very few of them can—or want to—deal with what that actually looks like.

For this exact reason, Maya spent the first five months of her pregnancy wearing loose-fitting tops and shoving saltines into her mouth whenever she felt a wave of nausea at the office. She so desperately tried to keep her pregnancy a secret, especially from her male colleagues and the board. It took her fainting in the middle of a company meeting for her to finally break the news.

Dev squeezes her hand in support as they walk toward the nursery, but just when her mind starts quieting down, she feels that telltale twitch in her breast.

"Damn it. I have to pump. Now."

TRENDING:

#MAYAPATEL

@CarrieCodes: Anyone hear more about what's going on with Medini and its founder? Sounds out of control! [Posted July 28, 2019, 7:03 PM]

@TheElusiveTechBro: I worry that a lot of these older millennial founders don't understand how to really run a business. That being said, I liked what I knew of Patel. She seemed to lack the entitlement and privilege of some of the other founders who get so much fucking money from investors.

@CarrieCodes: Yeah and now she's just gone? How does that even happen?

@GOMITECH: I agree re: Patel. Can I say what I know some of us are thinking? What about her husband? Isn't it always the husband?

@TheElusiveTechBro: He seemed normal (I think?). But why isn't he saying more? It's weird.

@GOMITECH: A friend of mine who lives in their building said she saw them arguing in the lobby multiple times. And could sometimes hear them arguing from her apartment unit above them.

@CarrieCodes: I was going to say he gives off douchey trust fund vibes! I know someone who went to college with him, and Maya was supposedly an emotional wreck at their wedding for unclear reasons. AND he works at a place known for hiring toxic (and mediocre) men.

@Biohack23: I've been following this Maya Patel story and holy shit. I saw her out late one night with another man, just last month. They looked super cozy, if you know what I mean.

@CarrieCodes: DAAAAAAAMN. Do you think she was having an affair?

@TheElusiveTechBro: Tbh, I think all these influencer people are lying on their public profiles. She sadly wouldn't be the first.

@CarrieCodes: This unfortunately does provide more context since her disappearance.

@TheElusiveTechBro: Those couples who always post happy photos online are always trying to hide something IMO. I always thought they looked like they were trying too hard.

@Biohack23: Also super weird he hasn't posted or shared anything about her missing...

@GOMITECH: That's what I'm saying. Look more at the husband.

3

MAYA RUNS TOWARD HER BREAST PUMP with the fervor of a firewoman called to an emergency. Sure enough, milk has leaked through her bra and dress. She hooks up the portable pump and slips it through the slits in her nursing bra.

She had pumped when she woke up this morning and then again before the interview, seconds before Carol summoned her to the set. There's no need for a clock anymore. Her time is now measured by the last time she pumped.

Once she hears the whirring sound of the suction cups on her chest, Maya and Dev tiptoe back toward Shaan's nursery, where they find her mother cradling Shaan. She's singing the same Gujarati lullaby she'd sing to Maya and her younger brother, Tarun, when they were little. When Mom hears them enter, she looks up, gently holding a finger to her lips.

The two of them quietly retreat to the kitchen, and Mom joins them a minute later. "He's sleeping, so if it's alright, I think I'll head back to the motel. Your father's already called me twice. There's some medical convention in Metuchen and some of the overflow guests are staying with us. You know that man gets flustered if he has to make small talk with strangers for more than five minutes." Mom laughs, rolling her eyes.

Complaining about Dad is so natural to her that she doesn't even realize she's doing it. Unless they were around people other than close family, of course, in which case Mom would put on her best smile and act like her marriage was perfect. Growing up, Maya was never sure which version of her parents' marriage she'd get. Would it be the polite, socially acceptable one? The resentful, arguing one? Or the withdrawn, disdainful one?

"Mom, is everything okay with the motel? I feel like you and Dad are busier than normal."

"Everything is fine, beta," Mom says. "It's just been business as usual!"

Maya frowns, not buying it. As she stands beside her mother in the fluorescent kitchen light, she's struck by how much older Mom looks. She notes the deeper creases around her mouth and the multiple streaks of gray peeking out of her low bun.

Even at their age, her parents still work nonstop. The reminder floods her with guilt. She sends them grocery deliveries every two weeks and has tried to take them on vacations, but they always refuse. When she was younger and saw them working every weekend and holiday, she made promises to her future self. Someday, she'd be in the position to really take care of them. Someday, she would make sure they could finally take a step back.

"Are *you* okay, beta?" Mom asks, taking her out of her thoughts.

"Of course. Why wouldn't I be?" She's annoyed by the defensiveness in her own voice.

"If you say so… I'll be back as soon as I can." Mom wraps

her into a warm hug and Maya catches a whiff of her signature scent—Vatika coconut oil. Mom buys it on a monthly basis from Patel Brothers.

"By the way," Mom says, "your interview was just wonderful. I can't believe my baby was on television talking about *her* baby! And the way you answered those questions in front of all of those people… I just couldn't believe it!" Tears start to form in the corners of her eyes. "I'm so proud of you, beta. And I honestly don't know how you did it. All of it."

Because of you, Mom. She thinks back to the countless hours Mom spent helping her file, package, and mail Medini's first thousand orders. For a full year, the motel lobby's back office was stuffed to the brim with products, packaging tape, and envelopes.

Maya shrugs nonchalantly. "It was really nothing. And it went by so fast. Honestly, I don't know how you took care of two kids and ran the motel with Dad."

"Oh, we all make it work somehow, right?" Mom waves the compliment away as she collects her large black purse.

It takes everything in Maya not to beg her to stay. She can't imagine going the entire day without her. Ever since having a baby, she's felt like a child and adult at the same time, equal parts raw and responsible.

But she needs to get a grip. Women all over have been raising babies since the beginning of time. There's no reason she shouldn't be able to do the same.

And despite Mom's constant offers to come back to help, she knows she can never fully take her up on them. Unlike the other mothers Maya saw growing up, the ones who baked cookies and took their kids for long days in the park and asked details about school every evening, Mom constantly struggled to keep her head above water. Between managing the motel, working other part-time jobs, and caring for the array of family members who were always in town, there was no time or energy left over for nurturing. Maya knew the best thing she could do for her mother back then was to stay out of her way. When she found out she was pregnant with Shaan, she made a silent promise to the life growing inside of her: *You will never feel that way.*

Mom points to a stack of Pyrex containers. "I made you some methi dhebra and oat muffins. Sejal Masi said fenugreek and oat are the best ways to increase your milk supply."

Maya suppresses a groan. Mom takes every chance she can get to call out the postpartum rituals in India.

"I doubt that actually works."

"It does. You just have to try!" Mom proclaims, as if she's announcing a scientific breakthrough. "And you need to rest. The first month after the baby is born is for a mother to heal, not *work*."

"If you want to change, I'll wash these bottles and your pump parts before I head to the office," Dev offers.

"Isn't that nice? Dev, beta, you really are so *thoughtful*." Mom beams, her eyes lovingly shifting back and forth between Dev and Maya.

Every time he parents, Dev's lauded for being an exceptional father and husband. One time, an auntie literally clapped when she heard he changed diapers. The guy should go ahead and get his acceptance speech ready.

Maya retreats to the bedroom to take out her portable pump from her nursing bra. But despite the pain in her breasts and her now ruined dress, she barely produced any milk. Great.

She closes the door and scans her body in the full-length mirror. Loose skin lingers around her middle. Deep purple stretch marks hug her hips. Her nipples are now disc-shaped and darker than they used to be. As she stares at her reflection, she feels more like a stranger in her own body than she did when she was a pimply, wide-hipped adolescent.

Dev's voice is hushed on the other side of the door, and

Maya picks up on the words *stressed* and *distant*. Mom, who can't whisper if her life depended on it, blurts out, "To be fair, she's always been this way."

Maya shuffles to the bathroom with a new pair of mesh underwear, lining it with an ice-cold witch hazel pad. She then changes into her signature postpartum ensemble: flannel pants and a pajama top with a flap she can lift to breastfeed at a moment's notice. A far cry from her previous rotation of jewel-toned dresses, pencil skirts, blazers, and coordinated athleisure.

When she emerges from the bathroom, Dev's standing in front of the mirror, a concentrated look on his face as he fixes his collar. "Your mom just headed out," he says when he hears her come in. "I'll take over everything when I'm back so you get a break. And I'll be home as soon as I can." He does a final check in the mirror and walks over to give her a kiss goodbye. Dev's midway through shutting the bedroom door behind him when he pauses and turns back around. "I'm hoping I can give you a *real* break soon," he says.

Bainbridge technically has a paternity leave policy, though no one has actually used it. When Dev first told his coworkers about Maya's pregnancy, there was an obligatory round of grunted *congratulations*. Immediately after Dev's announcement, one of the guys chimed in to share how he'd started traveling *more* for work after his wife had a baby. So he could get some "time away."

Dev submitted his paternity leave request five months ago, but it's been "pending" ever since.

"I know it wasn't easy for you to request that," Maya says quietly, avoiding his gaze.

How could you ask your husband to take time off work when he's the breadwinner? And what kind of mother doesn't want to spend as much time as possible with her newborn?

She shakes the thoughts away.

"I had to," Dev says, shrugging nonchalantly. "It's about time the firm does what they've promised in writing. I just wish I could have taken it sooner."

He presses his lips against hers again for a full two seconds, and Maya feels an overwhelming rush of gratitude, thinking back to the promise Dev made to her two years into their relationship, when they started seriously thinking about the future. They were sitting in a cozy booth at their favorite wine bar in the West Village, when out of the blue, he ceremoniously clinked their glasses together. *If we decide to have a kid, I'll do everything I can to support you and your career,* Dev told her. Up until then, Maya knew she could see herself marrying him, but a part of her was still intimidated by the world he came from. A world of private schools, first-class tickets, fundraisers. She didn't see herself fitting in there. But from that night on, her doubts vanished. Dev has only been unwavering in his support of her and her dreams. When she'd finally made the leap and quit her consulting job, he took her out to a celebratory dinner, where they brainstormed a game plan to get Medini off the ground. And months later, when both their families expressed doubt over Maya's entrepreneurial endeavor, Dev defended her wholeheartedly. He always believed in her. And he had a way of making sure everyone else did, too.

Maya settles onto the light gray sectional in the living room from where she can see the large ficus in its round gold pot, the floor-to-ceiling bookshelf next to the television, and the navy blue ottoman with the gold tray (which has now become home to Shaan's burp cloths). Boxes of Pampers and wet wipes line the narrow space between the kitchen and living room. They had to put two of their side chairs in storage to make room for Shaan's play mat. Maybe Maya should've taken a note from Alaina's book and left the city when she got pregnant to find a bigger, more livable space for their growing family. She envisions herself in a quaint suburb somewhere, pushing

Shaan's stroller down clean sidewalks and rolling up to drive-throughs in an SUV.

A gnawing fatigue settles over her limbs. She's about to turn her phone off for a quick nap when, like clockwork, the screen lights up with a message from Tiffany, Medini's chief of staff.

Tiffany: I'm SO sorry to bother you but have you checked your email by any chance?

Maya: Not in the last hour. What's up?

This might have been the longest stretch of time she's gone without checking her inbox. She was that person who was sending emails as she went into labor. And she had no intention of stopping, either, until the anesthesiologist came to put in her epidural and said, "Um, you might want to stop working now."

Tiffany: If you have time, maybe you should take a look? It's about the Whole Foods deal. Just wanted to give you a heads-up.

The Whole Foods deal?

A year and a half ago, Maya spoke with Arteen Steinberg, the buyer for Whole Foods's mid-Atlantic region, at a conference. (Technically, she'd ambushed him during a lunch break to pitch Medini to him.) To her shock, he relented and agreed to look at some samples. By the end of the week, Arteen was in Maya's inbox with pages of feedback on Medini's branding and packaging. She took every single one of his suggestions. By that point, she'd already been rejected by so many tech accelerators and local retailers. Once Medini was on Arteen's radar, Maya had to do everything she could to keep it there.

Fast-forward six months and Medini's products got placement in two separate Whole Foods stores in New Jersey. For the first couple months, Mom, Dad, Tarun, Dev, and Maya would split up in teams to go to both stores and make sure Medini's shampoo bars and bamboo toothbrushes were actually selling.

Arteen and Maya were set to meet a couple months from now so he could give her a report on sales trends. In their few brief exchanges since, he'd never once implied he wanted to meet sooner.

Her heart races as she opens her slim silver laptop. At the top of her inbox, she sees the subject line: *Whole Foods Rockville Meeting.* She skims through the email at record speed and immediately calls Tiffany.

"What the fuck?" Maya hears her pulse thudding in her ears.

"I'm assuming you saw it?" Tiffany's typically calm and collected voice is shaky.

"Whole Foods wants to meet with us again? Why? When did this happen?"

"They reached out after your interview. You really made an impact!" Maya hears Tiffany's voice strain to soften the blow. Even in the heat of the moment, she can't help but feel gratitude for her.

"I was under the impression Arteen and his team would check back in after we got the sales report. Do you think something bad happened? Maybe we haven't been selling?"

"I highly doubt they'd want to meet if it was bad news?" Tiffany reasons. "But the thing is, the retail team can only meet next week, so Josh is going to book a flight to Rockville."

"*Josh* is meeting with Steinberg?" She must have misheard her. "No. Absolutely not. I'm the one who's been in contact with him, so I'm the one he needs to speak with."

Maya is the only person who is constantly researching reasons why Medini's products stand out in the market. Only she can best articulate why her company deserves to not only occupy but *keep* occupying valuable shelf space. She needs to be the one to oversee this conversation, otherwise... *Nope, not going there right now.*

"It's kind of weird nobody alerted you to this, right?"

"Yeah, it is," Maya replies through gritted teeth.

"Maybe nobody wanted to bother you?"

Oh, please, she thinks. *No one's had a problem bothering me plenty of other times since my leave. And I actually* want *to be bothered by this!*

Maya opens three more tabs on her internet browser, typing away furiously. "I'm sure Josh and the team are doing what they think is best. But I'll take care of this. Thank you for letting me know. Can you do me a big favor and look up flights to Rockville for next week?" She reopens her inbox to alert the team. At this point in her career, Maya's learned how to write emails that strike the perfect balance of assertive and personable.

In other words, she's perfected the art of the exclamation point.

"But...you're still..." Tiffany stammers on the phone. "Your baby." Right on cue, Shaan's high-pitched cries ring out from the other room.

"Tiffany, hold on a sec," Maya says before racing toward the nursery. Once she reaches Shaan's bassinet, his crying has escalated to full-out screaming.

"Shh, it's okay, sweetie, it's okay," she soothes, hoisting him up. Despite her swaying movements, his shrieks get louder. Each one grating more and more on her nerves.

And then the smell of poop fills the room.

Terrific.

Maya rushes to the changing table, removes his swaddle, unbuttons his onesie, and removes the dirty diaper. Almost there. She turns around for a split second to grab the baby wipes, and when she shifts her attention back to Shaan, she watches helplessly as yellow liquid pools under his onesie, slowly trickling off the table.

"No!" she cries.

In that moment, all she can think of is a video her ob-gyn recommended she watch during pregnancy. In it, a baby sleeps throughout the entirety of its diaper change, the faint noise of a piano instrumental playing in the background. Fuck that video. Did a man make that?

She changes his diaper, then his onesie, and throws the soiled one into the tiny white hamper.

Please calm down, she pleads. *Please, Shaan. Please.*

It doesn't matter that she got a full-ride scholarship to Columbia University, that she worked part-time shifts all throughout college, or that she built a successful company from the ground up. This six-pound bundle always knows how to humble Maya and make her feel as incompetent as ever.

She cradles Shaan in her arms and picks her phone back up.

"Sorry about that," Maya says, out of breath. She feels like she just finished a spin class. Not a diaper change.

"No worries!"

Through the phone, Maya hears Tiffany clacking away at her computer, along with the faint sounds of light conversation and the office printer coming to life.

What she'd give to be there instead.

"Oh! By the way, your interview was amazing!" Tiffany chirps. "We can't stop watching it. And our online orders are through the roof! The team hasn't stopped refreshing the numbers all day. You're really putting them to work. In a good way, obviously."

"Really? That's so great to hear," Maya says, balancing her phone between her shoulder and ear, a squirming Shaan on her hip, as she carefully steps over baby toys scattered across the floor. She manages to make it all the way to Shaan's DockATot—aka a so-called baby necessity that's essentially just a glorified oversize pillow—wondering if she could have been a trapeze artist in another life. Once she plops down on the couch, Shaan in the DockATot beside her, she lets out a self-satisfied sigh.

Then Maya remembers Tiffany's still on the line. "So, let me know once you've found some flight options and I'll touch base with Josh?"

"Sounds good. And seriously, great job today!"

They hang up and Maya spends the next half hour replying to unread direct messages. When she looks up from her phone, Shaan's sound asleep.

She snaps a photo of him and hits Post, with the caption Loving mornings with this little guy.

The comments immediately trickle in.

How precious!

Love his outfit!

What a cutie!

Maya puts her phone down and opens her written agenda to make a game plan for the rest of the day.

She can handle this.

All of it.

NEW YORK CITY POLICE DEPARTMENT

OFFICER RICHARDSON: Has Maya ever struggled with her mood? Or had periods of her life when she was more emotional?

MIRA PATEL: Never. She was always happy. Okay, maybe not happy. But easy. We never had to worry about her! Yes, she works a lot. Puts so much pressure on herself. And of course, having a new baby can be a big change and she was worried about his weight and feeding and all that. But she's been managing very well. And she always has a smile on her face.

OFFICER RICHARDSON: So, you're saying that big transitions or life changes tend to go smoothly for her?

ANAND PATEL: Perfectly. She's always been a star student, top performer at work. Sure, she was stressed about the board meeting and then everything that happened after was... Well, anyway, my point is, up until then she's never really struggled.

TARUN PATEL: Actually, that's not true.

ANAND PATEL: What do you mean?

TARUN PATEL: Maya had panic attacks in college.

MIRA PATEL: What are you talking about? No, she didn't! She was com—

OFFICER RICHARDSON: Ma'am, could you please let your son finish?

TARUN PATEL: They started her freshman year at Columbia.

I think it was hard for her to be around people with so much... well, so much everything. She felt like she wasn't good enough.

ANAND PATEL: Why is this the first time we're hearing about this?

MIRA PATEL: When did this start, Tarun?

TARUN PATEL: She didn't want you and Dad to worry... The first time it happened was after a group dinner. All her new friends were always wanting to try out these fancy restaurants, try every appetizer on the menu, get the most expensive entrée. Maya said they wouldn't even flinch when the check landed in front of them afterward. But the thought of paying the bill was dreadful for her. She told me she'd silently pray nobody would suggest they all just "split it," because she always made sure to order the cheapest appetizer as her meal. Sorry, am I saying too much?

OFFICER RICHARDSON: Is there anything else you can share from her childhood that could tell us more about her mental state?

ANAND PATEL: I don't think—

TARUN PATEL: She was always stressed about our parents' fighting. And our financial situation.

MIRA PATEL: Maya wasn't stressed about us!

TARUN PATEL: Mom, are you kidding? She's been stressed about you since we were kids.

OFFICER RICHARDSON: Some of her loved ones mentioned things became more difficult for her after having a baby…

MIRA PATEL: She's definitely been harder on herself than usual. But these changes can be difficult for anyone. And our community—where we come from—doesn't discuss things like this openly… Being a mother is only supposed to be happy and instinctual, and it's your duty as a woman.

OFFICER RICHARDSON: So, what I'm hearing is, it's possible she was struggling with things and didn't feel comfortable sharing them with anyone?

MIRA PATEL: I want to say no but now I'm not sure. I'm not really sure about anything anymore. Would you excuse me for a second?

4

BY THE TIME MAYA MAKES IT TO THE entrance of Brookfield Place to meet Liz for coffee, she's running twenty minutes late.

It didn't matter that she timed Shaan's morning routine down to the second, that she'd laid her outfit out the night before, or that they'd picked a café *two freaking blocks* from Maya's apartment—at Liz's suggestion—so that she and Shaan could have some added "buffer time."

None of this mattered, because it took Maya five minutes, not the usual thirty seconds, to orient the straps on the baby carrier. And it took her fifteen minutes, not the usual five, to put her screaming, resistant newborn into said carrier. Just as Maya checked her watch and let out a sigh of relief because they'd actually be on time, Shaan's self-induced motion sickness from all his twisting and turning made him vomit all over himself and his carrier. And Maya.

So now, as Maya pushes the stroller past a group of women

sporting Lululemon attire and sipping on green juice, all she can do is pray that her oversize Medini sweatshirt and tattered leggings give off an effortless-athleisure-chic look, and not a woman-in-need-of-basic-grooming vibe. But based on their darting, not-so-subtly judgmental looks, suffice it to say she's the latter.

She spots Liz in a trendy, flattering denim jumpsuit, sitting at a round table overlooking the water. Her wavy bleach-blond hair falls effortlessly around her ears, accentuating her gold hoop earrings, and her perfectly manicured hands are cupping a steaming cappuccino. Aside from a light pink matte lipstick, she's not even wearing any makeup.

The first thing Maya wants to say to her is *How in the world can you be as busy as you are and still find the time to look this good?*

"Maya! I'm so glad you made it!" Liz says when she notices her. Maya prepares to go in for a handshake, but Liz immediately pulls her close for a hug.

"Liz, I'm so sorry we're—"

"Nope, no apologies necessary. In fact, according to 'mom time'—" she pauses to fake a look at her blush-pink Apple Watch "—you're actually early." She winks and her eyes fall to the stroller. "And look at this little guy!" She bends down and grins at Shaan in his adorable pale green onesie and matching socks.

Thanks to Botox, a disciplined skin regimen, genetics, or all of the above, there are no wrinkles around Liz's eyes when she smiles.

"Thanks for being so understanding *and* setting this up. I can't tell you how pleasantly surprised I was to see your name in my inbox. I'm such a big fan." Maya lets out a nervous laugh.

Liz waves her hand away. "Oh, please. Look who's talking!"

Maya's face flushes. Did Liz just compliment *her*?

Liz peers at her intently, and Maya instinctively covers her mouth with her hand.

"Is there something on my face? In my teeth? I had to rush out of the apartment—"

"You know, you have great skin," Liz interrupts. "And no under-eye circles. I should hate you."

"Oh!" Maya's hand rushes back to her face in surprise. "You'll have to thank my concealer for that." She laughs nervously.

"Which one do you use? I was sent this vegan, organic one from a new start-up but it isn't doing shit." Liz rummages through her purse and pulls out a compact mirror and the concealer in question, then dabs some on her chin. She rolls her eyes. "See? Nothing."

Maya laughs. "Oh, come on, your skin's perfect. If that's what you use, then sign me up!" Liz asks her again which one she uses, and Maya feels a prick of excitement when Liz jots it down in her notes app.

She shifts her eyes to Shaan to see him fidgeting in his stroller. "I'm keeping my fingers crossed this little guy lets us chat since it's almost time for his nap." She starts wheeling his stroller back and forth from where she's sitting.

"Oh yeah?" Liz looks down at her watch. "Why don't we walk and talk? My kids always fell asleep in their strollers at that age."

Maya's eyes light up in relief. "Actually, that would be great."

"Wait, you know this thing can go completely flat, right?" Liz reaches toward a latch on the back of Shaan's stroller.

"It can?" Maya watches in disbelief as Liz pulls on the latch and Shaan's seat becomes horizontal.

"Yep! Might also help him fall asleep faster."

"I can't believe I didn't know that. You're a lifesaver."

As they walk in step along the waterfront, they discuss anything and everything, ranging from Liz's kids, who are soon off to summer camp (*and thank God for that!*), to Women Rise's upcoming line of sleep supplements (*I'll send you free samples*), to Medini's Whole Foods test buy (*fingers crossed!*).

Maya can't remember the last time she had such an easy rapport with someone outside of her close circle.

"So…how *have* you been?" Liz asks once they reach a vista point overlooking the Hudson River.

Maya laughs. "Didn't we just dish that all out?" She gestures behind them to signal their walk. When she turns back around, Liz is raising a perfectly groomed eyebrow.

Her first thought is *I wonder if she waxes or threads.*

Her second is that Liz is looking at her the same way Alaina does whenever Maya is in her people-pleasing mode—which is basically all the time. It's a look that says *cut the bullshit.*

Maya lets out a relenting sigh. "Okay, you win. Honestly, I'm *exhausted.*" She brings Shaan's stroller to a stop and pauses a moment to take in her surroundings. The boats dotting the water, the New Jersey skyline in the distance, the nannies pushing UPPAbaby strollers, the high school students who are clearly playing hooky, the couple cuddling on a park bench. She breathes in the fresh air and feels a rare semblance of peace.

"Of course you are," Liz says in validation, gently touching her arm. "You're the only person who can do the things you're doing. That's the twisted irony, right? You're the only person who can be the mother of your child *and* you're the only person who can run Medini. You can't just be substituted in either role."

"Exactly! I've been trying to explain that to my husband and my best friend, but they…" Maya's voice trails off.

Liz nods her head through the silence in understanding. "They don't get it."

Maya nods. "They really don't. They try."

"I'm sure. But nobody can really get it unless they're in our exact shoes. And in their defense, it's not easy to be. The system's set up so that being a mom has to seem like this exhausting, self-sacrificing *feat*, making women feel like they're in constant limbo between their jobs and kids and relationships and, frankly, everything."

It could be the steady doses of stress and sleep deprivation, but Maya legitimately considers the possibility that Liz is her fairy godmother, a figment of her imagination. She can't remember the last time she openly aired out her grievances and was met with so much compassion and shared empathy. This is a woman who gets it, gets *her*.

At the break in conversation, Maya tiptoes to the front of the stroller, where—*oh my God*—her baby boy is sound asleep. She turns to Liz in amazement and stretches her arms toward the sky, mouthing *Hallelujah!* Liz joins in her dramatics.

They move to settle down at a table by the water, the whirring sounds of helicopters buzzing in the distance.

They sit in comfortable silence for a while, until Liz says, "You should know that when I saw you on the *Today* show, I felt like I was watching a version of my younger self. When I was first 'coming onto the scene,' I was way more confident and self-assured…before I started to get weighed down by everyone's opinions of me." She looks out toward the water, lost in thought.

When Liz turns back to her, she has a smirk on her face. "*So*, how'd it feel? I mean Taylor. Fucking. Rutherford!"

Maya's face lights up. Liz's energy is infectious. "It felt good. No, it felt *great*," she corrects.

"I bet it did. And your answers were all perfect—inspiring and concise. Speaking of…" Liz trails off, then says, "I've been in this space for a long time. I know there were things you weren't saying on the segment. Things you're still not saying now."

Maya tries to ignore the tightening in her stomach, the solid ball of dread that seems to get heavier with each passing day. She's been terrified to speak these thoughts out loud to *anyone*, let alone to a woman she's idolized for so long. But when she looks up, Liz's expression is only curious and warm. There's not the slightest hint of judgment in her eyes.

Maya didn't expect to feel so at ease. With Liz, specifically, but also in general. She's so used to always being "on" in some way, ensuring she's likable and palatable enough for everyone around her, that she forgets how much relief she feels when she's just allowed to be *Maya.*

She takes a deep breath in. "Umm..." She chews on her lip, fighting to keep the tears at bay. "Things have been...challenging."

"Of course they have. How could they not be?" Liz reaches her arm across the table to squeeze Maya's hand. "It was like that for me, too."

"It was?" Maya wipes at the corners of her eyes and bites down hard on her tongue, a trick Mom taught her when she was younger so she wouldn't cry in public. "Because honestly, I feel like I'm out of my depth here. Sometimes I worry I'm not cut out for all...this." She gently nods in the direction of the stroller. "I don't know. Ever since I went on maternity leave, I just feel like I'm always letting someone down. If I'm at the office, I'm away from Shaan. If I'm at home, I'm away from the office. I just feel constantly torn between 'work Maya' and 'mom Maya,' and it's starting to feel more and more impossible to be both people at once. I feel so out of the loop at my own company, and breastfeeding isn't working, and all the doctors say..." Maya trails off.

The tears grow heavier behind her eyes as she feels the guilt that's been burrowing inside of her for weeks. Her still-sore postpartum body that flinches at Dev's touch every night they crawl into bed. Shaan's tiny face looking up at her when she tries—and fails—to get him to latch. The number of unanswered calls, texts, emails, FaceTimes collecting on her phone.

Liz reaches for her hand again. "Hey, you're not alone. The guilt women are so susceptible to feeling, especially on maternity leave...it's not something I'd wish on my worst enemy.

And if I could help *one* woman avoid that bullshit rabbit hole…" Liz pauses and looks back out onto the Hudson River. "I don't know. If I could take that away for just one other woman… all the pain I felt when *I* was going through it will have been worth it."

Now Maya's the one reaching for Liz's hand. "You said something just then…*the bullshit rabbit hole of guilt.* That's exactly it. You just put what I've felt for weeks into words. It's the guilt that's the most debilitating, and sometimes I just have this negative thought spiral running through my mind on a loop. *You don't love your baby enough. You're a bad mother. And a bad founder.*" She shakes her head. "Is that what being a mother is? Feeling guilty 24/7?"

Liz's expression shifts. "Well, yes…and no. But there are *some* things that can help with that."

I swear to God, if Liz tells me to meditate, I'm jumping into the river right now.

"Okay…like what? Trust me, I've tried *all* the mom hacks." Maya pauses. "Alright, well, maybe not that one you showed me earlier," she says, gesturing to Shaan's stroller. "But I've got the bouncer, the white-noise machine, the burp cloths—the *nice* ones, even. None of that shit makes a difference."

"I agree with you. Those things won't change much." Liz's face remains unreadable. She does a quick look behind her shoulder and leans in close. "This *has* to stay between us."

Maya nods, sitting up straighter in her seat.

"Years ago, I was trying to figure out which types of supplements to sell through Women Rise. I dug back through a lot of my old pharmacology research when I was doing my dissertation. And I came across something interesting. A lot of the products out there are treating symptoms but not getting to the root, emotional causes of why so many women feel overwhelmed and depleted. So I started thinking of a product that could change that."

"So you designed something new for your supplements line?" Maya asks.

Liz shakes her head no. "This is not your typical supplement. At least not the kind you're thinking of. There's no simpler way to say this, so I'll just come out with it. I've developed a supplement that can get rid of...guilt. Female guilt."

Maya smooths her hair out of her face. *Maybe I'm more sleep-deprived than I thought. Maybe Liz really is a figment of my imagination.*

"I'm sorry, I'm not following... A supplement that gets rid of guilt? As in, *guilt* guilt? Like, the feeling?" When Liz doesn't respond right away, Maya lets out another nervous laugh. "I can't tell if you're messing with me."

"Maya, I know how bizarre this sounds. But trust me when I say this has come from years of asking women what they need more of, what would make their lives seem more manageable. When I was devising Women Rise's next product line, I realized that in all of my interviews with women—women like you—the one thing they kept bringing up was guilt. How without it, they would say *no* more, they'd ask their partners to step up for once, they'd set boundaries with in-laws, with employers. Moral of the story, they'd give fewer fucks. More than a few of them said they daydreamed about getting mildly injured so they could be in a hospital bed for a few days, just so *they'd* feel taken care of for once. Can you believe that?"

"Honestly...yeah, I can." *I've had that thought myself.* "And it's horrible," Maya quickly adds. "But how can something just—*poof*—get rid of guilt? I mean, that's impossible, right?"

"But it's *not*," Liz says, her eyes lighting up. "I've finally figured out how to suppress the female body's internal guilt response. I had learned a long time ago in pharmacy school that there are specific parts of the brain that become activated when we feel guilty. And my work with an incredible panel of neurobiologists has taught me that we have a 'doing' part of our brains and a 'feelings' part. Now I could bore you with the nitty-gritty—prefrontal cortex, limbic system, all that fun stuff—but basically, I've created something that prevents some of those guilt-fueled activations in the 'feelings' part. We started trial runs all over and have only heard rave reviews. In fact, I just heard back from some clients out in Silicon Valley—two moms—and they said this has been life-changing."

"And it's okay to just tinker with a human emotion like that?"

"I know this can sound extreme at first. But when you really break it down, it's no different than some widely used supplements or medications that are already out there. They either enhance or suppress what our bodies are already doing. Take melatonin, for example. It's a natural hormone your brain already produces in response to darkness. Melatonin supplements just give you an external boost of it. On the other hand, SSRIs like Prozac or Zoloft just stop our neurons from reabsorbing serotonin. We have parts of our brains that get activated when we feel guilt. My pill suppresses that activation so it's not as… you know, overwhelming. And guess what happens? Women are finally able to shift their focus to what needs to get done. It's amazing what we can accomplish without guilt dragging us down."

Maya chews on her bottom lip, considering. "But…don't we feel guilt for a reason?"

"Why do you think doctors prescribe antianxiety medications? Your body and brain aren't always on your side, Maya. Not every human emotion is necessarily healthy, especially in such large doses like you've been experiencing with guilt. Not to mention, a lot of the guilt women feel is socially constructed."

Liz lets out a deep exhale. "Let me ask you this. Are there moments where you don't even recognize your own life? When it feels like your husband can just go out the door without a second thought, because he knows, deep down, everything will be taken care of by the time he gets back? Taken care of by *you*?"

Maya's silence answers her question.

"Are there times when you've been so hyperaware of other people's comfort levels that you compromise your own? Have there been instances when you've wanted to accept help from others, but just can't bring yourself to do so, because you don't want to bother *them*?"

Maya mentally checkmarks empty boxes in her mind, running through the past week, the past month. Her entire life.

"Well, it doesn't have to be that way," Liz says to segue. "And I'm not saying this is some magic wand that's going to just *poof*—" she winks at Maya when she says this "—make everything all better. You'd be amazed by how much easier life becomes when you're no longer bogged down by guilt. I mean, how do you think I've gotten as far as I have?"

Now she's listening.

What Maya would give to have her shit together like Liz does—in her job, her marriage, her social life, motherhood. She closes her eyes to picture that life for herself.

"Maya, some people have advantages because of the color of their skin or the family they're born into. And other people, they have to take their chances when they're handed to them. I'm handing this to you." She reaches into her bag and holds up a small, translucent brown glass vial, filled to the brim with hot-pink pills.

"If you think these might come in handy, be sure not to take more than one a day. The effects last six to eight hours and there's a potential for minimal side effects—stomachache, nausea, headache—but nothing major. And once your body gets used to these—" she shakes the bottle in her hand for emphasis "—they should resolve quickly. And they don't pass into breast milk, in case you were wondering."

Maya's eyes are entranced by the little pink pills as they sparkle in the light, knocking into one another until they settle at the bottom of the vial.

Liz looks down at her watch. "Oh jeez, I'm running late to a meeting. I just had too much fun chatting with you! Let's keep in touch, yeah? I know we've just properly met and all, but I'm here for you. Seriously."

Maya smiles. "Thank you, Liz. That means more than you know."

"Oh! I almost forgot." Liz nudges the bottle across the table. "Here, you can have this. Obviously, this goes without saying, but I never want to pressure you into using something you're not comfortable with. So feel free to think on it, or don't! As you wish. Anyway, I just thought you might be interested."

They part ways, and as Maya's pushing Shaan's stroller back to Brookfield Place, all she can hear is the sound of the pills rattling around in her bag.

THE CUT

Can Parasocial Relationships Be Dangerous?

By Amanda Friedman
Published July 30, 2019, 8:45 AM EDT

Parasocial relationships, or one-sided relationships where someone emotionally invests in another person who doesn't know they exist, can be complicated. Many have debated whether they're unhealthy, or even toxic.

But is it possible that a parasocial relationship can also be downright dangerous?

The recent disappearance of Maya Patel, CEO and founder of Medini, new mother, and popular Instagrammer, has raised questions about how well we truly know the people we follow online. Patel's Instagram page highlights snapshots of her life, whether it's at home with her infant and husband, out with friends at social events, or at work conferences, celebrating victories for Medini. Patel frequently features products that have helped her along the way, ranging from an organic breastfeeding pillow to a vegan leather diaper bag. All of which, she's pointed out, are products from female-founded companies. Many of Patel's fans have turned to her because of her relatability and inspiring nature. "I finally see someone who looks like me in this space," one follower commented on Patel's most recent post. "If only I'd had a role model like you when I was younger."

However, recent speculation concerning Patel's disappearance indicates marital tension, mismanagement and toxicity at her company, and her personal struggles with early motherhood. Is it possible that the cracks in her carefully curated facade have finally caught up to Patel? Does anyone even know who the *real* Maya Patel is?

"Social media may trick us into believing we know people

far more than we do. But regardless, we would all benefit by giving people, even the ones we admire, space," notes Dr. Teresa Cavanaugh, a licensed psychologist and *New York Times* bestselling author of *Exploring Parasocial Relationships*.

It's important for all of us to remember that even when we *think* we know someone online, we never really do. After all, it's who they are off-screen that ultimately matters.

@MillennialMama: Yeah, no shit people didn't know Maya Patel. I was so into her pregnancy and boss woman content and now feel pretty duped.

@TheNewMaryOliver: Another influencer faking it. So original.

@Rebecca_Martin: I went to high school with her. She was really nice. A little aloof but honestly a good person who never created any drama.

@Chad_NewYork: I don't know... I heard she was an intense boss. Maybe got tired of keeping up her good girl act?

5

THE PLANE RIDE TO ROCKVILLE FEELS like a day at the spa. Maya gets to recline her seat, sip on a cup of coffee that's still hot, and watch an entire episode of *Sex and the City* uninterrupted. All she's packed is a gray weekender bag. No stroller, no burp cloths, no backup onesies, no car seat.

This is bliss.

Maya adjusts her AirPods and focuses on the show. In it, Carrie is upset about Aidan's boxes blocking one of her bathroom doors. Maya lets herself get lost in their steady back-and-forth argument, the way it ends with Carrie at a Starbucks with her laptop.

But when she unlocks her phone screen to an image of Shaan, a prickly sensation covers her body. The pit in her stomach grows heavier as she hands her empty coffee cup to a flight attendant walking by.

She's so far away from him. What if Shaan's crying in distress because he has no idea where she is? And what if Mom doesn't know the best way to soothe him?

And while we're at it, what kind of mother feels so relieved to be apart from her newborn baby? What do you think it says about you, Maya, that you feel more like yourself right now—alone—than you do with your own family?

She starts feeling claustrophobic and can't concentrate on the episode in front of her. She sits in her thoughts for what feels like a lifetime, until they finally land.

She can't get off the plane fast enough. Once she's in an Uber, she checks Shaan's diaper-and-bottle log and immediately texts her mom.

Maya: How's everything going? Can you send me a picture or video whenever you get a chance?

There's no response until she pulls up to the hotel.

Mom: He's been a little slow with his feeding.

Above the text, Mom's sent a picture of Shaan, and even though he's smiling in it, she knows he's been crying. His face is red, and she can make out a fresh tear at the corner of his eyelid. The guilt expands upward, becoming a solid weight on her chest.

Get back to him now.

She starts looking up return flights to New York City. She can't do this. Josh will have to handle it after all.

"Sir?" Maya says to the driver. "I need to go back to the airport."

She changes her trip so it takes her back to the airport. If there isn't traffic, she'll be able to catch the last flight back to New York. She pictures Shaan's face lighting up when he sees her walk through the front door.

And then her chest cramps. *Kill me now.*

Maya hoists her pumping bag onto the seat and removes the Spectra pump, then attaches the suction cups to her chest. After twenty minutes of sitting there, her bottles are only one ounce full. How is that possible? The moms in her Facebook group are always posting photos of their freezer stash. She hasn't even made enough to fill a shelf on her fridge.

Her phone buzzes with a text.

Tiffany: Just heard from Arteen's team. The meeting needs to be moved up.

Maya: To when?

Tiffany: Now.

Maya: WHAT?!

Maya quickly puts all her pump parts back in the bag, paralyzed with indecision. If she goes to the meeting, that means more time away from Shaan. She won't be able to catch the earlier flight back home. But if she doesn't meet with Arteen, she'll be flaking on the most important sales conversation Medini has ever had. And if he has bad news about Medini's products in the stores, she should be the one to convince him to give them another chance.

Her grip is white-knuckled on her bag. Despite the adrenaline cascading through her body, she's frozen. A pressure builds on her chest. Her breath becomes quicker. Is she having a panic attack?

And then she hears it—a faint echo of Liz's voice: *You're the only one who can be there for your baby* and *run your company. Nobody else really gets it. It doesn't have to be this way.*

She opens her black crossbody bag and removes the little

brown glass bottle. And before she can talk herself out of it, she swallows one hot-pink pill.

Instantly, her heart rate palpably slows down, the way it does after a yoga class. Her thoughts decelerate. A warmth trickles into her limbs as she walks with purpose toward her laptop bag.

Maya feels the same way she did when she got transition glasses in middle school. Like she's seeing everything clearly for the first time. And she knows exactly what she needs to do.

She throws a printed copy of her slides, her laptop, and a tiny makeup pouch into her bag. "I'm sorry," she calls to the driver. "We'll actually have to go back to the hotel."

"You made it! It's so good to see you!" Josh extends his arms out to her for a hug. He's switched out his staple hoodie-and-joggers combo for an off-white button-down and beige slacks.

"It's so good to see you, too," Maya says, actually meaning it. She can feel her mood lift by the second as they enter the conference room. She refrains from asking Josh how bad things must be going for Arteen to call an impromptu meeting.

Maya first met Josh at a networking event five years ago. From the second they met, she could tell he was COO material, from his charismatic demeanor to his in-depth market knowledge. At that point in time, he had just launched an incredibly popular boxed-salad restaurant chain. As the son of an investor and spoken-word poet, Josh knew exactly how to command the room and influence people. *He could have been a politician in another life*, Maya remembers thinking at the time.

She was pleasantly surprised to discover the parts of Josh that could only emerge as they worked closely together—especially while sharing a box of greasy Two Bros pizza after hours at the office. Late into the night, the sounds of the city growing quiet all around them, Maya came to learn that Josh has three sisters he speaks to weekly on the phone (and sometimes serves as a faux therapist for), his ex-fiancé left him for his best friend, he receives exclusively literary fiction from his Book of the Month subscription, and he feels an existential crisis whenever he attends a comedy show (he used to do stand-up during and after college, and often wonders about what could have been).

As Maya really got to know Josh, she remembers feeling ashamed that she'd initially dismissed him as just another "tech bro," when clearly there was so much more to him.

The Whole Foods meeting starts right on time. Maya sits at the head of the table, Josh on her right. Three sales reps from the Whole Foods team sit between her and Arteen, who's at the opposite end of the table.

But where her nerves should be, Maya feels only a burst of conviction. The fog that's clouded her thoughts for the past six weeks has miraculously cleared.

"I know Josh and I are here to hear from you." She motions to the Whole Foods reps. "But before that, I thought I'd share a strategy I made over the past week. If things aren't going as predicted with our products, I've got an updated marketing plan that we can put into motion immediately."

The presentation flies by in a blur, and when she's done, she's buzzing with passion and enthusiasm.

But when she looks at her audience, she sees Arteen staring at the final slide for what feels like several minutes. Arteen, a self-identified stoic, has one of those unreadable faces with his pin-straight brows and relaxed shoulders. The expression he's wearing in this very moment could be interpreted as boredom, anger, annoyance, or satisfaction. There was no way of knowing.

Finally, Arteen clears his throat. "Well, that was really *something*," he says, clasping his hands. "I've gotta say, Maya, I'm very impressed. I've been impressed since the beginning. And the people in this room know it takes a lot for me to ever say that." He looks around the room and his sales reps laugh along with him, proving his point. "I originally wanted us to meet because Medini's products are doing so well that we should expand to more stores—"

"They *are*?" Maya interrupts, unable to contain her excitement.

Arteen nods. "And now, after seeing your plan, I say we think even bigger…" He pauses, letting his words sink in. "Let's expand Medini to be in sixty of our stores."

"Sixty?" Maya asks as Josh echoes the same. "Really?"

Arteen nods. "To be honest, I was already contemplating this based off the sales in Jersey alone. But after all that?" He motions toward the screen. "It's clearly the obvious next step."

The following morning on her return flight, and then again in the Uber from the airport, reality starts to sink in. She just won over Whole Foods. She single-handedly transformed Medini's trajectory.

In the back seat of the car, Maya picks up the crossbody bag on the seat beside her. She opens it and takes out the brown bottle, watching the hot-pink pills glitter like tiny jewels. And for a moment, she envisions a life with the guilt pill. A life that's lighter and freer and clearer.

She shakes her head, bringing herself down to earth, and shoves the bottle back into her bag under a pile of crumpled receipts. She can't take some unreleased medication she knows nothing about. No, Maya Patel is never reckless. She's an eldest daughter. A CEO. A mother.

She's being silly. As soon as she's home, she'll toss out the bottle and its contents.

It was all a placebo anyway.

TECH SCENE

Interview with Medini COO Josh Kaplan

By Katie Higgins

Published July 31, 2019, 10:33 AM EDT

TECH SCENE: Was the company having more problems than people were led to believe?

JOSH KAPLAN: I can't presume to know what people were led to believe.

TECH SCENE: You released statements about how much money you were raising, your retail partnership with Whole Foods, among other things. The public perception was that Medini was thriving.

JOSH KAPLAN: All of those things are true. It's also a company's job to keep people excited about the products and to speak openly about our successes.

TECH SCENE: And your CEO, Maya Patel, how was she through all of this? There are rumors about office conflicts, mismanaged leadership, and both overt and covert signs that she was experiencing sexism and racism.

JOSH KAPLAN: Maya was clearly struggling more than any of us realized. She has always had a lot on her shoulders, and I don't know, maybe the pressure became too much.

TECH SCENE: How would you describe your relationship?

JOSH KAPLAN: Honestly, we worked really well together. She was brilliant.

TECH SCENE: Was?

JOSH KAPLAN: Sorry, *is*. I don't know why I said it like that. It's just that, I don't know, it's like she turned into a different person over the past weeks.

TECH SCENE: Have you heard from her since she went missing?

JOSH KAPLAN: I have not.

6

"DOES THIS WORK FOR YOU? WE CAN go somewhere else if you want." Liz motions around the inside of Bluestone Lane. She's straightened her blond hair since Maya last saw her and she's wearing a flowy blue-and-white dress that's been dubbed a "nap dress." It certainly doesn't look like Maya's loungewear, that's for sure.

"This is perfect." Maya pushes the giant stroller toward a table near the entrance. If Shaan starts crying, she can rush out of here and be home in five minutes.

"I almost suggested we go somewhere for mimosas but didn't want you to worry about your pumping schedule and..." Liz keeps speaking, but all Maya can focus on is the giant plant directly behind her. The more she stares at it, the more it seems to move.

"You okay?"

"Oh. Yeah." She forces a smile. "Just tired. This little guy kept me up all night."

Liz gives her a soft smile. "Let's get you a coffee and some food," she says, waving down a waiter.

Once they have iced lattes and two avocado toasts sitting between them, Liz asks, "So, have you celebrated yet?"

Mid-bite, Maya gestures her fork toward her mouth to excuse the pause. "Sorry, celebrated what?"

"Rockville!"

Since their first coffee date, Liz has routinely checked in on her to see how she's been managing with Shaan, with Medini, with everything. It reminds her of how things used to be with Alaina before she moved to Jersey and took that ER job that has her working all hours. Maya forgot the comfort of being so in touch with a friend. To not only keep another person constantly in the loop about your day-to-day, but to have them actually care to ask.

"Oh, right! Uh, not really. To be honest, I was on a high after that meeting and it's just been back to the grind since," she says, shrugging it off.

"Maya, a move like that deserves to be celebrated. You did the damn thing!" Liz raises her hands in a mock cheerleading gesture. Her two gold Cartier Love bracelets slide down her arms. "On second thought, maybe we *should* have gone out for mimosas."

Maya laughs and takes a long sip of her latte. "I *was* proud of it. I mean, I am. But I don't know. I have this nagging sense that I'm still not going to get the credit I deserve with the board for closing the deal with Whole Foods."

Liz puts her fork down and props her manicured hand under her chin before leaning in closer. "It's your board, isn't it?"

Maya's heart drops. "Wait, how'd you know? Are people discussing this?"

Liz laughs. "Nobody *told* me. No one had to. I've been around this shit long enough to pick up on a thing or two."

Maya does a quick look behind her shoulder and lowers her voice. "It's *some* of the board members. They're constantly doubting my decisions and leaving me out of the loop. And it's always been like this. I can't even tell you how many pitch meetings I've sat through where everyone in the room has turned to our COO, Josh, for information about Medini's valuation, growth, and product plans. Some of our initial investors even asked Josh more specific questions about the company than me! When I'm the founder!" She throws her hands up in frustration but remembers herself and quiets her voice back down.

"Liz, I had to *insert* myself into going to Rockville. Josh was going to go alone. I'm sure my board would have *loved* that. Honestly, if my chief of staff hadn't given me the heads-up, I probably wouldn't have known about the meeting at all until it was over." She throws her head into her hands.

"Okay," Liz starts, pressing two fingers into her temple. "Just so I'm understanding… Your board consistently tries to override *your* authority at Medini, when you are, in fact, the reason it exists?"

Maya slowly nods.

Liz leans in closer. "Let me guess—have they been subtly implying that your maternity leave's holding you back, maybe even holding the company back, as a manipulation tactic to keep you under their thumb?"

She sighs. "Subtly and…um, not so subtly, yes. The worst part is, they're not wrong. I mean I *have* been out of the picture more."

"Maya, you're on maternity leave! You just had a baby! What do they expect? This is such discriminatory bullshit. Have you told anyone else about this, like Dev? Or your best friend… sorry, what did you say her name was again?"

Maya sighs. "Alaina. And no, not really. Dev still doesn't think I should have pushed myself to go to Rockville in the first place. Turns out Alaina agrees with him. They both have made that clear to me since the trip. So I don't think they'd want to hear about any of this anyway."

Liz frowns. "Wait, Dev doesn't think you should have pushed 'yourself'? Give me a break. You really think he'd be so concerned about you spreading yourself too thin if he didn't have to think about child care while you were away? God forbid a man has to learn how to change a diaper." She rolls her eyes in frustration, then catches herself. "Sorry, obviously I haven't met the guy, and I don't mean to sound anti-Dev or anything. I'm sure he's wonderful."

Maya looks down at her lap. "He wants to be more involved. I don't know…it's harder for both of us than we realized. His job is really demanding. And it's also the reason we're able to pay our bills. I still find myself getting annoyed, and then upset about being annoyed, whenever he says he's tired."

"Tired," Liz says. "That word used to get me, too, when Owen said it. Like *he* was the one waking up every two hours. And Alaina, you said her kids are older, right? She probably doesn't even remember what this phase is like. Plus, she isn't an entrepreneur. It's easy to judge when you're no longer in the trenches yourself."

"No, I didn't mean to make her sound like that. She's not judg—"

"Maya," Liz interrupts. "I think it's sweet you're giving everyone the benefit of the doubt. But we both know things need to change."

Maya gives her a confused look.

"Trust your instincts. I'm telling you from my own experience that this inflection point, right after a child enters the picture, is a critical one, specifically in terms of your job. Dev and Alaina may mean well, but they're not giving you good advice. And I'd maybe be careful about how much you share with others about everything going on at Medini because the *last* thing you need is more opinions thrown on you right now. The less room for self-doubt, the better."

Maya fidgets uncomfortably in her seat. *But I tell them everything*, she thinks. *I always have.*

"Because Maya, your *board*—" Liz lowers her voice "—they have their own agenda. They always do. Right now, they probably want you to be more removed from Medini, take a load off. But you know what that's going to do? It will isolate you from your own company until your authority is worth shit all. And once you're off your leave, guess what? Medini's not your company anymore. It's theirs."

Well, fuck. Maya anxiously picks at her nails, not knowing what to say. Her head is spinning.

Liz sighs and gives her a knowing look. "I really do see so much of myself in you. My younger self, at least. I used to be kinder, more trusting. I worked with people because I *liked* them, not because they were good at what they did." She glances away, lost in thought. "Look, I know what's written about me. What people say behind my back. That I'm cut-throat, ruthless, aggressive, robotic, narcissistic. And I don't blame them. I know it may have seemed that way, especially after my first company shut down. The countless employees I had to let go, the customers we let down. The friends I lost along the way." Liz bites her lip, her eyes watery.

Anita.

"Just because I don't talk about it, doesn't mean I wasn't hurt." Liz reaches for a tissue and dabs the corners of her eyes. "Sorry, I guess it still bothers me. All I'm trying to say is there's a lot that people *don't* see, let alone care to see, about what it's like for female founders. How much we've sacrificed to make a name for ourselves in such a male-dominated space."

She pauses for emphasis.

"But what I can tell you is that it's critical you act *now.* It's time for you to get back in the driver's seat at Medini."

Maya takes a moment to mull over everything that was just thrown at her. "I hear what you're saying… And I understand it, in theory. But what about Shaan? I can't just have a one-track mind when it comes to work now that I'm a mother."

Liz's eyes drift up in thought. "Have you considered a nanny?"

Ugh.

She was afraid she'd ask that, even though it's more than

a reasonable question, especially in New York. But how can she even begin to explain that her own mother was so frequently outsourced to other families to help pay the bills, leaving Maya and Tarun to fend for themselves? Or that every time she pictures Mom working between the motel and other people's homes, Maya wants to burst into tears? Or how the most traumatic… No. She's not going there right now.

"I know it's easier said than done," Liz says, a softer tone to her voice. "But just something to think about. You're at the precipice of something *big* with Medini. You have a compelling story as a founder, and now all you need is more eyes on you than ever before. You can start small. Maybe you drop by the office unannounced at some point this week, just to remind everyone you're still the boss? And then keep building the momentum for Medini, with *you* at the helm. Leverage the *Today* show and Rockville into…more. Insert yourself back in the narrative."

Maya lets out a nervous laugh. "I wish I could just snap my fingers and make that happen."

Liz smirks. "I *might* have an idea in that department. And the timing couldn't be more perfect." She sits up in her seat and clasps her hands together. "My publicist arranged a profile with *Vanity Fair.* The assigned reporter asked if I knew of any other founders on the rise who might be interested in doing it with me. I hope it's okay, but I sent her your information. I think you'd be perfect for it."

Maya's jaw is on the floor. "You thought of me? Really? Wow… Liz, that's so kind."

Liz waves her off. "It's nothing. You deserve it. Let me just confirm the date and time…" She taps her foot as she pulls up her Google calendar, tilting her phone screen toward Maya. A quick glance confirms that Liz's calendar is exactly as Maya pictured: color-coded blocks for meetings, media features, networking drinks. Meditation.

Maya jots down the date and time.

"I'm in."

NEW YORK CITY POLICE DEPARTMENT

OFFICER KENT: When did you last hear from your wife?

DEV MEHTA: Like I've already told you, we were together Friday night, before she left. Why? Have you heard some—

OFFICER KENT: Sir, we need you to focus. Have you received anything suspicious since then? A call from a random number, maybe? A text?

DEV MEHTA: No. Nothing.

OFFICER KENT: Her cell phone is off. She hasn't used any credit cards.

DEV MEHTA: There must be something that tells us where she is. This isn't like her at all.

OFFICER KENT: There have been reports of her struggling the past few months.

DEV MEHTA: Well, yeah, we have a baby, and her job has always been stressful. And she's sometimes coped by… I don't know, shutting down. Closing herself off.

OFFICER KENT: Meaning…? Has something like this happened before?

DEV MEHTA: You're asking if my wife has a habit of leaving her husband and son?

OFFICER KENT: Sir, I'm trying to get a clearer picture of the situation.

DEV MEHTA: No…she's never left us.

OFFICER KENT: Us? Okay, then what about just *you*?

DEV MEHTA: There was one time…after we got married. I'd rather not get into it. It's a long story.

OFFICER KENT: We have time.

JUNE

before

7

"YOU'VE BEEN NOTHING BUT ON THE go. The *Today* show. Liz. Rockville. It's hard to keep up with you." Dev laughs, but there's a slight edge to his voice.

"I know, I know, I know. You didn't want me to go. But I didn't have a choice."

He finishes fixing his tie in the mirror and comes over to sit beside her on the bed. "Josh was ready to go for both of you. That *is* his job while you're on leave."

"Don't you realize that I had to be in Rockville *because* Josh was going alone?"

Dev gives her a quizzical look, not catching her drift.

"How many times have vendors looked directly at him in meetings, *only* him, as if he's the CEO?" She sighs. "Look, do we really have to go over this again? It's done. It's over. I'm tired of talking about it. Moral of the story is that we're going to be in sixty *fucking* stores. Can't you just be happy for me?"

"Of course I'm happy for you. I'm so, so happy for you and

proud of you. You're incredible," Dev says, reaching for her hands. "But sometimes you just..."

Maya narrows her eyes. "I just what?"

"You always think you have to *go, go, go*. You can never just pause and take it easy, even for a second."

Despite how much he tries, Dev just doesn't get it. She doesn't have the luxury of taking a step back, knowing her status and authority at Medini will be fully restored once she returns to the office. She can't just "take it easy," because she doesn't know how. From working at the motel every weekend as a student, to getting an Ivy League education, to conceiving the idea for Medini, to cold messaging over a hundred chemists on LinkedIn to help manufacture her products, to pulling off a flawless first-pitch presentation minutes after a potential venture capitalist tried to grab her ass.

Taking it easy has never been an option for her. And it isn't one now.

Dev sighs, signaling the end of that conversation. "I'm glad your mom was able to help out with Shaan while you were away."

Maya lets out her own exhale and nods in agreement. "I know. I couldn't have done it without her."

"Do you want to see if she can come back this weekend?" Dev suggests.

"Honestly, I'd rather not." Maya shakes her head. "She clearly has enough to worry about as it is."

"What do you mean?"

"She barely responds to my texts, and when I call her, she sounds extra performative. More than usual, at least. Like she's overcompensating. I feel like she's hiding something."

Dev smirks. "Hiding something? You make it sound like you're the mother and she's the daughter who's been sneaking behind *your* back."

Maya stifles a giggle. "I'm telling you, something feels off!"

"What does she say when you ask what's wrong?"

"She says something about how the motel needs work or that Dad has a family member in town who she needs to entertain, so on and so forth. She has an excuse for everything. Tarun claims that's just who Mom is, but don't you think she's tired of always worrying about everyone else besides herself? She's been doing it her whole life. And I don't know, maybe I feel bad asking her to take care of one more person. Even if it is her grandson." She looks over at the nursery.

"I get that, honey. I do," Dev says, pulling her in for a hug. "And if you don't want to put more on her, I understand. But like mother, like daughter." His voice is muffled in her hair.

Maya pulls out of the embrace and narrows her eyes at him. "And what do you mean by *that*?"

"Don't you think you *also* could use some 'me' time? What if my mom came over? I know she's free."

"Come over? Does that mean you finally feel comfortable telling her not to give so much unsolicited advice?" Maya feels a stab of irritation as she thinks back to all the times her mother-in-law has inserted her unprompted opinions on how to "correctly" raise Shaan.

Dev doesn't say anything.

"That's what I thought," Maya snaps. She's never understood this paradox. Her husband can be a father to their child, advise people on how to handle their finances, and win over clients in minutes. But he can never speak up to his parents.

Dev continues to stare at her in silence, likely wondering why she felt the need to poke at the one, constant sore spot in their marriage when he was just trying to help. If Maya was in a better place, a more rested, grounded, feeling-like-herself place, maybe she would have even agreed with him. Why *did* she have to snap like that?

"I guess I should get some work done." Dev grabs his navy blue laptop bag and settles into the living room.

"Yeah, you do that," Maya mutters under her breath. Even after scoring the Whole Foods deal, why does it still feel like she's not doing enough? When will things start feeling better, or at the very least, more manageable?

Her phone rings.

"Mom! Where have you been?" Maya says when she answers the call.

"Here! Where else?" Mom says, as if she hasn't been impossible to get in touch with lately. "Your kaka and kaki are visiting from California, so I've been taking them everywhere—the sari shops in Edison, Hindu temple, Patel Brothers. They're going to the beach today and I'm almost done packing their snacks and dinner."

Maya sighs. "Mom, you don't have to make food for them. They're grown adults, they can manage on their own."

"Maya, they're our guests. I can't let them go hungry." She mutters something under her breath, but Maya doesn't catch it.

"What was that?"

"Nothing, beta." Her tone seems off.

"What's wrong?"

"What do you mean?" Through the phone, Maya can hear the hiss of the pressure cooker, the splash of something being dropped into a pot. She can vividly picture her mother in this very moment, hunched over the stovetop, a cloud of cumin and ginger suspended around her. Once they hang up, Mom will probably spend the next fifteen minutes or so putting dry snacks into freshly washed Ziploc bags, wrapping rotlis in foil, and pouring fresh chai into a steel thermos.

"You've seemed more, I don't know—" Maya searches for the right word "—tense or something."

"I'm not tense. I just..." Mom sighs. "I think seeing Shaan, seeing *you* with Shaan, it's making me think about a lot."

"Like what?"

"I just didn't think I'd end up here. Doing this."

Maya frowns. "You didn't think you'd end up making food for Kaka and Kaki today?"

"It's not just that. I didn't think I'd have two kids who are all grown up, but *still* spend my days telling guests when to check out or swiping their credit cards or washing their used sheets. I thought..." She trails off, sounding wistful. Maya can picture her gazing out of the kitchen window above the sink, the one overlooking the side of the motel parking lot. "Can you believe I once thought I'd be traveling around the world, meeting people, writing their stories? Isn't that ridiculous?"

"No. Not even close."

"Of course it is! I haven't done anything."

"That's not true at all," Maya says, a pang of sadness taking up space in her sternum. "You've done so much. Dad wouldn't be able to run the motel if it wasn't for you. Do you know how many times he's said the bookkeeping and customer service would have fallen apart without you?"

"Yeah, yeah, I've done that. But..."

"But what?" Maya presses. She's always been able to sense her mother's deepest emotions—jealousy, fear, anger—no matter how much she tries to bury them.

"But sometimes it just wasn't what I pictured when I was younger." She sounds like she's going to elaborate but a second later, she clears her throat. "Anyway, I don't need to sit here and feel sorry for myself. I'm just tired."

As Mom proceeds to update her on the past couple of weeks at the motel, Maya's half listening, her mind preoccupied as she drafts a text message.

Maybe she's still on a high from Rockville, or it's the exhaustion in Mom's voice, but before she can second-guess herself, she presses Send.

Maya: Mom seems tired from everything she's been doing. Kaka and Kaki can manage on their own today, can't they?

Dad: Where is this coming from?

Maya: She just seems exhausted lately and I think she could use a break.

Dad: Did she say something to you?

Maya: I can just tell she's extra tired today. You know she never wants to let anyone down, especially family. But I think she needs a day for herself. Why don't you get takeout for everyone? I'm sure Tarun can help with the motel if you need backup.

Dad: OK...fine...

Dad: Still not sure where this is coming from...

Maya: Great! ☺

How can her parents run a literal business together but be so out of touch when it comes to the other's state of mind?

If Maya divided her life into a pie chart, the largest chunk would be "explaining my parents' feelings and behaviors to each other." By the time she was in third grade, Maya learned to expect Mom's and Dad's separate vent sessions to her—always concerning the other—and accepted her role as messenger. She didn't realize this wasn't the norm until she started going to friends' houses for sleepovers and noticed the ways other spouses interacted, not just among themselves, but with Maya's friends, too. There was a clear divide between parent and child that wasn't present in her own home. By the time she got to college, the only time her parents had ever formed an alliance was when it came to Tarun: *Your mother and I would like you to tell your brother to try harder in school. Your father and I were wondering why Tarun doesn't want to play soccer. Does Tarun have a girlfriend? He won't tell us.* Each time, Maya went through the same motions. She listened. She absorbed. She advised. She felt drained and then guilty for feeling drained. She replayed the conversations over and over in her mind long after they were over.

"So, your kaki was going on and on bragging about how her—"

"Mom. Sorry to interrupt, but I texted Dad. He said they'll be fine without food. And that you can go take some time for yourself. He'll handle everything and maybe enlist Tarun to help out."

"You did *what*? Why would you do that?" Maya can hear the panic in her voice.

"Because I knew you wouldn't. Now go do something just for you. Maybe get your nails done? Or go to the bookstore? The mall? You're always saying you just wear the same clothes, right?"

Mom scoffs. "I can't just do that."

"Yes, you can."

"Oh really?" Mom mocks. "You think it's that easy, huh?"

"I do, actually. I think you've been made to feel that it's not, that you're supposed to just forget about *you* the second other people need something. But you're allowed to say no sometimes, too."

The wisdom in her own words surprises her. This whole "female guilt" ordeal has been passed down intergenerationally. She imagines it taking up space in their tightly coiled DNA. A family heirloom of sorts.

"And what will Kaki and Kaka think when they realize I'm out and about, instead of preparing them with a nice meal?"

"Who cares?"

Mom scoffs again. "Maya! What has gotten into you lately? It's not like you to act like this."

What's gotten into me is that the last two weeks have made me see how much women are controlled by guilt, Maya wants to say. *And on the other side of that, there's lightness! Freedom! And you deserve to feel that, too. You always have.*

"Do you ever hear Dad or Tarun asking if they can leave or go somewhere when family is in town?"

"No," Mom says flippantly.

"So then why do you hold yourself to such high standards?"

"It's different for them. It always has been."

"That doesn't mean it needs to stay that way now," Maya reasons, rolling her eyes at her mother's choice of words. *It always has been.* Words too often used to justify toxic and oppressive expectations.

"Do you even hear yourself? And don't act like you haven't had to make sacrifices as a wife. It's different for us."

"What does *my* marriage have to do with this?"

"Do you remember that spa day we had before your wedding, just the two of us?"

"What about it?"

"Do you remember the conversation we had in the Jacuzzi? I warned you about the duties that come with being a wife and a mother, especially for Indian women. But you just kept telling me that your marriage is going to be different. That *Dev* is different, giving you the space and energy to focus on your own work, your own needs, your own *wants*."

"I still don't know how any of this is relevant."

"Do you see how you were wrong?"

"How was I *wrong* about that?"

"Is Dev there with you?" Mom asks.

"No, he just left for work."

"Aha, my point exactly! Dev just left for work, and you're the one staying home to be with Shaan. Even though you have things to do at Medini. See? When it comes down to who will sacrifice, whether that's for a marriage or taking care of a child, it's always the woman." Mom sounds so pleased with herself, and Maya's annoyed she gave her the perfect opening.

But when she takes a second to process what Mom just said, the words hit her like a slap to the face. "Actually, you know what? You're right."

"I am?"

"Yes, you are. I've been spending the last six weeks just making sure I don't step on anyone's toes, that I make sure Dev has enough sleep and enough energy to do his job, while rationalizing that it's fine for *me* to work on no sleep. That *I* have to be the one to always monitor every single thing Shaan does. So thank you for this conversation, it's been very…illuminating."

"You're welcome?"

"I've been wanting to bring Shaan by the office for weeks, but I keep delaying it because I'm worried about messing up his routine," Maya says, on a roll now. "But you're right. I should take my own advice." A plan starts to materialize in Maya's mind. She hears Liz's words from when they last met. *Remind them you're still the boss.*

"Maya, I didn't mean that—"

"Sorry, Mom. I have to go. Love you. Thanks for the chat."

As soon as she's off the phone, Maya prepares to do something she should have done days ago.

NEW YORK POST

Tech CEO and new mother Maya Patel may have been living a double life

By Renata James
Published August 1, 2019, 5:05 PM EDT

Maya Patel, CEO of Medini, has been reported as missing. She was last seen at her apartment in Tribeca, where she lives with her husband, Dev Mehta, and their six-month-old son, Shaan.

Patel founded Medini, a sustainable toiletry start-up that's been on an upward trajectory ever since the company announced a funding round of $5 million two years ago. As the daughter of two Indian immigrant motel owners, Patel's rags-to-riches story has been captured by multiple media outlets. She came up with the idea for her company after years of witnessing the amount of waste that collected from standard hotel products.

Former Medini assistant manager of customer retention Erica Bird reports, "During our team meetings, she sometimes shared stories from her more humble beginnings, like what it was like growing up in her family's motel, or how she helped her parents cut coupons every week as a kid. She's always had to work twice as hard as everyone else."

But there may be a darker side to this respected founder's life.

An anonymous insider source speculates that Patel "was really struggling after having her baby" and seemed "desperate to prove she could do it all." According to the source, the rumors around Patel's substance abuse issues "seemed unbelievable at first. But when I think about how much she's changed in such a short period of time, the things that don't seem to add up...it starts making more and more sense."

When asked for any final remarks, the insider source shared

a widely felt sentiment on the ongoing case. "I just hope that wherever she is, she's finally at peace."

Patel's family has not yet responded to requests for comment.

@KatieK: Wow. That's horrible.

@Caryn: Shocking, huh? You never know what someone's *actually* like in real life.

@BijalShah: Drugs? Her?! My mom always refers to her as the perfect Indian woman.

@Caryn: I know. I can't believe it either. So awful.

@Jinamama: OMG!! I follow her on Insta and noticed she hasn't been posting! I hope it's not drugs... 😟

@KatieK: This isn't the first time I've heard rumors re: drugs. Maybe there's some truth to it after all?

@Mukesh: Who even is this person? I'm brown and I've never heard of her.

@Karen: probably just doing it for the attention

@Brittany: that was low and unnecessary.

@Karen: idk some of these influencer people will do anything for a story lol

@KatieK: She's a businesswoman, not an influencer.

@Arti: sadly not surprised a brown mom and businesswoman is someone you're trying to tear down...people like you are what's wrong with the world. get help.

@Karen: it was a joke lol y'all need to chill

@Jinamama: Her poor baby ☹

8

AS MAYA PUSHES SHAAN'S STROLLER across Sixth Avenue and toward 23rd Street, she starts having second thoughts.

She's about to see her colleagues again for the first time in almost two months. What if they look at her differently? What if this is premature? What if people don't even *want* to see her?

Maya catches her reflection in a shop's window, and her black maternity athleisure is scrunched around her still-enlarged stomach. She's become so used to not wearing any makeup that she completely forgot to throw some on before leaving the apartment. Not even concealer to hide the very visible bags under her eyes.

Great.

Shaan whimpers in his stroller.

You're being selfish. You're messing up his nap schedule. All you care about is yourself.

Maya shakes the thoughts away. Mom may think sacrifice is the status quo for women, but not her.

"Shh, it's okay, you're okay," Maya whispers as she leans forward and pats his round belly. She's not sure if she's trying to comfort her baby or herself. "Mommy is just going to get the latest numbers on our spending, celebrate the Whole Foods deal, and remind everyone she's the boss. Then we can leave, okay?"

Medini's office is on the third floor of a nondescript Manhattan building. There's a revolving door on one side of the entrance and a heavy industrial door on the other. The side she's on just so happens to be the heavy-industrial-door side. *Why aren't there more automatic doors everywhere?* It's only after having a kid that she's realized how much infrastructure is lacking for parents, not to mention anyone with a mobility aid.

Maya struggles with the door, trying to use her back strength to keep it open as she does a reverse-walk into the building, Shaan's stroller out in front of her.

She's sweating by the time she makes it inside. Maya pushes Shaan's stroller through the building lobby and into the elevator. She's hyperaware of everything: the women in the elevator glancing at Shaan, the thud of the doors closing, her baby's body now at ease. So many of the things she used to do before without thinking—riding the subway, getting a cup of coffee, navigating crowded New York city streets—now feel more high-stakes when she's doing them with Shaan.

I can do this. I can do this. I can do this.

When the elevator doors finally open onto her office floor, Maya takes a deep breath in and walks up to the office entrance.

She scans her Medini badge and pushes the double glass doors through.

Medini's director of social media, Jackie, looks up in shock from a white front desk positioned at the front of the office. "Maya? Oh my God! You're here!" Her eyes grow wider as she takes in the stroller. "*He's* here!" She steps out from behind the desk to give her a hug.

Jackie squeals as she gets a closer look at Shaan, taking in his white onesie and blue-striped pants, an ensemble gifted by Dev's parents. (An outfit that Maya felt was *way* too expensive for an infant, or quite frankly, for anyone. Her son isn't even half a year old, and he already dresses better than most people she knows.)

"He's even cuter in real life!"

"Thank you!" Maya grins. She didn't realize how proud she'd feel hearing someone compliment her son.

Jackie pauses her game of peekaboo with Shaan to squeeze Maya's arm. "It's so great to see you."

"You, too. You know, I thought I'd just drop by to say hi and surprise everyone." Maya shrugs, feigning nonchalance.

Behind Jackie, Maya sees Ralph, a member of the customer service team, and can faintly hear him on the phone with a customer. She subtly repositions herself to get within better earshot. (One employee review on Glassdoor described Maya as "sweet" but noted that she "makes a habit of micromanaging every little thing that's going on at the office." When Maya read that comment, her first thought was *Wait, is that a bad thing?*)

"Your order came after your trip even though you paid for faster shipping?" Ralph types notes from the call into the company's customer service software. "Uh-huh. Okay, so I'll refund the shipping and also send you some of our new wooden combs. No, thank *you* for your understanding!"

She shifts her focus back to Jackie. "So, how is everyone?" Maya asks. "I thought I'd check in with the team ab—"

"Maya." She's interrupted by Travis Schmidt, one of their largest investors and a board member. Oh, and certified douchebag.

"Travis."

He raises his bushy brown eyebrows. "What a surprise to see you!"

"Likewise," Maya says, straining to keep her smile intact. Travis is never at the office.

Travis was the lead investor into Medini after Josh convinced Maya he was one of the most "highly sought-after consumer VCs in New York." He and Travis were both part of the same Yale alumni group, and Josh thought Travis could help give Medini more credibility. But all he's given Maya is higher blood pressure.

What is he doing here?

Before she can think of the politest way to ask that exact question, Travis says, "So how's your vacation going?"

Maya blinks twice. "Um…you mean my *maternity leave*?"

"Right," Travis says, snapping his fingers. "Of course. That's what I meant." He holds up his palms in mock surrender.

Maya makes a mental note to vent about this to Dev and Alaina later. She fights the urge to roll her eyes or, better yet, curse Travis out right now. It would be so cathartic to unleash all her pent-up frustration from the past weeks on this entitled asshole.

But this entitled asshole has also given her company massive funding, so she bites her tongue, takes a deep breath, and even manages to flash him a grin. "Oh, it's busy. I can assure you, taking care of this tiny human is no vacation! I'm sure things were busy when Emily was home with your little one last year."

"Yeah, yeah, I'm sure," he says, typing something out on his phone.

"So, is everything good with you?" Maya asks. "I didn't expect to see you here."

Translation: *What the fuck are you doing here?*

"All smooth sailing," Travis says, his irritatingly cool, calm demeanor resembling that of someone who is, in fact, about to go sailing. Travis has a beach house—correction, a beach *mansion*—in the Hamptons. He's one of those guys who has always been wealthy, his childhood chock-full of "rich white people" experiences that Maya only saw in movies: sailing yachts, playing polo, even traveling by private jet.

Shaan starts to grumble. Maya pats his legs, then glides the stroller back and forth. *Please don't cry here.* He gives her a complacent smile, as if he's thinking *Fine, but just this once!*

Until now, seeing Shaan smile filled Maya with an all-consuming warmth. But today, her son's two rows of gums and the lightness in his eyes gives her something more: courage. It's the two of them against everyone. There's no need for her to be intimidated by Travis.

"Was I interrupting something?" Maya's gaze shifts toward the people lingering outside the conference room, some of them shooting her wary glances. Medini's vice president of finance (Brad), the vice president of marketing (Margaret), and a couple members of the finance team are all staring at her inquisitively, like she's an outsider. Intruder.

"We were just reviewing some of the financial projections for the upcoming months. You know, since the Whole Foods deal is going to shift things," Travis says, taking a quick look around the office before lowering his voice. "It's not looking good, Maya."

"What are you talking about? This deal is a great thing for us." She orders herself to stay calm, but her stomach's twisting in knots. She pushes Shaan's stroller back and forth in what she hopes is a soothing rhythm for him, but she's doing it for her. Maya needs to keep her hands busy right now to resist the temptation to punch Travis in the face.

"You…" Travis clears his throat, starting over. "*Medini* is going to be burning way more cash than what was projected by now. It's not sustainable. You didn't negotiate a lower cost per unit for bigger orders with your manufacturer, so now Medini is going to be spending even more money trying to fulfill the massive Whole Foods order. And they pay a lot slower than the average customer. It's a *lot* of cash, Maya."

Stay calm, stay calm, stay calm. Don't give him the satisfaction. "I'm sure you do remember me saying months ago that I should negotiate for a lower cost per unit in case we ever needed to make more products, but I was told, by *the board*—" she pauses for emphasis "—to not do that and lock in a better base rate. And I was also advised to hire more people in marketing and spend more on R&D. So yes, we've been spending."

It takes her a second to fully comprehend the impossible situation she's been put in. She was told by her investors to *spend, spend, spend* to prove she had big plans for Medini. In fact, she was specifically told *not* to waste time negotiating rates even when there was always the possibility that Medini's products would be in higher demand than initially projected. It's clear as day to her now that the only reason the board would have ever told her not to negotiate a lower cost per unit for massive orders was because they never truly believed they'd *get* massive orders. Despite all their talk, on some level, they never imagined Medini would be this successful. They pushed her to spend according to their vision, not hers. And now she's to blame for it.

Travis shakes his head. "Look, what I do know is that we're going to have to make some changes around here. Fast."

She frowns. "What are you say—"

"Is that Maya? Look at you!" Josh's bellowing voice echoes down the hall.

Shaan smiles up at Josh, who squats down until he's eye level with her son. "And this little guy! What a cutie!"

Maya relaxes for a second, grateful for Josh's contagious enthusiasm.

But then her mind drifts back to Travis's comments.

"Travis mentioned that there are concerns about our burn rate?" She tries to ignore her negative gut feeling. Something is wrong. And the fact that nobody gave her the heads-up that some of Medini's investors were stopping by the office couldn't have been an honest mistake. She was intentionally left out of the loop. And maybe Tiffany was, too.

Josh clears his throat as he stands back up. "There have been concerns, yeah."

"And you all met right now to discuss this?" Maya impatiently taps her foot and crosses her arms.

"A few of the guys just happened to be in town, so decided to have a few of them swing by the office to chat." Josh shrugs.

"Why didn't anyone tell me?"

"You know, because of your..." Travis interjects, motioning toward the stroller. *"Situation."*

"What do you mean, my situation? As in the fact that I gave birth?"

Travis shrugs, but then nods, doubling down. "Since the start of your vaca—"

She shoots him a very pointed look.

"—your *leave*, we've had the chance to think about Medini's future."

Maya can't believe the words coming out of his mouth right now. What would Liz do? She'd demand an explanation, that's for sure, and tell everyone they have no right to meet without informing the CEO of the company. And she certainly wouldn't let them weaponize her justified absence.

Years ago, she absorbed a harsh truth: she wasn't the type of founder that was typically banked on. Sure, investors enjoyed sharing their affiliation with her as "proof" of their DEI initiatives. *Look, we gave money to a brown woman! Of course we're inclusive!* But she was still going to have to prove herself every step of the way. For some time, she considered changing the way she dressed, or how aggressively she made her points.

Her mind jumps to the number of times she feigned an interest in golf, or smiled through never-ending happy hours, or sacrificed sleep so she could peruse every article published on specific venture capitalists. Each one of the VCs she connected with pushed their opinions on her, from how they wanted her to run Medini to how much of her company they expected to own. To bypass this, some well-meaning people in her network suggested she "self-fund" or ask for financial support from her family. Maya never knew how to tell them that simply wasn't an option.

"I'm still very much here," Maya says through gritted teeth. "So what exactly *is* the issue here?"

Josh lowers his voice. "Maybe we should discuss this pri—"

"Just tell me," Maya cuts him off.

He shoves his hands into the pockets of his jeans, and Maya feels another stab of anger, but this time at Josh's ability to wear such casual work attire to a meeting with their VCs. She must have spent thousands of dollars over the years on blazers, blouses, jumpsuits, you name it, all in the hopes that she'd get taken more seriously. But clearly, her efforts were futile. No matter how many fancy blazers she buys, she'll never be as respected as Josh, even when he's wearing a stained old pair of blue jeans.

"Brad looked at all of our numbers." Josh sighs. "At the rate we're going, we have five months of runway."

"*Five months?* You're telling me we have five months left to survive at the rate we're going?" The words are a kick to her stomach. "Please tell me you're joking."

He looks down at the floor. "I wish I was."

"Is that why I hadn't gotten the numbers yet?"

"We wanted to come up with some sort of plan before reaching out to you on your leave. We've gotta keep spending at our current rate, at least for the foreseeable future, to fulfill the Whole Foods deal. And even though everyone is already working well past capacity, they're still struggling to keep up. The customer service team keeps saying they can't handle the number of calls and emails coming through. Operations isn't even able to confirm when our inventory will physically arrive at the warehouse." Josh runs his hands through his curly blond hair in distress.

"Like I said, it's bad," Travis chimes in.

"Yes, I think I get that," Maya snaps. "Okay, then we need to figure out a way to cut costs ASAP."

"And think about if we want to raise more money," Josh adds.

"Funding was hard enough for you the first time," Travis cuts in, only looking at Maya when he says this. "So let's not assume that's a guarantee of anything."

She hates that he's right.

Josh glances down at his watch. "Look, I'll call you and we

can talk this through in more detail. I've gotta run to another meeting right now, but let's set up a time to chat, okay? It was great to see you!" He pulls her in for a quick side hug.

Before Maya can even think of a response, he jogs over to his office and closes the door.

Later that night, when she's attempting to feed Shaan, Maya feels her eyes start to flutter. She pinches her forearm in a feeble attempt to stay awake.

"C'mon, buddy, we can do this," she whispers as Shaan twists away from her nipple.

She looks outside the window and all she sees are dark apartments and the golden tint of streetlights. There's an occasional sound of a car driving by, probably dropping off some twenty-something who's been out partying. Other than that, this part of Tribeca is fast asleep.

Never has she ever been so envious of her neighbors.

All of a sudden, Shaan's entire body shakes and he erupts into an ear-piercing scream. *You're not cut out for this.*

She tries to shift Shaan's face toward her chest, grabbing her breast "like a hamburger," as the lactation consultant told her to do.

Shaan's screams intensify, each one louder than the last. She rubs his back and tries a soft *shh*. Anything to stop his screaming. She can't take any more screams.

You're not cut out for this. You're not cut out for this. You're not cut out for this.

"Shh, okay, I'm sorry," Maya says, desperately trying to keep her voice calm. If she shows irritation—or God forbid, anger—she will "scar him forever." At least according to every parenting book on her nightstand.

Maya closes her sore eyes. She doesn't need a mirror to know they're red and sunken. It's been like this with Shaan every night. A blur of delirious wake-ups and failed attempts at feeding.

His screams slowly start to soften as she sways back and forth. The light gray rocking chair underneath her looked so serene, so aspirational, when she first saw it at Room & Board. Now it just reminds her of all the sleepless nights she's spent in this very position. And of her failure as a mother.

She wipes the tears collecting on the tips of his long eyelashes. According to that Facebook moms' parenting group she joined when Shaan was born, she's supposed to continue breastfeeding—or at least try to—even if the baby doesn't immediately latch. The second she stops, it's game over. Her efforts as a mother will directly determine whether or not her baby will starve.

She pictures Shaan decades from now, sprawled across a therapist's couch and dragging on a cigarette. *My life really started to go downhill when my mom stopped breastfeeding me. Maybe if I had those extra antibodies, those extra nutrients, I would have gotten into Harvard and made something of myself.*

She grabs her breast again. But the second Shaan whimpers, she retreats.

"Please don't scream again. I can't bear it," she whispers. "I'm sorry, I just can't."

As she cradles him and walks to the fridge to get a bottle of pumped milk, the voice is back. *You're not cut out for this. You're not good enough. You're selfish. You're a bad mom.*

The thoughts gain more and more momentum as her mind plays a memory reel from the past two months. The condescending look on her mother-in-law's face when she said she'd refused to even *buy* bottles when her sons were born. A mommy influencer's Instagram post of her holding her smiling, healthy baby, proudly announcing she's successfully breastfed for two years. The doctor's strained smile at Maya's most recent checkup when she handed her a printout of a breastfeeding study and its long-term health benefits for infants.

Shaan starts crying again.

Maya clutches the bottle, tears pooling in the corners of her eyes.

Her heart starts to race as a *thump, thump, thump* resounds in her head. She's completely on edge and frozen at once. Shaan's cries slowly fade into the background, a never-ending noise machine.

A distant, internal voice urges her to take a deep breath and try not to panic.

But all she can pay attention to is the louder voice in her mind, one that's becoming meaner by the second.

You're a failure. You're not strong enough. You're starving your child.

Despite her urge to feed her crying son, she's paralyzed. She has to snap out of this. Now. She tries telling herself that her self-critical thoughts are just a function of the patriarchy and internalized capitalism and all of these other forces out of her control. Just like Liz said. Nothing more.

Liz.

Maya forgot to throw out the bottle.

With Shaan still cradled against her, she reaches into her bag and rummages through the pile of receipts at the bottom until her hands find the tiny capsule.

She doesn't want to stop to think about it first. Maya's done too much thinking already. With a sip of water, she swallows the pill. And just like in Rockville, the effects are immediate.

The chaos that just ensued seems like a distant memory in her mind. She feels firmly rooted in the present in a way she hasn't in a long time, maybe ever. She takes in Shaan's tiny nose and soft cheeks. The curl of his fists. Why doesn't she slow down during precious moments like these? Moments full of wonder and cuteness and awe?

Is this what parenting is *supposed* to feel like?

Shaan looks up at her, his eyes searching. Maya slips the bottle into his mouth, and shockingly, he downs it in seconds. Once he's all fed, she swaddles him and tucks him into his bassinet. He instantly falls asleep.

And for the first time in weeks, so does she.

TRENDING:

#MAYAPATEL

@Doc_Rad: I've gone down a Maya Patel rabbit hole and she definitely gave signs of drug abuse. [Posted August 1, 2019, 12:14 PM]

@MelissaRW: Do you think it's possible she was sick and nobody knew? She seemed okay on her Instagram...

@Bina_Mehta: People can have a lot of illnesses and "look okay," lol.

@Doc_Rad: I'm just saying, she fits a lot of the telltale signs of high-functioning drug use. I wouldn't be surprised if she uses a lot of cocaine or other stuff. Have you heard of those so called "canna moms"? There are so many people who say pot apparently makes them better parents.

@Kaira1234: Um, maybe that's because being a mom is brutal??? And I don't think a *man* (I see your profile pic) should judge a woman, a MOTHER, for what she feels she has to do to get through the day.

@MelissaRW: Then shouldn't her team release some sort of statement? Why is Medini, or her publicist, okay with this type of press?

@Kaira1234: Oh, because her health is *our* business now?

@Bina_Mehta: To be fair, she puts herself online. When you choose to be public facing, it comes with certain responsibilities.

@Kaira1234: So she doesn't deserve human privacy? Wtf is wrong with our world?

@Bina_Mehta: you need to chill, lol. It's not like you knew her personally.

9

WHEN MAYA WAKES UP TO SHAAN'S CRIES two hours later, she notices it.

Or rather, the absence of it.

She doesn't feel panic, she doesn't feel dread. She doesn't even feel resentment toward the sleeping figure beside her. Maya just feels…calm. At peace. It's the same warm, buoyant sensation she felt as a kid when her family would occasionally take a day trip to the Jersey Shore. It was the only vacation they could afford at the time, and Mom and Dad didn't want to spend more than a day away from the motel. So for those short-lived moments she spent floating in the Atlantic Ocean, Maya felt untethered. Free. She forgot what that felt like.

Until now.

Shaan's tiny feet kick into the air, barely visible through the netting of their overly priced bassinet, known as the Snoo. It's been lauded in the New York parenting circle for its "magical ability to rock and soothe every baby to sleep." Every baby except Shaan, that is.

"Honey?" Dev rolls over toward her, his eyes tight with sleep. "Are you getting him?"

"You can do it. I'm tired," Maya says, the words just slipping out. Her hand rushes to her mouth right away. Did she really just say that? *Out loud?*

The clock on her nightstand reads 6:30 a.m. How long did Liz say the pills would last?

"What was that?" Dev speaks in the bewildered tone of someone who was interrupted mid-dream. She can tell he's still half-asleep.

"I meant, can you get Shaan this time? I'd like to close my eyes for a little longer. I have a big day ahead of me."

"Oh, sure. Of course I can get him, honey." Dev robotically sits up in bed and marches toward the bassinet. He hums a lullaby as he picks Shaan up and carries him to the kitchen.

Maya pulls the down comforter over her head, inhaling its scent of laundry detergent.

Holy shit.

Was it really that simple? Has it always been? She immediately picks up her phone from the nightstand and sends Liz a text.

Maya Patel: OMG, this pill is amazing.

Since she's already on her phone, she does a quick scroll through Instagram. The first picture on her Explore page is of a woman cradling a baby. They're wearing matching floral, light gray outfits. The caption: Enjoying every second with my sweet girl. The photo directly underneath that one is of a woman standing in her kitchen, flour on her face as she angles a freshly made pizza toward the camera. She's surrounded by six children, each wearing sauce-covered aprons and holding up a pizza roller: There can never be too many cooks in this kitchen!

She laughs out loud. Ever since Shaan was born, seeing these kinds of "quintessential nurturing mother" posts filled Maya with first guilt, then fear, always in that order. Guilt that she's not "that" mom now, quickly followed by the fear that she'll *never* be that kind of mother. But all she can think in this very moment is *Who the hell needs six pizza rollers?*

Maya smiles at the thought, and seconds later, her eyelids close.

When her alarm goes off two hours later, she feels a looseness in her muscles, an alertness about her. Is this what a good night's sleep feels like?

She grabs her phone from the nightstand and sees a text from Liz.

Liz Anderson: OMG! I'm so glad it ended up coming in handy. Noticed a change right away?

Maya Patel: It was subtle but definitely there. I let my husband take our baby. (Usually try to make sure he sleeps since he has to go into the office all day.)

Liz Anderson: That's so great. We need as much energy as possible for when we meet with Paula today. Proud of you for standing up for yourself. See you later! xoxo

Maya Patel: Actually, do you have time for a quick chat?

Her phone rings a second later.

"What's up?" Liz immediately asks.

"It's about Medini."

Maya doesn't even know how long she's been venting for by the time she's done with her long-winded rant. All she knows is that it's so cathartic to voice everything she's been feeling lately, uninterrupted. No mansplaining, no condescending laughs, no comments like *Why can't Josh just handle it?*

When she's finished, Liz says, "Is there anything else?"

"Nope, that's pretty much it..." She checks the time and realizes she's been talking for ten minutes straight. "Sorry, I know I just talked your ear off."

"Don't be sorry," Liz reassures her. "But you might not like what I'm about to say. You're behaving more like head of HR instead of company CEO. You're playing too nice."

An executive coach had told her something similar years ago, after a week of observing her on the job. *You care too much about people's feelings and not what's best for the company.*

"Is it bad to not want anyone to get hurt?"

"It's not about whether it's good or bad," Liz says. "It's about the fact that that's not going to change anything."

"So, what are you saying exactly?"

"You're going to have to fire people."

"Wait, *what*? I can't do that. Some of these people—most of them, actually—have been with me since the beginning. They're good at their jobs. And they have families to support."

"I hear you. I do. And as I've said before, I've been there." Liz pauses. "But this is business, and it comes with the job."

"There has to be another way."

"It's just food for thought. You don't have to make any big decisions now. And I'll see you later!"

When they hang up, Maya exits the bedroom and finds Dev and Shaan sprawled across the sectional.

"This little guy and I had a nice start to the day," Dev says when he sees her. "Did you get some rest?"

"I did, actually. Thanks." Maya blinks, registering everything in a way she hasn't before. Her husband and their baby. The sun peeking out through the living room blinds. The white-noise machine droning on in their bedroom. This is her life. She's so lucky.

She assembles her pump parts and sits down next to Dev, who holds Shaan on his lap and softly pats his back to elicit a burp.

"Success!" Dev says when Shaan burps a few seconds later.

Maya laughs. "I don't think I've ever heard a burp celebrated that much."

"Oh, you better believe I'm cheering for that one. It was taking so long I thought it wouldn't come at all."

It's good that they're spending time together, she thinks. *It's important.*

Maya wraps her arm around Dev's neck and kisses him on the cheek.

His eyes widen in surprise. "What was that for?"

"For being you."

Dev looks at her with a warmth in his eyes she hasn't seen in weeks and shifts closer to her. "I love you."

"I love you, too."

He links his hands through hers and squeezes tight.

When Dev leaves the couch to get ready for work, he says, "You seem more like you today. It's nice."

"You know what? I think I agree with you."

Maya's smiling up at him, but there's a sudden pit in her stomach, signaling that her eight hours of bliss are now up. She hates keeping secrets from Dev.

Besides, she doesn't want to ruin this moment, this lovely morning they've had together. As he kisses her one last time before heading out the door, she silently promises to be more grateful for what she and Dev have always shared. She doesn't need a pill to remind her of that.

This was the last time.

No use worrying him over nothing.

★★★

"I'm so glad she wanted to interview us together. That doesn't usually happen!" Liz's gold hoop earrings catch a glint of sunlight.

They're sitting at Amelie wine bar, a place Maya normally associates with her and Dev's date nights at the start of their relationship. They used to cap off those evenings with a slice of Joe's pizza and a long, meandering walk home. She smiles at the memory.

"You're a pro, so I know you've got this." Liz squeezes her hand. "Oh, but one quick thing… Maybe we omit what we talked about on the phone this morning? And everything you heard at the office?"

Maya quickly nods. "Oh, absolutely. Don't worry, there's no way I'll go there. I don't *want* to go there. I'm still processing the news myself," she admits, trying to ignore the growing pit in her stomach whenever she thinks of Medini.

"Of course you are. That's a lot to take in! And hey, we're going to figure it out," Liz says, before abruptly shifting her attention toward the bar entrance. Her eyes light up in recognition and she waves her arm in the air. A woman starts heading in their direction and, based on her glamorous appearance—the tailored black blazer and pleated trousers, thick black glasses with a cat-eye frame, and that signature bold red lipstick—she needs no introduction. Maya knows it's Paula Goldberg, the acclaimed writer from *Vanity Fair.*

The three of them order a round of cocktails, and as soon as the drinks appear in front of them, it's down to business.

"Should we get started?" Paula opens a black Moleskine notebook and presses the record button on her iPhone.

She kicks off her questions with some low-hanging fruit, like what a day in the life as a founder looks like, if they always knew they wanted to start their own companies, and who they looked up to the most when embarking on their entrepreneurial journeys.

Then she pivots to how Liz and Maya first met.

Maya glances at Liz to see who should speak first, like they're an old married couple tasked with answering that same question. "We're new friends," Liz jumps in, flashing Paula a professionally bleached smile.

"Well, I mean of course, we've followed each other's successes over the years..." Liz trails off, subtly nudging her arm as an indication for Maya to take over. (Translation: Maya followed Liz's successes, not the other way around. She appreciates the white lie.)

Maya jumps in. "But we really connected after I did a Mother's Day segment for the *Today* show. Liz reached out to me afterward, and the rest is history!" She laughs. "Let's just say she's been a lifesaver, as both a professional colleague *and* a friend. As a new mom, I don't know how I could have balanced it all—work, motherhood, a social life—without Liz's advice and guidance."

Paula perks up at that last comment. "Ooh, tell me more about that. I'm interested in that shared intersection—life as a founder *and* as a mother. You're creators in more ways than one. I'm picturing you both holding babies and wearing high heels!" She lets out an excited giggle.

Trust me, it's far less glamorous than that.

Maya sits up in her seat. "Oh, it's a juggle, that's for sure. And let me tell you, motherhood has made me face my relationship with optimization in ways I didn't think possible. Now, I consider myself a pretty good multitasker. But when you throw early motherhood onto running a company, it can be exhausting. Liz and I are just trying to normalize that being a founder *and* a mother is certainly possible, but it's also not one-size-fits-all. It looks different for different people."

Paula jots down something in her notebook, and Liz takes

the opportunity to give her a subtle thumbs-up. Maya grins in response. She can already picture that last statement as an isolated pull quote when the feature runs.

Maya thinks they're about to wrap up when Paula says, "Just one more thing. I'd like to talk about hardships. Maya, how are things *really* going at Medini? I know your company's socials, and even your own, talk a big game, but I've heard some rumors that this might not be the entire picture..."

Just like that, the persistent rock in her stomach is back. And this time, it's a boulder.

Breathe. Just breathe, she commands herself.

She digs her white sneakers into the floor and says, "Running a business is much more complicated than anything I, or anyone else, could possibly capture in a single post online. There are just too many moving parts. Have we experienced uncertainty, a couple of curveballs, this year? Of course we have. But is our more-than-capable team prepared to handle it? Absolutely."

Paula nods, taking notes. Sure, Maya's nonresponse may or may not have resembled that of a politician. But she clings to Beth's words. *It's the story that matters.* It's how you spin the facts, how you project an assured confidence in what lies ahead. Fight through the internal dissonance as you lie through your teeth.

"And," Liz chimes in, "as we very well know, there are *always* rumors circulating. That's par for the course, especially for us founders whose business practices and approaches may seem unorthodox to some, simply because we're bringing something new to the table. But conformity doesn't effect change." She pauses, taking a beat to let Paula's pen catch up with her words.

"Now, I hope Maya doesn't mind me saying this—" Liz shoots a quick glance at Maya "—but Medini is scheduled to release some *very* exciting news in the near future. If people want to talk, let's give them something tangible to chew on. Stay tuned!"

Paula pauses from writing to turn to Maya, her eyebrows raised. She smiles, hoping that's confirmation enough.

Please don't ask me to elaborate. Paula, I beg of you.

"Well, you've definitely piqued my interest!" Paula smiles back and asks Liz a couple more final questions. Once they wrap up their conversation, Paula stands from the table and reaches for her jacket.

Oh, thank God. It's over. She can breathe again.

A moment later, after they've said their goodbyes to Paula, Liz orders two glasses of champagne.

"I think you know you deserve that," she reasons before Maya can protest.

"Thank you…for including me in the feature. And for saving my ass."

"You did that just fine on your own," Liz says. "And trust me, we are all tired of those takedown profiles on women. You have no idea how many times I've been the subject of a Most Powerful list, only to get blasted the next day in a sexist Should Women Lead? piece. I wasn't about to let Paula head down that route."

Maya smiles. "I appreciate that. And one thing I've learned is that when I fully own something, instead of just outright denying it, it can't be used against me."

"Cheers to that." Liz clinks their glasses together.

Maya takes her first sip of champagne, the bubbles tickling her throat. The stress of the last few weeks starts to blur into the background. She can do this. She can convince others—herself included—that everything's fine because it will be.

It has to be.

VANITY FAIR

Liz Anderson's Bold Past, Present and Future

By Paula Goldberg
Published June 12, 2019, 10:00 AM EDT

A tech mogul turns a complicated past into an empowering future.

One of the first things Anderson said to me when we sat down for drinks was "I want to change the world. For a long time, I felt that I had to deny that. But I'm done keeping parts of myself small just so others are comfortable."

That bold perspective has become Anderson's signature. Her hard work and loyalty to her big visions have led to her becoming one of the most recognizable women in business. As the cofounder of Limitless and Women Rise, Anderson has made a name for herself by expanding what's possible in women's wellness. For the past three years, she's been on *Forbes*'s 50 Women to Watch list. Her inbox is full of requests for keynote speeches, panels, and podcasts.

The name Liz Anderson is its own brand in and of itself, and the acclaimed #girlboss boasts 15 million followers across social media. Her fans applaud her for using her platform not only to show that it's possible to be both a mother *and* succeed professionally, but also that you can look sexy doing it. Anderson's feed is full of everything from advice on sleep training to the best unisex diaper bag to photos of her holding her children while typing emails. No matter what it is, you can be sure that Anderson's beach-blond waves, killer body, and signature pursed lips will make a frequent appearance in her photos.

While some claim Anderson's public persona is a way to distract from her controversial past and questionable business practices, Anderson's made it clear that she stands behind every decision she's made.

"I have no regrets in the choices I've made," she noted in an earlier profile for the *New York Times*. "Yes, I have high standards for my employees, and yes, I know when it's time to pivot and move on or break ties. Women are constantly judged for how likable they are. I'd rather be respected than liked."

On maintaining a work-life balance with such a jam-packed schedule, Anderson says, "I work a lot, but on the weekends, I prefer to focus on family and fun." She lives in Manhattan with her husband, financier Owen Humphrey, and their two six-year-old twin daughters.

For many, being at the top can often also mean being lonely. But not for Anderson.

As a constant champion for other women in business, she's not only made angel investments in several female-founded start-ups, but she's also taken numerous female founders under her wing, helping them build a name for themselves.

One such mentee is Maya Patel, CEO and founder of Medini, an ecofriendly toiletries company inspired by Patel's upbringing in a motel. The two connected after Patel's appearance on the *Today* show.

"We've been in touch at least once a day…more if you count Instagram DMs," Patel said, laughing. "Liz has normalized a lot of my conflicts about being a founder and new mother. She brings the same boldness to parenting that she does to work."

Patel notes that Anderson's boldness is contagious, and it shows. Later this year, Medini is expected to announce something "very exciting," but Patel's keeping it a secret for now.

There's clearly a lot in store for these two. And what's better than a power couple?

A power friendship.

10

FIVE MONTHS. FIVE MONTHS. FIVE. FUCK-*ing. Months.*

Those two words have been running on a constant loop in Maya's mind. Can her company really only survive for five more months at the rate that it's spending?

"Maya? Did you hear me?" Alaina asks.

"Sorry, what did you say?" Maya asks. "I zoned out for a second."

The two of them are standing in Maya's kitchen, their voices soft enough so that their husbands in the living room can't hear. Alaina and Ryan had brought over a giant pot of spaghetti and a bottle of Pinot Noir. The second Maya saw them on the other side of her door, reinforcements in hand, she thought, *Those are true friends.*

"Do you really think this woman understands any of the shit you're going through?"

Maya scrunches her eyebrows in confusion. "What? Who?"

"Liz!"

"Oh, um, yeah? I do." Maya feels a surge of defensiveness. "Liz has built a company. No, *companies*! Plural. You know how much I've looked up to her over the years. And she's really trying to make a difference with her line of supplements. They're helping women all over."

"I'm just saying, maybe you don't need to glorify her so much. I mean, what do you really know about those companies? About her?" Alaina presses. She's donning her standard uniform of leggings and an oversize T-shirt, her hair thrown into a messy topknot.

"What are you talking about? You've never even met her."

Alaina's face shifts into that hesitant expression she always gets when she's about to deliver a harsh truth. Tongue in cheek, eyes downcast toward one side. She pulled the same face when Maya told her she was considering getting back together with her toxic ex-boyfriend in college, and then again when Maya debated shutting Medini down after one failed round of fundraising.

"A nurse at work said that her supplements are a total joke and that that other company of hers just suddenly 'shut down.' I mean, don't you think that's weird? Sketchy?"

Maya stops herself from taking a sip of wine. Even though some alcohol is technically fine, she shouldn't take any more chances.

"I know Liz has an *interesting* reputation… But I *also* know, from my own experience, how women tend to get criticized for every little thing they do. Am I wrong?"

"No, that's true. But I don't know. She gives me those vibes of those women who claim sticking a jade egg in your vagina will heal you."

"She's a *pharmacologist*," Maya emphasizes. "You know more than anyone how the health care industry caters to men. She's creating cutting-edge supplements to boost women's health and wellness. Speaking of which..."

Alaina gives her a look. "Oh God. I was going to say you sound like an infomercial but now that segue scares me."

Maya doesn't fully trust her liquid courage right now, but she continues. "She gave me this new supplement to try. It's different from her other ones but wow, it's been helping me a lot."

"Which one is it? I've probably heard of it."

"It hasn't been released to the public *yet*, but she just has to iron out some stuff before it's more widely accessible."

"Oh my God. *What?* The woman gave you drugs?!"

"Alaina! Shh!" Maya shoots a furtive glance toward the living room. "She didn't give me *drugs*. It's a supplement. Look, she's spent years working on it, and it's all backed by extensive research. Like I said, nobody's really supposed to know about it until it's fully cleared, so don't tell people or anything. But Alaina, I'm telling you. It's fucking awesome."

Alaina shakes her head in disapproval. "What the fuck even is this thing?"

"Well, it's..." She hesitates. If Alaina is judging her this much now, she's only going to judge her more if Maya tells her the truth. She takes another large gulp of wine to buy herself more time to come up with a white lie. "It's like a stronger melatonin but doesn't make me sleepy. It's just supposed to slow the nervous system down. Plus, it doesn't have addictive properties or any bad side effects."

Her attempts at sounding nonchalant are overridden by the fact that she's rambling and has no idea what the fuck she's talking about.

"Ohhh, well, in that case, it sounds totally legit!" Alaina scoffs, not bothering to mask her sarcasm.

Maya stares at the ground.

"I mean, what the fuck? Are you kidding? Literally nothing you just said makes any sense. Not even a little bit. You're taking a pill from some random woman who *used* to study pharmacology back in the day?"

"Not some *random* woman. She's my friend," she says defensively, knowing she's dodging the first part.

"Right, I forgot. Because Liz is your pharmacological guru."

She should have known Alaina would react this way.

"Can you stop? It's really nothing. And you literally just said I was doing great!"

"That was before I knew you were taking some weird-ass unapproved drug!"

"Shhh!" Maya darts her eyes back over to the living room and nods her head to a farther corner of the kitchen.

When they're well out of earshot, Alaina says, "Why didn't you ask me about it first?"

Maya looks down. "I didn't think to."

"You didn't think about consulting your best friend, who just so happens to be an ER doctor, before taking some under-the-table drug?"

"I… I just…" She hates how backed into a corner she feels right now. "I didn't think I needed your permission. And trust me, it's safe."

"*Trust* you? Based off what, exactly? Where are Liz's medical credentials? Has she done drug trials? Have you gone through her research? Talked to other people taking this?"

Maya's cheeks flush. "No, I th—"

"And what does Dev think about all this?"

"I, er, haven't mentioned it to him yet," she says quietly.

"WHAT?" Alaina's eyes widen. "Why not?"

"I didn't feel the need to since I've only taken it a couple times. The first time I took it was during the most stressful work trip. Rockville, remember? And then I took it again one night when Shaan wasn't latching. And get this, after that second time, I gave Dev the baby for the first time ever so *I* could sleep. And I stood up to my dad for my mom. And then I surprised everyone by showing up to the office. Which I'm glad I did, by the way, because there's definitely something weird going on there."

Alaina shakes her head before letting out a deep exhale. "Okay, fine. Whatever. I don't want to spend the first time I'm seeing you in forever arguing… It was there. You took it. Just promise me you won't do it again. Not until it's at least vetted."

When Maya doesn't say anything, Alaina gives her a look. "Maya, I'm serious. Don't fuck with something you know nothing about."

"Okay." Maya takes a deep breath in. "I promise. No more supplements. I just… I just want you to know I've only taken it because everything has been kind of a blur since Shaan was born. I've felt so out of control and overwhelmed." She can feel her eyes watering and bites down on her lower lip.

"Come here," Alaina says, her tone softening as she pulls Maya in for a quick hug. "You just had a baby *and* you're still trying to run your company. That sounds impossible. Why don't you get some help with Shaan?"

When Maya doesn't reply, Alaina adds, "I've told you this before and I'll say it again. I get the sense that you think you have to do everything by yourself. Like it's you against the world or something. I'm sure Dev's told you this before."

"He has. He just did a few days ago," Maya says. But she doesn't feel like getting into that right now, so she pivots with "Enough about me. Oh, wait! How's couples' therapy?"

Alaina groans, leaning against the fridge. "I don't think it's working."

"Why? Did something happen?" Maya turns to look at her halfway through setting the table.

Alaina joins the effort and takes out four bowls from the pantry. "No, that's the problem. *Nothing's* happened. Or rather, nothing's changed. We keep having the same arguments over and over."

"About…?"

"Everything? Nothing?" Alaina shakes her head. "I don't know. I've realized I've been so resentful of him for being able to just focus on work and, frankly, do whatever he wants ever since the girls were born. Everything it takes to run our family falls on me."

"That's so unfair. Seriously. I'm so sorry it's been like this for you."

Alaina takes a long sip from her wineglass and lets out a satisfied sigh. "Like, the other day," she continues, "I was sitting in the Trader Joe's parking lot, and I just started thinking about *everything* I used to want when I was younger, and how much pressure I put on myself to achieve those things. All of it was supposed to make me happy."

"And it does, right?" Maya tries hiding the concern in her voice. "I mean, I know you're going through a rough patch with Ryan, but overall you're still happy with how your life turned out. Right?"

Alaina shrugs. "Honestly, most days, I'm too overwhelmed or exhausted to even process how I'm feeling. But when I do find the time to wallow in self-pity, I remind myself this was all my own doing. So then I tell myself to be an adult and grow up. Welcome to the real world, where everyone's tired and overworked."

Maya shifts her weight back and forth. "Okay…that doesn't exactly answer my question. Are you happy? Because from where I'm standing, you're living the dream. *Your* dream, to be exact. Ryan, the girls, the beautiful house. And you're about to start your dream job!" Alaina texted her a couple days ago when she got the job offer to be program director at New Jersey Medical's Emergency Medicine Residency Program. It's a role she's wanted since before she even started med school.

"I know, I know," Alaina says, nodding. "But you're asking me if I'm happy? I honestly don't know. I mean, I have so much to be grateful for and that's good enough, right? Isn't happiness such a reach, anyway? It's greedy to strive for that, right?"

Maya frowns. "I wouldn't say that…"

Alaina takes another—longer—sip of wine. "I'm fine, really. Fine enough. But happy? I'm not sure I've been *happy* for a long time."

Maya's heart drops for her best friend. She takes in the slump in her shoulders, the downturned corners of her mouth. She looks so depleted.

"I'm sorry." Now Maya shuffles closer to her. "For how you've been feeling. And for the fact that I had no idea."

"No, that's not your fault. Guess you're not the only one keeping secrets." Alaina gives Maya a smirk. "I didn't even really tell *myself*, honestly. Plus, it's so hard to talk openly about this with you if the girls or Ryan are around, or when I'm so exhausted from my shifts. I can barely keep my eyes open on the drive home, let alone articulate all this to you on the phone."

Maya nods in understanding. "Well, it sounds like we need to make more of an effort to see each other. More one-on-one quality time." She wants to say so much more, to tell Alaina she's missed her, that she wishes they were as close as they used to be, before marriage and kids and life got in the way. As grateful as she is for her life, she misses the time when a close friendship didn't require so much effort and energy and planning.

"Ah, what am I even going on about? I'm fine. Overreacting." She waves her hand away. "It's just one of those weeks. And I think this whole couples' therapy thing is bringing up a lot for me…and for Ryan, too, obviously. Until now, we hadn't ever really taken the time to examine our lives both as a couple and as individuals. I didn't realize how miserable he's been, either."

"He's *miserable*?" How did she not pick up on that, either?

Ryan has always been the life of the party; in fact, Alaina has been credited for bringing that side out in him once they started dating. When they were in med school together, every time Alaina or her friends would see him in the library, they'd text the group chat things like *Hot Guy is studying alone again. Who is going to convince Hot Guy to come to happy hour with us? Do you think Hot Guy actually talks?*

"I mean, we've never been the romantic couple like you and Dev are," Alaina says, gesturing toward the living room. "We're more the show-love-by-leaving-each-other-alone type. Like, I would never post anything like this." Alaina takes out her phone and opens Maya's Instagram page.

Her most recent post is a selfie of her in a blush-pink sweatshirt, thick black glasses, her hair tangled up in a bun. In the photo, Dev's fast asleep on her shoulder. His glasses are at an angle at the bridge of his nose, and the hood of his navy blue sweatshirt is scrunched around his head. The caption: Lounging with my favorite. He fell asleep while we were discussing how many ounces our little man consumed today. This counts as date night, right?

Maya unlocks her own phone and scrolls through the hundreds of comments already, many of which are some variations of "so cute," "the best couple," and "relationship goals."

"And I mean, good for you and Dev," Alaina says as Maya keeps scrolling. "This is how it should be after you have a baby together. Ryan had to work back-to-back shifts after Jade was born, and he didn't even know what was going on at home most of the time. I'm so glad it's better for you. Really, I am."

Maya feels a twinge of guilt looking at the picture. It's not that the caption of her last post isn't true. It's just not the *whole* truth. Maya omitted, for example, how Dev fell asleep when she was trying to fill him in on her day with Shaan. Or how, minutes before she posted that picture, they were arguing about finding child care for the hundredth time that week alone.

You're not the one who actually has to deal with everything, she had said to Dev. *Your job isn't ever going to be threatened because we had a baby. Your mom and my mom think you're a hero for doing basic parenting. You never have to go through what I do.*

As if to prove her point, Dev fell into a deep sleep minutes later while Maya stared at him, seething, until she was interrupted by Shaan's crying every three hours for the rest of the night. At three a.m., Dev was smiling mid-dream. Three a.m., she's learned, is dangerous. Three a.m. is when all of her bottled-up resentment becomes ravenous, on a mission to seize anything that'll help it grow.

Alaina's gaze shifts to the packages at the end of the marble counter and she laughs. "I can't believe you get sent all this free shit. Are these the perks of being an influencer?"

Maya's cheeks go red. "I'm not an *influencer.* I just document parts of my life on social media for Medini's sake and they get a lot of traction. So sometimes companies send me their products."

"Tomayto, tomahto. Well, whatever you want to call it, I clearly picked the wrong line of work. Did I tell you that when I was leaving my ER shift yesterday, a random guy spit on my shoes?"

The two burst out laughing. "You know," Maya says, "that could be your whole brand. A behind-the-scenes look at a day in the life of a mom who's an ER doctor."

"Oh yeah, I can picture that now." Alaina takes a small bow. "Hello, I'm Alaina, the influencer you know and love as Modern Superwoman. Oooh, look at my messy house and the bags under my eyes!" She gestures toward her body like a game show host. "Isn't this all so *aspirational*? If you click the link in my bio, you'll have access to all my secrets on how to never have your shit together!"

"Hey, it could work! People love it when you're 'authentic,'" Maya says, thinking about the weight of that word. She's only ever heard women be criticized for not being "authentic." She gestures to the stack of packages. "Anyway, you can take whatever you want from that. I'm going to give most of it away, as usual."

Alaina walks over to start rummaging through the boxes. "Do any of these products help someone not be constantly pissed at their husband?"

Maya laughs and uncorks another bottle of red. Even though she hasn't had much, she should definitely pump and dump tonight. "You know, it's funny, there are so many products out there that are supposed to make having a baby easier, but so few of them actually do."

"Oh wait, that reminds me!" Alaina turns to face her. "How does Dev like that baby carrier we sent? It was a little much for me, but Ryan swore by it when the girls were little."

Maya calls out to their husbands to take their drinks and plates to the living room coffee table for dinner, then whispers to Alaina, "We haven't actually had a chance to discuss that, or anything, really, since I came back from Rockville."

"Seriously? I feel like that was ages ago." When Dev and Ryan enter the kitchen, Maya hands them their wineglasses. "And I'm sorry," Alaina continues, "but couldn't someone else have gone to Rockville?? Someone who's not, you know, *postpartum*?"

"That's exactly what I said!" Dev extends his hand toward Alaina in gratitude.

"Sure, they could have. Josh was all too eager to fill in." Maya rolls her eyes. "That's literally *why* I went, so that wouldn't happen."

"I get that you want to do a lot right now," Alaina says, audibly choosing her words carefully. "But if you're going to keep going at this pace, shouldn't you get some help with Shaan?"

Dev claps. "Another thing I've been saying. But she doesn't want to."

"Hey, I'm right here, no need to talk about me in the third

person," Maya says sarcastically, doing a mock wave at Dev. "And I'm fine. I can handle this, okay?"

As they head over to the living room to take a seat, Dev says, "It's not about whether you can handle it, Maya. It's about the possibility that an extra hand with Shaan could give you the support you need." He steals a glance at Alaina for support.

Despite them being the two people who know Maya better than anyone, neither of them has ever been able to fully grasp the fact that spending money, no matter the situation, has and always will fill her with a mixture of guilt and self-loathing. *Especially* when it comes to child care.

"I, for one, think it's great Maya closed the damn deal at work, all things considered. Can we all cheers to that?" Ryan raises his glass.

"Oh, how very nice of you to celebrate *Maya's* choices," Alaina mutters under her breath, loud enough for him to hear.

"Her choices that help her keep the lights on at her company? Yes, how awful of me to want to celebrate that," Ryan retorts, fiddling with the collar of his sky-blue polo shirt. "And at least Maya doesn't jump at the chance to complain about everything she's doing."

"What? Like *I* do?" Alaina challenges. "Like my 'complain log' suggests?"

Dev shoots Maya a look and she can tell he wants to play peacekeeper. *Don't,* Maya mouths.

On the phone last weekend, Alaina told Maya that their therapist had asked her to log every time she says something negative. It turns out her list was pretty long. Way longer than she, Ryan, and even the therapist thought it would be.

But in this moment, she has to play pretend, as if she has no idea what they're talking about. She and Alaina have an unspoken understanding where they'll act like they know nothing about each other's marriage when the four of them are together. Ryan would be horrified if he found out what Maya knows about him, including but not limited to the fact that he failed his medical boards on the first try, he sometimes cries after having sex, and he once accidentally sent a dick pic to his aunt (her name is also Alaina).

"I didn't say that." Ryan sighs in exasperation. "I didn't say *anything* about your complain log."

"You might as well have," Alaina snaps, twirling spaghetti around her fork with laser-like focus.

Ryan doesn't respond. For several seconds, the only sounds are the clinks of their utensils and Dev clearing his throat as he reaches for the bottle and refills each of their wineglasses.

"Actually, you know what?" Alaina tears her eyes away from her fork. "Maybe I do complain a lot. But I'm exhausted all the time, taking care of the girls, coming off a twelve-hour shift, wasting my time going to ther—"

"Hey, hey," Maya interrupts, holding up her palms. This is going down a dangerous path. "For what it's worth, I complain a lot, actually." She steals a glance at Dev, whose eyes are glued to his plate, neither confirming nor denying. "And Alaina, of course you're exhausted. All of this shit—" she gestures around her to signal life in general "—this whole business of making it through each day, *is* exhausting."

Ryan sighs. "I thought this whole job-offer thing would make you so happy, Alaina. But you've only seemed more… on edge. Even your mom thinks so."

Maya shoots Ryan a warning look. Bringing up Alaina's mom is the *least* helpful thing he could do right now.

Sure enough, Alaina immediately scowls. "I really don't care what my mom thinks, thank you very much. She was barely around growing up, so her opinion doesn't carry much weight in my decision." She scoffs, refocusing her attention on the spaghetti dangling from her fork. "Besides, it's not like she's ever respected any of my choices anyway," she mumbles.

Alaina's parents met when Alaina's dad moved from Germany to Jamaica for work, saw Alaina's mom on the news, and called her for a date. Alaina's mom, Rita (Auntie Rita, as Maya calls her), relocated to Jersey soon after to start a life with him, where she got a job at the local news station. Auntie Rita threw herself into her work and frequently pressured Alaina to follow in her footsteps, excel in her career. Alaina has repeatedly told Maya over the years that she feels like, no matter what she does, she'll never live up to her mother's impossible expectations for her.

Ryan nods in mock understanding. "Right, so I can't have an opinion, and your mom can't have an opinion. Got it!" He rolls his eyes as he leans back into the sofa.

He sounds so much like Dev in that moment.

"You're *always* pissed about stuff from the past, *always* saying nobody gets it," Ryan continues.

Maya tries to catch Alaina's eye to give her a comforting glance. She's no stranger to the tricky nature of resentment, how it festers and has a way of being immune to time. But Alaina's eyes are too busy shooting daggers at her husband.

"You know what? I think I'm going to head out." Alaina aggressively puts her fork down on the coffee table next to her half-finished bowl of spaghetti and stands up from the couch.

"Wait, what? Right now?" Maya makes a move to get up from her seat.

"Yes, really. Enjoy the rest of the meal. And, um, sorry, guys." She gives her and Dev an apologetic look. "I'll see you both soon, I'm sure."

"Well, guess that means I'm out, too," Ryan mumbles, getting up from the sofa.

"No, *you* can stay. Take an Uber home. Do whatever. I don't care."

Before anyone can say anything else, Alaina slips on her white sparkly sneakers and walks out the front door.

NEW YORK CITY POLICE DEPARTMENT

OFFICER KENT: We are trying to learn more about Maya's emotional state after having a baby.

ALAINA BROWN: She was excited. And overwhelmed, maybe a little scared.

OFFICER KENT: She didn't want a child?

ALAINA BROWN: That is *not* what I said. Maya was overwhelmed the way any new mother would be.

OFFICER KENT: Did she say anything that led you to believe she wanted to leave her son?

ALAINA BROWN: *What?* No. Never.

OFFICER KENT: To your knowledge, has she ever run away before? Or disappeared for a day or two without telling anyone?

ALAINA BROWN: I'm not sure if I—

OFFICER KENT: Please answer the question, Ms. Brown.

ALAINA BROWN: Back when we were roommates, there were times when she would get really overwhelmed or stressed...and she'd sometimes go off the grid without telling me, or anyone. But she always came back. That's just how Maya is. She self-isolates and takes her space when things get hard. She hates asking for help.

OFFICER KENT: Is there anything that could suggest this time is different? That Maya won't come back?

ALAINA BROWN: Of course not. How could you even ask me that?

OFFICER KENT: You just said she was scared to be a mom.

ALAINA BROWN: You know what? I think we're done here.

Maya: We need to fix this situation ASAP.

Josh: I know. My guess is the board is going to want us to scale back on retail and focus all of our efforts on D2C.

Maya: It's too late to go back on the Whole Foods deal. And if I have to repeat that to them ten more times, I'm prepared to. But we do need to figure out a way to cut costs.

Josh: There's always the last-resort option...

Maya: Cutting team members?

Josh: Yeah.

Maya: We can't do that. Everyone's been working around the clock and sacrificing so much.

Josh: I know. I'm just having trouble thinking of other options, other than cheapening our products. It would save us money...

Maya: And compromise the integrity of the entire brand? No way. We'd alienate all our loyal customers.

Josh: I know.

Maya: Let me think on this and get back to you.

She darkens her phone screen. Her minds blanks as she tries to think of ways to decrease Medini's spending. But it's like her brain is stuck in molasses, unable to form a single productive thought.

Once again, Maya's confronted with the terrifying reality that if she can't think of a plan to save Medini, and fast, she will have wasted every dollar she's ever invested in her company. Every hour of her employees' lives spent toward keeping her company afloat. Every minute she's spent trying to prove every person who doubted her wrong, from the snide aunties to the jerk investors.

Fuck.

Maybe Liz is right. Maybe this is really the only option. But the thought of laying off her loyal, hardworking employees makes her nauseous.

Her eyes slowly shift toward the nightstand drawer next to her side of the bed, where she's hidden the little glass vial behind a pile of Strand bookmarks, bobby pins, old glasses, and an eye mask she could probably get some use out of lately. Keeping the bottle in her everyday bag was too tempting. But as she's lying in bed, entertaining the thought of laying off some of her dedicated employees—who have been with her since the start—she couldn't have picked a worse new hiding spot.

Alaina's words come back to her. *Don't fuck with something you know nothing about.*

She tears her eyes away from the nightstand and forces herself out of the bed.

Five minutes later, she's hooked up to her breast pump. The whirring sound grinds on her nerves as she taps her foot impatiently. She checks the bottles hanging off the end of the tubing to see some progress.

But they're practically empty.

How is that *possible*? How does she make no milk at all?

An ear-piercing scream yanks her from her thoughts.

"I'm coming, Shaan!" Maya calls out in frustration, detaching the pump parts.

Shaan's cries escalate, each one activating a primal panic in her. She speedily puts the barely filled bottles in the fridge and runs over to the bassinet.

He was up just two hours ago for his 3:00 a.m. feed. Shouldn't he be sleeping for longer stretches by this point? Surely, she's read about babies going for several hours by the time they're two months old. And how the hell can Dev sleep through all this screaming?

But once she approaches the nursery, her face goes white. Shaan's lower face and neck are completely covered in puke, his white onesie wet and clinging to his chest. He must have lost his entire last feed.

"Oh my God. I'm so sorry," Maya whispers to him.

Shaan cries louder as she removes his clothes and attempts to wash the sour smell from his skin. She holds him to her chest as she paces around the living room, hoping the motion will soothe him.

"C'mon, baby," she urges, her heart racing, "You're okay now. Shhh, I promise you're okay."

After what feels like hours, Shaan's cries subside. Maya keeps rocking him, worried they'll start again if she moves the slightest inch.

"Are you okay?" Dev appears in the living room a couple minutes later, clean-shaven and dressed in a light gray suit.

So you had time to get all dressed for work, but not to calm down our screaming child?

"Are you serious?"

"Yeah?" Dev starts setting up the Nespresso machine, not a fucking care in the world. This is what their interactions have looked like all week. Quick in-between moments, both of them too tired to discuss anything beyond child care logistics. They only offer each other their most drained selves now.

"Oh sure. *Now* I'm okay," Maya snaps.

"What do you mean, *now* you're okay?" Dev's not even looking at her as he absent-mindedly types something out on his phone.

"I *mean* that Shaan threw up everywhere, and I changed him and cleaned everything up."

He immediately stops what he's doing to finally meet her gaze. "He did? Is he okay? Why didn't you wake me up, or ask me to come help?"

If her blood was boiling before, now it's erupting. "I don't want to have to *ask* you. I want you to already be aware that I'm dealing with him every morning, and that when you hear ear-piercing screaming, it might be a good idea to come and parent *our* child with me."

Dev slumps his shoulders to face the hardwood floor. Maya's always the reactive one.

She used to love that Dev could keep his emotions under control, but today, she wishes he would react. Say something. *Anything.*

"So that's it, then?" Maya presses. "You're not even going to say anything?"

"I don't know." Dev sighs. "I can't win."

She hears exasperation in his voice, something that wasn't always there. Something that's been there every day this week alone, she realizes.

"This isn't about winning," she says, her tone softer.

"Then what's it about, Maya? I try to help, you get mad. I don't help, you get mad. What can I say that will actually make things better?"

That you don't consider it "help" when you're parenting our child. That something about your life has to change, too, since we had a baby. That you understand how much I'm trying to manage in a single day even though I have so little to show for it. That there seem to be a million fires for me to put out at my company, but I can't single-handedly focus on work the way you can. That you love me and you're sorry.

But none of that feels right. So she settles for a transactional but somewhat related response. "Have you heard anything about your paternity leave yet?"

"No, not yet. I'm sorry. I'm trying. I really am," Dev says, picking up his messenger bag.

More silence follows. Maya realizes there are two different wives in her right now with two opposing desires. One wants to wallow in her anger and let her husband feel a version of the guilt she experiences on a daily basis, while the other wants to pull him into her arms, apologize for snapping, and express her needs in a more productive way.

The latter sounds like the safest bet. They're not supposed to be this type of couple. She walks toward him, ready to wrap her arms across his broad shoulders.

But then Dev's phone lights up. "Damn it. Not again."

"What's wrong?"

"My morning meeting got moved up again. I have to get to the office right now," he groans.

"Right," she mumbles in reply.

He gives her and Shaan rushed kisses. "Love you both. I'll see you at his appointment in a few hours."

Later, they'll be at Shaan's third doctor's appointment since he was born. Despite having her vagina ripped open and bleeding for weeks, her breasts continuing to swell and leak, and intense hormonal changes, Maya only had one postpartum checkup, six weeks after giving birth.

She pulls up her Google calendar to confirm the time with Dev. But right as she looks up from her phone, the heavy apartment door shuts.

Maya soaks in the quiet, trying to process what just happened. Why did she have to respond in that way when Dev was only trying to help?

The guilt hits her like a slap to the face. She feels it cascade through her bloodstream and coat her organs. As her brain drifts back to that little brown bottle, she reminds herself over and over that she is a responsible person. She has made it through many difficult times in her life without the use of experimental supplements. Maya can learn how to control her days instead of letting her days control *her*.

Her phone pings, taking her away from her thoughts.

Liz forwarded her a meme on Instagram: To anyone who tells me to sleep when my baby sleeps, how about I'll work when the baby works? Clean when the baby cleans? Pump when the baby pumps? Yeah, that's what I thought. The meme's bold cursive font and millennial-pink backdrop are surprisingly comforting in that moment.

Maya Patel: You have no idea how much I needed to read something like this right now.

Liz Anderson: ♥

Later, Maya follows a nurse past the waiting room door to an exam table. Dev's already standing there, texting at rapid speed.

"You can remove everything but his diaper," the nurse instructs. "We'll weigh him, check his temperature, and I'll write down any questions you may have for the doctor."

Shaan predictably screams when Maya unzips his onesie and pants and places him on the scale. Dev tries to get him to look at the pictures of zoo animals on the wall, and when that doesn't work, tries singing him a lullaby.

"Wow, he's an unhappy fella, isn't he, Mama?" The nurse flashes her a tight, thin smile. Maya's sure she means well, but regardless, it stings. And why did she only direct the comment to her?

"Dr. Karp will be with you in just a moment." The nurse quickly jots down Shaan's weight, length, and head circumference, and leaves his chart on one side of the sink before closing the door behind her. On the other side, there are glass jars filled with cotton balls, tongue depressors, and Q-tips. The wall above the sink has a guide for how to wash hands properly, illustrated with paintings of characters from *Sesame Street*. Maya stares at it in concentration to distract herself. *First comes water, then comes soap…*

To Maya's surprise, she quickly hears a knock on the door and in walks Dr. Karp. His broad, stocky build and wide grin immediately put Maya at ease. She loves this doctor.

He examines Shaan from head to toe, unfazed by his ear-piercing screams and wriggling body that resists each and every part of the assessment. When the checkup is over, Maya dresses Shaan and cradles him in the crook of her elbow, bouncing her knee anxiously. Dev notices and rubs her arm gently.

Dr. Karp rolls a stool toward Maya, Shaan, and Dev. "So, how's this little guy doing with his feeds lately?"

"He's taking milk every few hours," Maya says confidently. "And I'm pumping as much as possible."

"Is he getting any direct breastfeeding?"

Maya shifts in the hard plastic chair while Dr. Karp scans through Shaan's chart. "I'm trying, really trying," she says in response, then gestures between herself and Dev. "*We're* really trying. But it's been a bit of a struggle." Dev squeezes Maya's hand in support.

"I see," Dr. Karp says after what feels like a lifetime. He's still smiling, but his tone has changed.

"Is something wrong?" Maya asks.

She waits for Dr. Karp to say, *Of course not, Maya, you're doing great! Shaan's the healthiest baby I've seen all day. Keep up the good work.*

But instead, he furrows his brows. "Shaan's weight has dropped from the twenty-fifth percentile to the fifth percentile."

"What?!" Maya feels her stomach drop. For weeks, her life has revolved around Shaan's feeds. And when she isn't feeding him, she's pumping, or thinking ahead to the next feed.

"And you're sure about this?" Dev asks the doctor, squeezing her hand harder.

"Unfortunately, yes." Dr. Karp points to the growth chart in his hands, tilting it for them to see. "Now, if you look at the height and weight here, when he was born, and then we move back here—" he points to a different spot "—you'll see there's been quite a drop."

"But… I've been… I don't understand." The pressure of tears builds behind her eyes. She tightens her grip on Shaan and slips her finger into his tiny fist. He's been struggling this entire time. And she had no idea.

"Now, as for his crying." Dr. Karp motions to Shaan. "I know I've mentioned the possibility of colic, but I'm convinced now that it has to be hunger. I'd suggest you stop trying to breastfeed or give pumped milk and switch to formula immediately. And if he's resistant to taking larger portions of milk, I recommend feeding him more frequently. Every two hours."

"Every two hours," Maya repeats, her head spinning. It's

impossible to fathom how she will stick to that routine during the day and at night. It's hard enough as it is.

"We'll start that right away, Doctor," Dev confirms, rubbing Maya's back in solidarity.

Dr. Karp scoots his chair back and rises to his feet. "Rest assured, babies with failure to thrive can catch up, especially when they have such caring, hands-on parents like yourselves."

"Failure to thrive?" Maya blurts out. "Our son has *failure to thrive*?"

Dr. Karp's somber expression is confirmation enough.

Maya remembers coming across that phrase in some of the books she'd read during pregnancy. It sounded scary but seemed so extreme to her, such a worst-case-scenario outcome, that she hadn't bothered investigating it further.

Dr. Karp's mouth is moving, but his voice fades into the background. All she can do is stare at Shaan. Her vulnerable, tiny baby boy.

She's failed as a mother. Her body is supposed to know how to nourish her son and it can't. *She* can't.

"I'm sorry," she whispers to Shaan after he gets his shots. The nurse mentions something about Shaan possibly developing a fever tonight as a result, suggests they have some Tylenol on hand. But Maya doesn't process any of it. She feels like a zombie as she walks alongside Dev back through the waiting room and into the elevator.

Dev hugs her when they're outside the office. "It's going to be okay."

"You don't know that."

"I do," he promises. "I really do. It'll all work out. Please try not to worry."

Please try not to worry. Worrying is all she's been doing since Shaan was born. It's the only thing she's good at when it comes to motherhood. Her life these past two months has been a constant roller coaster, her feelings rapidly shifting between excitement, exhaustion, hope, resentment, rage. She isn't sure how to hold all of them at once.

They walk in step toward the subway, Dev pushing the stroller and giving her a sideways glance every few seconds.

"Just say what you're thinking," Maya groans.

"I'm thinking that we're going to put him on formula, and he will be okay." He smiles and kisses her cheek. "We'll take care of this."

"But I'm supposed to *already* be taking care of this, of him." She makes the mistake of peering over the top of the stroller to catch a glimpse of his little face. All she wants to do right now is curl up into a ball and sob.

"Don't do that to yourself, Maya. You can't blame yourself for this."

"How can I not? My only job as a mother, the bare *minimum*, is to keep him healthy. But I can't even feed him." As they continue walking down Sixth Avenue, they pass people clutching iced coffees, adjusting their AirPods, and talking animatedly on the phone. How does the rest of the world just carry on when hers is so rocked, so out of control?

Dev kisses her forehead. "Let's just get home, honey. Maybe you can take a power nap while I give him a bath."

But once they're home, her mind is running a mile a minute and there's nothing that can quiet her racing thoughts. Not the soothing sounds of running water, not Dev's humming from the bathroom, not a mindfulness exercise. Not even her head hitting the cool, smooth pillow.

Your son is starving. It's all your fault. You're a bad mother.

She presses her palms over her ears, willing the thoughts to stop.

You will never be a good mom. You're not good enough.

She opens her nightstand drawer and holds the bottle in her hands.

Failure to thrive. Failure to thrive. Failure to thrive.

Before she can talk herself out of it, she shakes out another pill and dry swallows.

The relief is immediate. Her breathing slows down, the muscles in her neck loosen.

Maya tucks the bottle in the back of the drawer and leans against the wall, letting out a deep exhale. As today's sequence of events has shown, everything that's happening in her life right now is completely out of control. Out of *her* control.

She lets this thought sink in, and that's when it hits her. Yes, many things are out of Maya's hands at the moment.

Many things, but not everything.

As the pill keeps working its way through her body, the gears start turning in her mind.

Maya knows exactly what she needs to do next, and before she can talk herself out of it, she finds her phone. He picks up on the first ring.

"Josh, we have to let people go."

TECH SCENE

Interview with Medini CFO Brad Mosby

By Katie Higgins

Published August 2, 2019, 2:05 PM EDT

TECH SCENE: At what point did Medini's upward trajectory take a turn?

BRAD MOSBY: Honestly, we should have seen the layoffs as a warning sign. Things only went downhill from there.

TECH SCENE: In her interview for *Tech Crunch*, Ms. Patel claimed they were necessary. I believe the exact word she used was "essential."

BRAD MOSBY: Maybe it seemed like it…at the time. But it all just happened so fast. It wasn't like Maya to make such an impulsive decision like that, especially when it came to her employees' livelihoods.

TECH SCENE: Meaning?

BRAD MOSBY: Meaning that she, more than anyone, emphasized team camaraderie and morale. She had to know that letting people go meant putting more strain on the ones who remained. But she seemed, I don't know, desperate to keep Medini afloat.

TECH SCENE: Desperate? Isn't it a founder's job to keep a company running?

BRAD MOSBY: Well, yes, of course.

TECH SCENE: Do you think there's credibility to her numerous statements claiming, and I quote, "Female founders have it harder"?

BRAD MOSBY: I'm not sure what that has to do with this?

TECH SCENE: Please answer the question, Mr. Mosby.

BRAD MOSBY: Yes, I think there's truth to that.

TECH SCENE: And do you think that being in a male-dominated environment may have personally affected Ms. Patel?

BRAD MOSBY: I'm sure it did. I mean, don't get me wrong, it's not like we were some kind of "boys' club." But I guess it'd be unfair for me to assume it didn't feel that way sometimes for Maya.

12

"MAYA, YOU KNOW I'M THE SOLE EARN-er for my family," Jackie, Medini's director of social media, says through heavy sobs, her face crumpling as she reaches for another tissue from the box on Maya's desk.

"I'm so sorry. Trust me, I really didn't want it to be this way. I know how much you've done for Medini, and I want you to know how appreciative I am of your years of hard work."

Maya's words sound hollow. Weak. When she called Josh about layoffs, he recommended they set up a time to chat before moving forward, but she told him her mind was made up. *The sooner, the better. I'll come in on Friday. Let's start with the marketing team and go to customer service.*

It's so much easier said than done. Especially when you're literally face-to-face with the consequences of your actions.

"Why are you doing this?" The tears keep trickling down Jackie's face.

"I know this is hard. But I have to do what's best for Medini.

I wouldn't be doing this if it wasn't necessary. And you can expect a glowing recommendation letter from me, as well as a long list of people in my network whose companies I think you'd be a great fit for. I promise you I will do my part to make sure you end up in a good place."

"But I thought…we were friends," Jackie says, looking at her as if she's a monster. She pushes her chair back and grabs her bag off the floor.

"Jackie, please wait, I—"

The glass door shuts behind her.

She looks at the schedule Tiffany put together on her calendar. Ten more conversations like this are ahead of her. And the pit in her stomach tells her she only has so long until the pill wears off. Either way, she's not a robot. This is excruciating.

She needs a pep talk.

Liz picks up right away. "Maya! How's it going over there? I know today isn't easy."

"No, it's not. That's actually why I'm calling. This is hard. *Really* hard. I don't know if I can do this. I still have ten to go and I'm getting really in my head. I feel so terrible about this, I honestly think I might be sick."

"Listen to me," Liz says, her voice authoritative. "You're doing the right thing. It comes with the job. You're looking at the long term, not the now. And yes, it's hard, but you know what would be harder? Letting your company go under."

I'm the sole earner of my family. We were friends. Were.

Maya goes pale at the thought of Jackie packing up her desk at this very moment, putting her family photos in her bag, trying to think of the best way to tell her husband and the kids she just got let go.

You're a monster. You're ruthless. Your employees trusted you, and you betrayed them.

The air feels too hot, the office too small. Her breath starts to quicken, and she grips her desk to ground herself.

"I can't go through with this, I'm sorry. I thought I could, but I can't. I really feel like I'm going to be sick." She pulls the trash can toward her as a precautionary measure and tries to take slow, deep breaths.

"Maya, you didn't happen to bring the pills with you today, did you?"

"Actually, I did because I was running late this morning and brought it—"

"Take another pill."

"I wish I could, but I already took one this morning. You said maximum one a day, right?"

"Today can be an exception. You need the boost. I promise this will only help you get through everything ahead. Trust me. I only want to help."

Maya slowly reaches for her bag.

"Liz, I don't know—"

"When's your next meeting?"

Maya looks at the time. "Five minutes. God, I really need more time."

"It's going to be okay, trust me. Take an extra pill right now, and you'll thank me later, promise. You've got this."

Liz hangs up and Maya's alone with her thoughts again. She takes out the brown glass vial.

You're ruthless, Maya, ruthless. You're a corporate sellout. You're a bad person.

Her head's spinning, her breath growing shallower. She can't take the noise anymore. She just can't. It's debilitating. Unbearable.

She dry swallows another pill just as Ralph, a member from their customer service team, knocks on the door.

Please work. Please, I need you to work now.

"Um, hi, Maya."

"Hi, Ralph. Please take a seat."

Why aren't you working faster? I need you!

"What's going on? Jackie just walked out crying, and I saw other people packing up all their things earlier. You're not..." He looks up at her, and his face falls when she doesn't make a move to reassure him.

"Oh my God. Is this for real?" Ralph asks, his eyes wide.

"Unfortunately, it is." Maya's voice is deadpan as she nudges the tissue box closer to him, her heart rate finally slowing down. "I'll write you a recommendation letter. I'm sure you're disappointed, but I'm confident that with time, you'll see that this was the right move for the company, and for all involved."

Ralph stares at her in disbelief. "You're sure I'm *disappointed*? Is that what you really just said? While you're *firing* me?"

"I really didn't want this to happen. And I hope you know I exhausted every other option first. This was by no means an easy decision." Maya shifts her focus to aligning and reshuffling the sheets of paper in front of her. Anything to avoid looking him in the eyes.

"*Wow.* You are not who I thought you were." Ralph shakes his head at her and leaves.

Her heart aches, but in a manageable way. She can get through the rest of the conversations. When she turns to her laptop, an email is waiting for her at the top of her inbox.

Good job on making the right call.
Travis

Her phone buzzes with a text from Tarun.

Tarun: Have you talked to Mom or Dad?

Maya: Not in the last couple of days. Why?

Tarun: I stopped by the motel and Mom wasn't there. Dad said she's been leaving early every day this week with no explanation. Isn't that weird?

Maya: Really? Yeah, that is weird. Did Dad say anything else? Did you ask him what's been going on?

Tarun: No.

She knew he'd say that. Tarun never probes with her parents. Even though Maya sometimes wishes he would, she knows that she's contributed to this emotional distance between her brother and parents. Ever since they were kids, Maya made it her job as older sister to shield him from their parents' arguments. She's always been caught between protecting her brother and envying him at the same time.

Maya: Okay, let's go there this weekend. Shaan hasn't had a proper trip to the motel anyway.

Tarun: Sounds good. I'll meet you all there.

Maya puts her phone away and presses her black heels into the floor. To her surprise, all she feels is curiosity about the situation with her parents. Clear, direct curiosity. Nothing else. No pull to call her parents and mediate their latest argument. No pang of regret for not being able to go to the motel right now. Instead, she's all logic and focus. Conviction and action.

Damn. The pill is more powerful than she even thought if it can dampen new-mother guilt and founder guilt *and* daughter-of-immigrants guilt.

The rest of the day passes by in a blur of difficult conversations, tissue-box nudges, and well wishes for the future.

Later that afternoon, when she's on the subway back home, she waits to feel the heaviness of the day.

But it never comes.

★★★

"You're serious? You let all those people go?" Dev is pacing their living room back and forth. It's putting her on edge.

"I had to. I didn't have a choice."

"Damn. I mean…that's going to be a shock for a lot of people."

"I'm aware."

Dev leans against the fridge and unbuttons the top of his creased salmon-colored shirt. "So, when did you come to this decision? I had no idea you were even considering doing this."

"I wasn't planning on it. With the Whole Foods order coming through so quickly, we were going to burn through our cash too fast. I have to buy Medini more time. And you know how stressed I was about the company's spending even before that."

Dev sighs. "I did know, Maya, and that's kind of the point. We'd usually talk about something like this. And now you've made a huge decision affecting your company, and this is the first I'm hearing about it? After it already happened?"

"I would have talked to you, but it all just happened so fast."

He scoffs. "Letting go of a sizable portion of Medini's team 'just happened so fast'? Do you hear yourself right now?"

"That's not what I meant. I had been thinking about it but the final cho—"

"Exactly." Dev points his finger at her. "You *had* been thinking about it. And I had no idea."

Maya rolls her eyes. "Oh my God. Why are you so upset right now? Where is this even coming from?"

"It's coming from my wife keeping me in the dark about things."

"Stop it. I'm not doing that."

"You are. You've been doing this since we met, and you know that. We've talked about this *way* too many times. And

I know you know what I'm referring to." Dev takes off his glasses and rubs his temples.

"How can you say that? How can you act like nothing's changed between us since that day?" She hates it when either of them weaponizes past arguments they've resolved—or at least *she* thinks they've resolved—as ammunition for new ones.

"Because some things *haven't* changed!"

They stare at each other in silence. Maya's face remains stone-cold while Dev's starts to soften in what she thinks—hopes—is remorse.

Dev sighs. "I'm sorry. You're right, I shouldn't have gone there."

She lets out a deep breath and feels her body release some of its tension. "I'm sorry, too. I should have told you about the layoffs. You've always been the first person I go to about anything Medini-related, and you've been in this with me from the start. I get why you felt in the dark."

She takes in the slope of his shoulders, his full lips that she wanted to kiss the second she first saw him. That spark has persevered through career changes, family drama, pregnancy, parenting. Her Dev, the love of her life.

"I've missed you. And us. I don't want to fight," she says.

Dev stares at the blond wood floor for several seconds. He ruffles his hair, a signature boyish gesture of his that he's never been able to shake. It instantly reminds her of those framed high school yearbook pictures she saw at Dev's parents' house the first time she visited.

Maya had always wished her younger self could have known the younger Dev. Maybe things back then wouldn't have been as hard as they were if she had someone like him in her life.

"I miss us, too, honey."

Maya slowly walks toward him, and he meets her halfway, wrapping his arms around her to pull her in close. She sinks into his chest, savoring the moment.

For an instant, she feels the contours of it: the couple they used to be. The one they were just months ago. *This is the real us*, she thinks. As Dev cups her chin, she closes her eyes.

If this were a romance movie, they'd lock lips, only pulling away to gaze into each other's eyes. Dev would grab her hand suggestively and lead them out of the living room. *Let's make the most of this time while Shaan's still asleep*, he'd whisper in her ear.

But since this is real life, all they hear are Shaan's cries from the baby monitor.

"I've got him," Dev says, kissing her forehead before taking purposeful strides toward the nursery.

And just like that, the moment's gone.

NEW YORK CITY POLICE DEPARTMENT

[...]

DEV MEHTA: No...she's never left us.

OFFICER KENT: Us? Okay, then what about just *you*?

DEV MEHTA: There was one time...after we got married. I'd rather not get into it. It's a long story.

OFFICER KENT: We have time.

DEV MEHTA: My parents were visiting us a few weeks after our wedding. Maya heard them make a comment before they left. Something about how she was just with me to elevate her status and—damn it, it's so infuriating when they say those things, and I wi—

OFFICER KENT: What happened next?

DEV MEHTA: Right, sorry. Once they were out the door, she was upset. Really upset. And rightfully so. Our wedding planning and everything leading up to it was already so hard on her, so when that—

OFFICER KENT: So you had an argument about your parents, and then what happened?

DEV MEHTA: It was one of those arguments where one thing led to another and then...it just blew up. We were both angry—no, we were livid. We brought up stuff that wasn't even relevant. She told me she needed space and walked out the door. I assumed she was blowing off steam, but a few minutes later, when I tried calling her, her phone was off. And she wasn't in our apartment lobby. I ran the blocks around our building—maybe, what, ten times?—hoping to find her.

OFFICER KENT: Where did she go?

DEV MEHTA: To her office. She slept there overnight, which I should have figured. She uses work to cope with, well, everything.

OFFICER KENT: So how long was she gone, in total?

DEV MEHTA: Um, I think she left in the mid-to-late afternoon and came back the following day around lunchtime. So if I had to guess, a little under twenty-four hours.

OFFICER KENT: Were you worried?

DEV MEHTA: Of course I was worried! I was worried sick. For all I knew, she was out in the streets of Manhattan all night. Who knows what could have happened? After it turned dark and I still hadn't heard from her, I contacted her family and best friend to see if they'd spoken to her, but they hadn't. I was ready to file a missing person report right then and there, but her brother urged us to hold off until the morning, assuring us she sometimes just needs a little space. And the next day, she came home. It was fine. I overreacted.

OFFICER KENT: Mr. Mehta, how has your marriage been these past few months?

DEV MEHTA: What are you suggest—

OFFICER KENT: Please answer the question.

DEV MEHTA: It's uh, well, it's complicated.

13

THE NEXT MORNING, ON THE DRIVE TO the motel, Maya says, "So, I guess we'll finally see what's going on with my parents."

"Yeah, do you still think it's stress? Or maybe something with Tarun?"

"I have no idea. I can't believe he's been in touch with them more than I have," she mumbles, wondering if guilt is like a limited resource in her family. If she feels less of it, does it finally allow Tarun to feel more *of* it? Guilt, guilt, guilt. It's all she can think about lately.

A loud ringing sound reverberates through the car. Maya turns to face Shaan, whose scrunched-up eyebrows seem to ask *What the heck is that?*

A second later, her mother-in-law's voice booms through the speaker. "Hello! I just wanted to check if the car is working okay."

Part of Maya feels gratitude for her in-laws' offer to borrow their Porsche Cayenne, but the other part feels deep discomfort over sitting in such an expensive vehicle. It's the kind of car Dad would have pointed out to her and Tarun if it passed them on the Garden State Parkway.

"It's great, Mom," Dev says. "Thanks."

"Of course. And how's my baby boy doing?"

"*Shaan* is great," Maya chimes in. She can't help herself.

"Hm. And how has his feeding been?"

"Fine. Perfectly fine," she lies. "We're just glad he's calm right now and that we don't have to pull over to feed him. Just getting him into the car was a hassle!" Maya forces a laugh and prays Dev's mom will change the subject.

"You know, I took Dev and his brother to India by myself," her mother-in-law says for the hundredth time. Her voice screeches through the car speaker, and Maya fights the urge to turn the volume down. "*That* was a lot of work. A car ride is nothing."

"Right," Maya says, rolling her eyes.

"Anyway, it sounds like you're having trouble managing everything, Maya. I think it'd be best if I came and stayed for a couple of weeks. Help out."

Her face grows hot. It's not lost on her that her mother-in-law specifically said Maya, not Dev *and* Maya. Even though the extra help with Shaan would make Maya's life easier, her stomach clenches at the thought of sharing their tiny apartment with Dev's mom. "Um, that's very nice of you, but no need. We're okay."

"Please! I can clearly see that you're not. I'll be able to get Shaan on a better feeding schedule," she says definitively.

She's not sure if it's the vision of her mother-in-law measuring every bottle to the ounce while shooting condescending looks at Maya, or if it's her overall exhaustion, but she curtly says, "We're good. Besides, Dev should get approved for paternity leave any day now."

"*Paternity* leave? Is that a real thing?" Now it's her father-in-law's voice coming through the car's speaker. *Great, so he's been listening in on this, too?* Maya can picture him post-golf, probably in a white polo shirt and khaki pants, stretched across the recliner and sipping an Old-Fashioned. He's always reminded her of a character from *Mad Men*.

"It's very real," Maya says as Dev turns into the motel parking lot. "And should be more the norm. Dev put in the request when I was pregnant."

"You're telling me other men have done this at your workplace, Dev?" her father-in-law pries. "What, they just don't do their jobs? They stop working?"

Maya clenches her fists. "He's going to be the first to set a very impor—"

Dev cuts her off. "Actually, they got back to me this morning."

Once the car is in Park, he turns to face her and lowers his voice to a whisper. "It's not going to work."

"I'm sorry, what?"

"They're making excuses to not give me leave. I'm so sorry, honey."

"And you're just telling me this now?" She doesn't even care that her in-laws are still on speaker.

"I was going to tell you when we got back home tonight," Dev says, keeping his voice low. He clears his throat to say, "Mom. Dad. We're here. I'll call you later."

Once he hangs up, Maya shifts her body to face him. "You're kidding me, right? You've got to be fucking kidding me."

"Look, I'm going to push back. But you know how they are. You know they'll find a way to take it out on me in some way."

"This is so unfair. I've been doing everything. *Everything.*" She throws her head into her hands.

"I know. I'm sorry. I wish there was more I could do. But we need my income."

Of course. Since he's the breadwinner, she's not allowed to expect more involvement from him, right?

Before she can say anything, Mom rushes into the parking lot and taps on Dev's window. He rolls it down and she says, "You both made it! I'm so glad!"

"We did," Maya grunts. "Barely."

"How are you? Do you want chai? Snacks?" She keeps her voice a whisper so as not to wake Shaan, blissfully unaware that Maya's fuming at her mom's golden boy. "I made your favorites, Dev." Mom winks, a self-satisfied smirk on her face.

"You really are the best," Dev says, getting out of the car to wrap his arms around Mom's shoulders.

Wonderful. Maya has to fight for her life in heated interactions with *her* mother-in-law, while Dev's treats him like a king.

Dad and Tarun are waiting for them in the lobby, which has, for the most part, remained unchanged her whole life. It has the same beige-tiled floor, the same apartment she grew up in at the far end of the hall, the same cream walls decorated with a mix of artwork (some store-bought, some illustrated by Mom). There are a few "renovations," so to speak, like the light fixtures that were drilled into the wall after a group of young boys stole lamps from three of the rooms. Or the stock of towels and toilet paper behind the front desk (next to a designated written log) ever since a young couple requested extras the night before Halloween, only to get drunk and trash the entire lobby. Her family's entire livelihood, the subject of a Mischief Night prank.

But no matter how much time has passed or how many slight alterations they make, standing here always takes her back to that day: the *thump, thump, thump* of her light-up sneakers on the floor, blue and red lights splashing the front doors, the ambulance's wail first growing louder, then softer after leaving the motel parking lot.

She blinks the memory away.

As Dev catches up with Mom and Dad, Maya takes Shaan over to her brother. "Still working nonstop?" Maya asks, tousling Tarun's hair, which seems to have more silver in it than just a month ago.

Tarun smirks. "You know it. That's the banker bro way."

Maya rolls her eyes. "You're allowed to have a life outside of work, you know."

"Ha, that's rich, coming from you!" Tarun laughs. "And I do have a life, thank you very much." The combination of his grown-out hair and large, pointy nose so strongly resembles a younger version of Dad.

"I mean a life outside of barhopping in Murray Hill every weekend with your college buddies," Maya teases.

"What's been going on with *you* at work?" Tarun asks, changing the subject. "I feel like I see something new every time I open social media."

"It's…a lot. It's been a lot."

"How is that Liz woman you've become friends with? She has an…" Tarun's eyes shift as he searches for the right word. "*Interesting* reputation."

Here we go.

"Why, what have you heard?"

"Some guy at work told me that employees at Women Rise are divided into different teams. Apparently, you're not supposed to talk to coworkers who aren't on your team about what you're working on."

Maya laughs. "Oh, come on, seriously? That's ridiculous."

He shrugs. "That's what I heard. Rumor has it they track people's emails, too, to make sure there aren't conversations happening that they don't 'approve' of. Sounds pretty toxic if you ask me."

"I mean, yeah, that's weird if it's true," Maya agrees. "But it's *not*. And even if it's partially true—which I still doubt—

it's probably taken completely out of context. Liz has told me before how hyperaware she is of potential copycats after she faced a similar issue back at Limitless. So maybe this is her way of making sure nobody can rip off her company's products, or share the ingredients with a competitor?"

"Look at you, getting defensive," Tarun says in a singsong voice. "If I were saying this about anyone else, you'd be agreeing with me."

"I'm not being defensive," Maya counters. "I just know from experience that there's usually more to the story."

"Riiight. Anyway, it does sound like your plate is really full. Maybe you should finally get some help, like a nanny?"

"Funnily enough, I was actually thinking that on the car ride here." She lowers her voice to a whisper. "Anything to prevent Dev's mom from inserting herself and to avoid hearing her unsolicited opinions on parenting. And we do need the help." Maya sighs. "I don't know. It feels too soon and not soon enough at the same time."

"Hey, you're going to have to do it at some point," Tarun reasons.

"I know. It's just…harder than I thought it'd be."

"It's going to be fine." He playfully bumps her with his elbow.

"I know," she lies.

But for the second time that day, all she can hear are the wailing sirens, her parents' raised voices that escalate into screams. Her own racing heartbeat.

Maya's almost relieved when Shaan starts screaming. She needs a distraction.

"Is he okay?" Tarun turns to his nephew, who is wrapped in a white blanket like a burrito. A very angry burrito.

At the sound of the commotion, Mom, Dad, and Dev start walking over to them from the other side of the lobby.

"Oh, he's fine," Maya says, waving it off. "He just cries when his nap is cut short...or when he's not in motion...or when he's hungry. Or always."

"Maybe it's gas? Or colic?" Tarun suggests. "I heard lactose can be hard to digest at this age."

Maya raises an eyebrow. "And where did *you* hear that?"

"I've been reading some articles on babies and stuff." Tarun shrugs.

"You? Reading about babies?" Maya tries to picture her brother—her sports-loving, beer-drinking, head-in-the-clouds brother—pulling up websites about infant health.

Unfortunately for him, Mom's within earshot by that point. "Does that mean you're thinking of settling down?"

"Moooom, no," Tarun groans, dragging out the word. He sounds like he's thirteen again. "I'm just trying to understand my nephew."

Mom nods and looks away, unsatisfied. She and Dad call Maya at least once a week to get intel on Tarun's dating life. Or rather, lack thereof.

Dad holds his fingers to his lips as he leans toward Shaan. "Shhhh. You're okay. You don't have to yell. Although...your mom was the exact same way at your age!" He chuckles, gesturing a thumb in Maya's direction.

"Your mom was like that since she was in my *womb*!" Mom exclaims. "I felt her kicking and punching at all hours, whereas this one—" she nods at Tarun "—just glided." She gazes wistfully at Maya. "I used to walk with you in my arms all night."

"After a day of running the motel and cooking all our meals?" Maya shakes her head. "I really don't understand how you did it all."

"Why don't you ask Alaina what she recommends for a baby who cries nonstop? She must know what to do," Dad suggests.

Mom and Dad trust Alaina with everything, which, Alaina claims, is one of the many reasons she enjoys spending time with Maya's parents more than her own.

Shit. How long has it been since she last saw Alaina, or even called her? Was it that dinner party from hell?

Maya shakes her head. "Her kids didn't do this. Some babies do and some don't. The ones who do grow out of it eventually," she says, unsure if she's trying to reassure Dad or herself. "I'll ask the pediatrician at his next appointment."

"Come on, little guy." Tarun picks Shaan up and rocks him back and forth. "Let's give you the grand tour. See this big empty space here?" He points to the lobby. "This is where we used to play soccer when it was cold outside!"

Tarun's voice has a light quality to it that Maya's never heard before. Ever since he was little, her brother was content on his own, lost in his own thoughts to the point that many relatives and family friends thought him "detached" or "aloof." But when he's with his nephew, he's engaged and untethered at once. Maya watches as Tarun parades Shaan throughout the small lobby, past the entrance to the dining room, past the shelf full of pamphlets and brochures for visitors, past the sitting area and coffee table that's stacked with old *People* magazines.

As Tarun and Shaan circle back, Maya walks toward them and reaches for Shaan. "Let me show him our hiding spot!"

As she heads off in that direction, Tarun calls out, "Wait, why don't we do that later?"

"Yes, wait, Maya!" Dad calls. Behind her, she hears the echo of quickening footsteps.

But she has a head start and she's already made her way to the back office. In the far corner, she sees the giant "American-owned *and* operated" sign Mom made two months post-9/11, after more than a few people left racist reviews on the motel website. They openly refused to stay in a motel run by "people like them."

She holds Shaan close to her and points to a large wooden table in the corner of the room. "Your uncle and I used to hide under that table whenever guests checked in. That's also where all of us packaged everything for Mommy's company. Isn't that nice?"

Shaan coos in response. She loves showing him things, imagining the world from his curious, unbiased perspective. She takes in the familiar smells—the vinegar cleaning solution Mom's always used, the lemon air freshener—and watches Shaan's gaze continuously shift from the cluttered desk beside them, to the window overlooking the parking lot, to the framed sepia-toned photo of her family dressed up for Diwali. Maya picks up the frame, reading the date written on the back: *1998*. In it, Maya and Tarun wear matching outfits, him in a brown kurta and her in a mocha lengha. They're frowning, and if photos could talk, they'd be saying, *Please get us out of these outfits*.

"Oh! And that's the calendar your nani and nana have been buying from the Indian grocery store forever." Maya gestures to the spot on the wall where the same style calendar has been hung up her entire life. Each month has a photo of a Hindu god or goddess. July's goddess is Kali. Maya moves closer so Shaan can see Kali's four arms and the fangs protruding from her open mouth. She used to find Kali's red eyes and disheveled hair so scary as a kid, but now, as her eyes linger on her skirt made of human arms, her tight grip on a man's bloody head, Maya has a change of heart. Kali was aware of her power and unafraid to use it. Maybe if more women were encouraged to be unapologetic about their own power, the world would be a different place.

"Wait a second, what the..." Maya scans the last two rows of the month, where the words *DEAL MEETINGS* are written across each day of the week in Dad's signature block handwriting.

Out of the corner of her eye, she sees Dad appear in the office doorway.

"Dad, why do you have deal meetings scheduled every day for the rest of the month?"

"Oh, those? Just, you know, meetings to discuss future logistics and that type of thing."

Maya tears her eyes away from the calendar to face him. "What does that mean? Is something wrong with the motel?"

Tarun catches up, Mom on his heels. Dev awkwardly stands at a distance behind them. When Mom enters the room, she mutters, "You know I wanted to tell her, so go ahead."

"Tell me *what*?"

"Beta…we're selling the motel." Dad fiddles with the collar of his off-white button-down, the same one he got from Marshalls over a decade ago and continues to wear on a weekly basis.

"You're selling the *motel*?" Maya can't believe her ears. "You're kidding. Why would you ever do that?"

Dad and Mom exchange a look.

"Look at this place," Dad says, motioning around the room. "Look at *us*. We're so tired, beta. We're here day in, day out, and have been for years. It's time."

"This is coming completely out of nowhere," Maya says, shaking her head in confusion. When neither of them responds, she adds, "Is something else going on?"

Dad sighs. "It's a lo—"

"Nothing else," Mom interjects.

Maya frowns. "Do you have an offer?"

Dad nods. "We do. Someone reached out to us."

"And?"

"And…he says he'll take it for half of what we're hoping."

"Half?" Maya laughs sarcastically. "No. Absolutely not. You can't accept that. That's a total rip-off."

Dad gives her a look and she knows what he's thinking. It *is* a rip-off, but they've been ripped off many times before, in so many different ways. Her parents bought the motel thanks to a loan from Maya's paternal grandparents. The implicit understanding was that Dad would help his two younger brothers get settled in America, using the money he made from the motel. Once they were established, his siblings would help him expand, each of them pitching in to run this newfound family enterprise. Maya's grandparents back in India had heard these immigrant success stories all the time from their friends and family. But within three years, one of Dad's brothers got diagnosed with a brain tumor and had to stay in Baroda. The other wanted to pursue medicine in Delhi, allegedly needing Dad's help in paying for graduate school. (They later found out he was using the money for booze.)

Their entire childhood, Maya and Tarun watched from the sidelines as their extended families visited them for varying periods of time, always in need of some type of financial support. Even when it became clear that nobody, neither in Dad nor Mom's family, would come settle in America after all, her parents continued to send remittances. Someone always needed something from them.

"So who's making this wonderful offer?" Maya asks derisively.

Dad sighs. "It doesn't ma—"

"The Lyons. Those cheapskates down the street!" Mom blurts. "They've had their eyes on this place for so long and I *knew* they would pounce on us the second they could. Now, don't you worry, I gave them a piece of my—"

"Yes, you did, Mira," Dad cuts in. "And that's why they're no longer willing to negotiate with us."

Maya frowns. "Well, from what I'm hearing, Mom had good reason to speak up. Somebody needed to!"

Mom enthusiastically nods her head in agreement.

"Regardless, I just want to be done with all this," Dad finally says. "And this is what makes sense for us in the long run. We won't make as much as we hoped from this offer but at least it'll be something."

Maya's mind drifts back to her middle school self, who used to sit in the lobby doing homework while her parents checked guests in. She saw so much from her vantage point in the sitting area: the endless paperwork Dad filled out, the absurd requests from entitled guests, the multiple loads of laundry Mom did in a day. She promised herself back then that she'd do everything she could to create a better life for all of them—Mom, Dad, Tarun, and herself. But all she's done is leave her parents in an even more dismal situation.

A heavy wave of guilt settles over her, heavier than she's ever felt before. It feels like a horrible menstrual cramp, but she hasn't had her period since before she was pregnant. She felt it this morning, too, when she woke up and thought about the layoffs, but thought it would go away after taking a guilt pill. She's been taking it daily and up until now, it was getting her through the entire day.

Maya shakes her head. "But if this is really what you want to do, you deserve to make a profit from it. You don't have to be ripped off just because someone's put in a modest offer."

Unlike her and Tarun, her parents never lament the ways they've been shorted over the years. No, they wear their hardships as badges of honor. They seem to take pride in putting up with crap.

"You can fight for more. You should," Maya emphasizes. "And I'll help you."

"We've tried," Mom says. "At some point, especially as I'm getting older, I have to decide what's worth my energy and what isn't. I've fought enough, beta. And you know I'm tired." She has a far-off look in her eyes.

Maya scrambles for the right words. "But...you can't just give up. You still have a life, you know!"

"Don't worry about us," Mom says. "I know you think you

always need to get involved, but you don't. You have plenty of other things to worry about."

"That you do," Dad chimes in. "Speaking of, I can't believe you let all those employees go. Dev just told me a few minutes ago."

"You *what*?" Mom and Tarun say in unison.

She shoots a pointed look at her husband, whose eyes are to the floor. "I had to. I bought Medini more time, but we still need to come up with more cash." Maya's heart sinks as she pictures the financial projections for the next quarter, the guilt taking up more and more space in her body.

Why isn't the pill working today?

"*More* cash?" Dad shakes his head. "Beta, it's important not to get too rash. Don't ruffle feathers or cause problems. Or be too greedy."

Maya rolls her eyes. "Dad, I'm not being greedy. And anyway, this isn't about me. We're talking about you and Mom. I feel like there's still something you're not tell—"

"Maya, enough." Mom raises her palm as a firm sign that the conversation is over.

"Why don't we all walk to the Dunkin' Donuts?" Tarun suggests, a forced cheer in his voice.

"Let's do it," Dev agrees. "A change of scenery could be great."

As they leave the tiny back office, Shaan in Tarun's arms, Maya slowly trails behind them, feeling the worst kind of loneliness.

The one you feel when you're around the people who are supposed to know you best.

ROOSEVELT HIGH SCHOOL CLASS OF 2004

ANNA DAVIS: So sad to hear about our classmate Maya Patel. Was anyone close to her? [Posted August 2, 2019, 8:24 PM]

KENNETH ROSEN: I remember she always kept to herself. Seemed super stressed and in a hurry.

TIFFANY KOCH: I remember that, too. I'm shocked. Her life seemed like it got a lot better after graduation, especially in the past few years.

MARIA MARTINEZ: She *was* super stressed. Worked at her parents' motel after hustling in classes all day. IMO, that would make any teenager tired, don't you think? We were in AP Calculus together and she was obsessed with getting perfect grades. We had a couple sleepovers at my house, but she never invited me to her place.

ANNA DAVIS: Her mom seemed nice. I remember Maya telling me she and her mom shopped for knockoff Laura Ashley dresses, but she seemed so embarrassed as soon as she said it. I was so surprised when I saw she married some rich guy, started a company, and now lives in Tribeca. Thought things really turned around for her. But I agree, she always seemed super stressed.

KENNETH ROSEN: I always wondered if she struggled with depression? My first thought when I heard she was missing was that something awful happened because she felt so shitty.

MARIA MARTINEZ: That's terrible. I didn't even consider that but now that you say it, that makes too much sense.

14

"DEV! SHE'LL BE HERE IN A FEW MIN-utes!"

"I'm almost out of the shower!" he calls, his voice muffled by the water pressure.

Maya puts Shaan in his DocATot and rushes to her nightstand. If there ever was a moment to get some use out of this pill, it's now.

A steady rush of calm cascades through her body.

Please work, she wills the pill. *I really need you today.*

She does one final check of her makeup and outfit in the mirror. If someone were to see her in this very moment, they'd assume she was getting ready for a job interview.

Which she is, in a way. She's just the one doing the interviewing.

Maya grabs her pages of notes, walks into the living room, and calls the doorman to let their visitor in whenever she arrives. Dev is already on the living room couch, dressed nicely in a light blue button-down and gray shorts. Shaan is perched in his DocATot wearing the same outfit as Dev.

She thought it'd be cute, but now it just seems like overkill.

Maya takes one last glance around the living room. She'd scrubbed and dusted the whole apartment yesterday during Shaan's nap. A tray at the center of their coffee table contains mugs, a carafe of coffee, and pastries she picked up from Bluestone Lane on the way home. The scent of bergamot wafts from a candle Liz gave her throughout the apartment.

"What are those?" Dev asks, motioning to the stack of paper tucked under her arm.

"Interview questions. And some notes about Shaan's schedule."

"Oh, crap. I didn't think to prepare questions. Let me look some up now." He pulls out his phone. The glare of the screen reflects in his glasses.

She feels a surge of annoyance. "I've already got them. I did hours of research this week on things you should ask a potential nanny."

An internal voice urges her to stop there. But she can't help herself.

"I also made sure our place was clean. Oh, and that's right—I scheduled the interview in the first place."

"Seriously? You're doing this now? She's almost here." Dev motions to the door.

"You can't just pray for someone to appear out of thin air and take care of your newborn. That's not how it works."

He takes a sip of his coffee. "You didn't tell me you were doing all this homework. I would have helped."

"I shouldn't *have* to tell you that. This is a big step for both of us. All three of us. You should have known better."

"Jeez. Look, I really appreciate that you took the time to do this. But you can't get angry with me when I didn't know you were doing all this behind the scenes. You *just* told me you were on board for a nanny last weekend, when we got back from the motel. I wish you would have discussed it with me earlier so we could have split it up."

A memory materializes in her mind. Mom vigorously scrubbing their tiny wooden dining table that they got from a garage sale, yelling at Tarun and Maya for spilling maple syrup all over it. Tarun biting his tongue the way he always did when he was about to cry. Maya squeezing his hand under the table. Mom always seemed to get set off over the smallest things, and her mood was often unpredictable.

Now Maya wonders if it was more nuanced than that. Maybe Mom had to hold in her anger so often that it was bound to explode at any given moment.

And maybe Maya's doing the same thing now.

"Split it up?" She crosses her arms. "When? All you did was suggest we find a nanny in the first place. And then your work was done. You just knew I'd take care of the rest."

Maya hates this side of herself, and she's seen so much of it lately. She just feels so goddamn irritable all the time since giving birth. It's like she can't help her built-up resentment from erupting all over her marriage.

"You think this is easy for me?" Dev challenges. "I'm slacking so much at work because I want to be there for our family, but nothing I do is ever good enough for you."

The tension in her jaw loosens and her stomach tightens. Maya opens her mouth to respond when they hear someone knock.

She quickly runs over to the door, takes a deep breath, and opens it. "Nina! Come in!" Her jaw hurts from forcing an *aren't we such a happy family?* smile.

The nanny looks exactly like the photo Liz sent Maya last weekend. She learned early on that Liz has spreadsheets and directories of everything imaginable: baby products, nannies, language tutors, schools. Nina's brunette hair is pulled into a low bun, and she's wearing a mint-green blouse and dark jeans. No jewelry. Little makeup. She's pretty.

"And this must be Shaan!" Nina's lips curl into a smile when she sees their son. "How are you, cutie-pie?"

She already likes this woman.

They settle into the living room, Nina on the armchair, Maya and Dev on the sectional.

Nina declines coffee but takes a chocolate croissant from the tray.

"I have some questions we can start with," Maya says, jumping right in.

"Yes, of course!" Nina takes a paper napkin and dabs the corners of her lips, straightening her posture.

They spend the next half hour going through all of Maya's notes.

After they're done, Nina takes a final bite of the croissant.

"We would give you a tour of our place, but this is pretty much it." Dev laughs, his sole contribution to the entire conversation.

"It's great." Nina smiles and stands up, doing a quick glance around her chair to make sure she didn't leave any crumbs. Then she extends her arms toward Shaan. "May I?"

"Oh! Of course," Maya says, trying not to seem caught off guard. Or territorial.

"Aw, you're such a sweet little guy, aren't you?" Nina coos. Shaan settles into Nina's embrace, smiling up at her and reaching for a fallen strand of her hair.

Maya forces herself to look away. She thinks she's going to be sick. The cramp in her lower abdomen is back.

How can you just leave your baby all day? You're just going to… what? Be apart from your newborn son for at least eight hours at a time? Let someone else take care of your *baby?*

"I'm very comfortable following a schedule, feeding him,

and putting him down for a nap," Nina assures them. But Maya's only half-listening.

The worst-case scenarios play on a loop in her mind. What if Nina falls asleep? Or accidentally leaves a sharp object around him? Or leaves the window open during a thunderstorm?

She's transported back to that day. The little white onesie and tiny socks. The sound of her own voice screaming.

No, she commands herself. *Don't go there. Not here, not now.*

Maya goes through the motions until Nina's out the door. She shakes her hand, offers her an extra pastry for the road, and promises to be in touch.

Once she's gone, Dev says, "She seemed really great."

"Yeah, she did. I liked her."

"So, should we finalize it, then?"

"Um..." Her throat feels constricted, her stomach in knots. "I just need to think on it."

Maya follows Dev into the bedroom with Shaan in her arms, inhaling his scent of milk and cream. She tries to savor the feel of his tiny fist curled into her neck, but it only makes her feel worse.

Dev stands in front of their closet, his back to her.

After a long pause, he turns around. "Okay. Fine. Whatever."

"Whatever?"

But as he turns back to face the closet and sifts through shirts to change into, she decides it's better if they don't talk. If they unpack this, she might feel backed into a corner and have to finally tell him why she's so terrified of leaving Shaan with someone else.

And then they'd have to acknowledge the state they're in as a couple. She'll have to come to terms with the fact that no matter how much they've been through, part of her still doesn't feel comfortable confiding in her husband about certain things. And he'll recognize how truly incapable and flawed Maya really is, despite all her efforts to convince him otherwise. They'd never be able to bounce back from that.

Maya sighs when he doesn't respond. "Oh, by the way, I have to go into the office tomorrow."

"Tomorrow?" Dev asks.

"I have a presentation for work. About next steps for Medini in the wake of the Whole Foods deal and the layoffs." Maya props Shaan onto her shoulder and softly bounces him up and down.

"Um, what about Shaan?"

"We can figure it out. Maybe see if you can work from home or ask if one of our moms is available. I mean, that's what I've been doing on my own every day, right?"

As soon as the words leave her mouth, she realizes how true they are. She doesn't have to be the only one who worries about all the invisible but essential tasks that keep their family running.

Dev stares at her in silence, as if she's some foreign creature he's trying to identify. He turns back to face the closet and pulls out a long-sleeved navy blue button-down, then slips it on over his T-shirt. "I'm meeting a client for lunch. Then going back to the office."

"So we won't see each other all day, then." Her surprise morphs into something else, something flatter. Indifference. Detachment.

"Yeah, I guess not." He leaves the room.

She fixates on a rug stain, the air carrying traces of Dev's natural woodsy scent.

Maya finally gets up after a couple minutes to clear the tray of coffee and chocolate in the living room. On her way there, she notices Dev's messenger bag is no longer by the door.

She didn't even hear him leave.

A marriage and a baby have this in common: when things get too quiet, you start to worry.

JULY

before

15

THE NEXT DAY, TRAVIS IS FLIPPING through the printed pages of the presentation Maya just finished. "Looks like you've finally got things under control."

"That's right. And now we can fully focus on fulfilling the Whole Foods order."

"And what about the team?" Travis asks, his eyes still on the sheets of paper. "I imagine Medini's employees are feeling overworked, maybe even a bit discouraged, since the others were let go, don't you think?"

Josh is about to chime in, but Maya interrupts him. "We're confident they can handle it."

She can never win with this asshole.

Travis nods. "Right, then I think we've covered everything."

Everything for now, Maya thinks. She knows it's probably not the best time to announce the idea she's been mulling over for a couple of weeks now.

Tiffany types the last of the meeting minutes frantically as the others push their chairs back. They grab bagels from the basket at the center of the table and make small talk in one of the conference room's corners.

"Oh, and Maya," Brad says, looking up from his laptop. "Lotta great press coming in. Keep it up."

Maya smiles. "Thank you. And look out for a note from me about golf soon!" They share a wink.

As she exits the conference room, Josh catches up to her. "*Golf* soon?"

Maya shrugs. "I figured it's a low-key way to stay connected. You, Travis, and all our investors have been playing together for years, right?"

"Uh, right. Sounds good," Josh says, his voice fading behind her as she quickens her pace and grabs her jacket from the coatrack.

It was never enough for Maya to show up to work and do her job, no matter how well she did it. No matter how many sleepless nights she'd spend at the office, or how many business books she'd read on weekends, just trying to gain equal footing with her male counterparts. Because for every inch of progress she'd make, Josh surpassed her by a mile. While she buried her head in her work, he was networking out on the golf course every Saturday. When she stayed up late on Fridays drafting pitch emails, Josh was sitting in a dimly lit bar, clinking whiskey glasses with key stakeholders and investors. *That's* where the magic happens, where the deals are made. And she deserves a seat at the table.

Maya turns around to flash a smile in his direction. "I've gotta run. Great to see you!" She's out the door before Josh can say anything else.

The pill she took right before she left the apartment is still floating in her system. The city seems lighter. Happier. She knows she's running out of time and takes quick steps to the address Liz sent her last week.

Alaina calls her right as she's settling into the salon's cushiony black swivel chair.

"Girl, you are blowing up," Alaina says. "A *Glamour Magazine* feature? I can't believe that's *my* best friend!"

"Yeah, it's still surreal." Maya reaches into her satchel and removes her copy. She skips to the center of the issue, where there's a two-page interview covering everything from her childhood at the motel, her first consulting job, her early days with Medini, how she met Dev, and what it's like being a new mom. The feature is surrounded by photos: one of her first professional headshots, the black turtleneck dress maternity photo, a few bamboo toothbrushes, a zoomed-in photo of the Medini logo, Shaan's first baby photo that's currently her phone's home screen.

"How did that happen? Does a magazine basically just call you and say, *Hey, we'd like to profile you*?"

"Sort of. Liz knows the editor in chief."

"Right. Liz."

Maya smirks. "You're saying *Liz* like you usually say *the flu*."

"Let me guess. You're still subscribing to what she says... and does."

"If you're referring to the supplement, I'm not taking it."

"Really?" Alaina asks.

"Really. It was only for a once-in-a-while boost, anyway," Maya says, taking in every syllable of her lie.

Greg, the hairstylist Liz claims has changed her life, holds up a sleek hair dryer. "Can I turn this on?"

Maya nods at him. "Hold on a second, Alaina. I'm getting my hair dried."

"You're getting your hair dried? Where are you?"

"This new place. Salon Ruggeri. You should check it out," Maya says, looking around at the brightly colored artwork, a gallery wall of black-and-white photos of celebrities, and Fornasetti candles.

"Yeah, maybe sometime," Alaina mutters. She fills Maya in on the latest news at the ER: two nurses are quitting and one of the only physicians who works nights was poached by another hospital. Maya fills her in on their visit to the motel and her parents' plan to sell.

"Your mom wants that? Seriously?" Alaina asks.

"Seriously. You should have seen her face. You should see her in general, she looks so tired. All that lifelong hard work and sacrifices, and this is what it amounts to for her? It's… I don't know, it's a lot."

"What's a lot?"

"Just seeing how disappointed she is with her life. How exhausted. And of course, my dad is exhausted, too, but the amount my mom has had to constantly give up because that's what was expected of her… It's just hard to take in, you know? If this is what a life led by guilt looks like, I don't want any part of it."

"I get it. I don't want to end up like my mom, either. But nobody says your life has to be like that."

"But isn't that what inevitably happens? Plus, a couple weeks ago at my place, weren't you the one who said that following everyone's blueprints and expectations just leads to this feeling of emptiness?"

"Yeah, so? That doesn't mean the answer is to adopt Liz's way of life. You have to face your own."

"This *is* me facing it, by trying a new way."

"Really? That's what you want to call it? Because it seems more like avoiding by taking on someone else's rules."

There's silence, until Maya says, "I'm not avoiding at all. I'm delegating for once."

"Maya, I've been where you are. Overwhelmed with a new baby, a new life. You need help at home. And the way you're going about it, the way you're thinking about this in general, isn't sustainable. You can't just amp up at work and be all in as a new mom. You're going to break."

"But I'm not breaking. I'm actually thinking clearly for the first time in years, maybe ever. I know you're not a fan of Liz but maybe she's figured out a couple things."

"Yeah? Has she?"

"She has. And she's helping me figure things out for myself," Maya says. "I was literally just at my office, facing the board, and now I'm going to go home and brainstorm Medini's next steps with Dev."

"Dev, your husband, who's at home, trying to work and take care of your baby because you just *had* to be at the office?"

"Yes, I did. And what about the fact that I've been at home and trying to work for weeks all by myself?"

Alaina goes quiet. "I'm not saying it's fair. I'm just saying that the Maya I know would have considered how her actions impact the person she loves, instead of justifying all of it."

Now Maya's quiet.

"You're so damn hard on yourself," Alaina mutters. "But now it's like you can't even see straight."

"You know what? I think I should go."

"I think so, too." Alaina hangs up.

Maya grips the sides of her chair as pressure builds in her chest. She should call Alaina back and apologize.

But then she catches a glimpse of herself in the mirror. Her sleek hair that's now five inches shorter and streaked with shades of honey. Her matching lavender blazer and pants. Her bright eyes. For the first time in months, when she looks at herself, she feels something resembling satisfaction. (Wait, is it anti-feminist of her to like being pretty? She'll have to explore that later.)

Maya's no longer googling things like *when will I feel like myself again after giving birth?* or *why is it so hard to leave my baby?* or *how do I make sure I get credit at work?* With just one pink pill, she's limitless. Fuck the rules. The rules weren't made to benefit people like her.

But despite her resolve, Alaina's words ring in her mind as she leaves the salon and waits for the light to change at 23rd Street and Broadway.

Maya stops at Eataly on the way home to pick up a bottle of wine and Neapolitan pizza for dinner. She can't wait to tell Dev about her day at the office, knowing he's going to lose his mind over the "golf comment." She feels a burst of giddiness at the night ahead. Dev on the sofa, Maya unpacking the board meeting to him in detail as they drink wine in the bulbous glasses from their wedding registry. They just need some quality time together to get back on track. They've always been each other's favorite person to talk to.

But as soon as she enters their apartment, she's caught off guard by an all-too-familiar high-pitched voice.

"Maya, you're home," her mother-in-law says by way of greeting, craning her neck to look at her.

"Oh, um, hi," she says, frozen in the doorway. As if *she's* the one intruding in someone else's house. That's the way her in-laws have always made her feel, like she belongs on the outside.

"How are you, beta?" she asks. Her pursed lips and downturned eyes remind Maya that her mother-in-law's kindness always stems from obligatory politeness, not genuine warmth.

"Fine. You?" When she doesn't respond, Maya adds, "I didn't know you'd still be here when I got back."

"My son is here alone, handling *everything*," she says, dramatically raising her hand to her forehead like those women in old Victorian paintings. "He had an important business meeting this afternoon, so I had to stay later than planned. Look at how much he's managing on his own!"

Maya clenches her fists.

"And I've been *so* worried about Shaan," her mother-in-law

continues, smoothing down her blush-pink blouse that she's paired with white linen pants. She always looks elegant in an understated way, like a woman straight out of an under-eye cream commercial. *Nobody in this family would ever work at a motel*, Maya thinks.

Thankfully, Dev arrives home a minute later. He lingers in the doorway, a concerned look on his face as he picks up on the energy in the room.

"Shaan is doing really well," Maya says, not making eye contact as she brings the stuffed Eataly bag into the kitchen. *Of course I got takeout today of all days*, Maya thinks as she puts the food in the fridge. The pizza slices and store-bought wine are just further proof to her mother-in-law that she doesn't have a domestic bone in her body.

"Is he?" Dev's mom squints at Shaan lying on his play mat. "I feel like he looks thinner, frailer."

"Are you staying for dinner?" Maya asks, ignoring the question.

"No, no, I'll be going. I made chole and daal and kulfi at home, so I should get back to it... I hope you enjoy your pizza. Make sure to reheat that."

"Will do," Maya says through gritted teeth.

"Oh, and this place is a mess." Dev's mom scoffs. "I'm going to have to swing by more often to keep it in better shape."

Maya bites her bottom lip. Anger constricts her throat as she thinks of all of the moments she's held her tongue to keep the peace. *Don't engage, Maya. Don't engage.*

Don't. Engage.

But the words come out before she can stop them. "You know what? I think we've been handling a lot. And it'd be great to hear some acknowledgment of that instead of your constant judgmental, belittling comments."

Her mother-in-law swivels her neck and shoots Dev a look that says *Can you believe her?* "Excuse me?"

Dev's jaw is wide open, panic written all over his face. "Maya, honey? You okay?"

Yes, I'm okay. I'm better than okay, damn it. Stop avoiding conflict all the time and stand up to your mother. Why don't you try defending me for once?

Her mind plays a reel of all the other times in her life she's felt like this. A middle school teacher frowning, telling her parents she's "too opinionated" and "talks too much," right in front of her. Her ever-present, innate desire to never be a difficult woman, to never take up space. She hears Dad's voice from just the other week. *Don't ruffle feathers, Maya. Don't be greedy.*

But thanks to the pill, she doesn't let her listen to him or even parts of her old self.

"You heard me," she says, turning to face Dev's mother. "And you know what, I should have said something before. So that's on me." When she sees her mother-in-law's face drop, she softens her tone ever so slightly. "We appreciate your offers for help and your...advice. But sometimes it feels like you're only pointing out what we're doing wrong."

Dev clears his throat. "Maybe we can talk about th—"

"No," Maya interrupts. "We can air this out right now." She gestures between her and Dev. "We're the parents, okay? And you—" she motions to Dev "—are being bullied unfairly at work about your paternity leave. It's unethical. I think you need to push back. And we're getting a nanny." She pauses, realizing what she's just agreed to. "Look, my point is, we're trying our best, and your comments aren't helping in the way you think they are."

When she's finished, her resolve starts to dissipate, and the room starts to blur.

Dev's lips are moving but she can't hear anything he's saying.

Focus, she commands herself. *Listen.*

But she's overcome with exhaustion, and...something else. The period-like cramp is back with a vengeance, and she starts feeling faint, sweat trickling down her back, her stomach turning in nausea. A tingling sensation spreads through her feet like they've fallen asleep. And then it hits her, in full force, like a rough wave that's pulled her underwater.

How could you speak to Dev's mother like that? Doesn't she hate you enough? If Shaan doesn't have a relationship with his paternal grandmother, it's all your fault.

She almost keels over in discomfort. This is exactly how she felt before Ralph's exit interview.

Until she took an extra pill.

"I'm going to go," her mother-in-law says, slowly packing up her purse.

As Maya takes in her painted pink lips and French-manicured hands, she catches a glimpse of a woman who simply loves her son and grandson with all her heart. A woman who worries that not being needed is the same as not being loved.

"Wait. Can we please talk?" Maya asks, her tone soft.

"I'd rather not. I'll see you all soon." Her mother-in-law gives Shaan and Dev quick kisses and then she's out the door.

Before Dev can say anything, Maya goes to their bedroom.

When the door is locked behind her, she finds the back of her nightstand drawer and removes the brown bottle.

NEW YORK CITY POLICE DEPARTMENT

OFFICER RICHARDSON: How much did you interact with your daughter-in-law?

REENA MEHTA: Maya? Not a lot. I tried but she's never been very receptive.

OFFICER RICHARDSON: Can you elaborate?

REENA MEHTA: She doesn't make much of an effort to have a relationship with me. Or for me to have one with my own grandson, for that matter. I've told her I want to FaceTime with my grandson every day but she's always "too busy."

OFFICER RICHARDSON: Ma'am, I'm asking how often you spoke with *her*, not with your grandson.

REENA MEHTA: Not often unless she's with my son when I call him. She's always at the office or has her hands full with this, that, and the other. And my son is often home with our baby when *she's* the one on maternity leave. But when she *is* home with Shaan, she seems so overwhelmed, but then hates it when I try to give advice on early motherhood. I'm just trying to help. But off the record, I'm not sure what the big deal really is. I raised two boys just fine.

OFFICER RICHARDSON: So, you *were* aware that your daughter-in-law was struggling?

REENA MEHTA: Struggling? Struggling with *what*? Maya has everything. Her own company *and* a baby, all thanks to my son, who helps all the time with their newborn. I certainly didn't have that as a new mother and don't remember complaining.

Nowadays, all of these young women have so much trouble just being adults!

OFFICER RICHARDSON: Ma'am, please try to stay on track. Have you noticed any changes in your daughter-in-law recently?

REENA MEHTA: No, I have not. She's always been like this. Never fulfilled by or grateful for what she has.

OFFICER RICHARDSON: Ms. Mehta, do you think there is some truth to the statement that motherhood was too much for Maya?

REENA MEHTA: I do. Maya never seemed to have that... maternal instinct. I don't think motherhood comes naturally to her. And honestly, I don't think she even enjoys being a mother all that much. At least it doesn't seem like it.

OFFICER RICHARDSON: Ms. Mehta, do you think Maya's feelings of inadequacy as a mother, or her lack of "maternal instinct," as you put it, could have something to do with her disappearance?

REENA MEHTA: I don't know. I can't even begin to fathom why a mother would abandon her newborn baby. It's inexplicable.

16

"YOU HAVE TO KEEP TAKING MATTERS into your own hands." Liz pauses when their food arrives. It feels like they only placed their order a minute ago, but their Greek Market salads, cappuccinos, and Bloody Mary cocktails now sit on the table between them. It's like Liz gets VIP treatment everywhere they go.

"With Dev? Dev's mom? Or Medini?" Maya sips her cappuccino and keeps her hands around the warm, heavy mug. She usually loves being at the Ace Hotel and its library-meets-bar aesthetic. But today, she just wishes she stayed in bed.

"Both. Everything. All of it." Liz digs into her salad. "This is unfortunately how it is. As shitty as things are for moms, they're also shitty for dads who want to be involved."

"I'm being reminded of that every day. I just didn't think I'd be so constantly annoyed with him. Am I supposed to want to throw things at my husband every day since we've become parents?" She regrets her words as soon as they leave her mouth.

They may be true, but saying them out loud to anyone other than Alaina feels like a betrayal to Dev.

"Of course you are." Liz laughs. "I felt the same way with Owen."

Maya takes a moment to reflect. "It's funny, my best friend told me she was pissed at her husband all the time, too, when the kids were born, but I thought..."

"You thought you and Dev would be different?"

"Yeah, I guess I did," Maya says, realizing how presumptuous that sounds. Wouldn't stress and resentment corrode *any* couple over time? Who was she to think that her marriage would be stronger? She remembers her conversation with Mom about a woman's inevitable sacrifice in marriage and motherhood.

"But it can't just stay this way," Maya continues. "I think Alaina was right. I have to do something to make our marriage better. For me, for him, for Shaan. For all three of us." Maya thinks back to her pregnancy days when she would envision their life together after having a baby. Shaan sleeping soundly in the bassinet next to them, while they sipped wine and engaged in deep, meaningful conversations about the wonders of parenthood. Dev sitting next to her, rubbing her back while she effortlessly breastfed. The three of them going for pancakes at Bubby's, followed by a peaceful walk along the West Side Highway, where they'd fawn over their baby's every move and milestone. Instead, they give each other whatever little they have left at the end of each day. She learns and processes the most about parenting from social media. Not from a shared bonding experience with the father of her child.

"I get that. I really do," Liz says. "But here's the thing. We're parenting in a totally broken and fucked-up system. How many times have you and I talked about misogyny and sexism this past week alone? Mothers are on their own. You have to do what you can to make it more manageable. And the sooner you accept that, the more manageable it becomes."

"So, accept that it's shitty?"

"Sort of, yeah. And do what's in your control to make it better." Liz reaches into her periwinkle Telfar bag and pulls out a brown bottle. "For starters…"

"I already took one this morning," Maya says quickly. "I couldn't leave Shaan without the extra help, even though I know my mom will be fine with him. But that reminds me… Honestly, I think these pills might be messing with me."

Liz frowns. "How so?"

"I don't know. I mean, I've definitely been able to get more shit done when I'm not bogged down by guilt or how my actions affect others. But isn't that inevitably at the cost of everyone else around me, especially the people I love the most? Who love *me* the most? And I've been so irritable lately. I don't feel like myself. Maybe I just need to call it quits with these," Maya says, shaking her head.

"Call it quits with…what?" Liz props a manicured hand under her chin. The inquisitive look on her face coupled with her chic white blazer and delicate gold jewelry makes her look like a talk show host. "Quit making decisions that are beneficial for your company? For your family? For you?"

"I shouldn't need a pill to do all of that."

Liz leans back in her chair. "Ideally, you shouldn't. You're right. And society shouldn't make being a mom and getting through the day so damn difficult. But it does."

When Maya doesn't reply, Liz says, "Maya, do you know why I reached out to you in the first place?"

"Because my experience of being a mother and a founder resonated with you?"

"Yes, but that's not the entire reason. I also felt compelled to reach out because I was drawn to your story of why you got into this. Your family. Your vision. Your *purpose*."

Liz takes a long sip of her Bloody Mary before continuing. "I don't tell people this, but my parents owned a convenience store when I was young. It barely broke even for years. I was in and out of there all the time, just like you with the motel."

"Really?" Maya hadn't even considered the fact that Liz also had a difficult upbringing. She assumed that it resembled Dev's. A childhood made up of exclusive private schools, lavish vacations, and upscale restaurants.

Liz nods. "My mom worked the cash register, cleaned the aisles, the bathrooms. She did all this while cooking for us, checking my homework, everything."

"I'm so sorry. I had no idea."

"Most people don't." Liz smiles softly, but her eyes are watering. "One day, my dad decided he didn't want to be with her anymore. So he abandoned the two of us and made sure she wasn't left with a cent. And then he met someone else. My mom didn't think she deserved to fight for more. She thought she had to take whatever life handed to her. There was this one time..." Liz's voice breaks, but she pushes through. "My mom put me in the car and wouldn't tell me where we were going. All I could see was her splotchy face, all red and covered with tears, in the rearview mirror. She drove us to my dad's new house. I don't know how she even found out where he lived, but she made me wait in the car. I saw scooters in the driveway, chalk, bicycles with cute little white baskets attached. That's when I knew that... Sorry." Liz pauses to clear her throat, dabbing at the corners of her eyes with a napkin.

Maya shakes her head. "Please don't apologize. *I'm* sorry you went through this."

Liz takes a long sip of water. "That's when I knew he had started a new family, a 'better' one. He didn't just replace my mom, he replaced me, too. I could see things getting heated at his front door, both of them gesturing wildly. And I could hear the muffled sound of yelling from inside the car. I rolled down the window a crack, and that's when I heard her ask him—no, *beg* him—to come home to us. I couldn't hear his response, but I can only imagine what it was, because he slammed the door in her face a minute later. And we never saw him again."

Maya reaches for her hand. "Liz, I… I don't even know what to say. I can't imagine how that must have been for you."

"I think I repressed it for a while, to be honest," Liz admits. "But it didn't take me long to realize that wherever I looked, women were getting cheated in some way. And all too often, they blamed themselves for it. I knew then that I wanted to spend the rest of my life trying to protect as many women as possible from feeling a lifetime of that unwarranted self-blame."

Liz pauses, then adds, "It's okay if you take advantages when they come your way, Maya." She pushes the brown bottle across the table.

"I already took this advantage a few hours ago." Maya laughs nervously and pushes it back toward Liz.

"How many?"

"Um, just one. That's the maximum dose for these, right? Except for that one time you told me to take two, during the layoffs."

And then when I self-prescribed an extra after the blowup with Dev's mom.

Liz has a serious look on her face when she says, "Given everything you're dealing with, I think it could be a good idea to up your daily dosage."

"Wait, *what*? I didn't even know that was a possibility. Is that even safe?"

"Perfectly safe. I've specifically designed it so that women would be able to take it multiple times a day if needed. I started you on a low dose as that's just standard practice for these kinds of things. But you haven't had any major side effects, right?"

Maya bites her lip. "I mean, like I said, I've been feeling kind of weird… Nauseous at times, even faint, sometimes. And there's been this stabbing pain in my lower abdomen. Kind of like a bad period cramp? And like I said, I've definitely been more irritable."

Liz waves her concerns off. "All of that is actually quite normal. The pill has some serotonin activity, which can cause some gut discomfort, but everyone else who's been on it far longer than you said those side effects go away pretty quickly. And honestly, the irritability, the anger, those are signs that you're paying more attention to what pisses you off. And as you become more hyperaware, you'll probably feel it more. So going up on your dose could help block out guilt's 'noise,' so to speak."

Liz pauses, allowing Maya to take it all in. "And in terms of irritability, I want to make room for the possibility that you're conflating irritability with self-assertion. You're standing up for yourself! You're noticing what you refuse to tolerate! But when women set limits, it's seen as 'aggressive,' 'bossy,' or even 'bitchy.'"

Maya's silence encourages Liz to continue.

"But I get it. The thought of increasing the dose of something, even something as mild as this, is scary. So you should know that we've completed another round of trials, and my initial hunch was correct—there's nothing wrong with taking more than one pill a day. Between us, I have some clients who are taking up to five a day, and they're totally fine. No, more than fine. They're great!"

"Wait, so does that mean it's almost cleared for public use, or…?"

Liz nods. "We're nearly there. But this kind of thing takes so much time. It's honestly just a matter of getting some technical documents to just show what we already know. But in the very near future, any woman should be able to grab this from Amazon or GNC or wherever she gets her vitamins."

"Imagine that." Maya loses herself in thought. "A world where women just don't feel guilt."

What would Maya's life look like? Her mother's? Alaina's?

"Plus," Liz adds, "you've got your work cut out for you these next couple of weeks. I say you go up to three a day."

Maya bites her lip. "I don't know. My body is still in the process of getting used to taking *one* a day, let alone three."

"And does one a day feel like enough?"

Maya pauses at the question, thinking back to the numerous times within the last week or so when the pill either wore off more quickly than usual or just seemed less effective altogether. It's like she's on a high after taking one, excited about everything she can accomplish, but then she feels like shit. And if upping the dose could help with that horrible feeling in her stomach…

Her silence is answer enough, and Liz nudges the bottle closer to her.

Liz looks at her expectantly, and Maya removes two hot-pink pills from the bottle.

"So, an extra two? Right now?"

Liz nods.

Maya gives her a nervous glance between swallowing two pills with her Bloody Mary. Instantly—way quicker than ever before—she feels a warmth settle into her limbs. For the next couple minutes, all she focuses on is being fully present in her conversation with Liz and enjoying each sip of her drink. She takes in the buzz of conversation around her, slowly starting to feel more grounded. A remnant of her old self sparks back to life.

Liz nods toward the pill bottle. "You can keep that. You'll probably run out soon anyway, and now that you're taking more, you'll need the extra supply."

Maya smiles in gratitude and tucks the bottle into her cross-body bag.

"Oh, and someone will be joining us." Liz glances at her watch. "Any minute now."

"Wait, what? Who?" Maya suddenly feels hyperaware of her growing buzz from the alcohol, as well as her current appearance. She looks down and notices wrinkles in her plum shirtdress.

"And there he is!" Liz stands up and waves to someone.

He?

Maya follows her gaze to a fortysomething man with broad shoulders, salt-and-pepper hair, and a wide smile. The same smile she first saw from afar at a tech conference years ago, and more recently on a cover of *Tech News*.

"Wait, is that…"

"Mark!" Liz says, extending her arms out when he approaches them. "I'm so glad you could make it."

"Likewise." He gives Liz a hug and a kiss on the cheek before turning to Maya. "And you must be Maya."

Maya blushes. "That's me." They exchange a firm handshake. "Wow. It's so great to meet you, Mark."

Mark Stahlberg. Lead investor at Tribeca One, a top VC fund in the city. Which just so happens to be one Maya's investors thought was "out of Medini's league" just a few months back, when she'd suggested it as an option for their next round of funding.

Just days ago, Maya couldn't have even imagined cold emailing this man. And now here he is in the flesh, sitting across the table from her.

She takes a moment to dig through her mental archive of everything she knows about Mark Stahlberg. Columbia undergrad, Harvard Business School. Invested in some of the biggest health and wellness companies around: a spin studio with classes set to club music and instructors who shout motivational quotes, protein bars made of only three ingredients, a supplement that supposedly contains an entire day's worth of nutrients. (*Wait, now that I think of it, was that Women Rise? Is that how the two of them know each other?*)

"Mark and I were going to meet today anyway, so I thought this would be even better, because it gives you both a chance to connect!" Liz says, raising her eyebrows at Maya. A gesture that clearly says *So make the most of it.*

Maya smiles. "Well, then, I'm so glad this worked out." She capitalizes on a sudden, and very rare, burst of confidence and says, "I've been meaning to get in touch with you for a long time, actually."

"Oh, is that so?" Mark pauses to ask the waiter to bring him a glass of whiskey. When he turns back to her, there's a subtle smirk on his face. "You started the company with the bamboo toothbrushes, right?"

"Yes, Medini," Maya specifies. "We're an entire line of eco-toiletry products."

"Right." Mark snaps his fingers. "My wife was just telling me she's a big fan."

Wait, seriously?

Maya has looked up to Mark's wife, Lila, for some time now, ever since she found her on Instagram back when she was first researching (read: stalking) Tribeca One. Lila's feed is full of photos of her and their four children in matching pajamas, making chocolate-chip pancakes, and walking around Tribeca. Similarly to Liz, she makes parenting look not only effortless, but ethereal. Peaceful.

"That's so kind of her," Maya says. She suddenly remembers one of Lila's posts from just a few weeks ago of her and her kids building towers out of household items. In the caption, Lila wrote that this had quickly become one of their favorite activities.

Thank you, mental archive.

"Speaking of," Maya adds, "we're actually working on some new products for our Whole Foods launch. I'd love to make personalized gift boxes for Lila and your kids. Our recyclable packaging can double as toys." She winks.

"And not for me?" Mark says playfully, a glint in his eye. The waiter comes over and Mark rearranges his side of the table to make room for his drink. "I'm teasing. They'd definitely love that." He swirls the whiskey in his short glass. "It's funny you say this, actually, because my kids like any toy that isn't really a *toy.*"

"Do they? What a perfect coincidence!"

Checkmate.

The next hour passes by with them discussing everything from a company that IPO'd earlier that week to the season finale of a dark comedy on HBO.

Somewhere between their next round of drinks and their current conversation about working remotely with kids, Maya feels like a proper adult. A real grown-up in the outside world, not just someone who has spent the past months measuring out everything in ounces, staring at a hazy baby monitor, scrolling through online parenting forums, and barely leaving the house.

It's freeing to slip into a different self. She was so used to doing everything so precisely, so by the book, she didn't realize that for weeks she had been feeling—among everything else—*trapped*, almost. Just earlier this morning, pre-pill, she'd worried that if she ever admitted missing her old life, people would think Maya didn't love her son. She feels the edges of something she hasn't made space for in months, maybe ever: self-compassion.

But the haze has lifted. Of course it's normal to miss her freedom and independence pre-Shaan. It doesn't mean she's a terrible mother; it just means she's a human being.

"I'm not sure how you're even managing. I once changed a diaper on a work call and was worn-out for the rest of the day," Mark admits. His bright white teeth and chiseled nose remind Maya of a different Mark—Mark Consuelos, one of her celebrity crushes Dev occasionally teases her about.

Maya laughs. "Once? I do that every day!"

"I don't doubt it!" Mark joins in her laughter and so does Liz, shaking her head in amusement.

Mark's eyes linger on Maya's for a second too long before he excuses himself for the bathroom.

She tries to ignore the flicker of attraction she feels toward him.

Once he's out of earshot, Liz turns to her with a smirk on her face. "I think he finds you quite charming."

Her face flushes. "Oh, please. Me? No. That was just some standard schmoozing on both ends. And look at me!" Maya gestures to her greasy hair and wrinkled shirt.

Liz laughs. "Ha, okay. Whatever you saaaay… But don't pretend you're not hot. Own that shit."

When Mark returns, he tells them he has to head back to the office. Before he leaves, Liz pulls up her calendar on her phone. "So, I'll see you at dinner next week, then?" She turns to Maya and says, "Mark's dinners are just the *best*."

Oh, she's heard. Mark's famous dinners are notorious for their influential guests, which typically includes a mix of venture capitalists, founders, and executives. Come to think of it, Travis went to one last year.

"Yep, everything's all set," Mark confirms. "It should be a good one."

Maybe it's the added boost of the pill, Liz's infectious confidence, or the steely blue eyes still trained on her, but Maya suddenly blurts out, "I'd love to join if you have any space."

"Hmm." Mark inhales and stares at her.

Is this some sort of power tactic? Travis always lets silence build in board meetings just to make sure he has everyone's attention. And to remind them he's the most powerful person in the room.

But before she can reply, Mark breaks into a winning smile. "Of *course* I have space for you. Please come. And bring your husband. Liz will give you the details?"

Liz nods enthusiastically in confirmation.

Once he's gone, Maya turns to face her. "Holy. Shit."

"Holy shit is *right*," Liz says, sharing in Maya's excitement. "You know what you just did, right? You won over the most powerful investor in the city. Your board needs to remember who the fuck they're dealing with."

Maya can't stop smiling. "I forgot how much I loved this," she admits.

"And you're good at it. You know how to command someone's attention." Liz smirks again, and this time, Maya smirks back.

That night, when Dev takes off his glasses and crawls under the covers next to her, she shifts toward him.

"I don't want to rehash the past weeks or argue or talk at all, frankly," Maya says.

Dev starts to respond but she gently places her fingers over his mouth. "Let's not. I just fucking want you."

She reaches under the waistband of his boxers.

"Whoa, what is going *on*?" Dev spins his head around to face her, a grin on his face.

She answers by sexily slipping her hands under the worn cotton. When she feels him hardening against her palm, she keeps going. Dev pushes his tongue between her lips and their warm bodies press against each other. She bites his ear, then his shoulder, climbing on top of him. It's not that she's lost interest in sex or doesn't want to make time for it. If anything, she's been chronically *under*-fucked. And after the day she's just had, she's feeling empowered.

The grind of their daily lives recedes into the background as they press into each other under the sheets. She's no longer a woman worrying about her son waking up and needing two ounces of milk, or about the weight still lingering around her middle.

She's all movement and pleasure.

Release and relief.

"I'm not sure where this is coming from, but I love it," Dev says breathily, his voice low as he pushes into her.

Maya moves her hips back and forth, feeling sexy in ways she hasn't for a long, long time. "Me, too," she whispers in his ear.

And for the next hour, she shuts her brain off and lets her body do the talking.

GLAMOUR

Maya Patel: The Female Founder and "Momfluencer" Everyone's Talking About

By Miranda Sachs
Published June 26, 2019, 10:07 AM EDT

GLAMOUR: Okay, let's switch gears for a second and talk about your marriage. You and your husband always look so in love whenever I see pictures of you two on Instagram. For starters, how did the two of you meet?

PATEL: Aw, I'm so glad that comes across in my posts. Because it's true: we've had an incredible connection since we met and it just keeps getting better. The first time I saw Dev—which, gosh, must have been five or so years ago at this point—he was performing onstage with The Treble Makers, an all-male collegiate a cappella group at Yale University.

GLAMOUR: Your soon-to-be husband did a cappella? I didn't see that one coming.

PATEL: [*Laughs.*] Neither did I! He's a very good singer. I actually first started listening to The Treble Makers back in high school after my cousin, a Yale underclassman at the time, played me one of their CDs. Apparently, the group was known not only for their fun mash-ups of contemporary hits, but also for their nostalgic, boy-band-type harmonies, which, according to this *Huffington Post* piece I read in college, made fans "swoon."

GLAMOUR: And I'm guessing you were one such fan?

PATEL: I totally was. [*Laughs.*] Every spring, the group held a show with alumni at a bar in the East Village. My best friend,

Alaina, and her then boyfriend (now husband) begged me to join them at the event, instead of spending another Saturday night at home, watching Netflix.

GLAMOUR: You weren't much of a partier in your twenties?

PATEL: Not really. I spent the majority of my weekends helping my parents out at the motel, so whenever I had any free time, all I craved was mindless television and the solitude of my apartment. [*Laughs.*] But for whatever reason, I made an exception that night. I can still remember throwing on my go-to black dress from Target, touching up my face with smoky-eye makeup, and stepping out the door in Alaina's fancy designer heels.

GLAMOUR: You must have made *quite* the impression on your soon-to-be husband!

PATEL: It was actually the other way around! I spotted Dev before The Treble Makers even started singing. He was wearing this white button-down shirt rolled up to his elbows and plain jeans. I never typically noticed guys when I went out. That was more Alaina's domain. She would point men out to me if they seemed like "my type." [*Laughs.*] But I don't know, there was something about Dev that drew me in right away. I mean, obviously I was attracted to his confidence and his ability to perform onstage in front of a massive audience. But there was something about his wide smile and relaxed posture that also gave him an air of humility.

GLAMOUR: Wow, so you were really checking him out.

PATEL: [*Blushing.*] I swear I tried to focus on the other singers, too! I remember feeling embarrassed because my eyes kept hanging on him, but I couldn't help it. Alaina still makes fun of me for pointing out his glasses and beard. I don't know…he was handsome in this understated, intellectual way, different from the guys my friends were drawn to at the time. I had this sense that he didn't need to be the center of attention. He had this quiet confidence, something I found rare. We locked eyes in the middle of the first song and I immediately got butterflies. It felt like I was thirteen again.

GLAMOUR: [*Laughs.*] So did you just stare longingly at him all night, or did you go talk to him? Who made the first move?

PATEL: I did! I'm not sure if it was the three gin and tonics I had consumed by that point, the fact that I hadn't been on a date in months, or a combination of both, but after the performance, I found him near the bar—not in a stalker way, I swear—and asked if I could buy him a drink.

GLAMOUR: I love that you made it happen. That must have been so empowering. *I* feel empowered just hearing you tell the story.

PATEL: It was honestly the boldest move of my life. We started talking about the performance, and the conversation just flowed. We talked about our families, our favorite foods, our plans for the future. And then he asked me if I wanted to step outside to hear each other better…

GLAMOUR: What a line!

PATEL: [*Laughs.*] I know, right? Such a smooth talker, that one. We spent the next three hours leaning against the bar's brick entrance and chatting. He expressed his fears about becoming a workaholic like most of the men in his life. And I shared the mixture of desire and dread I felt at the thought of leaving my consulting job and starting something completely my own. I hadn't even told anyone that before. But I don't know, like I said, there was just something about him. He was—is—such a great listener. Dev felt familiar and exciting at the same time, and it just felt *right*.

GLAMOUR: Okay, we need a screen adaptation of your love story, like, yesterday. Last question: Who would you cast to play you and Dev?

PATEL: Ooh, such a fun question. I'd love to be played by a new South Asian actress in her first role, and for Dev, I'd say Dev Patel, and not just because they share a name!

17

WHEN THE WEEKEND ROLLS BACK around, Dev and Maya are standing together in front of the bathroom mirror.

"How are you feeling about tonight?" Dev asks, buttoning his crisp white shirt.

To an outsider, she and her husband are the embodiment of a blissful domestic scene: a young couple getting ready to go on their first night out since having a baby. But anyone who knows them would be able to detect an undercurrent of a perfunctory, even clinical, sense of detachment in their interactions.

"Excited. And maybe—no, definitely—nervous? Specifically at the thought of leaving Shaan with someone who isn't either of our moms." She looks over at Shaan's blurry, tiny body in the baby monitor. He does a light back-and-forth with his head and then settles again into stillness. She takes in the curve of his nose, his lips curled into a partial smile.

Her baby.

Ever since upping her dosage, it's like her brain has made space to fully absorb the wonders and joys of early motherhood. There are things she loves about Shaan that she didn't know she could love about a person, like the way he scrunches his forehead as though he's about to deliver a stern lecture, or how he puckers his lips before taking a bottle, or his big eyes that gaze up at her whenever she's holding him.

"He'll be okay," Dev reassures her. "Nina seems like a pro."

"I know. It'll just take some getting used to."

"That it will. And hey, tonight will be good for us to get our minds off of things," he says, squeezing her shoulder.

"Do you want to talk about...any of it? There's been so much going on."

Dev checks his watch. "I'm not sure now's the right time. Nina should be here any minute now."

He helps her with the clasp of her delicate gold necklace that has a pendant with the letter *S* engraved on it. He surprised her with it the week before she gave birth, when they finally landed on the name for their son.

She leans back into him, breathing in the faint citrus scent of his Le Labo aftershave, the feel of his button-down shirt on the back of her neck. He rests his head on her shoulder, and she stares at their reflection in the mirror, savoring the moment.

A thought quickly passes through her mind. *What if I tell him about the guilt pill?*

Surely, he'd understand. Dev's nothing if not understanding. In fact, that's one of the things she loves most about him. He has always openly accepted every single part of her, even the parts she'd prefer to keep hidden. But if Maya told him about the pill, she'd also have to explain why she felt the need to take it in the first place. Her feelings of inadequacy as a mother, as a boss, as a wife. It would only confirm what her mother-in-law has been saying all along. Maya isn't good enough for Dev, for their baby. And she never will be.

They hear a knock and share a deep breath before exiting the bedroom.

"Don't you two look nice!" Nina says when they open the front door.

"Ha, thanks. First dinner out since having the little guy. I forgot what it's like to get all dolled up," Maya says.

Dev kisses her forehead. "You look beautiful. And seriously, Nina, thank you so much for being here. We can't tell you enough how grateful we are for your help."

"Of course, I'm happy to be here! Let me just wash my hands."

They follow her into the kitchen, and after she dries her hands, Maya sees her eyes dart around the room.

"Oh! Shaan's in the nursery. I'll lead the way."

The three of them find Shaan stretching in his crib, his eyes slowly letting the world in.

"Hi, my baby," Maya whispers as she picks him up, then kisses him on the forehead. "I'm going to miss you. I'm going to miss you *so* much."

As Shaan rests his head in the crook of her neck, her gut wrenches.

How can you just abandon your son for an entire night? With a stranger, no less? Especially after what happened.

Nina must read the anxiety all over her face because she puts a hand on Maya's arm. "He'll be okay. I promise."

Maya nods. "I know he's in good hands. I just didn't think it'd be this hard."

"The first time's always the hardest. It'll get easier!" Nina extends her hands as a sign for Maya to give Shaan to her. "And I'll send you pictures and videos. You won't miss a thing."

Nina motions to Shaan again. "May I?"

"Oh, right!" Maya says, not moving a muscle. "Sorry. Just two more seconds."

Nina and Dev share a look that's equal parts amusement and

understanding. Maya gives Shaan one last tight squeeze before handing him over to Nina.

"I'm just going to use the bathroom to freshen up before we go," Maya says.

She takes quick steps to the bathroom and sprays her face with a rosewater toner to calm herself down. But as she takes in the distant sounds of Nina making Shaan a bottle in the kitchen and her son's high-pitched babble, the pang in her stomach comes back full force. She feels faint, clutching the sink tightly until her knuckles turn white.

You're making a mistake. You'll never get these precious moments back. Shaan will always remember you as the mother who wasn't around.

She's frozen. How is she going to get through the night? Her eyes well with tears, threatening to mess up her makeup. She steps out into the bedroom and her eyes flit over to her nightstand.

Liz's voice comes back to her: *I have some clients who are taking up to five a day, and they're totally fine. No, more than fine. They're great!*

What's one more?

Maya dry swallows a pill, and as soon as she shoves the bottle back in its hiding place, there's a knock on the bedroom door.

Luckily, Dev waits a minute before opening the door, so he doesn't see her jump like she's been caught red-handed. Or *pink*-handed.

She already feels so much better.

"You ready, honey?" Dev asks.

"Ready!"

The Uber pulls up to Gramercy Tavern. When Maya gives her name at the door, they're guided to the private dining room. It is the epitome of elegance, with rustic chandeliers, a wood-beamed ceiling, and fancily dressed waiters carrying trays of champagne. The center of the table is covered with an array of fresh flowers.

Liz is already standing at the large oval table, laughing at some comment while sipping on champagne. She looks right at home in her cream-colored silk Sachin & Babi dress, her hair perfectly styled in Hollywood-glam curls.

"There she is!" Maya points her out to Dev and threads her arm through his as they make their way to the table.

"Maya!" Liz exclaims. "And you must be Dev. I've heard so much about you. All good things!" She winks.

Not even a little bit true.

Dev gives Liz a polite smile. "Likewise. Great to meet you."

"Is Mark here?" Maya looks around the room.

"Not yet. He likes to make an entrance. Power move kind of guy, you know what I mean?" Liz laughs. "Anyway, *Vanity Fair* is apparently going to feature this dinner. Let's make sure we get a photo. And you both have to meet Owen!"

They follow Liz's gaze to a blond six-foot-three man in an off-white linen suit and Gucci loafers. All Maya can think when she sees him is that he'd be perfectly cast in any cologne commercial. He looks exactly like the kind of guy who could stare into the distance with a pensive look on his face before diving into the ocean to the sound of sensual music.

Owen turns around at the sound of his name and makes his way over to them. "Hello, hello! It's so nice to meet you both in person." Owen leans in to hug Maya and gives Dev a firm shoulder pat.

The four of them chat for a few minutes about work, their kids, the other guests who RSVP'd to the dinner. Maya finds Owen much more approachable than she thought he would be. "I'm just going to run to the restroom before more people get here," she says.

(Aka, she needs to do one final run-through of how she's

going to pitch Medini to potential investors without *sounding* like she's pitching Medini to potential investors.)

In the bathroom mirror, she clutches the edge of the sink. *You can do this,* she tells her reflection. *You've done much harder things before.*

She used to give herself these kinds of pep talks all the time when she first started pitching Medini. So many of the women in her favorite television shows hyped themselves up before conquering whatever was next. Olivia Pope. Dr. Cristina Yang. Leslie Knope. She conjures up these women in her mind, summoning their confidence.

Maya pats her face with a paper towel and reapplies her lipstick. The bright red shade matches her dress and nails. She's always felt the most confident when sporting bold colors.

As she's just about to cross the threshold into the dining room, her steps lighter and more self-assured, a man in her periphery motions to her.

Maya doesn't recognize him and hopes he introduces himself right away so she doesn't have to pretend to know who he is. His straight posture, graying sideburns, and perfectly tailored suit give off an air of importance. Is he a partner at one of the big funds? A CEO? He's standing with two other men, all three of them huddled directly outside the dining room. Judging by their boisterous laughter and bloodshot eyes, they definitely had drinks before dinner.

She flashes him a tentative smile. "Hello!"

"Hi, sweetheart. Can you get me another of these?" He holds up his cocktail glass.

What the fuck did you just say?

"Excuse me?"

"Another one of this drink that has, er, something fruity muddled in it? It was the third one on that menu someone gave me." He gives her an *I just can't remember* shrug.

Just a couple weeks ago, she probably would have frozen with awkwardness, maybe even apologized to *him* for the mix-up. But tonight, she clears her throat and points to the dining room.

"No, I can't, actually. I don't work here. I'm here for Mark Stahlberg's dinner."

"Oh…oh!" His expression shifts from surprise to mock recognition. But there's no embarrassment. Not even a *smidge*, as Mom would say.

He snaps his fingers as if making an important realization. "Right. Of course."

"Actually, no, you weren't right. You thought I was here to serve your drink. And while there's absolutely nothing wrong with being a server, that's simply not the case. I'm here as a guest, just like you."

"I see that now. My mistake." He does a faux bow.

"Yes, it really was," Maya agrees. "An unacceptable mistake."

It feels so good to stand up for herself after a lifetime of biting her tongue.

"Ah, a spitfire! I like that." He grins, elbowing the two men next to him, and takes a step closer to her.

Gross.

If only she had a nickel for every time a man has made her feel uncomfortable, especially at work events. Like at that one tech conference, right after she'd presented Medini's products onstage, when an investor pulled her aside and said, *Of course you'll get funding. You're gorgeous.* Or later that night at a cocktail party, when two male attendees asked her if she wanted to have a "brainstorm" session up in their hotel rooms. But of course she never heard from them again when she suggested they meet at a neutral location instead. Or the meeting with a VC partner that got moved from his office to a bar down the street. Over the course of an hour, he gradually shifted closer and closer to Maya until his thigh was pressing against hers.

"Honey?" Dev steps out of the dining room. "I think people are starting to sit down."

The man turns to face Dev. "Are we heading in?"

"*We*—" Maya gestures in the space between her and Dev "—are heading in. Now, if you'll excuse us."

"What was that about?" Dev asks, catching up to meet her stride as they file into the dining room. There's a hint of amusement in his shocked expression.

"I'll tell you later."

Mark asks everyone around the table to give a quick introduction, which takes an hour thanks to some people mentioning every publication they've ever been featured in. To her dismay, the man from before—whose name she finds out is Ted Davenport—*is*, in fact, a partner at one of the top venture capital firms. Maya's well-aware she probably just ruined Medini's chance at ever securing funding from his firm. *Whatever.*

The rest of the dinner passes by in pleasant side conversations around tech news and plans for future coffee dates. A managing partner at one of the top funds asks Maya to stop by her office in a couple of weeks. The host of one of the biggest tech podcasts, *Startup Success Story*, invites her to be a guest on the show.

She takes it all in like she's suspended above the room, an observer of her own life. So *this* is what true access means. Contrary to so many advice books out there, it has nothing to do with hard work. She's been surrounded by hard workers her entire life. This is about connections and privilege and leveraging whatever comes your way.

"I'm going to try to have a real conversation with Mark," she says to Dev, who is mid-conversation with a fellow Yale graduate and Treble Makers alumnus a few years his senior.

"I'll come with you," Dev offers, scooting his chair back.

She feels a hint of disappointment when he says this. And she hates herself for it.

They walk over to the head of the table, where Mark stands up to greet her. "Maya!" He notices Dev and adds, "And you must be the husband."

"That is true. I'm best known as Maya's husband." Dev laughs. "And occasionally, Dev."

Mark puts his hand on the small of Maya's back. "You're a lucky man, Dev."

A rush of heat crawls up Maya's neck and face. "Oh, please." She scoffs, lightheartedly rolling her eyes.

"I'm very much aware." Dev drapes an arm around Maya in a way that's equal parts affectionate and territorial.

Maya clears her throat. "We wanted to thank you for such a nice evening, and I just wanted to follow up on doing a formal pitch at some point. I'd love to discuss Medini more in-depth with you."

Mark nods, leaning in to lower his voice "Maya, I like you," he says. "But I have to be one hundred percent confident before I move forward with a company. I think we need to spend more time together. Get to know each other a bit more before we think about next steps."

He reaches into his blazer pocket and pulls out a thick white business card with *Tribeca One* written across it—in gold font, naturally. "Why don't you give my assistant a call? Let's get a meeting in the books."

"I absolutely will. Thanks so much, Mark!"

This could be *huge* for her.

When they walk back to their seats, Dev whispers, "What was going on back there? Between you two?"

"Nothing. That's just how he is," she whispers back.

He raises his eyebrows. "Huh, interesting."

She drains her glass of champagne and says, "It's getting late. Can you call us an Uber? I'm just going to run to the bathroom."

The buzz from her drinks gives her an airy, almost light-headed feeling.

On her way, a familiar voice—or voices—stops her in her tracks.

"I mean it, Liz. You need to do better. Especially after everything that happened at Limitless."

"I have it under control!" Liz says with exasperation, her irritation clear despite the low volume of her voice. "How many times do I have to tell you that? Women Rise is everything to me."

Maya can see them but hopes they can't see her. She grips the cool, smooth wall, willing it to stop her from making any noise.

"And our family isn't?" Owen snaps back. "You're putting us all in jeopardy *again*, Liz. You promised me you were going to stop this bullshit!"

"Oh please, Owen. Quit the dramatics. It's all going to be fine. It *is* fine. You need to stop freaking out. Now, can we get back in there? This isn't the time or place for this." Maya hears the rustle of silk, followed by one final annoyed huff.

She waits until they're both out of sight until quickly making her way outside, where Dev's waiting with the Uber.

NEW YORK CITY POLICE DEPARTMENT

OFFICER KENT: Sir, you said your marriage was healthy.

DEV MEHTA: It was. It *is*.

OFFICER KENT: But you've informed us of a time when your wife intentionally left you.

DEV MEHTA: For *less than twenty-four hours*. Sure, we've had some low points. But what marriage hasn't?

OFFICER KENT: There are rumors about your wife allegedly having an affair.

DEV MEHTA: Excuse me? An *affair*? No, that's not Maya. She would never do that. Where did you hear that?

OFFICER KENT: We've received tips from anonymous sources alleging that your wife was seen with another man, and that they seemed "friendly." He's described as a "colleague" of sorts. Does the name Mark Stahlberg ring any bells?

DEV MEHTA: [...]

OFFICER KENT: Mr. Mehta, please answer the question.

DEV MEHTA: That's bullshit. I'm not entertaining this.

OFFICER KENT: Sir, how well would you say you knew your wife?

DEV MEHTA: Look, Maya's complicated, okay? But our marriage was—*is*—good. Great, even. She's the love of my life and the mother of my son. And she's coming home to us. I'm sure of it.

18

THE SECOND MAYA'S EYES OPEN, IT HITS her all at once. The tightening in her chest and throat. Pangs of dread and defeat. A dull throb on the left side of her head.

Are these the shitty hangovers you're told to expect once you've hit thirty?

She feels like she's having some combination of the worst hangover anxiety (*drinker's remorse*, as her and Alaina used to call it) mixed with the most debilitating period cramps of her life.

But there's something else in there, too. Sure, there's the predictable pounding headache and the nausea. But this feels so much worse than anything she's ever felt after a night of drinking. It's a pain in her head, her stomach, *and* her heart.

You left your baby last night. Have you even thought about how negligent you've been with Shaan? How you just gave up on breast-feeding? And have you realized you've stopped weighing him every day because you've been sooo busy with work? What kind of mother is too busy to take care of her child?

Maya sits up in bed, alert, propping two pillows against their light gray headboard. Dev's sheets are still rumpled in his shape. She runs her hands across the linen and wills herself to take deep, heavy breaths. She was up every two hours to feed Shaan after they came home last night. On some level, she hoped that the predictability of the task would anchor her.

What was that mindfulness exercise she relied on in college? Something to do with observing her surroundings, naming what she sees and smells? She takes note of the slanted raindrops streaking the window. The stack of unread novels and parenting books on the windowsill. Dev's scent still lingering on the bed.

But the thoughts don't stop.

You're supposed to be making sure that your son has a better childhood than you but here you are, losing yourself in work just like your parents did.

Did you seriously flirt with Mark last night in front of your husband? Who are you becoming? You're a bad wife. A bad mother. A bad person.

The covers are hiked up to her chin, her heart racing. There's a brief respite, where her mind just goes completely blank. Maybe it's over. Maybe that was the worst of it.

But then comes the kicker.

You know, deep down, that if the people you love actually *knew who you really are, they wouldn't love you.*

Maya presses her hands over her ears and screams into her pillow. The guilt sits on her chest, heavy, making it hard to breathe. She tries forcing herself out of bed to splash cold water on her face, anything to shock her system, but she's completely frozen.

She can't get through the day like this. She can't even get out of bed.

Maya stretches toward her nightstand and removes four hot-pink pills. Four made such a difference last night, and she needs all the help she can get.

Hurry up and work. Hurry up and work. Hurry up and work.

The relief is immediate as her thoughts progressively come to a stop. She always forgets how good the heady sensation feels as soon as she pops a pill.

The baby monitor shows a still-sleeping Shaan.

She calls Liz, who answers right away. "Hello, hello! Recovered from last night?"

"Barely." Maya's voice is hoarse.

"Well, you sure made the most of it. Did Gary's team reach out about recording?"

Maya opens her email and finds a message from *Start-Up Success Story* at the top of her inbox. "Yes, actually! They already did."

"Amazing! One episode with him can grow your profile in an entirely different way. I mean, I think he officially has the number-two podcast in the country now. Isn't that wild?"

"It is. I've been listening to it for years and never thought I'd get the chance to be a guest on it." There's so much about her current life that a younger Maya could have only dreamed of.

Maya cuts Liz off before she can continue. She feels bolder than usual this morning. "Listen, I actually called because I heard you and Owen fighting last night on my way to the bathroom."

"What?" Liz sounds like she has no idea what she's referring to.

"Outside the bathroom. I was waiting to go in and then realized you were both in a conversation that sounded pretty heated. I just wanted to check in to make sure everything is okay."

Liz is silent, until she finally says, "Ah, that. Um, yeah. We got into it last night."

"Do you want to talk about it?"

Liz sighs. "Owen's stuck in another era. Every time I bring up my work, he has something negative to say. He always claims it's because he wants me to spend more time with the kids, or with him, but c'mon, I know what he's implying. He's resentful of me. Of my success. He wants me to cut back at Women Rise, stay at home with our girls, and be his perfect little fifties housewife, so *he* can be the center of attention, the clear breadwinner. It's so obvious he feels emasculated by everything I've accomplished. He always makes my wins about him."

"You really think that's true?" Maya wasn't expecting that. "I mean, surely Owen never could have thought that a 'fifties housewife' was in the cards when he married *you*."

"You're right, that was never in the cards for him. And I made that crystal clear from the very start. Owen thought it was sexy at first, the way I wanted to 'disrupt the status quo.' But you know what I've realized? Sometimes people are attracted to one thing, but what they really want—no, *need*—is something else entirely."

Liz sighs again. "I don't know, I guess I thought Owen was different, more like Dev. But I think having kids changed him, or at the very least, made him realize what he really wants. And it's not me." She pauses. "Who knows? Maybe he was lying to the both of us all along. Men lie all the damn time."

"So, all that stuff you post about him empowering you… I thought you were so happy." She's brought back to her conversation with Alaina on spaghetti night. Why has she been so dismissive of her best friend's concerns?

"Please. It's all social media bullshit. Investors like it when female founders play the 'good wife.' It makes us more palatable to them or something. And Maya, I *am* happy. Just not with him. I have to put up what people want to see. And regardless of who's on my profile, they're not coming to me to get *marital* advice. They're coming to feel inspired, like they can escape their humdrum lives. You know people like us have to keep posting and sharing to feed that goddamn algorithm. It's all a game we agreed to play. I mean, look at you now compared to when we first met."

When she doesn't respond, Liz adds, "You're telling me everything you post is one hundred percent accurate?"

"Well, it's not a blatant *lie*. I can say that much."

"Oh, come on. You might think you're not 'playing the game,' but you are. You have for months. If I took a look at any one of Medini's platforms right now, I'd immediately assume that the company's thriving. Am I wrong? I mean, you certainly gave that impression last night when you networked all around the table. But that's not true, is it?"

She has a point.

Liz isn't finished. "And posting pictures of Dev on your shoulder, when you've been fighting so much? Or posting videos of Shaan giggling after he was up every hour the night before, crying? *That's* playing the game, Maya."

She remains silent for what feels like a long time. That last one hurt.

"I should go check on Shaan," Maya finally says.

"Of course. I'm sorry if I seemed super harsh. And I'm not blaming you, or myself, or anyone for it. This is just the way it is. Anyway, I won't keep you. I'm glad we got a chance to chat!"

Liz cheerily ends their conversation as if she didn't just basically call Maya a fraud.

But she can't ruminate on that right now. She's got shit to do.

Maya pulls out her computer from under the bed, sends an update to Josh about the dinner with Mark, sets up drinks with Travis, and texts Mark a thank-you for dinner.

Dev's on speakerphone when she steps into the living room.

"Yeah, Mom, I'll check that... Uh-huh, uh-huh... Yeah, I'll ask his pediatrician... Okay, yes... I have eaten that." When he registers Maya's presence, he gives her an awkward smile, and she knows how badly he wants to take his mom off speaker.

"Hi!" Maya calls out a little too forcefully to the phone.

"Oh, hi, Maya," her mother-in-law says, her voice tight. "Dev, I have to run. I'll talk to you later. Love you."

"Okaaay," Maya says when he's off the phone. "Do you think I should ask her if she and I can talk about that situation from the other day? One-on-one?"

Dev sighs. "You know that isn't really her style."

Of course she knows. His entire family has always just swept things under the rug like they never happened. She used to envy their constant polite and pleasant exteriors, but based on Dev's pathological conflict avoidance, it now seems like it's not a great way to go through life after all.

"Why did you have to go off on her last time?" Dev asks quietly.

Because I took something that helped me give less fucks. Her whole life, guilt has kept her quiet, even when she's had every right to speak up.

Maya's about to apologize, but something stops her. It slowly dawns on her that, on some level, she thought that having a baby meant her in-laws would finally accept her.

But they didn't. And they never will if they don't have an honest conversation with her.

"It's important for these things to be discussed openly if your mother and I are going to have a better relationship. I know this isn't the way she's used to doing things, but it's the way it has to be from now on."

"I appreciate what you're saying, I do, but I don't know, Maya..." Dev shakes his head. "You're different. There's always something with you lately. I don't know if you're in the best place for a conversation like that."

Dev's sexiness has always stemmed from his stability. His strong but soft hands. His black-rimmed glasses. His ready, wide smile. The calming presence he brings into every room he enters. He's always been the peacekeeper, the tension diffuser.

But right now, his constant aversion to ruffling feathers, especially when it comes at the cost of his own wife's well-being, infuriates her.

"Always something? Seriously?" Her phone rings with a call from Mom and she sends it to voicemail.

"Yes, seriously. I mean, what was even going on last night between you and Mark?"

"*Nothing* was going on. I was networking!"

"Ohhh, networking? Hm. I've never seen it look like that. I've never seen *you* look like that."

Maya rolls her eyes. "Sometimes these guys with big egos need to be a little buttered up. And if I want Medini to not only thrive but *survive*, I have to con—"

They're interrupted by Shaan's cries.

"I've got him," she snaps before exiting the room.

In that moment, she relishes the monotonous tasks of parenting. Rock the baby. Change the diaper. Prepare formula.

Once Shaan's comfortably cradled in her arms and she hums him a lullaby, her nervous system finally slows down.

Until it doesn't.

What were you doing with Mark? Have you noticed how your husband looks at you lately? What if Liz was right about people being attracted to one thing but needing another? What if you're not what Dev wants, let alone needs*?*

She tries to distract herself by fixating on Shaan's long eyelashes and round nose, but that quickly backfires.

Look at him, he's still underweight. You stopped trying to breastfeed and you quit pumping and he's not a healthy baby. And it's all your fault. You're so selfish. And a terrible mother.

Her headache worsens, and it's as though someone is squeezing her head with superhuman strength. And this time, she *does* keel over in pain when the cramp attacks her stomach.

How is this happening? She took four this morning, and all at once. What was it that Alaina told her back when they were roommates? Maya wills the answer to come to her. Alaina was studying for her medical boards and said something about a chapter she just read, relating it to her experience with taking ibuprofen. Something about pain tolerance, lower baselines, rebound pain that's worse because it's overtreated? She can't remember the details.

All she knows is she needs quick relief.

Maya puts Shaan in his bouncer and peeks into their bedroom, where she hears the shower running.

Perfect.

She runs to her nightstand and throws back another pill at the exact same time Dev turns the water off, the rod squeaking as he removes his towel. She quickly sneaks back out of the bedroom to return to Shaan and put him on his play mat. He gazes first at the tiny bell, then at the swaying wooden toy that's meant to help his hand-eye coordination.

With her gaze half-fixated on Shaan, she pours two glasses of prosecco and empties a bag of sea-salt popcorn into a sky-blue East Fork ceramic bowl they'd received as a wedding gift. They need to talk. *Really* talk.

A few minutes later, Dev steps into the living room in a white polo and jeans.

"You're leaving?"

"Yeah. I'm meeting some people from work." He reaches for his keys and wallet.

"You are?" Unlike so many of her other friends' husbands, Dev is never the type to make plans on a whim without consulting her, especially since Shaan was born. She used to feel uncomfortable when she went to dinners where everyone complained about their husbands and she had nothing to contribute.

Maya tries to pinpoint the myriad of emotions rising within her. Surprise over his decision to leave her and Shaan right now.

Sadness that he definitely wants space away from *her.* Hopelessness about the state of their marriage.

Based on her parents' example, Maya assumed for years that a series of explosive, cyclical arguments were what eroded a marriage. Now she sees that relationships can also fray during the quieter moments, too. Moments like these.

"I won't be long. See you later." Dev walks toward her and gives her a quick kiss on the cheek. It feels forced. Distant.

The following hours pass in a slew of tasks that she performs on autopilot. Wash bottles. Play peekaboo. Change diaper. Wipe spit-up from chin and neck. Change clothes. Adjust burp cloth. Cradle and rock. Order formula. Open app and log Shaan's diaper changes, ounces consumed, and weight.

Weight.

Maya places him on the changing table and presses the button she's been avoiding for the past two weeks.

Her breath catches when she reads the screen. She weighs him again. Then again. But the number doesn't change.

Shaan hasn't gained any weight since their last appointment.

No, no, no. How is this possible? She's been waking up all throughout the night, *every* night, to feed him. She even followed up with Dr. Karp to make sure she's maximizing his calories per ounce with the formula.

Her heart races as she looks up contact information for a nearby pediatric gastroenterologist.

Can't you see that you're unfit as a mother? Dev's mom was right about you all along. This is concrete evidence that you're failing your baby.

She holds her hands over her ears again.

Stop. Please, stop.

Suddenly, Maya's back there. She smells the bleach of the cleaner they used for trashed motel rooms, the artificial vanilla in the hand soaps stocked in every bathroom, and her brother's syrupy skin.

Please, I beg of you. Don't do this. Please.

She's sobbing now, clutching Shaan against her chest and fixating on the feel of his hands on her stomach. The tiny weight of his head against her chest. After a few minutes pass, Maya's breathing evens out.

She *cannot* drift off to that place again, especially when she's alone with Shaan.

And there's only one way to make sure of that.

Maya heads to her nightstand.

NEW YORK CITY POLICE DEPARTMENT

OFFICER KENT: How often did you see Ms. Patel interact with her son?

NINA JENKINS: Pretty often. I'd arrive at her apartment every morning and she usually stuck around for a bit before leaving for the day.

OFFICER KENT: Did you notice anything specific about Ms. Patel's demeanor with her son?

NINA JENKINS: She's very caring… And very concerned. She checked Shaan's feeding and sleeping log all the time. Sometimes I got the sense that she put a lot of pressure on herself. She seemed to like taking charge and overseeing everything. And then other times… Sorry, never mind, it's not relevant.

OFFICER KENT: Please finish your sentence, ma'am.

NINA JENKINS: I was just going to say that, um, other times, she almost seemed like she was elsewhere, in her own world. But I'm sure she was just tired.

OFFICER KENT: And Ms. Patel and Mr. Mehta? How did their marriage seem?

NINA JENKINS: A child can bring a lot of stress into a marriage.

OFFICER KENT: Please answer the question.

NINA JENKINS: I remember finding them very sweet the first time I came over. And then, I'm not sure why, but it seemed like things became more distant between them. Mr. Mehta once told me he didn't recognize his own wife anymore...but I'm sure that was just in the heat of the moment. He said it in passing after a big fight between the two of them.

OFFICER KENT: How have you liked working with Ms. Patel and Mr. Mehta overall?

NINA JENKINS: Could I please have some water? I think I need a minute.

19

FIVE PILLS.

Yes, that's exactly the amount she needs for a packed day like today. One pill every four hours and she'll be good to go. She keeps one in her nightstand for later today and puts the other four in the inner pocket of her workbag.

Her mind jumps to an old episode of *Saved by the Bell*, a show she hasn't seen in years. She pictures Jessie Spano opening her caffeine pills in front of Zack Morris and singing, "'I'm so excited! I'm so excited! I'm…so…scared.'"

She laughs despite herself, even though she's nothing like Jessie. Sure, Tarun may have compared her to the character back in high school, thanks to Maya's and Jessie's shared obsession over their GPA, or their constant stream of self-doubt. But Maya's a different person now. She's the kind of self-assured woman who makes plans and executes them, regardless of what others think. She's a *doer.*

"I'm sorry I have to leave you again," she says to Shaan after taking her first pill of the day. She kisses the top of his head and waves goodbye to Nina.

He'll be just fine. Besides, she doesn't want her son growing up to think motherhood means sacrifice, or that a good mom is one whose identity is solely defined by how much she does for others. She wants Shaan to see her as a fulfilled parent, a woman who doesn't lose herself after having a baby.

By the time she reaches the 1 Train, she finds a renewed sense of purpose and speedily responds to Slack messages whenever she gets service.

When Maya gets off the subway, she savors the first sip of her street-cart coffee, watching as passersby power walk beside her, distractedly texting on their phones. She soaks in the scent of pastries wafting out of Eataly and the fresh-cut grass in Madison Square Park. She's seeing New York City the same way she used to as a little girl. While Mom and Dad scoured the streets for a parking spot that would fit their giant gray minivan, Maya would stare out the window, mesmerized. Even then, she knew the city would one day be her home base.

Her phone buzzes in her bag.

Josh: You almost here? Board is in the conference room.

Maya: Just a couple minutes!!!

As she takes the elevator up to Medini's office, she feels empowered. Important.

Everyone is waiting for *her* to arrive. It's a refreshing change. When she enters the board meeting, she immediately walks to the head of the room's large, rectangular table and places her bags down beside her to mark her territory. The center of the table is filled with their usual stash of chickpea crisps, a bowl of clementines, and water bottles emblazoned with the Medini logo.

She feels everyone's eyes on her. The ambient noise of small talk dissipates as she sits and smooths down her hair, then adjusts her silky tan blouse and navy pencil skirt. She waits until the sounds of shuffling paper and rustling chip bags subside, then clears her throat to get everyone's attention. "Are we ready to start?"

Medini has a board meeting every quarter to review and evaluate the company's strategy for the rest of the year, while also addressing any concerns that may have bubbled up since they last touched base.

"I think we should jump in with how things have been going," Travis starts. Today, he's wearing a perfectly ironed button-down shirt and charcoal slacks. His heavily gelled-down hair reminds Maya of one of the T-Birds from *Grease.*

"They're going," Maya replies. "People are overwhelmed. As was expected after letting so many go and making no adjustment to our remaining employees' workloads."

"So, we need to hire more people, then," Travis says point-blank.

"After we just did layoffs? Is 'hire and fire' our thing?" She uses this phrase on purpose, having heard it from countless investors in the past. Maya always found this business approach volatile and inconsiderate. She still does.

"That was nice of you to send old team members care packages," Brad offers, gesturing toward Maya.

"You did *what*?" Travis looks appalled.

"Thanks, Brad. And yes. I sent care packages to the employees who were let go," Maya says.

"Care packages? Like they're hospital patients or something?" Travis snorts derisively.

She sees the other attendees' eyes awkwardly dart back and forth between Maya and Travis.

"No, Travis. Like they're people who got the rug pulled out from under them. People who put in a lot of time here." Maya pauses for effect. "And anyway, going back to your original point, we need to raise more money before growing the team. We must be very intentional with any next steps. We have to *act*, not react."

"Well, since you brought up raising more money, this seems as good a time as any to ask if you pitched Medini to Stahlberg?" Travis raises his bushy eyebrows.

Maya straightens in her chair, taken aback. "I didn't officially *pitch* Medini. If you're asking if I told him about the company, then yes, I did. We were at a big dinner, not a one-on-one meeting."

"So what I'm hearing is, you didn't talk up Medini's vision or imply we want him on board."

"We are going to see over time if it feels like a good fit." Maya clenches her fists, feeling like a teenager forced to explain her whereabouts. "I'm sorry, am I not allowed to discuss *my* company at an industry gathering? Josh, you have impromptu discussions with VCs all the time, don't you?"

Josh fidgets awkwardly. "You and I still talk about it." His voice is soft, reminding her a little too much of Dev right now. "Usually beforehand, but definitely after," he adds.

"I was going to tell you all once I heard back from him," Maya says, hating the defensiveness that's crept into her voice. "When I'd have an actual update to share with the team."

Travis once again puts her in the hot seat. "Did you tell him about Medini going into more Whole Foods stores?"

"He asked about my vision for the company, so yes, I did."

"I thought we agreed at the last meeting that we were going to see if this Whole Foods thing was even sustainable, let alone scalable, before going full-fledged into retail. And obviously before telling other people about it," Travis says, scanning his notes to prove his point.

So that was a trap.

"We didn't agree on that," Maya retorts. "And I know we

haven't talked through a plan for our next round of funding yet, but it's important to make sure some of the name-brand VCs know who we are."

"Name-brand VCs?" Travis tightens his jaw. "So Mark Stahlberg's not an anomaly, then? You're sure you want to aim that high? It was hard enough for you to get funding last round. I don't know if there's reason to think it will be smooth sailing this time."

She feels a reflexive *what if he's right?* form of self-doubt, quickly overcome by a burst of anger. The anger is surprisingly comforting. Refreshing, even. She wishes she could clutch it in her palms and throw it right in Travis's face.

Somewhere, deep down inside of her, a faraway voice tells her to take a deep breath and let the moment pass.

But that's the old Maya talking. She's hit with a series of moments from her life, like when she was told by some higher-up she didn't "look like a founder." Or when she was repeatedly left out of dinner and drink plans with coworkers after a long day of work at *her* company, or when she was told to smile more during meetings, or when she even considered changing the pitch of her voice so others would take her more seriously.

Each memory builds more and more pressure inside of her. Rage coats her throat as she clutches the edge of the table. "Just so I'm clear. You're saying I shouldn't follow up with someone who expressed interest in our company because you don't think Medini is good enough. Am I right?"

Travis's expression remains the same, with everyone else looking down at the ground.

She continues, "There are founders out there who have lost investors tens or even hundreds of millions of dollars, and they go on to raise plenty of money for their next companies. Somehow, their track records don't hold them back, yet I'm always having to defend mine. Now, why do we think that is?"

Her words hang in the air again, heavy.

From her periphery, she sees some of the board members glance nervously at each other. One of them looks at the door as if he's contemplating getting the fuck out of there.

"What's gotten into you lately, Maya?" Travis asks. "You make these decisions, you don't communicate. You're so…" He waves his hands in the air for emphasis, and she knows which words are right at the tip of his tongue. *Intense. All over the place. Aggressive. Hysterical.*

She can't win. When she speaks up, she's too aggressive. And when she doesn't, she's too timid.

"I haven't made any decisions," Maya calmy responds, folding her hands. "I've been working to do what's best for all of us, and as the CEO, founder, and largest shareholder, I'm well within my rights to do so. And don't think I'm unaware of the fact that you, *all* of you," she says, motioning around the conference room, "dodged my question. It wasn't meant to be rhetorical. Remember a year or so ago when I circulated that article on female founders? The one exploring how female founders are assessed on past performance, whereas male founders are assessed on future potential? I'm sure no one wants that to be the case here, correct?"

Silence builds in the room. She feels the weight of everyone's eyes on her and remembers something Dev once told her: *Don't let the silence make you so anxious that you ramble to fill it.*

"Josh, what are your thoughts on all this?" Miriam, their most recently appointed board member, asks.

Why do you always fucking ask what Josh *thinks? I'm the one who built this fucking company!*

"I think Maya has always had a set vision for the company and it's gotten us to where we are," Josh says carefully.

She waits for the *but.*

"But I also think it's important for everyone to be on the same page about how we move forward."

There it is.

"I've got to be in midtown in twenty minutes." Travis swaps out his reading glasses for his sunglasses and looks down at his Rolex. "We're going to have to set up a time to discuss all of this further."

"Among other things," Brad mutters under his breath.

Tiffany pulls up the Google calendar. "I'll coordinate dates with everyone."

"Thanks, Tiffany," Maya says. Oh, how she wishes she could just work with Tiffany all day and never deal with people like Travis.

Once they confirm the new date and time, Maya puts it in her own calendar. She opens her notes app and jots down reminders to order more baby formula, to email Mark's assistant, to finish folding Shaan's laundry, and to call her parents back. There's always an endless to-do list. Running a company meeting—even one as stressful as this—somehow feels more manageable, more intuitive, than everything going on at home.

She exits the subway and checks her watch. It's well past 5:00 p.m., so Dev's probably back from work already. She's desperate to rehash the meeting with him and breathes a sigh of relief when she envisions him perched on their sectional with Shaan in his arms, the Daniel Tiger soundtrack playing in the background.

But when she rushes into the apartment, he's not at his usual spot on the living room couch.

"Honey?" she calls out, putting her things down by the door. She peers into the living room, the kitchen. Where is he?

It's not until she reaches the bedroom that she sees him, hunched over the nightstand.

Her nightstand.

"What are these?" Dev asks, his voice eerily calm. He's holding the brown bottle in his hands, which is now only a quarter full of hot-pink pills.

Heat rises up her throat. She watches in slow motion as Dev opens the bottle and pours the pills into his hands, an unreadable expression on his face.

"Where did you find them?" Maya asks nonchalantly. She tries to feign indifference, even ignorance. But either way, it's an admission. She's confirmed they weren't meant to be found.

"I was looking for an extra charger and these were pushed to the back of your drawer. Almost like you were trying to hide them."

When she doesn't say anything, he presses, "Were you?"

"I'm sorry."

"Maya, what *are* these?"

His voice remains calm, which makes it even worse.

What can I say that will make him ask the least amount of follow-up questions?

"They're these, um, pills, I mean, supplements. I've been wanting to tell you about them but I just—"

"You just what? You just forgot to mention to your husband that you're taking some new medication? And not only that, but you intentionally hid it from me? What the hell are these for, Maya?" Her heart breaks as she watches the expression on Dev's face shift from confusion to anger to blatant disappointment.

"They're nothing. They just help me feel better sometimes."

"Feel better *how*?" Dev holds the bottle in a white-knuckled grip, using his free hand to anxiously comb through his wavy black hair. His signature *what the fuck do you want me to do with this information?* move.

"They…they make things feel less intense."

"Where did you get them? Did Alaina recommend them?"

"No, she didn't. But I mentioned them to her."

"You mentioned them to her without telling *me*?"

"It just came up."

"And?"

"And…she wasn't a fan," Maya concedes. "But she's not, like, *concerned* or anything."

Dev shakes his head. "You still haven't told me what this even is."

Fuck. What *did* she tell Alaina they were again? She can't remember.

"They're CBD tablets."

Dev raises his eyebrows. "CBD? You've never even smoked weed."

"I know. But they're helping me. At least for now."

"You don't need this kind of help," Dev says, shaking the pill bottle.

"I do, actually," Maya snaps, her voice hardening. "In case you haven't noticed, I was doing everything on my own those first weeks—no, the first *month*—after Shaan was born. And it's been hard. *So* fucking hard. I've been working my ass off at home and at work and didn't expect how overwhelmed I'd feel all the time. So when Liz told me about these supplements that could help a little, I thought they were worth a try. And I was surprised as anyone when they actually worked, but they did." She pauses. "And they're totally safe."

"Oh, well, if Liz told you about them! Liz is what, then?" Dev asks. "Your coach? Your therapist? Your doctor?"

"She's my *friend*," Maya snaps, her muscles tensing. He sounds just like Alaina.

"Interesting. So Liz can tell you what to do but I'm not even allowed to know?" Dev furrows his brows. "Are these why you've been acting so different lately? And doesn't CBD help people feel calmer?"

"I'm acting so different lately because I'm *exhausted*!" Maya throws her hands up in exasperation. "Ever since we had Shaan, my life has felt so out of control. Everyone gives me shit, no matter what I do. These supplements are the *one* thing that's helped, the *one* thing that makes me feel better. God forbid I just want something to block out all the noise for a while, and not feel like such a fucking disaster all the time!"

Her words hang in the air. The only thing breaking the silence is the low hum of the sound machine.

"I think we need to get you some help," Dev finally says.

She narrows her eyes at him, shooting daggers. "We have Nina."

"No, I'm not talking about Nina. *You* need support. I've been saying it since Shaan was born, and I feel more strongly about it now."

He stares at her with a sad look in his eyes that borders on pity.

"You're telling me to see a *therapist*?"

After Maya and Dev's first ever fight when they started dating, her big takeaway was that it's still possible to be kind to your partner when you're arguing, something her parents never modeled growing up.

But she doesn't want to be kind right now.

"So you think I suck at this, all of it. Just say it." She glares at him, pacing at the foot of their king-size bed.

"I've never thought that, Maya," Dev says, his voice full of hurt. "Do you know you always do this? You don't face what's really bothering you. You shut me out, then blame it on being 'busy' like that's some sort of Band-Aid. And you keep spiraling and spiraling until you reach a breaking point. And then you take it out on me."

"Who said I'm reaching a *breaking point*?" Maya shouts, clearly contradicting herself.

"I think all of this is getting to be too much for you if you need stuff like this to get through the day." The pill bottle rattles in his hand as he gives it a light shake.

A month or so ago, she stopped confiding in him about the grittier details of her days. But in her defense, she could tell he didn't have the energy to listen to her the way he used to. He didn't have the capacity to create space for her emotions.

"It's nothing. Really. But if you're *so* worried, I'll just stop taking them, okay? It's literally fine."

But she knows it's a false promise as soon as she says it. These pills have helped her do things she's struggled to accomplish for years. They've given her clarity and room to breathe when she's stricken by crippling anxiety and self-doubt. They've made her feel alive and present in a way she's never known before.

They've given her an advantage. Something she's never had before. And if she tells him how much she really needs them, he'll see how broken she truly is. So she has to lie.

"I'll stop," she repeats. "But can we please still talk? I just feel like you don't even understand me lately."

"You're right," Dev says, shaking his head as he exits the bedroom. "I really don't."

He gives her one last look then shuts the door behind him.

SOUTH ASIAN FEMINIST BLOG

Have We Done Enough for Maya Patel?

By Karishma Kohli
Published August 2, 2019, 10:05 AM EDT

The recent disappearance of Maya Patel has sparked many questions. What happened to her? Did she leave by choice?

And…if she wasn't a South Asian woman, would her disappearance be treated differently?

"Maya was frustrated whenever she wasn't taken seriously," a close friend notes. "She was told she didn't look like a businesswoman many times. And there have been so many moments when people still assume she's not the head of her own company."

The latest theories on Patel's disappearance speculate that she left of her own accord, which raises important questions that have plagued so many of us before:

Who determines how our narratives get told, or which conclusions can be drawn?

Who gets the last word?

If Maya were white, would she be painted as a victim? Would there be more effort put toward finding her?

"Women of color are held to higher standards and get less grace," says Nadia Amin, founder of Indi-Glam, a boutique South Asian bridal company. "We have to look perfect, excel in school, be polite, be perfect wives and mothers… It's exhausting and oppressive. I wouldn't be surprised if Maya found it all to be too much. I certainly do on many days."

When you search the name *Maya Patel*, you'll find competing narratives on Patel's character. One source will describe Patel as a "loving mother," while the next will accuse her of "living a double life." Even the coverage of Patel's disappearance helps paint a portrait of how women are constantly wrestling contradictory expectations and judgments.

And as more questions emerge, one consistently remains: *Was Maya Patel struggling far more than her shiny, cheerful social media profiles let on?*

20

"OH. YOU'RE HERE," ALAINA SAYS AS she opens her wrought-iron double doors.

"Yes, you did invite us..." Maya laughs awkwardly.

"No, of course. I just meant that you've arrived." Alaina flashes her a tight smile. "And don't *you* look fancy?"

Maya's hand rushes to her blown-out hair. "Oh, I guess we haven't seen each other in a while."

"It sure has been an eventful couple of weeks!" Dev says sarcastically. He walks past Alaina and carries Shaan inside, his tiny legs swinging out from underneath him.

Maya rolls her eyes.

"You guys okay?" Alaina asks tentatively once Dev's out of earshot.

"We're fine," she replies tersely.

She feels subdued, like her brain's in a fog, even though she took a guilt pill—her fifth that day—before leaving the apartment. Lately, a dull numbness has settled over her body like a weighted blanket. She's felt more and more detached as of late, and while it isn't necessarily uncomfortable, it's definitely unfamiliar.

She probably needs more sleep.

As they walk through the front door, Alaina turns to her. "I keep meaning to call you and ask, have you talked to your parents or Tarun lately?"

"No, actually, I haven't." Maya envisions the missed calls from them collecting on her phone. "I want to, but then the day just gets away from me. Before I know it, it's two a.m.," she says.

"Maya, they're your *family.*" Alaina gives her a pointed look. "Maybe try to call them."

"You're right. It's just been a little crazy lately. I'll call them later tonight."

"You okay?" Alaina frowns. "You seem kind of dazed."

"I'm good. Just sleep-deprived." She tells herself to snap out of it.

"Well, come in and put your feet up. And please don't mind our appetizer of Goldfish crackers. Or our sweatpants." Alaina leads the way inside. "I know they're nothing compared to the fine dining you've been used to as of late, but they're tried-and-true." Her tone is lighthearted, but Maya knows her best friend well enough to sense a defensiveness in her tone.

Part of her wants to ask Alaina point-blank if she thinks she's a sellout. Maya has always valued the blatant honesty in their friendship, the unfiltered way they interact with one another. *I think it's time for an eyebrow threading appointment. You're out of his league. You're acting weird.*

But right now, she doesn't have the energy for that conversation.

A heavy silence builds between them, the only sound coming from the occasional chirping bird. Maya revels in the peace and quiet of the suburbs. She takes in Alaina's manicured front lawn with its purple hydrangeas and weeping willow tree. It's the kind of front yard Maya and Tarun wished for growing up, and yet both of them ended up in city apartment buildings. Maybe being raised in a motel made it difficult to live in a bigger space that was entirely their own.

As they enter the living room, Maya says, "Ha, I love Goldfish crackers," then quickly adds, "and being here. Always."

"You're going to love them, too, someday, little guy!" Alaina bends down to wave at Shaan, who's sitting on Dev's lap on the couch. He smiles up at her. "I haven't seen you in too long, buddy."

Maya feels a pang of remorse, quickly overshadowed by gratitude. For all the societal emphasis on family, there's not enough put on the people you choose. The people you intentionally keep in your life, the people you *want* your child to know. She needs Alaina around, not only for her, but for Shaan.

"By the way, do you want to put him in a Pack 'n Play or on a play mat? I've got it all!" Alaina says as the two of them move into the open foyer. "I may even crawl in there with him. My shift last night went over by two hours because someone came in at the end with what we *thought* was a stomachache. It ended up being a massive bleed that required a transfusion and surgery."

"Damn. I really don't know how you do it," Maya says, shaking her head in disbelief.

Alaina waves her hand away. "We all do what we must. Oh, I almost forgot." She disappears into a nearby closet and pulls out a giant box labeled *Baby Stuff.*

"Here, take a look and see if there's anything for Shaan in there," Alaina says, placing the box at Maya's feet. "There are a couple hand-me-downs from the girls, but maybe some of it could work for Shaan, too. Oh, and *lots* of toys. Too many."

Maya crouches and starts sifting through the box. "I didn't realize how convenient it would be to bring Shaan along to a house with kids," she says. "I don't have to lug my SUV-size gear around. You have all the things."

"Yeah, *too many* things. Promise me you'll never go up to my attic."

Maya laughs, relishing that things with Alaina feel normal for the first time in weeks. She holds up one of the girls' old baby onesies to get a second opinion, but Alaina's no longer facing her. "Ryan's in the back," Alaina calls out to the living room. Out of the corner of her eye, Maya watches Dev pick Shaan up and walk toward the entrance to the screened-in porch.

"MOMMY! I didn't know Maya Auntie was here!" Jade, Alaina's younger daughter, scampers toward them.

"I wanted to surprise you!" Maya says, picking her up and spinning her around.

Jade's wearing tan pants and a neon green T-shirt that says *I may be small, but I'm still the boss.* "Want to eat chocolate-chip cookies with me, Maya Auntie?" She sticks out her lower lip in an exaggerated pout and tugs on Maya's hand, her signature move that's always made Maya melt. Alaina always says toddlers know how to get their way more than anyone else. *Cute and cunning.*

"Of course you can both have cookies, sweetheart!" A cheerful, booming voice comes from the top of the stairs. A second later, Auntie Rita, Alaina's mom, is standing beside them. Maybe it's her forty-year career as an anchor on *ABC7*, or just an innate elegance, but Auntie Rita always looks so put together, from her silk emerald-green dress, to her gold studs, to her freshly manicured pale pink nails. Maya tries not to laugh at the stark contrast between Auntie Rita's appearance and Alaina's look. Her best friend's sporting plain black sweats coupled with Ryan's *New Jersey Ob-Gyn* T-shirt. They're quite the pair.

"Maya! It's so good to see you!" Alaina's mom extends her

arms and pulls Maya in for a big, warm hug. She catches a whiff of Auntie Rita's signature floral perfume.

"You, too! What an amazing surprise." Maya grins at her. "It's been way too long."

When she and Alaina used to live together, Maya spoke to Auntie Rita on the phone multiple times a week, asking her about everything from how to negotiate a salary, to how to prepare for a podcast interview, to where to find understated, delicate gold jewelry. Alaina always came up with an excuse to bow out of these conversations when Maya would put Auntie Rita on speakerphone.

As they make their way to the living room, Alaina's mom turns to her and says, "I've been following all your recent success, of course. I just told Ala this morning that those pictures you put on your Instagram stories are the *best*." She makes a dramatic hand gesture for emphasis, her huge diamond ring catching a glint of sunlight. "And then your *Today* show interview and all your media features! Oh, I'm so proud of you! And didn't you just love Taylor Rutherford? She's even better in person, isn't she?"

"She really is!" Maya exclaims. She always wondered what it would be like to have a mom who could take the time to pay her so much attention.

Auntie Rita proceeds to ask Maya about her early postpartum days and how things are going with Medini.

Maya gives her the CliffsNotes version, and Auntie Rita nods in understanding throughout the entire recap.

"Look, I'm sure you're already seeing this..." Auntie Rita's voice lowers. "But once you have a child, you have to be even more fiercely protective of your work. And of your time."

"Oh, I'm *seeing* it. I'm seeing it more than I ever anticipated."

"I'm not surprised, honey," Auntie Rita says, squeezing Maya's forearm. "I know how hard it is, how impossible it can feel. As women, selflessness is forced upon us at a young age.

And once we're grown up, we've been so conditioned to sell ourselves short, or downplay our accomplishments, that it becomes second nature. But we're allowed to hold on to what makes us feel whole. Being a mom doesn't mean you have to leave your dreams and ambitions behind. They're still a part of us, too, you know."

Maya sighs. "You're right. It just feels like the entire system is built against mothers." Even post-guilt pill, Maya is still a split self. She's just gotten better at navigating her different roles and obligations, making sure they don't bleed into each other. But she certainly doesn't feel whole.

"Hey, but you're keeping it all afloat! And that deserves a lot of credit, okay?" Auntie Rita gestures toward the kitchen, where Alaina's setting the girls up with dinner. "Now go knock some sense into your friend over there, won't you?"

"Oh, no need. She's doing great," Maya says, smiling in Alaina's direction. "I don't know how she balances such an intense job with two kids at home, but somehow she manages."

"Sure, if 'managing' means leaving your dreams behind." Auntie Rita scoffs.

Maya frowns. "What do you me—"

"Mom, I'm not leaving my dreams behind." Alaina sighs as she emerges from the kitchen and joins their conversation. "I'm just trying to create a new path for myself."

"So your new path is rejecting something you've worked so hard toward? Do you know what this job opportunity could lead to? All the connections, the doors that will start opening up? Think about it. In a decade, you could be running the entire hospital! Or you could even be one of those television doctors!"

"I don't want any of that anymore. And what if I'm done hustling just to prove something? I'm *exhausted*. There's no rule book that says I'm supposed to feel so drained all the time," Alaina says, flopping onto the couch.

But isn't there? Maya thinks to herself. Isn't that the unspoken agreement for living in today's world, to always do more and push more and exhaust yourself more?

Then again, maybe Alaina's right, and real courage comes from abandoning your ego to pursue what actually makes you happy. Maybe that's how you can stop capitalism, perfectionism, and all of those other isms from dictating your life.

"You're being safe," Auntie Rita says, her eyes flashing.

"I'm being *smart*," Alaina counters.

Maya stops herself from asking what they're talking about.

Auntie Rita snickers. "Once you've gone through everything I have, we can have a debate about what's 'smart.' You think the world's just going to wait for you? You think these once-in-a-lifetime opportunities will be here later, when you finally come to your senses and seize them? Well, they won't. Especially not for people like us, Ala. We have to work twice as hard to get half as far."

"I'm done with this conversation, Mom. For the millionth time." Alaina folds her arms across her chest. She may say she and her mom are polar opposites, but they do share the same stubborn streak.

"COOKIES!" Jade screams, running into the living room.

Auntie Rita bends down toward Jade. "Let's get you and Maya Masi some cookies."

"Actually, Mom, it isn't time for cookies yet." There's an edge to Alaina's voice as she hoists Jade onto her hip. "And Maya Masi is here to spend time with Mommy, and Grandma was just about to leave. Jade, honey, would you like to play with your older sister or read a book?" Alaina always gives her kids options instead of telling them what to do. Her favorite parenting guru doesn't believe in harsh rules or punishments, instead preaching that children should be empowered to make their own decisions.

Jade clenches her fists. "But I want cookies NOW!" she

says, before reiterating the message in Jamaican patois and then German.

Maya can't help but be impressed, even when Jade's giving attitude. She looks between Alaina, Auntie Rita, and Jade. If there's one thing that's certain, it's that Jade won't tolerate any bullshit without putting up a fight.

"I think she's being pretty clear about what she wants," Auntie Rita chimes in. "Is it so bad to give her cookies?"

Alaina grits her teeth. "Like I said, *Mom*, it's not time for cookies."

"Well, I guess that's my cue to leave!" Auntie Rita bends down to give Jade a kiss and shouts up to Amelia that she's leaving. (Alaina says that ever since she started fifth grade, Amelia wants nothing to do with "grown-ups" and prefers to read in her room.)

On her way out, Auntie Rita shoots Maya a look that says *I can't win with her.*

Maya responds with an awkward half smile.

Alaina bounces Jade up and down on her lap, her voice steady and calm when she says, "Honey, I understand you want cookies. But we have to wait, okay? We can share a cookie together later. For now, you can either play or go read. It's your choice."

Jade wriggles out of her mom's grip and stomps away, fists clenched. And to Maya's utter surprise, she makes her way to the pile of books strewn across the living room floor and plucks out a worn copy of *The Very Hungry Caterpillar.*

"Damn. You are such a rock star," Maya whispers.

Alaina widens her eyes. "Uh, I think you mean *mess.* I should get paid extra for the number of times I have to negotiate with my own kids on a given day. Damn you, modern, gentle, intensive, whatever-you-want-to-call-it parenting. Sometimes I wish I could just parent them like it's the nineties." She points her finger in a mock-stern gesture. "I don't care if you want cookies! Do you realize how hard I work for you?!"

Maya laughs. "You're amazing. Remind me to take notes for Shaan next time."

"Please." Alaina waves her hand. "You give me way too much credit."

"That's not true at all." Maya follows Alaina into the kitchen and drops her crossbody purse onto Alaina's granite kitchen counter. Her best friend is so confident in some parts of her life but so self-critical in others.

"Just ask my mom for confirmation that I'm not doing enough," Alaina adds over her shoulder.

"Your mom doesn't think that."

"Oh, yes, she does. Before you got here, she straight up told me my life isn't that hard and I don't have the right to complain about anything. Who says that to their own daughter? And of course she never takes even a minute to consider what it's been like for me as my parents' child. She and my dad *lived* at their workplaces for my entire childhood. She has no idea what it was like to have to grow up at such a young age to fend for myself and my little brother."

Maya bites her lip. *Well, that resonated.*

"You're right. She has no idea about that," Maya says in validation. "And for the record, you have every right to complain. I'm always here if you need someone to complain to."

"I know you are, but..."

"But what?"

"You've got your hands full. And you seem... I don't know, different."

"Different?"

"Yeah, zoned out. Almost like some of the patients I've seen who... Wait, you're not still taking those pills, are you?"

"Whoa, where did *that* come from?"

"I don't know. Never mind. I'm sorry." Alaina shakes her head. "I've just been trying to pinpoint what feels not *you* to me."

"It's been an intense time," Maya says defensively.

"I know. But it looks like you're managing it all perfectly on your own."

"That's not true at all. Trust me, what you see online isn't the full picture. You know that!"

She considers opening up to Alaina about everything—the dire situation at work, her marital strife, Shaan's health. The pills, and what they *actually* do.

But she can't, so she just changes the subject.

"About what your mom said back there... You're sure you don't want to take the job?"

Alaina slowly nods in response and says, "I really don't want to get into it right now, if that's okay."

Maya places a hand on her shoulder. "Of course it's okay. And if that's what you really want, I support you. I may not fully understand, but I'll always support you."

Alaina smiles. "Did you know you're the only person who ever asks me what I really want? You're the one who reminds me that, at the end of the day, I'm the one making the decisions about *my* life. These past couple weeks, I've often asked myself, *What would Maya say?*"

Before Maya can respond, a bellowing voice fills the living room.

"Hey, you two!" Ryan walks in, followed by Dev, Shaan in tow. Their hands grip sweating beer bottles. "I ordered pizza."

"That sounds *perfect*," Maya says. She loves being in Ryan's infectious presence. It's sometimes difficult to hear all of Alaina's grievances toward her husband, especially because this is the only version of him Maya gets to see.

Ryan plops down on the couch and playfully puts an arm around Alaina. "So, obviously you two are the only people we'd talk to about this, but...couples therapy seems to *finally* be working. It turns out that staring at each other for a weirdly long period of time actually pays off." He looks to Alaina for confirmation, but her face is unreadable.

"That's awesome." Dev leans forward and puts his beer bottle on their round coffee table, which is covered with errant crayon marks and partially unpeeled Peppa Pig stickers.

Ryan talks about their previous session and the latest homework assignment, which is to write a letter from the other's perspective about a particular rough patch in their marriage. He chose the first couple weeks after Jade was born, and Alaina picked the stretch of time when Ryan's private practice lost two doctors, tripling his workload.

Maya will forever be grateful for Ryan's vulnerability and how it encourages Dev to feel more comfortable opening up. Dev's never struggled to make friends, but he's had a history of keeping his connections safe and surface-level, especially in his male friendships. She's sure that gets lonely sometimes.

Just when the doorbell rings, so does Maya's phone.

"Start eating without me," she says, gesturing to her phone and heading into the laundry room.

She closes the door behind her. "Hello?"

The voice on the other end says something, but she can't hear over the massive washer's and dryer's rinsing, shaking, and loud humming. She couldn't have picked a worse room for a phone call.

"Sorry, what was that?" She puts her phone on speaker to hear better.

"Where are you?" the familiar voice asks. "It sounds like you're underwater."

It's Mark. And he called *her.* Her palms start sweating and butterflies form in her stomach. *Play it cool.*

She laughs. "I'm with my family visiting some friends in the suburbs."

"Ah, I see. I was hoping you were going to say somewhere more exciting."

Maya laughs again. "Sorry to disappoint. Was there something you wanted to talk about?"

"Yes. It's about your next funding round. But since you're busy, why don't we chat another time. Or better yet, let's grab a cocktail or two sometime next week?"

"I... I'll have to see," she says hesitantly.

"Don't keep me waiting too long." His voice is husky, and she can tell he's been drinking. A thrill of excitement rushes down her spine as she says, "Oh, I won't." The words come out flirtier than intended.

The door suddenly creaks open behind her, and she abruptly says, "Um, I have to go. I'll call you later!"

When Maya turns around, Alaina's staring at her in shock.

"Who was that?"

Heat travels up Maya's neck. "Just someone from work," she says, avoiding eye contact.

When she finally looks at her, Alaina's eyes are narrow slits. "Yeah, that sounded really *professional*."

"What is that supposed to mean?"

"Something's going on with you, something's *been* going on with you, and I have no idea what to make of it."

"What to make of it?" Maya sputters. "Why are you coming at me so much lately? Did I do something that pissed you off or something?"

"Maya, I *wish* I was pissed off, because then we could just hash it out like we always do. But this?" She gestures in the space between them. "This is something else entirely. Who even are you lately?"

"The same person as always," Maya snaps.

"No, that you're not. Look, I don't know what's going on with you, but I do know that this—" she gestures to Maya's body "—is not my best friend."

Alaina stares at her intensely, reminding Maya she can't bullshit her, no matter how hard she tries.

"What's the holdup?" Dev shouts lightheartedly from the other room. He and Ryan are standing at the entrance to the laundry room. Ryan is holding Jade piggyback style, while Dev has Shaan in his carrier. She and Alaina used to dream about a moment just like this before they had kids, their two little families coming together.

"Nothing," Maya calls out in response. "Let's eat."

They move to the dining room, where the table is set with stacked plates, Coke cans, and two open bottles of wine. Dev and Ryan enter the room as Maya sits down next to Alaina. "Oh, you know what? I forgot something. Be right back." Alaina stands up and disappears into the kitchen.

She returns empty-handed and takes the seat farthest from Maya.

DR. ALAINA BROWN @DOCTORMOMAB

INSTAGRAM DMS

@TheFemalePerspective: Hi Dr. Brown. We are so sorry about the news of Maya's disappearance. We were wondering if you would be interested in sharing thoughts about her in a profile we're doing about the pressures of being a female founder. We thought, as her best friend, you would have a unique perspective on what that's like. [Sent August 3, 2019, 11:47 AM]

@DoctorMomAB: Thank you for reaching out but I'm not interested. And just FYI, Maya has always been able to handle pressure, so not sure she's the right person to highlight for this, anyway. Not to mention, this feels like an inappropriate time to ask me that. Please give her family and friends some space.

@TheFemalePerspective: So she hasn't seemed different to you recently? There are rumors about her acting out of character.

@DoctorMomAB: We haven't been in touch as much lately.

@TheFemalePerspective: You grew apart?

@DoctorMomAB: I didn't say that. I'm saying that I know my friend. Maya isn't a quitter. That's not the kind of person she is.

@DoctorMomAB: Please think twice before you publish any information about Maya. And don't contact me again.

[Seen by **@TheFemalePerspective**]

21

"ARE YOU FEELING READY FOR YOUR next board meeting?" Mark asks when they sit down for drinks. "And does this one include your plan to present to us?"

"Do you think I'd be here if I wasn't ready?" Maya smirks, clutching her cocktail. The scent of spiced pineapple is heavenly.

Mark quickly downs his Nomadic Old-Fashioned, which, according to the menu, has "chai honey" as one of the ingredients. Mom would have a field day if she read that. *Chai honey? They take our drink and make it a honey?!*

Maya follows suit and takes a large sip from her drink, leaning back into the velvet booth. Dear Irving's dim lighting, gold beaded curtains, chocolate-brown ceiling, and gilded mirrors give it the appearance of a James Bond movie set.

"Anyway, I'm not here to talk about Friday. If I'm not mistaken, I should be keeping some intrigue for a proper pitch, so I don't want to say more," she says playfully. "Liz should be here soon, and we can talk more about work. Or not."

He takes a gulp of his drink. "Ah, she's not coming."

"She's not?" Maya scrolls through her texts with Liz.

"She just texted me that something came up at the office," Mark says, just as Maya's phone buzzes.

Liz: I'm stuck at the office. Shipment issue. I'll explain later. So sorry! Have an extra drink for me!

"Oh. Then I guess I should get going." Maya tries her best to hide her disappointment as she reaches for her bag. She was looking forward to tonight.

"What? Why? We just got here." Mark gestures to their two full cocktails.

"Ha, as fun as it sounds to stay, we were supposed to meet about work. I still have to prep for Friday..."

"Are you worried about it?"

She mentally runs through her board presentation, slide by slide. In just a matter of days, she'll show the team her big idea for how to get Medini back on track. She'll go through their updated projected sales—now that they're going to be in dozens of stores—their marketing strategy for the next year, and the amount of funding they'll need to back these changes.

"To be honest, no. I feel ready for it. I've always had to convince people Medini is worth their time and money. This isn't that new."

"Then what's wrong?" Mark asks. "I can tell something's up."

"It's...everything else." She takes a sip of her cocktail, the lime lingering on her tongue.

"Such as?" Mark gives her a look that's a mix between concern and curiosity.

Where to even begin?

The waiter passes their booth, and Mark signals for another round. She's not even halfway done with her first.

"No, really, it's fine." Maya takes another long sip. "I just sometimes wish I could escape from it all."

In the middle of the night, after she feeds Shaan and unsuccessfully tries to lull herself back to sleep, she finds herself flirting with the idea of leaving. Taking an Uber to the airport, scanning the departures list, and stepping onto the next available flight.

"Don't we all feel like that?" Mark's matter-of-fact tone comforts her. "But I also realize your situation's different, as a boss and a mother. And as a woman. You just had a kid, *and* you're preparing for a funding round. Maybe cut yourself some slack?"

"Well, when you say it like that..." Her lips curl into a smile.

"Let me guess," Mark starts. "You're exhausted. You've had to prove people wrong over and over again. And you've probably had a bunch of assholes tell you there's no way you're going to raise enough money for your company."

Maya looks at him in amusement. "Seems like you know a thing or two about how tech treats women."

"So, tell me. Which part resonated?"

"All of it?" Something about Mark's open and curious expression makes her want to open up to him.

She doesn't want to find solace in a man who isn't Dev. But he's not speaking to her much these days, and it's freeing to not have to justify why her work matters to her, or why she feels so overworked and overwhelmed. It's nice to feel validated for once.

Before she knows it, minutes have flown by, and she's shared her entire career journey with Mark. How she designed the first Medini products, the countless meetings where people assumed she was there to serve food or take notes, her need to build something worthy of all her parents' sacrifices.

Mark laughs. "Damn, Liz was right about you."

Maya raises her eyebrows. "How so?"

"She said you're really hard on yourself."

"My best friend, Alaina, says that, too. And my husband. But how can I not be?" Maya pictures Dev's face lined with concern, his four-day stubble showing new flecks of gray. Alaina looking at her with a mixture of confusion and disgust in the laundry room. "Honestly, I don't know how Liz does it."

Mark makes a face.

"What?"

"She doesn't. At least not in the way you do."

"What do you mean?"

Mark sighs, and she can tell he's conflicted about how much to share. "She has assistants for everything, for one. And let's just say it helps when you don't consider how your actions impact other people." He tugs at his formfitting sky-blue button-down, and her eyes drift down to his biceps. Maya catches herself, refocusing on his dark, ruffled hair and clean-shaven face.

"I know that's her reputation with some people, but..." Maya trails off, trying to find the right words to defend her friend.

"Ha, no kidding. Asking a bunch of your employees for a last-minute meeting and then telling them they're being fired immediately doesn't exactly conjure up warm and fuzzy feelings."

He's referring to Liz's famous firing incident a couple of years ago at Women Rise, with even *Forbes* and the *New York Times* covering the story. Maya remembers seeing some memes at the time that labeled Liz as the ultimate "#girlboss." Liz faced criticism for that for years.

"Does she have a responsibility to conjure up warm and fuzzy feelings? Or is she expected to, just because she's a woman?"

"Let's just say that she can be *quite* calculated when she wants to be. Remember those 'devoted mother' photos of her with her kids that flooded social media right after the firing incident? It was right before Mother's Day, too, when the *New York Times* was already set to run an exclusive feature on her."

Maya doesn't say anything.

"And you should ask her what happened with her first company," he adds. "Why she had to shut it down."

Maya racks her brain for what Liz told her about her first company and how it serendipitously led to Women Rise.

"What are you ta—"

"I shouldn't have said anything. She's your friend. But hey, you know what I think? I think you need to blow off some steam. There's a place next door that makes excellent Negronis."

"No, I should go..." She's suddenly hyperaware of their surroundings. It wasn't until now that she's fully realized how being alone with Mark in a dimly lit room, especially when alcohol is involved, is a very bad idea. A jitteriness takes over her limbs, making her feel like she's in free fall. The room becomes a blur of conversations and cocktails. She feels a pit in her stomach for flirting with him earlier, for letting him talk about Liz like that behind her back, for how physically attractive she finds him in this very moment.

Please, brain. Don't make me feel that rebound guilt again, Maya pleads. She coined the phrase to specifically refer to the horrible, debilitating, intense waves of guilt that emerge whenever the pills start wearing off. It reminds her of when Alaina described patients feeling more pain after receiving anesthesia than they did before it.

In a gesture so smooth she could have missed it, Mark shifts his hand so it's on top of her thigh.

Move it, a voice in her commands. *Tell him to stop.* But she doesn't do any of that. She doesn't *want* to. Her heartbeat quickens, a lustful desire building from the lower region of her body. She allows herself to feel the warmth of his palm against her.

And then a tsunami of guilt pulls her back under.

She squeezes his shoulder. "I'm sorry. But I really should go."

"Are you sure? The night's young. And so are we, right?" Mark playfully bumps his knee against hers.

Her surroundings become amorphous. Somewhere deep inside, she hears another voice. *A part of you wants to go. You can listen to it this once. When was the last time you had a carefree, late night out?*

But it's quickly followed by *You have a family back home. A husband, a newborn baby. Dev would never do this to you. You're a horrible, unfaithful, deceitful wife. And when he finally realizes this, he'll leave you for good. Just like his mother wants him to.*

Her head is spinning. She doesn't know which voice is the real Maya. Maybe neither is. She can't tell anymore.

"I'm just going to use the restroom," she says, excusing herself.

Once she's inside the bathroom, she grips the sink to steady herself, sweat pooling on her forehead. She immediately removes the bottle from her black clutch and dry swallows an extra pill. Anything to feel anchored again in her body and make the rebound guilt go away.

She splashes cold water across her face and reapplies lipstick. By the time she washes her hands, they're no longer shaking. She pats powder on her face and takes deep, heavy breaths.

It's okay. You're okay. Just leave the bathroom, say goodbye to Mark, and call an Uber.

On her way back, she sees their waiter take the tiny black leather booklet filled with their signed receipts. To anyone watching her, she's sure she looks poised and full of purpose in her bold lipstick and flattering black blazer. She pulls the Uber app up on her phone and sees all the tiny black cars on the screen that could take her right back to her apartment, right now.

But something stops her. Maybe it's the dread of going back home, where she and Dev will spend another night's sleep with their backs turned to each other. Maybe it's anticipating Shaan's cries waking her up in a matter of two hours. Or maybe it's pure, stark selfishness—she doesn't want to base her decision off other people's feelings. And maybe right now she doesn't have to.

Her heart rate slows down, and for the first time in hours, she stops overthinking. She closes the Uber app and walks back to their table.

"You know what? Let's get that drink."

NEW YORK CITY POLICE DEPARTMENT

OFFICER RICHARDSON: What was the nature of your relationship with Maya Patel?

MARK STAHLBERG: We were professional contacts.

OFFICER RICHARDSON: That's all?

MARK STAHLBERG: I'm not sure what you're getting at.

OFFICER RICHARDSON: There were sightings of the two of you at a bar late at night…sitting very close together.

MARK STAHLBERG: That was work-related.

OFFICER RICHARDSON: Is that how you interact with all your business colleagues?

MARK STAHLBERG: Yes. I mean, no. Maya and I got along really well. She's…special. Different.

OFFICER RICHARDSON: How so?

MARK STAHLBERG: She wasn't entitled, and she wasn't solely focused on money and success. She really was trying her best and, I don't know, in a world where there's so much schmoozing, it was refreshing to talk to someone who could be…vulnerable. Real.

OFFICER RICHARDSON: So, you were close?

MARK STAHLBERG: I didn't say that.

OFFICER RICHARDSON: She confided in you?

MARK STAHLBERG: She was managing a lot in her life and shared some of that with me, yes.

OFFICER RICHARDSON: Did your relationship go beyond the professional realm?

MARK STAHLBERG: I'm done answering any further questions.

22

"BETA," MOM SAYS. "WE'VE BEEN TRYING to reach you."

"And you're never available," Dad adds.

"I know," Maya says as she sits down next to them. "It's been busy."

Mom nods. "We know it has. And we know work comes first."

"So should this little prince, though!" Dad smiles when he looks in Shaan's direction. "He needs you now more than ever, Maya."

Please decide who you want me to be. Just pick one. I can't be both.

"I'm doing the best I can," Maya says.

The words come out robotically.

Feel shitty, she commands herself. *Feel the way you deserve to feel for being a neglectful daughter.* But she's met only with detachment. It's like her emotions have been suffocated, wrapped up in a blanket.

"Beta, are you okay?" Mom asks.

Dad and Tarun look at her with the same concerned expression.

"I'm fine."

"Are you?" Mom asks again.

"Yes. Totally. I was just thinking about work. We have that follow-up board meeting coming up and I still need to prep." She shifts her focus to Shaan and lifts him up in the air. He just finished his bottle. Maya's been holding her breath since his last sip, anxiously waiting to see if he'll spit it back up. Every time the regurgitated milk dribbles out of his mouth, her heart drops. Why is her maternal guilt the hardest to shake? The pills have been slacking in that department but working overtime in the others. Her throat tightens as she rubs her son's tiny back. *Please burp. Please, please, please.*

Dad frowns. "Are you sure you're okay? Because you see—"

"Let's maybe focus on why we're here?" Tarun interjects, taking the attention off her. He's always known how to read her in the way only a sibling could.

"Yes, thank you. I can't believe *you* got us together," Maya says, gesturing toward Tarun.

They're sitting on the rooftop of his apartment building at sunset. From this vantage point, they have a snapshot of Murray Hill, a neighborhood Maya always associates with a more carefree time in her life. Below them, Third Avenue comes alive with the sounds of cabs honking and people getting ready to barhop. She's hit with a sudden pang of nostalgia for the nights she and Alaina stayed out late, ordering bagels the next morning and spending the rest of the day watching rom-coms. But even on those days, a nagging voice from within kept asking her where her life was going. Her twenties were filled with equal parts freedom and uncertainty.

"Yeah, I'm glad this worked out," Tarun says to her once

their parents break off in a side conversation. "I know Mom and Dad have been wanting us to all be together so we can talk."

"*You* know that? Since when?"

"They keep telling me." He pauses, then adds, "On our phone calls."

"*You've* been calling *them*? Regularly?" She conspicuously gestures at their parents, unable to hide her shock, but they take no notice.

Tarun nods. "Yeah, I know it's a busy time for you, so I've tried to check in on them."

"Right. Okay, then." Their conversation is thankfully interrupted by Shaan's babbles.

"So, what's up?" Maya asks when the four of them regroup.

Mom and Dad look at each other, their lips a straight line.

"What is it? Are you sick? Is something wrong?"

"Nobody's sick," Dad reassures her. But his continued fixation on the fake grass beneath them does nothing to assuage her concern.

"Then what is it?"

Mom takes over. "You both know we've been wanting to sell the motel. And we're going to finalize the deal with the Lyons."

"You can't take that offer!" Maya interjects. "It's insulting!"

"We've already decided to because we're going to..." Mom looks at Dad. He gives her a nod so slight, Maya wonders if she imagined it.

She can't take this anticipatory anxiety any longer. Are they taking a trip around the world? Her parents aren't the spontaneous type. Despite their differences, the one thing they've always united on is their deep-seated belief that they should work to the brink of burnout.

"We're going to take some time apart," Dad finally says.

The words register in Maya's mind slow and muffled, like they're being dragged through mud.

"What? What do you mean, you're taking some time apart?" Her eyes dart between Mom and Dad. "From each other?"

"You're splitting up?" Tarun chimes in.

"Not splitting up," Dad clarifies. "Just doing our own things for a little bit. Mom is going to go to India for some time and I'll have some family come visit me here."

Maya scoffs. "That sounds like splitting up. Why...why are you doing this?"

"It just so happened to work out," Dad says, trying to keep things light. "My brothers have been wanting to spend more time in America, and Mom's been missing her family back in India." He extends his arms out to hold Shaan. Maya tentatively hands him over to Dad, Shaan's eyes lighting up when they take in his grandfather's face.

"So, you're going to help more family set up here?" Maya asks. "When you could be focusing on yourselves? You're not even going to try to work things out?"

Their silence answers her question.

"Why didn't you tell us any of this earlier?"

"We didn't want you to be upset," Mom says, reaching for her hand.

Maya pulls away from her. "It's a little too late for that."

Shaan seems to register her foul mood and starts crying. Maya takes him from Dad and walks with him around the seating area, toward a corner that's stained from pollution and time. She glances down at the street to see a couple holding hands, getting ready to sit down at an outdoor table. *Trade places with me*, she wants to scream down to them.

"We knew you'd jump in and try to fix it. Or at the very least, try to talk us out of it. Sometimes I think you forget *we're* the parents and *you're* the child." Dad laughs, and she knows he's thinking of the numerous times over the years Maya has checked in with her parents to make sure they're going to their routine doctor's appointments, or that they're eating enough, or that they're not driving too late at night.

Maybe that's why she felt such a palpable rush of freedom the first night alone in her dorm room at Columbia, having opted out of the welcome week's parties. As she settled into her floral-sheet-covered twin bed, all she could think was, *Do I really only have to worry about myself tonight?*

"Look, this is what works best for us, okay?" Dad says. "We have a plan, and we're happy with it."

"And please keep this between us for now," Mom adds, her voice a whisper.

"Of course. We wouldn't want anyone to know the *truth*," Maya mutters.

Dad gives her a pointed look. "Maya."

"She has a point," Tarun says under his breath.

Mom holds up her palm. "Look, you both need to let us be. We've got this, okay? Your father and I are grown adults."

"And you're okay with just letting go of the motel? Just like that?" Maya shakes her head in disbelief at this entire conversation. "The Lyons are totally ripping you off!"

"Yes, Maya, *just like that*. We don't have the energy to keep fighting," Mom says.

Dad nods in agreement. "Sometimes knowing when to walk away is the most important thing."

"I understand that," Maya says. In some ways, she understands her parents more every year. She understands how chronic exhaustion has a way of distorting your view of the world. Of yourself. She understands constant conflict can erode a relationship over time. She understands the sheer terror and fulfillment that can come from building something of your own and knowing someday you may have to let it go.

"Let's eat, na? You all must be so hungry!" Mom reaches into the giant cooler she brought from home, filled to the brim with homemade kathi rolls.

As she starts unpacking the cooler, Mom asks, "So, how are Alaina and Ryan?"

Classic Mom. She can pivot from life-changing announcements to casual chitchat in seconds.

Maya tries not to tense up at Alaina's name. "They're good. Keeping busy with the girls and work."

Mom nods. "I've always said that girl is smart," she says, wagging her finger for emphasis. "She does what she has to."

"Yup." Maya bites into a roll.

"Ay!" Mom jumps up. "We need some sriracha. Tarun, can I get it from your apartment?"

Tarun's face tightens. "Uhhh…"

Mom waves her hand. "Oh, don't worry. I won't look around."

"I wasn't worried about that." Tarun's defensive tone says otherwise.

"And I'll use the restroom," Dad says, slowly getting to his feet.

Once Mom and Dad are out of sight, Maya turns to her brother. "So, that was crazy."

"I know, right? What the hell was that?"

"And what about the motel?" Maya continues. "It's their *home*. They're just going to let that go? At such an unfair price? How are they going to support themselves financially?"

Pressure builds in her chest at the thought of her parents applying for jobs that require them to be on their feet all day, working grueling hours.

Tarun shrugs. "They've always figured it out, right? Heck, they've figured it out *too* well. I mean, all their relatives expect Mom and Dad to send *them* money. It just sucks that they're always hustling *and* selling themselves short."

"Don't you do that, too, though? Work yourself to that place?" Maya thinks back to the number of times her brother has sent her emails and texts from the office well past midnight.

"And you don't?" Tarun's expression is half smirk, half smile.

"Touché."

"I don't know if I want to anymore, though," he admits. "I don't know if I even went into banking for the right reasons."

"What do you mean?" Tarun was so excited when he got his first-choice summer internship before his senior year of college, and then again when he received job offers from three different investment banks. She, Tarun, Mom, and Dad had all gone to Woodbridge Mall together to find him suits and dress shoes.

"I did it because I was supposed to. Because it was stable. Mom and Dad always wanted me to be like you. Responsible. Communicative. *Married*." He laughs at the last one. "But I don't know. My job hasn't been enough for me. I don't feel fulfilled."

"If it's any consolation, Mom, Dad, and…everyone, really, only see me for what I accomplish. They enjoy being in your presence. You're the fun one."

Tarun shakes his head. "It's not like that at all. Sure, maybe I stir the pot every now and then. But you're the one they're proud of. I always wanted to be like you growing up."

Maya gives a self-deprecating laugh. "Trust me, it's not all it's cracked up to be. It never was. I couldn't afford to fuck up. You were able to actually enjoy being young."

"You can have fun, too." Tarun's voice takes on a serious tone. "It's not too late to live a little, you know."

"Ha! Live a little. That sounds nice."

"Alaina used to tell you that all the time," Tarun says, referring to the countless hours he spent at Maya and Alaina's apartment when they were roommates. Alaina missed her own younger brother, who had moved to Los Angeles by then. So much so, in fact, that she relished buying Tarun alcohol, ordering his favorite takeout meals, and letting him stay at their place for hours at a time just to talk or watch his latest favorite show on Netflix.

"And I know Dev still says it." Tarun takes a gulp of his beer. "I've been talking to him, actually. About leaving banking. Trying something new."

"You have? When?"

How is this the first time she's hearing of this?

Tarun shrugs. "In the evenings, sometimes on weekends. He's been really helpful."

"Oh. Good, I'm glad." She tries to hide the annoyance in her voice.

"What's wrong?" Tarun asks, noticing her face change.

"Nothing," Maya replies. Lately, when she feels like she has too much to say, it seems safer to say nothing at all.

They sip their drinks side by side, the sound of the city filling the space between them.

NEW YORK CITY POLICE DEPARTMENT

OFFICER RICHARDSON: Were you around your daughter a lot these past months?

MIRA PATEL: Of course! I tried to be with her and my grandson whenever I could.

OFFICER RICHARDSON: And how often was that?

MIRA PATEL: Um, well, not enough. My husband and I run our motel and it's hard to leave wi—

OFFICER RICHARDS: So she was on her own a lot?

MIRA PATEL: I guess so. Yes, she was.

OFFICER RICHARDSON: Any indications that she seemed different when you did see her? Were you worried about her mental health?

MIRA PATEL: She was stressed and tired. But she's a new mom. That shouldn't—

OFFICER RICHARDSON: There are reports from people close to her suggesting erratic behavior. Rash decisions. That she pulled away from people who were once in her inner circle. That she didn't seem like herself.

MIRA PATEL: Listen to me, my daughter is strong. *Very* strong. She can handle anything that comes her way.

OFFICER RICHARDSON: Your son-in-law claims he tried to get her more support. Do you think they were having marital issues?

MIRA PATEL: Dev and Maya? No, of course not! Why would you even say that?

OFFICER RICHARDSON: I'm just trying to get the full story, ma'am.

23

"YOU'VE TOTALLY GOT THIS," LIZ SAYS to her the next morning. Maya smooths down her off-white jumpsuit, which she's paired with tan clogs she recently read about in a *New York Times* article.

Maya grins. "You know what? I think I'm starting to believe you."

Liz tilts Maya's laptop so she can peruse the slide titled Long Range Plan. "Let's just add *world domination* at the end and I think you're done." She snaps a photo of their lavender hot chocolates and pistachio croissants, then posts it on her Instagram story. Maya takes her own photo and positions her laptop to be in the shot. She captions it: Sunday Funday or Sunday workday?

The floor-to-ceiling floral arrangements, blue-and-white teacups and saucers, stacks of buttery pastries and giant cookies, and customers rushing in and out of Maman's all infuse her with a renewed sense of calm.

But just as she's settling into work, a self-satisfied smile on her face, she hears it.

Good job, Maya, just keep throwing yourself into work like you always do. Maternity leave is the time you're supposed to, you know, be a mother?

She's already on her fourth pill this *morning*, and they're not doing shit.

Maya sips her hot chocolate, hoping her go-to comfort beverage will soothe her. She's always said hot chocolate should be a year-round drink.

The warm, velvety liquid glides down her throat. She only realizes her hands are shaking when she puts the teacup back on the saucer.

"I really think I need to stop taking these pills."

"What? Why?" Liz looks up from her phone in surprise.

"I don't feel like myself. And with everything going on lately, I think I need to get back to being the 'real' Maya before I forget who she even is."

"That's the point of the pills," Liz says, her voice light. "If anything, you're supposed to be *more* you when you're on them. A new-and-improved Maya who can reach her full potential without all the internalized bullshit holding you back."

The people at the table next to them crane their necks to look at Liz. Do they recognize her? Or are they also pulled in by her magnetic charm?

Liz notices the stares and dismisses them. In person, she has a nonchalance that directly contrasts her peppy, animated Instagram persona.

"Yeah, I don't know. I've just felt off. And honestly, I don't think I'm loving this person I'm becoming. Plus, the pills don't seem to be working lately. I upped the dose like you said, sometimes even taking an extra—" *or two,* Maya thinks to herself "—for good measure. But the rebound guilt comes back way quicker than it used to."

Liz leans in. "Do you think the old, guilt-ridden Maya would have been able to scale so quickly in Whole Foods? Or hired a nanny so she could actually get shit done and save her company? Or—" Liz taps Maya's laptop with her perfectly manicured sky-blue nails "—do you think she could have stayed resolute about her company valuation? And potentially secure that backing from one of the top VC funds in the city?"

A thrill of excitement cascades through Maya's body. She's heard of valuations like this countless times, but she never thought a number like that would even be in the realm of possibility for *her* company.

If she can pull this off, it would be life-changing.

And besides, there are more men than she could ever count who've convinced people their companies are worth much more than this. Were they ever told they were being too cheeky? Overconfident?

But then she thinks of Shaan's soft, round face, and Dev's silhouette turned away from her in bed all last night. Her parents' frowns as they scanned the wordy contract from the Lyons. The concern on her brother's face that day on the rooftop. Her internal alarm bells going off when Nina held Shaan for the first time.

Is it naive, even greedy, to expect to like every version of yourself when you're putting your own ambition above all else?

Reading her mind, Liz says, "I know this is hard. Trust me, I get it. And if you feel comfortable, I'd keep going up on your pills. I'm still not seeing any harmful side effects, and honestly, I've designed this so you can take as much as you need at any given time. I have three women taking two in the mornings and evenings, along with a couple more here and there throughout the day. Maybe you could try that? Here, I actually have an extra bottle of these on me. Take it with you."

"But that would bring me up to—"

"Wait, isn't that your friend who just walked in?"

Maya's eyes shift toward the café's entrance, where she sees Alaina crouched down, saying something to two young girls whose backs are turned to Maya and Liz.

"Oh, wow. Yeah, it is." She feels a weird anticipatory anxiety, the same kind she felt when she introduced Alaina and Dev for the first time. "I'm going to say hi." She scoots her chair back.

Liz stands up with her. "I'll come with you!"

"Alaina!" Maya says, aware of the forced cheeriness in her voice.

"Maya?" Alaina stands up and smooths out her shirt.

"What a pleasant surprise! What are you doing here?" She goes in for a quick hug.

"Maya Auntie!" Jade reaches for her, and Maya scoops her up in her arms. Amelia gives her a skeptical look, as if her mom's been filling her in on their recent beef.

"We decided to make an impromptu trip into the city. I was going to stop by your place after this to pop in and say hi. Since we're in the neighborhood."

"Hi, I'm Liz!" Liz juts out her hand, but then thinks better of it and goes in for a hug. Alaina's stiff-armed, awkwardly placing her hand on Liz's back to return the embrace.

"Hi. I figured. I'm Alaina."

"You should come sit down with us!" Liz offers, seemingly unaware of Alaina's standoffish demeanor.

"That's okay. We don't want to intru—"

"Oh, please," Liz says, waving a hand away. "Don't be silly. I feel like we're connected already, thanks to Maya!"

"Right. Uh… Sure." Alaina subtly looks between where they're standing and the exit.

The five of them head over to the table and pull up three more chairs. Alaina's eyes drift to the open laptop. "Are you sure we're not interrupting something? Because we can sit somewhere else."

"No!" Maya quickly removes her laptop from the table and puts it away. "Liz was just helping me with something for work."

Alaina curtly nods. "Wait, I keep forgetting to ask you—how'd your interview with the nanny go? Dev told me the two of you were looking into it."

Liz's face lights up as she turns to Maya. "Isn't Nina the *best*?"

Alaina shoots Liz a side-eye that she either misses or chooses to ignore.

"She's great. Really caring. Kind. Organized." Maya flashes a forced grin at each of them.

"That's great, I'm so glad. And how are you feeling about leaving Shaan so soon? I remember it being so hard when I came up on the end of my maternity leave, realizing I wouldn't be home all the time to look after the girls. I dreaded going back to the hospital."

"Really?" Liz chimes in. "I was the opposite. And I was going to say, Maya, if you know it's your last couple weeks at home, make the most of them! Especially now that you have Nina helping out. Don't let yourself get bogged down with premature guilt."

Alaina gives them a confused look. "Wait, she already started?"

Maya slowly nods, but before she can respond, Liz says, "Isn't that perfect? Now Maya has more time to ease back into work before she hits the ground running when she *officially* returns to office. The end of your leave always creeps up on you."

When no one makes a move to respond, Liz says, "Anyway, I'm so glad it worked out. That must be such a relief."

Maya bites her lip. The tension is palpable. "It's, well, um… Yeah, it is."

An awkward silence follows, and Maya darts her eyes between both of them, so badly wanting to fill the silence. Why can't she come up with a single thing to say to either one of them? Her two *best* friends?

She sends a silent *thank you* to Jade when she breaks the tension, adamantly demanding Alaina buy her a nutty chocolate-chip cookie.

"They *are* one of Oprah's favorites," Maya reasons. "You've got great taste." She gives Jade a high-five.

Alaina rolls her eyes in amusement. "Let me set them up," she says. "And, sorry again. We didn't mean to interrupt your 'girlboss' meeting." She raises an emphatic fist.

Maya makes a move to stand up. "You're not interrupting anything! Here, let me get the girls their cookies. You sit."

"Nah, I've got it."

Maya had pictured this exact moment many times. Some people like to play matchmaker in dating, but Maya always wanted to do that with friends. She had envisioned her, Liz, and Alaina lost in conversation for hours on end, effortlessly sliding between gossip, laughter, and deep heart-to-hearts.

But in reality, she's brainstorming conversation starters before Alaina and the girls return from their cookie venture.

Jade and Amelia run back over to the table, their fingers already covered in chocolate. Alaina slowly trails behind them before reluctantly plopping back down in her seat.

"So, what do you do?" Liz asks her.

"I'm an ER doctor."

Liz nods enthusiastically, waiting for Alaina to say more, but she doesn't.

Ugh, can't you both just like each other? I *like both of you!*

After another long, awkward silence, Liz reads the room and says, "I should head out. Give you both a chance to properly catch up one-on-one." She stands up and gracefully slides her chair back with her heel. "Wait! Before I forget. Do you know what you're going to wear for the presentation?"

Maya smiles sheepishly. "I decided to go with a cream blazer over my blush-pink dress."

"Attagirl!" Liz pats Maya's shoulder. "I'm going to send you this yoga stretch to do before your presentation. It *really* works, I swear."

After two cheek kisses and a playful wave, she's gone.

Maya watches Alaina's eyes follow Liz out the door, her face unreadable, and sighs. "Just say whatever you're thinking."

"Nothing." Alaina shifts her attention to breaking up Jade's cookie. "I'm not thinking anything."

"You're making that face."

Alaina feigns ignorance. "What face?"

"The one we used to call *focused boss*, remember? Where you narrow your eyes in this intense way—" Maya mimics Alaina's expression "—and look like you're about to get some shi…" She pauses, her eyes flitting over to the girls. "Get some stuff done." Maya conjures up an image of Alaina curled up on their living room sofa when they were roommates, sifting through fat medical textbooks.

"I mean, 'attagirl'? Really?" Alaina's eyes widen. "Are you fucking kidding me, Maya?"

"Mommy! You said the f-word!" Amelia declares with pride, clapping her hands.

Alaina waves her hands toward them. "Yeah, yeah, yeah, Mommy made a mistake, don't tell Daddy, you know the drill."

Maya frowns. "Am I kidding you about *what*?"

"That woman sounded like she was gentle parenting and single-handedly dictating your every move at the same time. You seriously can't see that? It's like she's got some sort of spell on you or something."

"A spell? Seriously? Come on."

"Seriously. And was she suggesting you do *yoga*? As if you need some white woman to tell you about the benefits of yoga!

Let me guess—does she also tell you you're exotic and resilient?"

"You're being so negative," Maya says. "Just because you're feeling bogged down by everything doesn't mean you need to spread misery to everyone else."

"Are you serious?" Alaina scoffs. "What are you even saying?"

"Things I probably should have said a while ago."

"Whatever. I really don't get you," Alaina says, shaking her head.

"Why do you keep saying that?!"

"Look around, Maya! Look at you. Look at your *life*," she says, making a sweeping gesture with her hand. "You're like some damn…influencer fembot or something."

Their growing distance is gutting her. Maya wants her best friend back. She wants to hear how work's going, if couples therapy is making a difference, if Auntie Rita has been less overbearing lately. And she wants to tell *her* everything. Her constant fights with Dev, her parents selling the motel, her parents' impending divorce, her big plans for Medini.

Or the very real, nagging fear that she has no idea what to do about her guilt anymore. Every time she feels it, she needs more pills. And when she doesn't, she's numb. Detached.

But as she watches Alaina wipe chocolate off each of her daughters' fingers, pleading with them to stay quiet for *just five more minutes*, Maya doesn't bother wasting her breath.

When it comes to the people she loves most, it's safer to not say anything at all.

TECH TIMES

Liz Anderson's Convoluted Feminism

By Yolanda Ashton

Published July 17, 2019, 11:00 AM EDT

Exactly eight years ago to the date, Liz Anderson announced she was shutting down her emotional wellness company, Limitless.

Among other things, Anderson is renowned for mentoring women in the tech space. "I want to uplift as much as possible," she's emphasized in countless interviews since first emerging into the spotlight. "I want to be more than an ally. I want to be a changemaker."

Anderson got her start at Limitless, the wellness company she cofounded with Anita Johnson.

"Limitless was the perfect combination of skill meeting market demand," Anderson said in an interview with the *New York Times* after the app launched. Anderson's background in health and wellness, combined with Johnson's expertise in data analytics, led to their collaboration in building a platform where women could track their moods, write empowering journal entries, and even share mental wellness updates with their therapists. The app provided a daily "mood score" and tracked an individual's score over time. For years, social media was flooded with status updates such as "Treating myself to a score boost, also known as a wine flight," or "Shout-out to everyone whose score dips whenever they've been ghosted."

The company announced it was shutting down six months after allegations were made by mental health professionals questioning the app's accuracy, its suggestions of medical diagnoses, and a data leak that exposed over fifty thousand users' personal information.

In response to these rumors, especially regarding Anderson's and Johnson's involvement in a space reserved for qualified medical professionals, Anderson stated, "We covered a lot of ground in a short period of time. Of course that's going to come with hurdles."

As for the split between Anderson and Johnson? "Ultimately, it came down to us having different visions. Nobody was right or wrong. And part of being a leader is knowing when something is over. I will always respect Anita as the brilliant businessperson she is, and I wish her all the best."

So where's Johnson now? She's been out of the public eye ever since Limitless's shutdown, but rumor has it she's hard at work building a new tech start-up. Multiple outlets have speculated about her next steps. Her team released the following statement at the end of last year: "Anita is busy working behind the scenes on something brand-new. She's very grateful for everyone's interest in and support of her endeavors. She will share more when she's ready." At this time, her team has declined all requests for interviews.

Looks like we'll have to be in the dark for a bit longer, but it sounds as if something *big* is on the horizon for Anderson's former business partner.

Speaking of tech empresses, Maya Patel, founder and CEO of her green-tech start-up Medini, has made quite the splash this summer. In a short amount of time, she was featured in outlets such as *Vanity Fair* and the *New York Times* Style section, among others—many thanks to her recent friendship with Anderson.

Like Johnson, Patel is also a female founder of color with a substantial social following, and her link to Anderson and her connections has only helped Patel gain more reach. Anderson's friendships with both women seemed to happen overnight, and in the blink of an eye, she and her "girlboss" best friend—whether it was Johnson or Patel—became tied at the hip. Anderson was rarely seen without the other at any given tech event.

Since the start of Limitless, Anderson has touted her commitment to "inclusivity" and making sure "women of color get their seat at the table." Although statements like these received applause at the time, there's now speculation about whether Anderson's brand of feminism has been—and continues to be—*performative*, rather than genuine allyship.

While there's still a lot to learn about these three founders and how they may or may not be intertwined, what we do know is this: Liz Anderson remains as determined as ever.

"I just want women to take over the world," she said in a press interview just last week. "That's when I'll know my work is done."

@WannaBeSteveJobs: Has anyone heard more about Anita Johnson? I read some article saying she turned into a recluse but tbh, that never sounded right after seeing how much she seemed to love the spotlight.

@Yvonne1234: And the way Liz kept Anita by her side felt so performative. Ick.

@TechWiz: Yaaaaas. Like she was saying, look at me with my woman of color by my side! I'm so inclusive! But it was all a PR stunt for her.

@WannabeSteveJobs: The woman does know branding. I took a couple of her workshops and she had a lot of great points about how to get people to notice you. I mean, she somehow turned being a pharmacologist into a mini #girlboss movement.

@Yvonne1234: Liz clearly taught both of them that what's online is all that matters. From an outside perspective, Maya looks like she's thriving. Living her best life.

@Tech Wiz: Let's see if any of that's actually true.

24

MAYA PUSHES SHAAN'S STROLLER TO A shaded section of the giant outdoor table at The Odeon, one of her and Mom's favorite spots to grab lunch. Despite the rare seventy-five-degree July weather, the place is empty.

She makes out the side profile of her mother sitting outside, facing the opposite direction. Maya starts walking over, and in classic Mira Patel fashion, she can hear every single word her mother's saying on the phone.

"Sejal, I've already made up my mind," Mom says. "You know some of what I've been through but if you *really* knew all of the things I've put up with, you'd understand why I have to do this… No, no. I've made my decision. Anand knows this is what's best even if he doesn't want to say it… The kids will be just fine. There's nothing you—"

"Mom?" Maya interrupts, making her presence known.

"Sejal? I have to go." Mom puts her phone on the counter and shoots Maya a tight smile. It was the same smile Maya gave her as a teenager whenever she was in the middle of texting boys—she wasn't allowed to date at the time—and Mom came into her room to say good night.

"So that's it, then? You and Dad are just splitting up?"

"Why do you have to say it like that? And hello to you, too," Mom says before getting up to kiss Shaan's cheeks.

Maya sits down, Shaan in the stroller next to her. She takes a sip of the "dirty" iced chai that Mom ordered for her before she arrived.

"I told them not to put concentrate in that, by the way," Mom says, a self-satisfied smirk on her face.

It's the type of afternoon she often imagined having with her mom and son during her last few weeks of maternity leave. Of course, she'd also imagined they'd be discussing their latest favorite show on Netflix or typical auntie gossip. Not her parents' separation.

"Because…it's a marriage. It's your marriage." Maya sighs. "You don't even want to see if you can work this out? If talking to a professional might help?"

"I have no desire to tell a complete stranger everything I've been through. Nor do I expect them to understand." Mom crosses her arms like a defiant little girl.

"I actually think everyone from your generation could benefit from a little therapy," Maya mutters.

"What'd you say?" Mom asks.

"Nothing. I just want you to have really thought this through."

She waits for Mom to say *Of course I have* or *You have to drop this*. But to her surprise, Mom looks off into the direction of West Broadway, seemingly entranced by the cabs sliding over potholes and the people on Citi bikes.

When she shifts her focus back to Maya, she says, "You know what? Maybe you have a point."

"I do?"

Mom takes a large gulp of coffee. "You're right, what *do* I have to offer outside of my marriage? My children?"

"You know I didn't mean it like that."

"I didn't accomplish *anything*." Mom's eyes are wet. "All these years and I have nothing to show for myself."

"That's not true at all, Mom," Maya says, reaching for her hand. "How can you say that? You've done *so* much."

"Did you know my mother felt the same way? And she told me—she *warned* me—this would happen."

"It's not too late," Maya says, her voice strained. "You can still do things."

"Like what?"

"Like… I don't know, anything! Whatever you want!"

Mom shakes her head and looks up at the sky, her signature gesture of defeat. Their conversation is briefly stalled when a waiter drops off their purple sticky rice bowls.

When Maya had graduated college and was torn about her life path, Mom confided in her that she'd been accepted into the top journalism program in Europe in her early twenties. But weeks before her deposit was due, she was arranged to marry Dad. She tried going back to school after she was pregnant with Maya but was told by her parents and in-laws that she couldn't. As a new mother, she was expected to be around at all times for her daughter, and eventually for her son. Maya remembers an analogy Mom used to describe coming to terms with her lot in life. Something along the lines of her feeling like she was driving a car, and she could see all her hopes, her dreams, her big plans in the rearview mirror, growing smaller and smaller.

Of all the different versions of her mother Maya's envisioned, this is the hardest one to come to terms with: the woman her mother wasn't allowed to become. Every time she thinks of the life her mother never got the chance to lead, something inside of her breaks.

If sacrifice is the status quo for women, she wants nothing to do with it.

"Mom?" Maya shifts her chair closer to the table.

"I know you're very attached to your father, but I swear to Ganesha, if you tell me to understand where he's coming from, I will lose it."

Maya laughs. "That's not what I was going to say. I was actually going to mention that I'd looked something up for you months ago. It was supposed to be a Mother's Day surprise, but I didn't know if you'd like it."

"What is it?"

Maya takes her phone out of her crossbody bag and turns it to face Mom. "Columbia has continuing education courses in journalism. I was going to sign you up for one. Maybe now's the perfect time!"

"No, please don't bother." Mom shakes her head. "It's too late for anything like that."

"It's not too late at all. You still have so much life to live!"

"No. I'm not like you, Maya. I'm not brave enough."

When Maya doesn't respond, Mom reaches for her hand.

"Beta? I know you're concerned about me, but what about you? Are *you* okay? Tarun's been a little worried about you lately. Is there something going on? Is it that board presentation you said you were stressed about?"

"It's that and, you know, other things." Maya stirs her drink with her straw, fixating on the perfectly squared little ice cubes floating around.

"Such as?" Mom raises her eyebrows.

"I'm not sure if I like the person I am, or the person I'm becoming."

Outside of Liz, this is the first time she's expressed this to anyone. Maybe it's hearing her parents' news, or Mom's peaceful presence, but Maya has an urgent desire to go back with her to the motel and fall asleep in her childhood bedroom.

The silence swells between them. Mom scans Maya's face from forehead to chin.

"What are you even saying, Maya? You've got everything!" Mom's expression quickly switches from concern to amusement. "You really don't sound like yourself right now. You've always done this, did you know that? You get overwhelmed and so in your head, but then it always ends up being fine. I think you just need some rest. Trust me, you've always been able to figure things out. Now, Tarun, on the other hand…"

As Mom keeps talking about the importance of sleeping eight hours, all Maya can think is that this is what happens when you're the rock, the person everyone else turns to for support. The second you drop the mask, proving you don't have it all under control like you've led them to believe, they can't handle it.

Because if they accepted that reality, then everything else would start unraveling, too.

This is why her deepest, darkest, most unlovable parts need to stay hidden. *Especially* around the people she cares about the most.

"Yes, more rest. That's probably it," she says, ending the conversation.

NEW YORK CITY POLICE DEPARTMENT

OFFICER RICHARDSON: Were there ever times Maya ran away? Or left you without any notice?

MIRA PATEL: No, never. She's the reliable one. Always helping us with everything.

OFFICER RICHARDSON: Her best friend, Alaina Brown, informed us that, in their twenties, Maya sometimes left their shared apartment for long stretches of time without telling anybody.

MIRA PATEL: Maybe she was with Dev? The two were inseparable when they started dating. I'm sure there's a reasonable explanation.

OFFICER RICHARDSON: Well, your son-in-law also claims that Maya's disappeared once before.

ANAND PATEL: She left Dev? When?

OFFICER RICHARDSON: That's not what's I am im—

MIRA PATEL: Are you trying to say this is what she does? How dare you imply anything of the sort when you should be out there making sure my daughter is okay!

OFFICER RICHARDSON: We're just trying to get as much information as possible, ma'am.

MIRA PATEL: All that's relevant for you to know is that she's not the type of person who leaves her family. Her *baby*. She just isn't. The fact of the matter is Maya's still missing. And do you know what day it is? It's August 3. She disappeared July 26. She's been gone for over a week! And what have you done about that, other than question her character? While you're asking these senseless questions, she's out there, probably alone and in danger! Or even— [Voice breaks in a sob.]

OFFICER RICHARDSON: Mrs. Patel, I assure you we are considering all scenarios related to Maya's disappearance. But as we've informed you, there have been no found indications of foul play, so we also have to take into account some other—

MIRA PATEL: Oh, so because there's no concrete evidence she was harmed, you just give up? DO something! Why are you all just sitting here, twiddling your thumbs, instead of searching for her? How are you not taking this case seriously? Is it because she's a missing brown woman, instead of a white woman?

OFFICER RICHARDSON: I can assure you, we—

ANAND PATEL: Officer, I think we're done here.

25

THE RICKETY SOUND OF THE TRAIN AS it cascades down the tracks. The muffled overhead speaker announcing each stop. A twentysomething woman across from her in burgundy fitness attire, lip-synching to a song on her AirPods. Two men in tweed, both of their legs crossed, sharing a hard copy of this week's *New York Times*. An elderly lady clutching a yapping chihuahua.

Maya can observe the scene around her in fine detail but feels separate from it. Like she's watching her life play out from behind a television screen.

She leaves the station on 23rd Street and walks toward the office. It's one of those rare, crisp summer days that feels more like fall. It immediately brings up memories of buying school supplies or curling up under a blanket with a mug of hot apple cider. Maya waits for the nostalgia to hit her, a warmth in her heart. A longing for Shaan to be near her.

But she feels nothing.

When she arrives at the office, the conference room is fully prepped. A flat-screen at one end reads *Medini Board Meeting.* The center of the large glass table has an assortment of Ess-a-Bagels, a giant carton of coffee, paper cups, and trays of cut fruit. Pressure builds in Maya's chest as she sees board members start to file into the conference room, some scrolling on their phones, others engaged in light conversation.

"Hello, hello!" Josh says, walking toward her, a big smile on his face.

Maya gives him a quick hug. "You ready to go in there?"

"As ready as I can be. Thanks for taking out so much time on the weekends to work on this. That couldn't have been easy with Shaan."

"It was fine," Maya says, instantly regretting it. "Actually, no, that's not true. It *was* challenging. But I'm glad we were able to get it done."

Josh leans closer to her and lowers her voice. "So, who do you think is going to freak out the most when we tell them the valuation we're going out with?"

Maya laughs. "Travis, obviously. Then again, I could see him respecting me for having big-dick energy. He can really go either way. But honestly, he can think whatever he wants about this presentation. I know it's what the company needs. You know it's what we need. He can get over it and decide to get on board whenever he's ready to put his ego aside for five minutes."

Josh whistles in response, then rubs his hands together. "Let's go, let's go, let's go!"

Maya stifles a laugh. He's acting like they're in a loud sports bar, counting down the seconds until the Super Bowl's opening kickoff.

They enter the conference room, which is filled to the brim with all of Medini's board members and leadership team. Most of the Ess-a-Bagels have been claimed, only whole wheat left. There goes her post-meeting breakfast.

Maya walks to the head of the table and clears her throat. "Are we ready to get started?"

Tiffany quickly takes attendance, then Maya launches right in. The next hour passes by in a blur, Josh chiming in here and there on the points they'd rehearsed together.

Throughout its entirety, she's not fazed by the multiple sets of eyes on her, doesn't get thrown off when her voice momentarily wavers. She's fully in the moment. And she's kicking ass.

While she presents, multiple board members are raising their eyebrows and nodding in pleasant surprise.

And then, just like that, it's over.

Her eyes scan the faces in the room, and it's suddenly hard to discern what anyone's thinking. A couple people raise their hands. Sweat pools under the maternity bra she should have probably stopped wearing by now.

Travis clears his throat. "Just so we're all clear, you're putting Medini at a *one hundred million dollar* valuation?"

"That's correct," Maya confirms. "We believe th—"

"How on earth did you come up with that number?"

Don't let him interrupt you. Assert yourself.

"I was just about to explain." It takes everything in her to keep her facial expression intact and not betray the built-up resentment she has toward this man.

Travis dramatically extends his hand, signaling her to go on.

"For starters, our expansion into dozens of new Whole Foods locations means our growth rate can accelerate faster than ever. New locations, new channels, exponential revenue increase."

Maya steals a glance at Josh, who catches her drift to chime in. "This aligns with other brands that have expanded in a retailer like Whole Foods, and at the same scale as Medini."

"But we're missing the real point here, aren't we?" Travis asks, looking around the room for group solidarity.

Maya raises her eyebrows. "And that is…?"

"That Medini's in a compromised position. And just because you put a valuation on a slide doesn't make it reality."

This fucking asshole.

Maya takes a deep inhale and says, "Yes, Travis, we're all very much aware that things aren't as great as they could be. That's why we n—"

"Aren't as *great* as they could be?" Travis laughs condescendingly. "No, Maya, they're bad. *Really* bad. They've been bad for some time now."

"Right. I think you've made your opinion quite clear." Maya keeps her lips in a tight, straight line. "And while we could sit here and ruminate on that for hours, I think it'd be a more productive use of our time to discuss a game plan."

"I agree." Brad leans back in his chair.

"Same," Josh echoes as he fiddles with the strings on his hoodie. (It just so happens to be the same hoodie Brad's wearing.)

Maya shifts her attention back to the rest of the room. "So, if we want to move on to funding…"

Tiffany hits the next slide.

"I know we've mentioned Mark and Tribeca One before, but I obviously don't want us to put our eggs in one basket," Maya continues. "I've also added some other potential places we can pitch for our next round."

She recites the list of VC funds on the screen behind her. It's a mixture of firms she's been in touch with before, the ones that have explicitly and publicly expressed their interest in funding more female-founded companies.

"That's quite a long, *ambitious* list," Travis notes. "Again, let's not forget how hard it was for you to raise money the first time. Plus, there's really no guarantee that any of these funds will want to come on board with this."

Ironically, it was Travis who convinced Maya not to go after too many funds during the first round. He told her it was better for her to retain some control of the company and not "give it all away to investors." She listened. She listened to what *all* her investors told her to do, thinking that if she pleased them, she'd be in their good graces. But all she's done is make them think they can walk all over her.

"Yes, I'm aware of that," Maya says through gritted teeth. She's instantly reminded of the string of meetings she's endured throughout her career, when the investor she was pitching to would either cut her off, ask her to "rework the deck," tell her he couldn't "relate" to her product, or worst of all, just direct all his questions to Josh.

"Some of these funds *are* extremely selective about the type of company they invest in," Brad says, agreeing with Travis.

Selective. He should just say what he's thinking. That she's a risky investment because of her gender, the color of her skin, and her products.

"Thanks for that, both. Like I said, I've thought this list through."

Brad furrows his brow at her in response, displeased.

Maya presses on. "And that's why I've brainstormed a variety of places to approach to ensure a *diversity* of perspectives. I'm happy to go through each one so we can all come up with a plan?" (And by *diversity*, she means people who aren't just men.)

"Actually, before you get to that, can we have the room? Board only and Josh, please," Travis interjects.

Maya clenches her fists under the table as people start filing out. What she'd give to just punch the wall right now. Or better yet, Travis.

"Here's what we're thinking," Travis says after everyone else has left. "Maya, you need to step down."

His words come to her in slow motion. She envisions them suspended over his head in block letters, or as a bubble in a comic strip.

"From being CEO," Travis adds, like she needed the clarification.

"Excuse me?" Maya's eyes twitch, an intense energy thrumming in her neck. She wants to scream, but it's like there's a hand over her mouth. The only sounds she hears come from outside the conference room. Soft conversation, the gurgling of the coffee machine, the beeping of the printer. "Did you seriously just ask me to quit my job at *my* company?"

"I didn't ask. I'm strongly advising," he says, sitting back in his seat and crossing his arms. Everyone's eyes are on her. The room feels way too hot.

Why isn't Josh saying anything? Or literally anyone? Was this discussed prior?

"Where is this coming from?" She hates that tears are threatening to pool in her eyes. She will *not* let this man see her cry.

"From a place of what's best for Medini. If you step down as CEO, you'll have the chance to focus on the things you're good at, like being the face of the company, maintaining its image… We can even consider moving you into some type of executive chairman—I mean, executive chairperson—role, so you still feel like you have a title in addition to founder, and someone else gets to deal with—" he motions around the boardroom "—all this."

"'All this' is my *job*. And my stepping down isn't an option. It never has been. Today is about moving forward as a team."

And you can fuck off for suggesting that in the first place.

Judging by the shocked expressions on several of the board members' faces, nobody had planned on her fighting back.

"Exactly. Move forward in the strongest way. Look, Maya, you know—we *all* know," he says, looking around at the other attendees, "that things have gotten out of control. The team is overworked. Costs are skyrocketing, especially since you committed the company to scaling. We can't let things go on this way."

How does Travis always find a way to blame her for everything?

Maya narrows her eyes at him, her face growing red. "The team is overworked *because* we let so many people go *because* our costs were going up *because* I was pushed to spend. And even then, I secured a deal for us to get into more stores. Not to mention all the press and publicity I've gotten all by myself." Warmth continues to creep into her face and she just lets it. She doesn't give a flying fuck if they think she's overreacting.

"Look, I hear you, but not every founder is meant to be a CEO. I've seen this time and time again." Travis shakes his head in the most patronizing way possible.

"I'm aware that several founders opt out of being CEO for many different reasons, Travis. Thanks for that valuable insight. I don't think that's relevant here."

"All I'm saying is that things work better when someone knows their strengths and their weaknesses." Travis runs his fingers through his silver-flecked hair, letting the words settle between them. The smoothness in his voice pisses her off even more. "It's always a good idea to choose what's best for the company over what's best for your ego. I think it's important to at least consider this, don't you think, Maya?"

"My ego? You're kidding, right?" Her face has reached beet-red territory.

Travis stares at her, his expression unchanged.

She can't believe this is happening. *Choose what's best for the company over what's best for my ego?* Is he kidding? How dare he speak to her that way! And why is everyone so fucking silent?

You aren't one of them. You'll never be one of them.

"All I've ever wanted is what's best for this company." Her voice comes out softer, weaker.

Travis clutches his coffee cup and pretends to fixate on something in the room. Maya knows this tactic. He's going to let the silence build until it's so uncomfortable that someone feels compelled to jump in and agree with him.

While he was talking, more than a few of the board members were nodding along. If this had happened two months ago, Maya would have taken their agreement with Travis's proposition as her reason to give up. She would have stammered out an apology, probably offering to think on it.

But she's not going to budge. Especially not with six pills in her system. All too often, the polite, people-pleasing woman gets taken advantage of. She's done with that tired narrative.

Dad's voice comes back to her. *Don't ruffle any feathers, Maya. Don't get too greedy.*

They won't make her another statistic.

"I'm going to come up with some *other* options and we'll circle back." Maya aggressively pushes her chair away from the table, adjourning the meeting. Her pulse pounds in her ears, but she somehow manages to keep her head held high as people file out of the room.

Once she's alone, her resolve dissipates. Did Travis really suggest they find another CEO, in front of everyone? And nobody stood up for her, not even Josh?

Fuck. Fuck. Fuck. Fuck. Fuck.

The word loops in her head until it doesn't even sound like a word anymore.

How long has the board been planning to drop this on her? Did Josh know this was going to happen? He had seemed so supportive when they reviewed the deck together. Is there really a chance she'll lose Medini?

She tells herself to breathe, to throw herself back into work, and to figure out logical next steps. That's what Liz would do.

But her vision starts to blur, and her throat becomes constricted. She feels faint, like there's a heavy weight over her chest. She runs out of the office space and into the stairwell, where her breathing becomes quicker and shallower until she can hardly breathe at all. Maya clutches her chest as tears burn behind her eyes.

I can't lose everything. I just can't.

Her entire career flashes before her eyes: sending the first Medini orders from the motel's back office, Dev framing a photo from Maya's first press interview, Maya holding her pregnant belly with pride and anticipation during team meetings.

In each of these moments, she felt a bubble of excitement that, one day, she'd be able to show her baby everything she's built for herself. She spent so much of her maternity leave working in the hopes that Shaan would grow up and think of his mother as a successful, well-rounded, fulfilled woman.

But all of it was for nothing. All that time spent away from him was for nothing. All those late nights working was for nothing.

Maya sits on the top step and buries her face in her hands.

I've failed. I've failed at everything.

Before she hears it, she feels it pummeling through her veins, collecting like a weight on her chest.

You've ruined everything. You've failed your colleagues, your customers. You've wasted everyone's time, energy, and support. You let everyone down.

Hot, salty tears stream down her face and into her mouth. She lets out a guttural sob, a sound so foreign she thinks it's coming from someone else.

She's interrupted by the stairwell door opening behind her.

Shit.

Maya turns around, face-to-face with five twentysomethings who work at one of the other start-ups headquartered in the building.

Typical. The one time she cries in this establishment, and she gets an audience.

Can't a woman just have some privacy when she's in the middle of a meltdown, dammit? She thinks of that *Sex and the City* episode where Charlotte cries at work and is forever taunted by her colleagues for it.

The male ringleader gives her an awkward look. "Oh…um, hey… I mean, sorry."

Before Maya can say anything, the girl behind him stammers, "We'll…uh…take the elevator." Her syllables echo in the stairwell.

"No need!" Maya puts on her most cheerful voice, wondering how splotchy her face looks. "I'm heading back in, anyway!"

She feels the weight of five pairs of eyes staring uneasily at her.

"Good to see you all," Maya says peppily. *See? I'm totally fine! You didn't see me having a breakdown. It was all just a big misunderstanding! We'll laugh about it later, trust me.*

Five minutes later, she's in the bathroom, splashing cold water on her face. Mom used to do this after heated arguments with Dad. When she'd finally emerge from the bathroom, met with Maya's concerned expression, she'd say she was fine, wiping remaining traces of water on her face with her sleeve. She wishes she could ask Mom if she did that because she was ashamed of her anger. Ashamed of being a normal person with human emotions.

Maya quickly pops back two pills, puts on her most confident smile, and takes the longer route to her private, glassed-in office. She deliberately makes eye contact with every single one of her employees when she passes their desks, reminding them she's right where she belongs.

And she's not going anywhere.

MAYA PATEL @MAYA_PATEL

INSTAGRAM DMS

@EnvironmentalParenting: I'd love to pick your brain about starting a company. Can you send me times you're available? I'm in a bit of a rush to get things going, so the sooner the better. [Sent May 20, 2019, 3:36 PM]

@EnvironmentalParenting: Just checking in on this. Thanks so much! [Sent May 30, 2019, 6:58 PM]

@HappyBaby: How do you think your baby will feel when he's older and realizes you've been sharing so much of his early life online? Do you think he wants pictures of himself, his milestones, and other personal moments showcased for all the world? And then, after all that, you abandon him? Maybe the reason you've gotten so far is because you put your own needs above all. But it's time to think of others for once, especially now that you're a mother. [Sent June 7, 2019, 1:21 PM]

@GetYourBodyBack: Hi! We've noticed you may be having trouble losing the baby weight. Our thirty-day cleanse is guaranteed to help you lose at least ten pounds. DM us if you'd like more information. We'd love to do a collab with you. [Sent June 28, 2019, 8:42 AM]

@GetYourBodyBack: Hi again! Just following up. Is this something you'd be interested in? [Sent July 12, 2019, 4:43 PM]

@TheRestedMother: Hello, Maya. You look a little more tired in your recent posts. Maybe catching some z's would help with your stress levels. Have you considered a sleep coach for you and your baby? We'd be happy to set up a call and send you some of our award-winning products! [Sent June 30, 2019, 2:08 PM]

@TheRestedMother: Hi again, Maya. Just following up here. I notice you haven't been active on socials, so please let me know if there's a better way for me to reach out. [Sent July 27, 2019, 12:04 PM]

@Marina123: Hi Maya, I used to be a big fan of yours but have been disappointed in you lately. You seem to be all about your public image and only interested in what benefits you. Then you just leave all your loyal followers in the dark? Going to unfollow you now. [Sent July 14, 2019, 8:12 AM]

@MissouriMom: Just wanted to say I've always loved your posts and appreciated your content. As the mother of a baby boy myself, my heart goes out to you and your family. I hope wherever you are, you're safe. [Sent August 3, 2019, 9:56 PM]

26

"I REFUSE TO TAKE THIS SHIT."

"You shouldn't," Liz insists. "You can't."

"Oh, trust me, I won't," Maya says.

"Travis is just trying to scare you. I always knew he was an asshole, but this is another level of fucked-up."

"I know," Maya agrees. "But I can't just wallow. I have to do something about this."

"Do you remember me telling you how, at my first company, they tried to push me out, too? Hell, I know there are even people I work with *now* who would do the same if given the chance. May I offer some unsolicited advice?"

Maya stares off, lost in thought.

"Maya?" Liz prompts.

She blinks, bringing herself back to the present. "Sorry, I zoned out for a sec. Long day."

"Could I give you some advice?"

Maya laughs for the first time since the board meeting. "Always."

"Whatever you do, don't let this get out publicly. You've been getting so much great press for Medini these last few weeks, so do what you can to maintain control over the narrative. This is *your* company. And you're the face of it."

Josh knocks on her door.

"I'll have to call you back." Maya puts her phone away and motions for Josh to come in.

"How's it going?" Josh asks.

"It's, well, you know." Maya shrugs. "You were there. And quite silent I may add. What's up?"

"I just got off the phone with Travis," he says. Her stomach drops.

"And?"

He takes a deep breath.

"Just say it." She puts her face into her hands and braces for the worst.

"He definitely wants you out and wants me to be interim CEO."

"WHAT?" She snaps her head up, her breath catching in her throat.

"I know." Josh sighs. "This isn't something I want. Or would ever want."

"Oh *really*? It's not?"

Why isn't there a pill to get rid of female rage, too? Liz and Women Rise are missing out on a real market there.

And why isn't that awful cramp in her abdomen going away? She's been feeling the rebound guilt more, the relief less.

"C'mon. You have to know it's not." Josh's voice is softer now, reminding her of their late-night conversations at the office.

She hates how much she hasn't trusted him, and after everything they've been through.

"I'm sorry," Maya says after a long pause. "I'm a little…all over the place, if you can't tell." She forces a laugh. "Thanks for letting me know."

Her emotions are an amorphous blob, one that changes its shape from one minute to the next. Her mind jumps to a meme she saw on some Facebook parenting page that said, *When you don't know if you need a nap, run, coffee, wine, or tranquilizer…*

He gives her a soft smile. "I have to go hop on a call, but here if you need anything. I'm sorry about…all this." He gently closes the door on his way out.

Only then does Maya realize she forgot to ask him the single most important question. *Did you say yes?*

A minute later, Maya gets a text from Nina and breathes a sigh of relief. A smiley photo of her baby is just what she needs to lift her spirits. Ever since Nina saw how nervous Maya was to leave Shaan for Mark's dinner, she's made an effort to update her throughout the day with photos and videos. Maya can already envision Shaan's bright eyes facing the living room window, glistening in the sunlight. Or his fist grabbing the edges of his mint-green burp cloth that's covered with images of tiny sheep.

But today, there are no photos, just words:

Nina: I'm so sorry to bother you. But I was wondering if Shaan seemed sick to you last night?

Maya: No. Why? Is something wrong?

Nina: He's been spitting up since I got here and just threw up his last feed.

Maya: I'm on my way.

★ ★ ★

Half an hour later, when she arrives home to find Shaan sitting up in his bouncer, all she can think is *I'm sorry. I'm sorry I haven't done better for you.*

The confusion on his face makes her stomach clench. He's probably wondering why his mother wasn't around when he was sick, or why she hasn't been around at all lately to take care of him.

Nina offers to stay, but Maya insists she go home. She lifts Shaan out of his bouncer and traces the velvet curve of his nose and cheek.

Once she's sitting on the sofa, Shaan curled against her chest, Maya fully absorbs how utterly exhausting this entire week has been. Nonstop emails about the Whole Foods purchase orders. Follow-ups from Travis regarding "next steps." The conversation with Josh. Being away from Shaan.

Her baby sinks into her, preparing for a nap. She knows she's supposed to encourage independent sleeping, but she needs his soft, tiny body pressed against hers right now. As her muscles relax, she sees her life spread out in front of her like a giant collage. Just one year ago, she thought she had it all figured out. At her baby shower, Maya told every auntie who asked that she had a guaranteed plan for how to "make it all work." She'd get the right child care, the right support at work, and maintain a strong, balanced partnership with Dev. Then they all moved on in conversation, keeping it light and sharing laughs about the size of Maya's belly.

She didn't have a care in the world back then.

And why would she? Nothing could have prepared her for any of this. There was no way of knowing back then the shit show waiting in store for her.

Her eyes grow heavier and heavier, and she drifts off into a deep sleep.

★ ★ ★

An hour later, she's jolted awake by a persistent buzzing sensation. As she slowly opens her eyes and takes in her surroundings, she does a double take when she looks down to find Shaan fast asleep. She didn't even register his weight on her chest.

She looks for her phone to send a follow-up to Dr. Karp, her body slow-moving as she attempts to reorient herself from her post-nap haze. She feels around the couch but can't find it anywhere. Moments later, the couch starts vibrating again, and she finds it wedged between a cushion and the back of the sectional.

When she unlocks her phone, she finds an endless number of notifications from multiple social media apps.

She rubs the sleep from her eyes and takes a closer look, scrolling through notifications from Beth, Josh, and Liz, missed calls from Dev and Tarun, a voicemail from Alaina, and a follow-up text from Dev saying he's on his way home.

Her intuition tells her to pull up Beth's message first.

Beth: Maya, don't worry about the article. I'm already on it and will get you the opportunity to clear the record ASAP.

The article? What article?

She skims through the other unread messages:

Josh: I swear I had nothing to do with this. Please call me whenever you're ready to talk.

Liz: FUCK THEM. I'm serious! This is not even worth your time.

What the fuck? She goes back to her texts with Beth and finds a link underneath her latest message.

She lays a giant blanket across the couch for Shaan and gently removes him from her chest, careful not to rouse him. Then she opens the link.

Everything blurs into the background as the words *BUSINESS NEWS NEW YORK* appear in big capital letters on her screen. Why would Beth send her this? She never mentioned their interest in profiling Maya.

But as soon as the article finishes loading, the headline comes into clear view.

Oh my God. No, no, no, no, no.

This has to be some sort of mistake. This can't be happening.

But when she closes her eyes and opens them again, the words on the screen remain unchanged: *Eco-toiletry company Medini is looking for a new CEO.*

Who would do this to her? To Medini?

She feverishly skims through the rest of it, her heart pounding in her chest.

It isn't until she reads the very last sentence that she has her answer.

BUSINESS NEWS NEW YORK

Eco-toiletry company Medini is looking for a new CEO

Published July 26, 2019, 3:30 PM EDT

New York–based start-up Medini has been making waves with its eco-friendly toiletries. Before its recent deal with Whole Foods, the company was reported to be valued at thirty million dollars. Medini's founder, Maya Patel, has been lauded in multiple media outlets for her ability to carve out a space in the start-up world, one that she claims is "too often dominated by men."

But earlier this week, *Business Insider* spoke to a source from inside the company who suggested things may not be as rosy as they seem. The source indicates that Medini is spending far more money than projected and that things have been "unstable for a long time."

Leaked Slack messages also indicate that Medini's investors have been pushing for the company to find new leadership:

(Screenshot, Medini's Slack #company-announcements channel):

Josh Kaplan: Hi, a few of us had an impromptu follow-up after that last board meeting, and I wanted to give everyone a brief recap of the team's takeaways: 1) Maya has no plans to leave. I know a few of you heard otherwise from a conversation with some board members, but please do not engage in conversations about this. 2) Please do not discuss this with people outside of Medini. 3) If anyone reaches out asking about any of the above, do not comment, and please let me know.

When asked for their overall thoughts on the situation, the insider source states, "Just because someone starts a company doesn't mean they're the right person to keep leading it."

27

"HEY, HEY, IT'S GOING TO BE OKAY," Dev says, rubbing her back in small circles.

"You really don't know that." Maya moves off the couch and picks Shaan up off his play mat to place him on his tummy. He stretches his tiny neck, then hangs his head in a gesture of defeat.

"What if you did an interview with *Business News*? Or put something on your social media that informs everyone you're still very much the CEO? Or..." Dev continues to rattle off ideas.

"I appreciate what you're saying, but I really don't want solutions right now. I just want to figure out how to even begin to process all of this." She's expressed this same sentiment to Dev over and over again since they started dating. His first instinct is to jump right into problem-solving mode, when sometimes all she needs is a shoulder to cry on.

"Okay." He hunches his shoulders and looks down at the floor.

Maya stares off into space. How did this become her life?

"Look, why don't we go have dinner in the park? Get a little change of scenery? I'll order salads," Dev suggests, right as his phone rings with an incoming FaceTime.

"Mom!" he says with forced enthusiasm. "We're just about to head out. Can I call you later?"

"Let me just see him."

Dev points the phone toward Shaan, who is on his back again, kicking into the air. Every few seconds, his feet hit the bell that's hanging over the play mat. They paid one hundred and forty dollars for their son to lie on this piece of fabric because it "encourages grasping" and "fosters development." Maya wonders if it was all a scam, just like so many other products geared toward new parents.

"Oh no, he looks so much *skinnier*!" Dev's mom cries. "I used to mix rice cereal into your brother's milk to get him more calories. Why don't you try that? And is he sleeping better? If Maya's doing the rocking method I showed her, it'll help. And please make sure she's keeping up with all of this, so we don't have a bad doctor's appointment again."

She observes the panic in Dev's face as he struggles with his phone, trying to take his mom off speaker.

Rage pulses through Maya.

STOP. GIVING. SO. MUCH. UNSOLICITED. ADVICE! she wants to scream. *Don't you think this is hard enough without us having to answer to you all the fucking time?*

Dev sends Maya a sideways, nervous look, his face twisted into a forced smile. "He's fine, Mom. More than fine. Anyway, I have to run. Love you!"

"I'm really sorry," he says once he's off the call.

"For what?"

He motions to his phone. "What she said."

"Which part?" Maya cocks her head, feigning ignorance.

"You know what? Never mind. I don't think we should have this conversation right now. We've both had an intense day already. Why don't we regroup in thirty and head over to the park? I already put our Sweetgreen order in."

Once Dev's preoccupied with Shaan, Maya immediately enters the bedroom and checks twice to make sure she's locked the door behind her. She needs some relief after the day she's had.

Her hands find the brown bottle.

An hour later, the three of them are at their usual spot toward the far end of Prospect Park, sitting on a bench overlooking the water. Before they had Shaan, Maya and Dev would sit here for hours, just watching the boats drift by. They can make out the New Jersey skyline on the other side of the water, the Statue of Liberty just visible in the distance.

She removes their salads and the lemon-flavored sparkling waters she grabbed from the fridge. They eat in silence, pausing only to rock Shaan's stroller.

Maya takes in her surroundings—the place that has always made her feel so at peace—and waits to feel something. Anything.

She fixates on Dev adjusting the pacifier in Shaan's mouth, her mind completely blank.

I know I love you, she thinks as she stares at her husband. *But for some reason I don't know how to access that love right now.*

He turns to her with an annoyed look on his face. "You're always upset about something. Always."

She now fixates on an ant on the ground that's carrying a crumb of bread. *Look at that little guy go.*

"Hello? Did you hear me?"

She looks up. "Sorry, what?"

He just shakes his head in response. She doesn't bother asking what was said.

Another minute passes in silence.

Dev finally sighs. "You make me feel so shitty."

Maya's body registers the anger, and her muscles tense up, her face reddening. But her mind doesn't. It's like her brain and body are two separate entities. One cares enough to be angry, and the other doesn't.

So she settles for something in between.

Pettiness.

"I make *you* feel shitty? I didn't realize it was so shitty for you to be able to live your life as if nothing's changed, while I'm over here drowning."

Dev grabs his hair in frustration. "Am I not allowed to have feelings, too? You make me feel like I barely contribute anything. And then when I try to offer suggestions, you don't want to hear them, let alone take them."

"Your suggestions are always for me to just outsource things and get someone else to help out. It's just not that simple. Besides, the person I want more help from, more initiative from, is you. But clearly you just want to absolve any and all responsibility."

"Right, right, of course." Dev nods derisively. "So when I try to suggest things that could help, that's not good enough. And then when I ask you to just tell me what to do, that makes you mad. I can't win."

"For the millionth time, I don't want to have to tell you what to do. I wish you would just do it."

"Yeah, well, unfortunately I'm not a mind reader."

"You don't need to be a mind reader to know you should coparent your own child."

It's physically impossible for her to empathize with her husband in the way he wants her to. It has been for some time now. That part of her brain is completely shut off to her, and she's too drained to try to revive it.

"Every day, there's something, Maya. No, every goddamn

minute. Whenever I take the subway home from work, I run through a mental checklist of what's going to bother you when I walk through the front door."

His words settle over her, filling the miles of space between them. She hears them but doesn't fully process them.

"I'm sorry to be such a goddamn burden," Maya mutters.

"Come on. I didn't say that."

"No, I get it, okay? You hate coming home to us. Sorry, to *me.* You hate that this whole motherhood thing didn't come as easily to me as it did to your mom, to Alaina, to all the other women you know. You hate that I complain and can't just pay my way out of problems like you learned to do growing up. You hate that I have to work nonstop. You hate that you married me in the first place, and you hate that I had your baby. Good talk."

Dev clenches his jaw. Another minute passes. Two. Three. Each daring the other to break the silence. This is their thing now, apparently.

"I don't even know what to say to you anymore," he finally says. "You're not happy with your life. With *our* life. I don't think you have been for a long time."

Maya runs her flats through the trimmed grass. The sky is tinted pink and purple. Usually, the late summer brings her relief. But now all it brings to mind is the end of her maternity leave. She has a few weeks to fix her marriage, her company, and her relationship with Shaan before she returns to work full-time.

The only thing waiting for her on the other side of this is more guilt. And the pill only gets her so far. It's not enough.

"What's so wrong that you can't manage to be happy, even for a day?" Dev continues. "Like, even with my mom just then, you got *so* set off. Are things really that bad?"

"So you're saying I have it so great, that I should just be, what? Fine? And you're seriously saying this right after I've been asked—no, *ordered*—to leave my own company?"

There it is. The anger has finally made its way up to her brain. And it's catching fire.

"I didn't s—"

"No, I am so sick of you minimizing my experience, or worse, being totally clueless about my struggles. So why don't I give you some insider info on what's been going on for me?"

Somewhere, she hears a faint voice. A relic of her old self. *Stop, Maya. Don't go down this path. This isn't you.*

But she can't stop. She isn't that person anymore. She's someone she no longer recognizes.

Within seconds, she's shouting, voicing every grievance she's harbored against him for months, years. His impossible mother, his privileged upbringing, his conflict avoidance, his false promises to her when they agreed to grow their family. She's rage and release, rage and release.

Out of the corner of her eye, she sees a nearby group of parents sprawled out across a white picnic blanket. One of the women from the group nervously glances over in their direction and says something to the people around her.

Then, and only then, does Maya stop to take a breath.

Dev's eyes have been downcast the entire time, and when he finally looks up at her, he's in shock.

A woman in a pink leopard-print sports bra and matching leggings jogs past them, doing that awkward, breathy "Hi." If they were the old Dev and Maya, this kind of interruption would have broken the tension, stopping the fight in its tracks.

But they're not the couple they used to be.

Dev's still staring at her, and in a voice so soft she almost doesn't hear it, he says, "Are you done now?"

She nods.

"Okay." He stands up. The smooth, even tone of his words stings far more than anger ever could, almost cracking through her hardened exterior to pave way for something much, much worse. *Almost.*

Dev grabs Shaan's stroller and starts pushing it toward the park's entrance.

Maya jogs after him. "Wait, where are you going?"

"Home."

"Come on. Don't go."

"'Come on, don't go'? Seriously? After everything you just unloaded over there?" He motions back to the bench they were sitting on. Their spot.

She takes a deep breath, her anger slowly waning. "I'm sorry for airing it all out like that. I think we just need to talk."

Dev shakes his head. "I think you just talked a *lot*."

"You know what I mean."

"There's nothing for me to say to you right now."

And just like that, she's angry again.

"Really? After all that, you have nothing to say? This keeps happening. I get upset and you completely shut down. And then we don't move forward."

Dev looks up in exasperation, taking a step away from her and lifting his elbows to the back of his head. "I'm sorry I'm not exactly in the mood to sit and chat after I just got chewed out like that." His voice is laced with an uncharacteristic sarcasm, a biting edge. "You're… I don't know what you are. You're someone else."

"I'm sorry."

Is she, though? She knows she *should* feel sorry. But knowing what to feel and actually feeling it are two very different things.

"You're always so angry. Always."

"No, I'm not. C'mon. We never want to end our days like this, remember?" She's referring to Dev's insistence that they never go to bed angry. Maya had heard this marital advice many times before—during wedding toasts, at bridal showers, in women's magazines—but she never saw it in practice until she met Dev. Mom and Dad went to sleep angry at each other almost every night.

Dev takes a step away from her and stares at the sky. When he looks back at her, he's squinting, studying her like she's under a microscope. And then his eyes widen first in recognition, then in fear.

"Oh my God. Alaina was right."

Maya rolls her eyes. "Okay, what does Alaina have to do with this?"

Dev starts pacing, tugging at his hair. "She called me after she saw you, that day you were at the café with Liz. She said you've seemed different lately and asked me if you were still taking those supplements. I told her no. Because *you* told me no." Maya can't tell if he's talking to her or to himself. "But you are, aren't you?"

She opens her mouth to respond but Dev says, "You know what? Whatever." He starts walking off in the opposite direction, pushing Shaan's stroller out in front.

"Wait!" Maya calls.

"For what?" Dev spins around. "For you to keep lying to me? What the hell is going on? How can I trust you?"

She wants to tell him so badly. She can't carry this heavy weight alone anymore. But he wouldn't understand—or worse, he'd keep tabs on her to make sure she never takes another guilt pill again. And she desperately needs them just to make it through the day. She doesn't want to face the person she's become on the other side of them.

He stands still for a long second, just staring at her, then shakes his head in disbelief, like he's erasing the image of her from his mind. "God, I… I don't know you. I don't."

"Dev, come on. Can we please just talk this out?"

"I don't want to." Dev sighs and after a few seconds, adds, "Maybe I don't want any of this anymore."

His words are a swift punch to her stomach. Her heart plummets.

"Did you actually just say that to me? And *mean it*?"

In all of their arguments, Dev's never said anything like that. Maya is the one who loses her cool, says words she wants to immediately take back.

But now, Dev's silence is all the confirmation she needs.

The things that are supposed to come naturally to people, like working a job, starting a family, being a parent, are breaking her. Maybe other people are meant for all of this, but she clearly isn't. The past few months are evidence of that.

She thinks back to an image someone had shared in one of those Facebook parenting groups. It was a map of New York City. A red dot indicated where a new parent who'd joined the group lived. When Maya first saw the map, she was reassured by the numerous red dots scattered throughout lower Manhattan. There were new parents all around her. She wasn't alone. But now she wonders if there could be a map that shows the whereabouts of the struggling mothers, the *what did I get myself into?* mothers. Where are they? Or is she the only one?

"I'm going home," he says.

Maya starts to close the distance between them. "I'll come—"

Dev holds his hand up. "Don't. Just don't. I'm serious, Maya."

All she can do is stand there, frozen in place, as his silhouette gets smaller and smaller in the distance.

Only when the sky turns dark and a chilling breeze fills the air does she start making her way back home.

BUSINESS BUZZ BLOG

Exploring Some Recent—and Worrisome—Patterns Among Female Founders

By Alexis Clear

Published July 27, 2019, 8:00 AM EDT

It has been a brutal year for women in business.

In January, Anna Gilbert stepped down from her women's underwear company, Improve Her, following allegations of employee misconduct. Just one month later, Sonia Bosworth announced she would no longer be CEO of her clothing brand, Refinery, after employees took to social media to reveal multiple instances of racism committed by Bosworth in the workplace. Three more prominent founders, Whitney Davidson, Selena Marsden, and Mary Sanders, have also stepped down from their companies this past year.

And, most recently, a recent *Business Insider* article indicates that Maya Patel, founder and CEO of Medini, may be next. Rumors about an intense work culture—to the point that employees have had to cancel vacations and take on extra work during off time—have been circulating for months. And while Patel hasn't been known for the same offenses allegedly committed by the other aforementioned founders, we've learned that it can take years for employees to feel comfortable sharing the truth of what it's really like to work at a certain company.

Of course, plenty of research has shown that women tend to be held to higher standards than their male counterparts. Male CEOs and founders can criticize team members and fire employees at a moment's notice. Oh, and no need for them to spend countless hours building a social media brand, because who would expect that of them, given their busy schedules? (Would anyone have cared if Steve Jobs wasn't on Instagram? Were people anonymously quoting Adam Neumann for berating employees?) Less than 2 percent of total VC funding goes to all-female founding teams.

But maybe there's something to learn from these female founders I've referenced here. Each of them quickly became the faces of their brands and gained big followings on social media. They also post content that reflects the stated values of their companies. Anna Gilbert and Sonia Bosworth were known for their prominent Twitter profiles, while Patel's Instagram account has over a million followers. Is it possible that by fusing their own image with their brand, the lines between work, personal life, and performance became too blurry?

The answer may be unclear for now. What we *do* know is that when women in business fail, the impact is felt far and wide. It only makes the tech landscape more challenging for current female founders and deters future ones.

28

THE SCENT OF HONEST COMPANY'S sweet orange-and-vanilla baby soap hits her the second she walks through the front door.

Down the hall, she hears Dev sing, "Bath time!"

Maya tiptoes toward the bathroom. The sound of running water almost drowns out the other voice. But not quite.

"Sorry I had to run earlier. We needed to eat," Dev says.

"It's okay, beta. Is Maya there?"

"No. She's not home yet."

"Okay, well, I'm not sure how to say this but..."

"What is it?"

"I've been so worried about Shaan."

"Mom, I know. But I told you, he's fine."

"Yes, but you know Maya has her own way of doing things. With him, with you, with...*everything*."

"And what's that supposed to mean?" Maya's heart lifts at the defensiveness in Dev's tone. Even after the worst fight they've ever had, he still wants to protect her.

"She's not like us," her mother-in-law continues. "I've told you that from the beginning. She's different—the way she thinks, her background. Her family didn't raise her with the same, let's say, *standards*, or values, as us. I've tried to hold my tongue before, but I just can't anymore. Because now it's affecting my grandson. And I'm worried about him."

Maya anxiously waits for Dev to cut his mom off, to tell her she's out of line and not to say anything like that ever again.

But after a long pause, he says, "I'm worried about Shaan, too."

Her stomach drops. *But he's been telling* me *not to worry this whole time!*

"And I think we need to make some changes. I might need your help with Shaan now more than ever..."

Maya's breath catches in her throat. Thanks to Shaan's babbles, all she hears are snippets of Dev's voice: *I need to think... rash decision...you were right.*

She can't bear to hear another word. All she can focus on is the *whoosh* of the water, the light splashes of Shaan kicking his feet. Just when she thought the day couldn't get any worse, it does. A lot worse.

She takes quiet steps to the bedroom and closes the door as hot tears trickle down her face. Maya glances around the room, feeling more out of place than ever in her own home.

They're better off without you.

Her eyes land on a framed photo from their wedding. She and Dev are draped in rose garlands matching their traditional red-and-white outfits. Pieces of rice are flying all around them. Dev's mouth is open mid-laugh. In the background, Mom's wiping tears of joy from her face.

Moments after the photo was taken, several aunties came up to her and told Maya she was lucky to find someone like

Dev. *Treat him well,* one of them said. *He's a gem. Make sure he's always taken care of.*

Her fingers trace Dev's framed face, his words ringing in her mind. *Maybe I don't want any of this anymore.*

She puts the photo back on her nightstand, her eyes lingering on the drawer underneath. In less than a split second, she locates the bottle pushed toward the back and takes one hot-pink pill. When that doesn't instantly make her feel better, she swallows another.

Maya brings the little brown bottle with her and sprawls out on the living room couch, her limbs stretched and heavy.

The water in the tub is still running and she faintly hears Shaan's splashes.

This morning, Dev woke up and cleaned the kitchen, then washed and dried Shaan's bottles. He hasn't gotten impatient with Shaan, or frustrated, or exhausted like you have. He's better at parenting. He's better than you. He's better.

The word cycles around different sentences in her mind, each one a punch to her stomach.

He's better. He can find someone better. They're better off without you.

Her head is spinning, and she has to sit down to fight the dizziness. She feels it settle into her body, taking up space in her sternum. She fills a cup of water and downs two more pills. Anything to make the noise stop. She takes another. Another.

And another and another and another.

They'll be fine without you. With Dev's patience and affection, he'll learn the ins and outs of child care in no time. Shaan will have a parent who's present and secure, calm and capable. You never deserved either of them in the first place.

Maya pulls out her phone and scrolls through her contacts until she finds the name she's looking for. She dials the number, but it goes straight to voicemail.

She waits for the tone, then says, "I can't do this anymore.

I'm so sorry. I just can't." The rest of the words come out in a jumble of syllables and stifled guttural sobs.

She hangs up and approaches the bathroom door like she's waist-deep in molasses. From a faraway place, she can hear her son giggling in the tub. The squeak of a rubber ducky.

Better off without you. Better, better, better.

Maya knocks once. Twice.

She hears Dev's muffled voice on the other side of the door. "One second, Mom. Maya?"

"I need some space tonight, so I'm staying at the motel."

No response.

"Did you hear me?" Her voice is monotone. Deadpan.

"I said one second, Mom," he repeats, irritation in his voice. "Maya, what did you say? It's really hard to hear you. I'm almost done with his bath. Just come in."

She can't. She can't go in there. Because if Dev takes one look at her, he'll know.

So she doubles down, her voice louder.

"I need some space tonight. I'm spending the night with my parents at the motel."

There's another pause, and then "Seriously? Shouldn't we talk about any—"

But before Dev has the chance to open the bathroom door, Maya turns around, grabs her packed bag off the kitchen counter, and leaves the apartment.

PHONE CALL

July 26, 2019, 9:44 PM EDT, 00:00:23

MIRA PATEL: "Dev, beta! How are you?" [*Background noise of a television.*] "We were just thinking about you!"

DEV MEHTA: "Has Maya gotten there yet?" [*Sounds of heavy breathing and pacing.*]

MIRA PATEL: [*Confused.*] "Gotten where? Is everything okay?"

DEV MEHTA: "Yes, please just tell me." [*The sound of typing.*] "I know she probably doesn't want to talk to me but can you please, please just tell her I'll be at the motel soon?"

MIRA PATEL: "I'm sorry, beta. I have no idea what you're talking about."

DEV MEHTA: "What do you mean? She's still not there?"

MIRA PATEL: "Maya isn't here. She never told us she was coming… Wait, what's going on?"

DEV MEHTA: "I'm not sure. I have to go but I'll call back as soon as I can."

29

MAYA'S EYES SLOWLY OPEN AND SHE'S in the back seat of a car. It takes her several seconds to register she's on a suburban road. The road looks familiar. *Very* familiar. She just can't pinpoint why that is.

The car pulls up to what appears to be a warehouse, but there's no sign out front. It looks abandoned. Weeds cover the bottom windows, opaque from pollution and time. Across the street, there's a Dunkin' Donuts that fills her with a mix of sadness and longing. A distant figure walks to their car in the lot across the street.

A faint alarm bell goes off in her mind, and she feels her brain working hard to pinpoint something, something important. Something that threads together all the unanswered questions in her mind.

She returns her gaze to the stranger on the other side of the street.

Help me. Please, help me.

NEW YORK DAILY NEWS

Breaking News

Published August 4, 2019, 12:33 PM EDT

At an early-morning press conference, the New York Police Department released an update on thirty-three-year-old Maya Patel's missing person case: earlier this week, a black crossbody bag was found on the corner of North End Avenue and Vesey Street. Forensic lab reports have since surfaced that confirm Patel's fingerprints.

"The bag was found in mint condition, near the ferry stop at Brookfield Place Terminal. The only thing we found inside was a small generic pill container with no label on it," Officer Kyle Richardson announced. "We are searching the water for any signs of Patel's whereabouts."

This is an ongoing investigation.

30

MAYA WAKES UP TO SUNLIGHT POKING through two dirty windows.

It takes her a minute to take in the white counters covered in test tubes and beakers. The trays with vials of blood. A couple microscopes. Boxes of blue latex gloves. An easel in the corner with a giant diagram of the human brain.

She has no idea where she is, no recollection of how she got here.

A jolt of pain travels from her head to her neck. Something's not right.

Where is she?

Maya tries to sit up and realizes she's in a hospital bed. She panics, frantically looking around the room.

There's someone else here. They're leaning against the counter farthest from her, fixated on something. From her vantage point, she can make out a white lab coat.

"Hello?" Maya tries to get out of the chair. "Can somebody help me?"

"You're going to be okay," a far-off voice says.

"I think I might be…" She trails off, too fatigued to get the words out.

"It's okay, you're in good hands now."

"Did I fall asleep?" When Maya tries to fully open her eyes, all she can see is an amorphous blue-and-gray blob. Her head feels like it's stuffed with cotton.

"You've been a little in and out since you got here. Don't worry. This will pass."

"I think I took too many pills… I feel really sick… I…" Her words slur as if she's had several cocktails.

"I know. You'll feel better soon. The situation's monitored and under control."

A primitive part of her brain warns her that something's wrong. Very wrong.

But a heaviness settles over her, and the world goes dark.

The next time Maya gains consciousness, her eyes snap open. She remembers.

PHONE CALL

July 26, 2019, 7:42 PM EDT, 00:00:23

CALLER: Hey, I just listened to your message. We'll figure this out. I'm ten minutes from your apartment and can pick you up. We'll get through this, okay? Are Dev and Shaan home?

MAYA PATEL: Yes. Dev's giving Shaan a bath.

CALLER: Okay, I'd definitely let Dev know you won't be home for the rest of the night so he doesn't panic. Otherwise, we both know he'd freak out. I'm turning onto your street, by the way. I'll be parked right outside.

MAYA PATEL: Okay.

CALLER: The Uber's here. See you soon. And hey, I'm here for you. Always. You know that.

[End of call.]

31

“OH GOOD, YOU’RE AWAKE. THAT TOOK longer than expected.”

A jolt of pain travels from Maya’s head to neck, and it feels like she’s being electrocuted.

Something’s not right. She tries to get up again and realizes it’s not her weak muscles that are the problem—it’s her legs that are tied to the bed.

“Where are we?” Maya croaks, her eyes slowly taking in her surroundings.

“My lab.”

“I thought your products were made in upstate New York?”

“*Those* are.” Liz swivels around in her chair. “But this is where the real magic happens.”

“Where’s everyone else?” Maya’s voice echoes in the vast emptiness.

“I keep things here as separate as possible from Women Rise. No one else knows about this place, except for my lab partner.

It's all mine." Liz runs her manicured hands across the counter as if it's a beloved pet. "Sometimes I can't believe it's all real."

A ball of fear settles in Maya's stomach. This can't be happening. Any second now, she'll wake up from this nightmare.

"Did you notice on the car ride here that we're in Jersey?" Liz continues. "After watching your segment on the *Today* show, I thought we were destined, in a way." She laughs to herself. "Your motel is right down the street from here. I first set up shop here years ago, and yet we never ran into each other. What are the odds?"

"Liz, please get me out of here right now." Maya tries raising her voice, but it comes out strained and soft. She pictures Dev holding Shaan, and her heart drops. "I need my phone."

"Not yet. We have to wait your reaction out. I gave you something that was supposed to counteract the addictive effect of the pills. But it isn't working for some reason." Liz squints at the beaker in concentration.

There's a lump in Maya's throat. She needs to get out of here. She needs to go home. "Why are you doing this to me?"

"*Doing* this to you? I'm *helping* you. I've been monitoring you and trying to treat your withdrawal." Liz's facial expression shifts from calmness to contempt. "But of course you want to play the victim. Even though you always knew you were taking something that wasn't in stores, that was unreleased to the public. You were so skeptical the first time I told you about it. I never anticipated you'd go so overboard."

Maya's head is pounding, and she battles wave after wave of nausea. "I trusted you."

"See, this is the problem with you, Maya," Liz continues. "When you find yourself in a difficult position, you don't take any damn responsibility."

"This was all a mistake. A big mistake," Maya says. Her head is spinning and she strains to get the words out. "I never should have taken these pills. You took advantage of me."

"You're kidding, right? By pushing you to advocate for yourself more so you could keep your damn company afloat, or by connecting you with one of the most powerful investors in the city? Is that me taking advantage of you?"

"You can't give these to anyone else. You have to stop." Maya wishes her voice was stronger, wishes *she* was stronger. But she still can't move. She considers screaming but knows that she can't, no matter how hard she tries. She can barely talk above a whisper.

Liz waves her hand, changing the subject. "I was going to tell you this weekend, but I got one of my contacts to place you in Oprah's Favorite Things list this winter. And I can get you back on the *Today* show like *that*." She snaps her fingers. "C'mon, Maya. Don't you want to make sure other women aren't held back by the same barriers as you?"

"Please, Liz. I want to go home. That's all I want, and I won't say a word about this to anyone. Please let me go."

She hates that the words shake as they leave her mouth, her cheeks warming as hot tears stream down her face.

"You know, I thought I saw something different in you. I thought you wanted more for yourself. That you wanted to have a great life and *be* great." Liz shakes her head. "But obviously I was wrong."

"I don't want any of this. Please, all I want is to go home." Maya's suddenly overcome with a wave of fatigue. She doesn't know how long she has until she'll lose consciousness again.

"I wish it were that simple. I expected more from you. I really did," Liz continues. "But now, you've become a liability. You could ruin my life's work."

Get out of here, an internal voice urges. *Do anything you can to escape.*

"Liz, I really don't feel well. I'm so weak. My hands won't stop shaking but I can't move the rest of my body. Please take me to the hospital."

"Trust me. The hospital won't know how to deal with this. Only I can help you," Liz says. There's an intense look on her face that Maya hasn't seen before. A darkness behind Liz's usual performative, lighthearted expression.

Her body sinks into the bed as if someone's pressing down on her shoulders. "Please, I'm begging you. I need to go to the hospital."

Liz ignores her.

"Please." She's sobbing now.

What if I never see my family again? Mom, Dad, Tarun? Dev and Shaan? Alaina and Ryan?

Maya finally summons the courage to ask the question she's been avoiding. "How long have I been here?"

"About nine days."

Maya's jaw drops. "*Nine* days? You've kept me here for over a week?"

"Does it matter?" Liz taps her foot to signal her impatience. "Nobody's looking for you. And if they try, they won't figure it out. I planted your black cross-body bag by Brookfield Place, close to the waterfront, then sent in a tip to the police. That'll be their primary search location for the time being. And the clock's ticking for you. The antidote to the pills isn't working. I thought it would be different this time."

"*This* time?"

Liz stands up and turns her back to Maya, preoccupying herself with something on the shelf. "I really thought I was being careful, that *we've* been careful," she says to herself. "Supplements don't have to be FDA tested, but we *still* got the pill tested out by a third-party lab. We made sure there weren't any contaminants or chemicals at toxic levels. But..." Liz's voice trails off.

Maya closes her eyes and wills herself to wake up. *Please be a dream. Please make these past three months one long, horrible nightmare.*

"I'm not sure where I went wrong," Liz murmurs to herself.

"Just tell me, Liz. Why me? Why did you target *me* specifically? And don't tell me it was a coincidence."

"For once, you're actually right. We haven't tested it on any new mothers or anyone from a diverse background. We needed to make sure it was just as effective in women of co—"

"You experimented on me because I'm a new mom who happens to be South Asian? Is this some kind of sick joke?" Maya's face heats.

"I strive to implement diversity and inclusivity in my work," Liz says point-blank.

"*Diversity* and *inclusivity*? Wow, you can't be serious. I've been the minority check-off before, but this is definitely a first."

"There you go again, playing the victim." Liz shakes her head. "I needed some way to know how much of the pill was *too* much. So I pushed you. And look at all that you've accomplished! You're welcome, by the way."

Maya's head is spinning. "Is this the part where you tell me you're the one who leaked Medini's search for a new CEO to the press, along with the Slack messages?" Maya asks. But she already knows the answer. She had filled Liz in on everything after her presentation, even sending her a screenshot of the company's Slack messages. Of course it was Liz. She's the one who's been pulling the strings from the very beginning.

"I knew you needed a push, so I gave you one. It was a win-win. I pushed you out of your comfort zone so you could save your company, and I got to see what the pill could do to someone on the highest of doses."

"How are you still able to spin this so that you're the hero? How fucking entitled are you? You can't use human beings as guinea pigs."

"Ha. You know, you're just like her," Liz says, lost in thought. "In more ways than one."

Maya knows exactly who she's referring to.

Liz scoffs. "Oh, Anita. She got so pulled into this from the beginning, before either of us even realized how effective this pill could be. And when we did, she wanted to bring in other people to make sure we were doing this the 'right' way—more rounds of testing, no experimenting on women without their signed consent, or without our mandatory disclosure on what our experiments entailed and what to expect. She was a real stickler for the rules. But unfortunately, the ones who follow the rules are rarely the ones who leave an impact."

"So you used another woman of color for your own gain. Where is she now? What ever happened to her?"

Liz doesn't say anything.

"No. You didn't... Oh my God." Maya thinks she's going to be sick. "Is she...?"

Liz just stares at her as if she said nothing at all.

Maya suddenly recalls all the different articles that were released in the wake of Anita Johnson's falling out with Liz and Limitless's shutdown. There was some vague public statement from Anita's team about her taking a break from the tech industry for a while.

But nobody has heard from her since. And Liz's silence couldn't be louder. The awareness settles over her and sends a shiver down her spine. Which stories will be spun about *her*?

Liz disappears to the far end of the room and unlocks a glass case full of lab equipment.

"What are you doing? Please don't do this. Please." Her heart is racing in her chest as Liz slowly walks back toward Maya, gliding across the floor. It's more terrifying than if she were to spring at her. Liz seems to be holding something behind her back, but Maya can't make out what it is.

She squirms in the bed, but she's tightly locked in. There's no way to escape this.

"You know, you don't look so great. I think you need to

get some rest. I promise this will all be over soon," Liz says, raising her arm.

That's when Maya sees the syringe.

"Please don't do this. I'm begging you. Liz, I'm a mother. A wife, a daughter. And my family—"

"I'm sorry things had to end this way. I really am."

"No! Please—"

Liz gives her one final, menacing smirk and Maya feels a painful sensation in her arm. Her eyelids become heavier, heavier, *heavier*, and the exposed pipes on the ceiling slowly fade to a blur. She vaguely catches a glimpse of the tail of a white lab coat billowing in the doorway and hears a faint buzzing sound.

The very last thing Maya sees is a shelf full of brown, translucent pill bottles.

And rows and rows of hot-pink pills.

32

THE FIRST THING SHE NOTICES IS THE stone under her bare feet.

Brass pots are hanging over the stove. The sky-blue painted walls are chipped. Okra seasoned with cumin is sizzling on the stove. Outside the barred window, a light gray monkey jumps across the trees.

Where is she? This isn't her home.

"Mira!" An older woman in a peach-colored cotton sari rushes into the kitchen. "They're almost here! What is taking you so long? The chai should already be poured!"

"I'm tired." A twentysomething woman, also dressed in a sari, slumps in a chair. "I've been cooking for them all day. I don't even know these people."

"If you don't do this, we have no other options." The older woman bends down to face her. "You have to make this work. Do you understand me?"

"Please, Mami," the young woman pleads. "I don't want to meet him. I don't want any of this at all."

"I know it's hard." The older woman's face softens. "But this is what we have to do, okay? And you'll make a better life for your daughter one day. Just as I'm trying to do for you."

Before the younger woman can say anything, the doorbell rings.

An infant boy and a young girl are sitting inside a large round clothing rack. The young boy crawls up the girl's leg.

"Shhh, we're hiding," she whispers.

He smiles, revealing two new bottom teeth.

"You lost them!" A man's voice echoes through the store.

"Me? You said *you* had them!" a woman replies.

The girl puts her hands over the boy's ears, then scoops him up.

"We're okay." The young girl giggles as they emerge from the clothes. "We were just playing hide-and-seek."

"You can't scare us like that," the woman says. "How did you even end up here?"

The girl's face becomes hot and the boy curls against her. "I saw a shirt I liked..."

"We can't buy anything from here. If you didn't find what you wanted from the clearance section, we have to go," the man says, guiding them all out the store.

A dry-erase board with a diagram of a pregnant woman.

Health class.

The people sitting around her are busy writing secret notes to pass to their friends or doodling in the margins of their composition notebooks.

On the bottom of the board are the following words:

A female fetus is born with all of the eggs she'll ever have.

When your mother was in your grandmother's womb, the

egg that eventually formed you was there. This means you spent months in your grandmother's body.

When she gets home from school, she's excited to share what she learned today, but her mother tells her it's time to learn how to fold towels. They're expecting more guests than usual this weekend.

The diamond on a young woman's left hand glitters as she walks to the table. Their pasta has arrived. The waiter is adding Parmesan cheese to the steaming plates. But the people sitting at the table haven't noticed her yet.

"And you're sure about this? About her?" a gruff voice asks.

A young man's voice replies, "Of course I'm sure. And I don't want to ever hear anything like that ever again. She's going to be my wife."

The young woman retreats back to the bathroom and stays until the young man messages her to ask where she is.

They're so excited for us, he tells her on the cab ride back to his place. *I knew they would be.*

A woman stands in a bathroom, the stick in her hand revealing two telltale blue lines.

She calls out to her husband in the next room over. "I think it's… Just come in here!"

She isn't sure how she's supposed to feel, but the second she sees him—the smile stretched across his face, tears starting to trickle onto his beard—she knows it'll be okay. With him, it'll all be okay.

He wraps her in his arms, engulfing her in his natural woodsy scent.

"You're going to be an amazing mother. I just know it." When she doesn't say anything, he asks, "Aren't you excited?"

"Of course I am." She puts on that winning smile she's perfected over the years.

I am. I am. I am.

The hospital bed.

"Two more pushes, honey. Give me two more." The doctor's kind and firm gaze is fixed on her.

She feels another contraction.

A guttural sound escapes her, one she didn't know she was capable of making. The room blurs into shades of blue. Scrubs, latex gloves, sterile drapes.

"Push and let go. C'mon, let's push and let go," the doctor says.

She pushes.

Let go. Let go. Let go.

In the distance, a grown woman watches two kids play outside. She squints at them in recognition. She knows them. They're kicking a soccer ball back and forth in a motel parking lot. Suddenly, the figures vanish, replaced with the blinking red lights of an ambulance. A mother and a father are sobbing, clutching a small child in between them.

I'm sorry, the woman cries. *I'm so sorry.*

But nobody can hear her.

NEW YORK NEWS

Breaking News

Published August 5, 2019, 10:47 AM EDT

In an early-morning press conference, the NPYD has confirmed that after a total of ten days missing, Maya Patel was found late last night in Edison, New Jersey.

The officers on the scene report that the tech CEO and Instagram personality was discovered in critical condition.

She was rushed to the hospital and is being treated for a drug overdose. An inside source reports that, as of this morning, she has entered a comatose state.

"Maya's been struggling for a long time," says the source. "It's good she's finally getting the help she needs."

This is an evolving story. Updates will be shared here.

AUGUST

now

NEW YORK NEWS

Breaking News

Updated August 6, 2019, 6:27 PM EDT

According to a recent update from New Jersey Medical Center, at this time, no conclusions can be made about the drugs in Maya Patel's system. Initial testing has revealed trace amounts of benzodiazepines, MDMA, and hypnotics. The combination found so far has not been linked to any other known pharmaceuticals. We are actively working with leading pharmacology experts and chemists to learn as much as we can about these substances and will release a statement once we have an update.

33

AT FIRST, THE LIGHT IS BLINDING. FOR so long, all she's known is darkness.

It takes several minutes for her eyes to adjust. She can make out the tiled ceiling and the bodies in swift motion around her. The air smells like a mixture of sickness and antiseptic. Her arm is punctured and bandaged and attached to a tube that's feeding her a constant stream of IV fluids.

"Maya? Maya, can you hear me? *Maya?*"

She recognizes the voice. She looks up to see a woman clutching Maya's bed rail. It takes her several seconds to realize it isn't just any woman.

It's her best friend.

"Alaina? What are you doing here?" Maya stifles a yawn, her eyelids fluttering. Exhaustion settles over her like a weight.

Alaina fiddles with the stethoscope peeking out of her lab coat pocket. Her name is embroidered on the right side. "You're in the hospital. We're still running tests, but it looks like you've had a very bad reaction to those pills you've been taking over the past few months."

"What day is it? How long have I been here?"

"It's Thursday, August 8. They found you and brought you here Monday night. But don't worry. You'll be okay, and your vitals are finally stabilizing. You should get some sleep."

Maya covers her eyes as she tries to remember the events of the past couple days. "What happened to me?"

"I can't really speak to the investigation, but I can fill you in a bit on the medical side of things. We're still not quite sure what these pills did to you, but you came in with severe withdrawal symptoms and intense emotional dysregulation. All we know for sure is that they likely had an addictive quality to them and were—are—potentially fatal in high doses. You've had multiple seizures since you've been here and you…you almost…" Maya watches her best friend's face scrunch up, and she knows what Alaina was about to say. "All that matters is that you're stable. You're safe now, and you're going to be okay. You're in good hands."

Maya slumps back into the stiff pillow.

"I'm so sorry," she says. She repeats it again and again, unsure of who she's even apologizing to at this point.

I'm so sorry. I'm so sorry. I'm so sorry.

So many of her emotions have been numb, practically nonexistent, for weeks, and now she feels all of them rising within her at full force. Guilt, for one. But also regret, sadness, longing. Love.

"Alaina, what happens next?"

"You'll to have to go into a detox program for a little while. I'll have another doctor give you information about that."

"Detox? Another doctor?" Maya asks, fear all over her face.

Alaina nods sympathetically. "You overdosed, Maya. We're not yet certain what the pills have done to your body. We just need to move forward with a clear plan. And I can't be your doctor. Forget that this isn't even my field of specialty, but I'm your best friend. I'm too close to the entire situation. I have to let someone else take over." She pauses. "But you'll be just fine with Dr. Saul. This is her area of expertise."

Tears well up in Maya's eyes. "I've really fucked up. More than I can probably even process right now. I'm so sorry. I know that isn't anything close to a sufficient apology for everything I did. But I really am sorry."

Alaina leans forward, her eyes soft. "I'm sorry I didn't know you were struggling this much. None of us did."

"I never told you. I thought I had it all under control." Maya bursts into tears. "Where's Shaan? And Dev? And my parents and Tarun?"

How could she do this to them? What kind of a mother, a wife, a daughter, just disappears and leaves her family behind?

"Dev and Shaan should be here any second. Tarun is with your parents at the motel."

"Are they okay?" Maya asks.

Alaina's silence is enough of an answer.

"Maya!" Dev emerges from the hallway and races toward them. He gives Alaina a hug and thanks her. Shaan is strapped in the baby carrier, his limbs dangling. The poor thing is probably in sensory overload from being in a hospital. Shaan smiles when he sees Maya, exposing two rows of pink gums.

"Oh my God. You're here. You're really here." Dev buries his face into her shoulder. He smells like a mixture of laundry detergent and baby lotion.

He smells like home.

34

HER SCHEDULE IS THE SAME EVERY DAY. She wakes up early, eats breakfast in the dining hall, and sits in a meditation group. Then she attends a group therapy session. Almost a week has passed like this.

Carol, a sixty-five-year-old mom who was prescribed oxycodone after a surgery but kept increasing her daily dosage, currently has the floor. "I was repressing the way I've felt over the years because nobody ever taught me how to manage my emotions. It really has been that complicated *and* simple the entire time."

Other group members nod along, some sharing words of empathy. Paul, an investment banker in his forties, chimes in to say he realized he was addicted to work in the same way he's been addicted to alcohol.

"Maya?" Kaitlin, their group therapist, faces her. "You haven't spoken much today. I'm wondering if anything is coming up for you?"

"Yes. Many things," Maya says, her voice echoing in the room. Her folding chair screeches as she moves closer to the inner circle. "I've tried to numb my emotions down, too, because I thought they were what was holding me back. But really, it's been the superhuman expectations I've always put on myself, in every area of my life, that made everything seem so unmanageable."

She wants to say more, but her thoughts are a blur. Even though it's been days since she was discharged from detox and moved to the rehab floor of the hospital, her body is all out of whack. The discontinuation symptoms are causing sharp pangs in her chest, fits of nausea, and a constant headache that creeps to the base of her neck.

But her dreams are the worst part. Because they're not really dreams, they're memories that come back to life while she sleeps. Images of Shaan's tiny, vulnerable body on the weighing scale at the pediatrician's office, Dev's form slumped in defeat on their sectional, Alaina staring at her like she's a complete stranger, herself sobbing in the stairwell outside her office, a never-ending supply of hot-pink pills.

After group therapy, she walks down the hall to meet with her individual therapist.

"Maya, you've got a visitor," Jean, the rehab unit's receptionist, says when she sees her. "I didn't catch her name but she said she's a friend. She's waiting for you in the dining hall."

Maya's breath catches in her throat. She's thought of all the things she wants to say to Liz but doesn't feel ready to share them yet. She clenches her fists and takes deep, heavy breaths. How dare Liz show up here at Maya's place of recovery? Recovery from *her*?

But when she enters the dining hall, the person waiting for her is in teal scrubs, her dark curly hair falling in ringlets around her shoulders.

"Alaina? You're really here?"

She shrugs in response. "I had to see you. Make sure you're okay."

"You have no idea how good it is to see your face." Maya hugs her best friend tight.

"I'm still pissed at you, you know."

Maya nods. "I know. I would be, too."

Alaina sighs. "But more than anything, I'm so relieved you're okay."

"I know you—"

"I thought you died." Alaina's eyes well with tears. "None of us thought you were going to make it."

Maya faces the floor, shame coating her entire body. "I'm so sorry for what I put you through."

She goes in for another hug, and for a long moment they just hold each other. When Alaina pulls away, she snickers. "For what it's worth, and I never thought I'd say this, but I think I'm starting to see what you saw in her. Liz."

"What?"

They sit down at an empty table. "I get why you were so drawn to her," Alaina continues. "You know, for a long time, I was annoyed at how enamored you were of her. Probably even a little jealous—okay, a lot jealous. But I get now how important it is for you to have people who understand your unique situation as a mom and CEO. I shouldn't have judged you so harshly for that. I guess I just saw you acting differently, plus we weren't talking as much. And then there was all that shit going on with me and Ryan… I just felt so distant from you."

Maya gently reaches for Alaina's arm. "I hate that we weren't talking as much."

"Me, too."

"I remember feeling that way after you had the girls," Maya says. "It was like your life suddenly changed. And I was happy for you—*so* happy for you—but sometimes it felt like we were on two different planets. You with your new mom friends in Jersey, and me in the city living the same life as always."

Alaina's face changes with realization. "I could tell things were different between us back then, but I couldn't pinpoint what exactly the issue was."

"Really? I didn't know you could sense that." Their friendship has always oscillated through cycles of forgiveness and faith, even if they weren't aware of it at the time. Maybe that's what marks a true friendship—understanding that even when both people fall short, they'll still always have each other.

"But we can't let that happen again," Maya says resolutely. "We have to keep trying, even when things get hard. We have to make time for each other. *Talk* to each other."

Alaina nods in agreement. "You're right. We do."

Maya has heard so much talk about how marriages require consistent effort on both ends, but friendships aren't so different.

This *is what it means to fully show up for another woman*, Maya thinks. *This is what female friendship looks like. This is love.*

She loves the Alaina who came home from overnight shifts in their twenties, exhausted and ravenous, but satisfied and proud. She loves the Alaina who argues with her mother any chance she gets. She loves the Alaina who constantly doubts her own mothering, even though she's only ever been an amazing parent to her two daughters. She loves the Alaina whose vulnerability and strength allowed her to commit to couples therapy. She loves the Alaina who demands to live life on her own terms, even if they don't always make sense to the outside world.

"So, how are you doing?" Maya asks. "With everything?"

Alaina takes a beat to respond, pulling her hair into a bun with one of Jade's scrunchies. "Let's not get into my shit right now."

"No, I want to know." Maya squeezes Alaina's hand, which has become perpetually dry from years of applying hospital hand sanitizers.

"Hmm, well, let's see." Alaina crosses one leg over the other. "I've finally realized that all along, I've only advanced in this job because it's what my parents—well, really, my *mom*—wanted for me. Speaking of which, I need to set some firm boundaries with her going forward and not let her get to me so much. Sometimes I'm so annoyed with her I can't even see when she's coming from a good place."

Maya lets out a whistle. "I hear that."

"I also realized I haven't been home as much for the girls and Ryan. At first this made me so angry because I felt like I had to be the overworked, cranky parent in those in-between moments when I *was* home, while he got to be the 'fun' parent. But instead of talking to him about it, I silently grew resentful." *Feel that one, too.*

"It's not your fault," Maya says, shaking her head. "You always had so much going on, you probably didn't even process it all until it escalated."

"That's exactly what happened," Alaina confirms. "And you know what? You've been right about the power of guilt. I'm not accepting the program director job because I've spent too many years feeling guilty. Guilty for being out of the house so much, then for being tired and short with the girls when I *am* home. Guilty that my mom spent so many years working hard to build a life for us, then guilty for not living up to her expectations. Not making her proud. It's like I internalized her guilt, combined it with my own, and forced myself to keep grinding until I was totally depleted."

Alaina pauses for a moment, furrowing her brow. "Don't get me wrong. I hate Ryan for not doing his part. But I also see that I chose to put so much pressure on myself and became a different, more bitter woman in the process. I'm certainly not the woman he started dating in med school."

Maya frowns, considering this. "Well, to be fair, he isn't the man you started dating then, either." She thinks back to all the times Alaina described Ryan as a nerd who didn't realize he was handsome until they began dating. It reminded Maya of a gender-swapped version of the romantic comedies she watched in high school, where the female lead got a big "makeover" (aka took off her glasses) and became an overnight shoo-in for prom queen.

"I know he's not. We've both done things that got us to this place. I mean, hell, I've spent years resenting the nonstop, contradictory expectations people have put on me—*Be the best at work! Get married! Be a perfect mother!*" Alaina sighs. "We're going to keep working on things. On us." She looks to Maya for approval. "Do you think that's silly?"

"No, not at all," Maya assures her. "I think it's brave. I'm really proud of you."

"Thanks." Alaina leans her head against her. "He's going to see how we can spend more time together as a family, and as a couple. We agreed that if we keep going down this path, we won't recognize each other in a few years. We need to do this for our little family. We *need* each other."

Alaina scans Maya's face. "What's wrong?"

"I remember thinking Shaan and Dev would be better off without me." Her voice is soft, almost muffled.

Alaina looks shocked and grabs her hand. "That is *so* not true. Not at all. How could you think that?"

Tears start trickling down Maya's face. "I felt like I was failing Shaan and Dev in every possible way. No matter how hard I tried, I couldn't get the hang of being a mom. I felt like I wasn't good enough for either of them. I love them so much, but I couldn't find a way to manage our new life together. It seemed easier to just not feel the weight of it all anymore, all the pressure."

"Hey, we've all been there," Alaina says, her eyes full of understanding. "I just wish I knew you were feeling this way."

Maya sniffles. "I thought I could handle it all on my own."

"*Nobody* is supposed to go through this alone, Maya." Alaina's beeper abruptly rings. "Damn it, I've gotta run. I'll check in on you later." She gives her a tight squeeze.

Jean comes up to her later that afternoon. "You've got more visitors! Boy, are you popular!"

Maya looks at her in surprise. "More people are here to see me?"

She heads back down to the dining hall and sees Mom, Dad, and Tarun standing together in the far back corner.

Maya runs up to them and pulls them in for a big hug. "You're all here! I can't believe it!"

"Of course we're here," Tarun says, rolling his eyes in amusement. "Did you really think you could get rid of us?"

"My baby," Mom says as she takes in Maya's presence and lets out a sob.

Dad wraps Maya in another hug. "We would never have forgiven ourselves if something happened to you."

"I'm okay," Maya says. "Really, I am."

"We could never lose you. Ever," Dad whispers. His eyes are wet, too. This is the first time Maya has ever seen her father cry, and her chest tightens.

"I know. And I'm so sorry for such a scare, but I promise I'm better. And I'm on a good path now." She pauses as a thought crosses her mind. "Wait—who found me? Was it one of you? No one's told me yet how I escaped or ended up in the hospital."

The three of them share a look, none of them speaking, until Tarun says, "We did tell you, when we first saw you. You must have forgotten because there was so much going on… Remember that day at the motel when we all walked to Dunkin' Donuts?"

Maya tentatively nods in confusion.

"A couple days before you were found, Bharat Uncle, Mom and Dad's friend who works there, heard some voices across the street when he was clocking out of work. He normally doesn't see anyone in the empty lot. The only thing there is a warehouse that used to belong to some company, but they relocated, and it's been vacant ever since. So when he saw two young women going into the building, he was surprised, but didn't really think anything of it."

Maya gives him a puzzled look. "I was across the street from that Dunkin' Donuts? I was right near the motel?" Some of it slowly starts to come back to her. The Uber ride and the streets that looked familiar. Liz saying something about their friendship being "fate" because of how close the motel was to her private lab.

It *was* fate. Just not in the way Liz thought it was.

"A couple days later, we visited the Dunkin' Donuts to ask him to put up missing-person flyers and to let us know if he saw or heard anything suspicious. And to pass the word along. We had to take matters into our own hands since the police weren't taking any of this seriously," Mom said with a scoff. "He racked his brain afterward to see if he could provide any valuable information, and that's when the wheels slowly started turning. He called us the next day and told us what he saw in the empty lot a few days before. We thought it might be a long shot, but we couldn't rule it out. So we notified the police right away." Mom's voice shakes as she breaks out into another sob.

"We have a lot of blessings to count," Dad continues. "These people—our *friends*—who have known us for years. Who would have thought that all those trips to Dunkin' over the years would one day be the thing that saved you and brought you home to us? We remember during times like these why community is so important."

"It really is," Maya says. "I'm so sorry you all went through that."

When her parents and brother continue to stare at her in silence, she says, "Now can we please talk about *anything* else?"

They all laugh in unison and sit down at a table, then spend the next hour catching up on everything from Shaan to the motel to Tarun's job to the food on the unit.

But then Mom's expression changes as she takes in their surroundings. "What could I have done differently?" she says. "To keep this from happening?"

"Nothing," Maya says, grabbing her hand. "There's nothing you or anyone could have done. I had to figure this out for myself."

Ever since she left the emergency room, Maya's wondered if, in some way, she needed to go through all of this to change her ways. She's spent her entire life buried in work, self-doubt, and stress. Maybe this was the only way to finally face herself. She's sure she would have reached a breaking point eventually, and the pills just expedited the process. *You have to break down to break through*, she remembers some life coach preaching in an interview. She rolled her eyes the first time she heard the words, but now she sees so much truth in that.

"You're the toughest person I know," Tarun says.

Maya smiles at him. Her incredible younger brother who gets her in ways nobody else ever could.

"How were you the first person in the emergency room anyway?" Maya asks him. Alaina had told her so earlier. "It took Dev over an hour to get to Jersey from the city."

Tarun fidgets uncomfortably in his seat. "I was already in Jersey."

Mom's ears perk up. "What? Why? You're never in Jersey."

"I wanted to wait until we were all together to share that..." Tarun does a light drumroll on the table. "I've been meeting with the Lyons and some other motel owners who are looking to expand their portfolios. And it's taken a lot of convincing, and soul-searching on their part, but I got them to pull out of the agreement, and I found a better buyer for both motels. A *much* better buyer, who wants both motels so they can build a larger complex. The value of the real estate is so much higher than the motel itself so it's enough money for Mom and Dad to live comfortably for a long, long time."

Maya's jaw drops. "Tarun, that's amazing!" She jumps up from her seat to hug him tightly.

He smiles. "I know I've been in my own world for...my entire life? But I knew I could do something here. This has been a couple weeks in the making, but I wanted to get all the details ironed out before I shared the news."

Before Maya can think of a response, he turns to look at her. "It shouldn't always be on you to take care of Mom and Dad. I know it may have felt that way, but that doesn't mean it's true."

"So, what you're saying is that you three don't need me anymore." Maya laughs.

"No. We just need you to not go AWOL again." Tarun smirks. "Sorry, too soon?"

Maya bursts out laughing. "Not soon enough. It's refreshing to be able to laugh about it."

Mom claps her hands. "And once you've settled the motel deal, you'll have more time to find a girlfriend!"

Maya and Tarun look at each other in amusement. The woman can't help herself.

"The point is, you two—" Tarun motions between Mom and Dad "—can finally take a break."

Tears pool in the corners of Mom's eyes. "I don't even know what to say." Mom glances at Dad, and something passes between them. Is it respect? Acceptance? Forgiveness?

Now Maya's crying. Each of them is. Dad's eyes are red as he puts a hand on Tarun's shoulder. "Beta."

"I'm not sure what we did to deserve this," Mom says. "And both of you wonderful children."

Dad smiles at Mom, nodding in agreement. "Me neither."

"Wait, but what does this mean for both of you? Where are you going to go?" Maya asks.

Mom grabs her hand. "I was going to stay nearby with Sejal Auntie for a bit before finding my own place but... I have news, too."

Maya and Tarun share a confused look.

"I may have signed up for some journalism classes..." Mom's eyes light up.

Maya gasps. "You did? I thought you said I was being too overbearing!"

"Oh yes, you were." Mom laughs, her face glowing. "But you were also right. And after everything that's just happened, how scared I was to lose you, I don't want to take my life for granted anymore. I want to keep learning and finally do something that's just for me."

"That's amazing, Mom. I'm so proud of you," Maya says, her eyes welling up again.

She used to wonder what it would be like to have a more "traditional" mother, one who wanted to wear matching outfits with her, take her to the movies, spend hours chatting with her about boys. The therapist she's been seeing on the unit even asked if Maya has been trying to compensate for her mother's shortcomings by setting impossible standards for herself as Shaan's mother.

But she sees now that her mother gave her opportunity. And maybe Maya even sensed that from a young age, which is why she pushed herself to always get good grades, to land a respectable career, to secure a happy marriage. Anything to help pay back what Mom gave up for her and Tarun.

At the end of the day, it was Mom who first taught her to demand more for herself. To honor her anger and use that fire inside of her to prove them all wrong.

"And I'm going to finally take that long trip to India to see my family," Dad announces.

"That's great, Dad!" Tarun says, Maya enthusiastically nodding in agreement.

"So, that's it, then?" Maya's eyes flit between Mom and Dad.

Mom smirks at her and they share a knowing look. "You have to understand that we were arranged to get married when we were nineteen years old. We were so young, practically strangers when we got married!" She turns to Dad for confirmation, and he says, "Your mother's right. We were worried what people would think if we didn't go through with the marriage, or if we one day separated. But now we know this is the right decision for us."

Her parents' marriage is over. Then again, maybe it was years ago.

All her life, Maya hated endings. But maybe some marriages are at their most beautiful when they come to an end. Maybe, when a couple finally accepts that their relationship has run its course, there's an opportunity to crack through the ossified resentment and anger that's been trapped within their marriage. And set it free.

Dad's voice softens when he says, "There are a lot of things we did that we're not proud of. But we must have done something right along the way to have you two."

When Maya was younger, all she wanted was for her parents to admit their faults. To confess that they were too strict or that they held contradictory expectations for their two children. But as she's met with her parents' vulnerability, her mindset shifts and she says, "You did everything you could with the lot you were given. It's okay."

Because it is. She understands now that it's okay to be angry at them for the things they didn't do. It's okay to mourn the childhood she never had and also know her parents did their best.

Mom runs her fingers through Maya's hair, kisses her forehead, and says a quick prayer in Sanskrit under her breath. Maybe it's a prayer for a healthy fresh start.

For new beginnings.

35

THE CONFERENCE ROOM IS FULL. SOME people are standing at the door, Blue Bottle coffees in hand, while others indulge in seconds from the bagel platter at the table's center.

She's hit with a wave of anxiety. The last time Maya sat in this very chair, everything went to complete and utter shit.

But she has to face reality. The pills kept her in a state of denial, a state that felt euphoric in the short-term but proved detrimental in the long-term. She needs to take the broken fragments from the past few months and patch them into something new.

"I know we've got a lot of work to do," Maya announces. "And I know there's a long road ahead. But we will get there."

She pulls up the notes she's typed out, but she knows she won't need them. She has the whole thing memorized. Maya had reviewed them every morning and every evening while in rehab. She found the routine shockingly grounding.

"The past couple weeks have given me the time and space to reflect on Medini and to look inward. As I move forward, I have to be certain that I'm upholding and modeling the values that's made this company so special and unique from its inception. I need to practice what I preach if I want to make the culture here transparent and communicative. So, here goes.

"I had a crisis that landed me in the hospital. When I'm ready to do so, I'll release an official statement to the press, but I wanted you to hear it from me first. Yes, I'm telling you this for context on why I've been MIA the past month, but also because it's important for me to explain how I got to such a low point in the first place. It all started with a deep-seated belief that I have to manage everything on my own. But I was wrong. And I'm really sorry that this has all led to so much stress for all of you. I'm sorry for how I handled the layoffs and for how abrupt they were. I'm sorry for pushing us into more stores and operating on my own terms instead of discussing as a team first.

"I started Medini because I wanted to create and distribute products I wish I had growing up. And in the span of just a few years, my dreams became a reality as we widened Medini's impact and team size. Somewhere along the way, though, while we were scaling, I lost sight of how to manage our growth and all of the challenges that come with it. I made decisions because of how they looked, not because they were the best moves for the company.

"To that end, you should all be aware of some key changes. Tiffany is being promoted to a new role where she will spend a hundred percent of her time on people operations, an area that aligns with her passion and experience, instead of primarily supporting me. And we're in the process of onboarding new members to our team. I know this is a lot to take in, so I've broken it all down here."

Maya shares her laptop screen with the projector behind her. "I've found a fantastic executive coach, Kyra Mendoza, to work with me individually and with all of us as a team. The first thing Kyra and I realized was that we needed to make some structural changes sooner rather than later based on themes we saw in existing feedback. First off, we're moving to a flex workplace. You can do up to two days a week from home if you want. Second, for those coming back from parental leave, you'll have protected time for pumping. If you feel comfortable doing so, feel free to even put 'pumping,' or whatever it is you're doing, as your Slack status. And for non-birthing parents, we're increasing leave time."

The women in the room laugh and share enthusiastic looks. During group therapy, Maya was hit with the realization that she was trying to get Medini to fit a business model created by men. But what if she created her own and made space for a different kind of workplace? One where women didn't have to make themselves smaller to get ahead?

"We are also going to cut our paid marketing spend to both conserve cash and slow down website orders until we feel we have a better handle on things. Travis will be assigning his board seat to Angelica Rodriguez, another partner at his fund with more extensive retail experience. Josh will officially be named interim CEO until my return in four weeks. He and Brad will be managing all communication with potential investors, including Tribeca One, as we get ready for our next funding round."

Maya thinks back to the message she sent to Mark when she left the hospital:

I've appreciated being connected over these last weeks but think that going forward, it'll be best for you and Josh to directly communicate.

Mark replied in seconds: I understand and wish you the best, Maya.

Some of her employees fidget uncomfortably as they absorb everything she's saying. A lot of them look shocked by all of this. She feels a heavy pang of guilt. How could she have made such a mess of things?

Acknowledge what you're feeling instead of judging it. Let it sit in your body instead of trying to push it away. Kaitlin's words from group therapy circle around in her mind.

She takes a deep breath and pauses for comments or questions. Tiffany tells Maya she's grateful for her vulnerability. Brad says he's happy with the ad budget cut.

Surprisingly, nobody looks like they want to rip her to shreds.

Maya was so used to always wearing a protective suit of armor that she lost sight of how relying on and trusting others is so often the right call. It's made her a better representative for Medini, a better wife, a better daughter, a better mother. A better Maya altogether.

She pulls up her calendar as her team breaks off in side conversations, checking to confirm she moved her last meeting of the day to tomorrow before retreating to her office. She's expecting an important call.

A half hour later, her phone rings.

"Is this Maya Patel?" a familiar voice asks.

"Officer Richardson? Yes, it's me." Maya's palms start to sweat. "Do you have an update?"

"I'm afraid not. We've paid numerous visits to the warehouse you've described, and nothing. When you were found, you were lying on the floor of an empty room."

Maya's stomach drops. "But that's impossible. Did you check all the rooms?"

"Yes, we have done a thorough and comprehensive search of the entire building." He's silent for a moment before saying, "You've been through a lot. Maybe you thought you saw—"

"No! I know what I saw. She—Liz Anderson—was there. Liz did this to me. We were both there, and so was the lab, with all her beakers and diagrams. Can't you just take her in for questioning?"

"Unfortunately, Ms. Patel, we cannot do that without a reasonable cause. There is currently no evidence of Liz Anderson's involvement. We've tried to send out a request for interview but have not heard back. And if she refuses, she's within her rights to do so."

Maya paces around her office, her head spinning. How could Liz have gotten rid of all the equipment so quickly? And where the fuck did she go?

"But...but she was there. I'm telling you."

She's again met with silence.

"The case is still ongoing, and we'll let you know if we find anything," Officer Richardson finally says.

"Okay," Maya says, but her voice comes out weak, her resolve fading.

If there's one thing about Liz, it's that she sure knows how to cover her tracks.

36

"MAYA, I'M READING SOMETHING ON your face. Do you want to share what you're thinking?" Dr. Li turns toward her.

The office walls are painted a comforting sky blue, with plants of varying sizes arranged all throughout the room. The coffee table between them and Dr. Li has two potted succulents, a scented candle, a box of tissues, and one of those mini sandboxes that she would love to play with right about now. The machine behind the therapist's chair emits the soothing sound of crashing waves.

"It's refreshing to hear Dev talk this much," Maya finally says.

"And why is that?" Dr. Li leans back in her scalloped tan egg chair. They're all the rage these days.

"When we argue, he usually shuts down. But to be fair, I

can be so reactive that maybe he doesn't have the chance to speak up."

"Is that true, Dev?" Dr. Li asks.

When he nods, she says, "Tell me, Dev, what was your parents' marriage like?"

"Fine." Dev shrugs. "Fine *enough.* My parents didn't fight much, at least not out loud. But they've always cared about how things looked to outsiders, which usually meant pretending nothing was wrong."

The therapist turns back toward Maya. "And Maya, you have mentioned that your parents argued a lot growing up and you were often tasked with mediating those arguments."

Maya sits up straight, rearranging her seated position on the couch. "I went back and forth between wanting them to stop fighting and wanting them to get a divorce." She pauses to look at Dev. "But our marriage is nothing like theirs."

"I see." Dr. Li pauses, choosing her words carefully. "I'm wondering more about your conflict management style in marital arguments, and if there are any parallels with what you witnessed growing up."

Maya can't believe that she's only realizing this now at age thirty-three. She didn't connect the dots between her parents' fighting and her own tendency to yell and retreat in fights with Dev.

"Becoming a parent can resurface a lot of memories and internalized practices from how you were parented," Dr. Li suggests. "And managing conflict in perhaps a healthier way can feel scary because it's so different from what you're used to."

Dr. Li pauses again, allowing her words to sink in. "Dev, I'm curious, what were your thoughts about fatherhood before your son was born?"

Dev looks down at the white shag rug. "I knew I didn't want to be like *my* dad, that's for sure. He was always working. There were multiple monthlong stretches where he was away on business trips."

Dr. Li glances at her notes. "You mentioned during our intake that your job got busier before Shaan was born. Not only did that put more of the child care on Maya, but it also may have made you feel like you weren't living up to your own expectations as a father."

Dev sighs, burying his face in his hands. "I wasn't. I knew I was disappointing Maya and failing as a father and husband."

Maya turns to him. "I never thought that. Why didn't you tell me?"

"I wanted to. I tried." Dev shifts his gaze back down to the floor. "But you were so angry. And you shut me out."

She feels an intense burst of guilt and welcomes it. "I know," Maya says softly. "I'm really sorry."

He turns to face her. "I know you are. It's just hard when it feels like it's never enough for you."

Dr. Li steps in and says, "Maya, is it possible you were angry with Dev because you felt he had it easier than you? Maybe even before having Shaan? You mentioned the unfair social pressures that only women face as parents. And you also mentioned Dev comes from a more privileged upbringing than your own."

Maya nods. "I feel like he sometimes just doesn't get it."

"And Dev, could you be open to the possibility that there may be some parts of Maya's life that you may need to approach with curiosity and understanding? The parts that make her feel 'othered'?"

He responds by scrunching his shoulders to his ears and letting them fall.

"Parenting can be incredibly difficult, especially that first year," Dr. Li continues. "There's a lot of change in your daily routines, your marriage, your social lives. Maya, I'm getting the sense you may have felt lonely after becoming a mother. Is there truth to that?"

Of course there is. That's one of the reasons she clung to Liz and her "magic" pills like a life raft. Why she was so desperate for anything to ease the burden, the guilt, the isolation.

She considers how best to answer that question.

"When I had our son, I wasn't the least bit prepared for how much it would affect me. I love him so much. Really, I do. But I didn't anticipate it'd be so hard to take care of him and be my own person at the same time."

Dr. Li nods sympathetically, and Maya wonders if she's a mother.

"How long have you felt like this?"

Maya sighs. "Honestly...since the beginning. I had a rough pregnancy and vomited almost every day until giving birth." She thinks back to the consecutive months she had to keep a plastic Duane Reade bag on hand at all times. "I thought I'd feel better once I had him. And I did, in many different ways. But I also felt other things I didn't expect, like a debilitating fear something bad would happen to him on my watch." Maya wipes tears from her eyes. "I love him *so* much," she reiterates. "And frankly, that scared the shit out of me."

"That must have been difficult. Not to mention, there is certainly an expectation for new mothers to be grateful and happy every second of the day. There's not much space given to embrace the full spectrum of emotions that often come with such a big life transition. And if you are someone who's a perfectionist, it can be quite difficult to deal with the unpredictable changes and chaos of motherhood." Dr. Li pauses and scans her notes. "Maya, what comes to mind when you think of your own mother?"

"My mom was always working. Always. I never saw her do anything just for herself. I never saw her set boundaries or ask anyone for extra help. Or God forbid, just sit and relax." Maya leans back into the soft cushions. "So I guess when I think of her, I think of hard work and sacrifice. Exhaustion."

"And your father?" Dr. Li prompts.

"He was always working, too. Neither of them ever took vacations. He learned all these new skill sets to run the motel—fixing toilets, hanging signs, accounting—so we could save on money. I can still vividly picture him with that giant bag of tools." She laughs at the memory.

Dr. Li gives her a soft smile. "You've also mentioned your younger brother in session. With how much your parents were working, would you say you took on a parental role for your brother?"

Maya nods. "When Tarun was born, I didn't leave his side. I sang him his favorite lullabies before bed, could tell apart his hungry cries from his tired ones, watched *The Lion King* with him on repeat until he memorized every line." She pauses, her mind searching. "I screamed at the kids who bullied him at school, covered his ears when our parents fought. I gave him the dollar bills relatives gave me on my birthday so he could buy an extra treat at Dunkin' Donuts." She laughs. "We've always been close."

"That sounds like a lot of responsibility to take on as a little girl," Dr. Li notes.

"Yeah, but I loved it," Maya says. "I took my role very seriously and it gave me a sense of purpose."

"It sounds like taking care of your brother, and your family in general, was important to you from a young age. Sometimes, the things that defined us back then can morph into how we measure our self-worth and capabilities as adults. Does any of this resonate?" Dr. Li asks.

Maya's stomach drops. But she finally feels ready to talk about it, so she takes a deep breath in. "There was an incident…

when Tarun was a baby. Sometimes, when my parents were really busy with work, they'd asked a distant family friend—a friend of a friend's grandmother—to come babysit us. One day, when she was over, I really wanted to read by the pool. Usually, whenever she was there, I remained glued to Tarun's side. I didn't trust anyone else with him. But that day I made an exception. When I came back inside an hour later, the sitter had fallen asleep while feeding my brother and..." Maya squeezes her eyes shut. She can vividly picture Tarun's tiny body smothered by an old, embroidered blanket from India. The stillness of his face. The thump of her feet against the thin carpet, then wood, as she screamed for her parents.

She feels Dev's eyes on her and she's sure he's wondering why she never told him this story before. "He ended up being okay, but he almost wasn't," Maya says, rubbing at her temples. "I was only thinking about myself that day and he could have..." She breaks into a sob.

"I'm so sorry you went through that, Maya. That must have been terrifying. But you were just a child," Dr. Li says gently.

You were just a child.

"What I'm gathering is that you were given a lot of responsibility as a child," Dr. Li continues. "Which could lead to your role as 'caretaker' in many different facets of life, not just in relation to your brother."

Maya nods. "That's true. I'm constantly keeping tabs on everything and *everyone.* To always make sure they're okay."

"Do you think it's possible that..." Dr. Li hesitates for a second. "Checking in with your loved ones has given you a false comfort or semblance of control? When we first spoke on the phone, you mentioned a habit of repeatedly checking your son's feeding log or checking the baby monitor to make sure he's breathing. Or losing sleep because you were so worried about him, and how resistant you were in leaving him under anyone else's care. I'm wondering if your childhood experiences have bubbled up to the present day, now that you're a mother, and if they have perhaps manifested into an intense anxiety."

Dr. Li pauses for Maya to fill the space, and when she doesn't, she adds, "Which would make sense. Because if you took full responsibility for everything pertaining to your son, you could feel some sense of agency or control over the things that happened to him. But do you think this could also result in self-blame for things that weren't your fault, or perhaps out of your control?"

Maya chews on her lip. "Maybe…"

It's true that she took full ownership for Shaan's incremental weight loss and all his trouble with feeding and sleeping. But isn't that just what mothers do? They hold blame and they nurse it. Her own mother certainly did. Growing up, if Maya talked back to a relative or if Tarun threw a tantrum at the temple, people would only ask Mom if she raised her children right, not Dad.

Dr. Li leans forward and says something Maya never could have anticipated. "You had a lot of risk factors for postpartum depression and anxiety."

Her breath catches in her throat.

"I know that might be a lot to hear right now," Dr. Li quickly adds when she's met with Maya's silence. "Perhaps you and I could meet separately, in addition to these joint sessions? I'd like the chance to continue this conversation one-on-one. Then we could come up with a plan for next steps together."

Maya nods and the session ends. She and Dev confirm they'll be back next week at the same time.

As they leave Dr. Li's office building, a memory pops up on her phone. It's a selfie of her and Dev during her first prenatal appointment. Maya's hair is pulled back in a low ponytail, the paper-thin gown stretched across her body. Dev's nose is buried into her hair.

The woman in that picture had no idea what was in store for her.

If she could send a message back to her, she'd say, *Some days, maybe even weeks, you'll feel like you're failing at everything. You'll feel lots of contradictory emotions your first couple months postpartum. Emotions about your marriage, your parents, your friends, your newborn. But you'll get through this.*

And you will be more whole because of it.

She walks alongside Dev in the direction of downtown, toward home.

"I'm sorry, honey," Dev says later that day, when they're lying next to each other in bed. "For everything."

"No, I'm sorry." Maya inhales his natural woodsy scent as he shifts toward her. She covers them with their thick down comforter, relishing this intimate moment with her husband. A eucalyptus-scented candle flickers on his nightstand.

They used to spend Shaan's naptime working or doing chores or checking things off their individual to-do lists. But they've started using it as time for just them two.

"I should have been there for you more." Dev strokes her hair, then the back of her neck.

"You tried," she says. "I pushed you away."

"Sometimes—okay, no, a lot of times—you do that." Dev laughs lightheartedly, then his face turns serious. "What made you push me away after we had him? When did it start?"

He has a far-off look in his eyes, and Maya can tell he's trying to pinpoint the exact moment things went south between them. But is it ever one moment? Or is it the accumulation of daily frustrations that threaten to erode a marriage?

Maya sighs. "If I'm being honest, it started pretty early on.

Even those first weeks after he was born, I was resentful that you still got to live your life, go to work, even *look* the same," she says, gesturing to his unchanged body.

She can see it so clearly now when she plays it all back. She was drowning. Day by day, she was slipping further and further below the surface. Every now and then, she was able to come up for air, thanks to Shaan's gummy smile, or five consecutive hours of sleep, or the weight and warmth of Dev's hand on hers. But it was always just a matter of time before something grabbed her ankles and pulled her back down again.

"Trust me, it wasn't all great." Dev stares at their white ceiling. "I didn't want to be this type of guy. When we decided to have a family, I was so sure I'd be different. *Involved.* Obviously, I know now it wasn't that simple." He fluffs his pillow and props it against their gray fabric headboard. "But there were so many times I felt like a useless dad."

He pauses before continuing. "And Shaan so clearly prefers you all the time, anyway. I mean, I get it because I've missed out on so much quality time with him because of work. I love seeing you with him, but sometimes I wish he and I had that same bond."

Maya absorbs his words, trying to think of the right response, but then Dev's voice shifts in tone. "I really thought I was turning into my dad."

She sits up. "You weren't. You never will. You're already a completely different father than he was."

The two of them didn't bring just *themselves* to parenting. They brought their own parents, too, along with the people their parents never were. They brought childhood memories they cherished and some they regretted. They brought their hopes and aspirations, but also their insecurities, their fears.

"I didn't know you felt that way," Maya says.

"I didn't either, until shit really hit the fan." Dev sighs. "I don't know, something about being alone with Shaan for that long *and* being scared out of my mind about where you were made me realize how I've fallen short. I really didn't think I'd be able to take care of him on my own, without you."

Maya sinks in closer to him, caressing his face. "Nobody would have known what to do if they were thrown into that situation. I'm sorry I put you there in the first place." The guilt is back and stronger than ever. It cascades through her veins, feeding every part of her body. She feels it all.

For so long, she was worried about being an unloving mother. But she misunderstood maternal love. Love is changing Shaan's diaper when she's weary-eyed. Love is rocking him back and forth during his screaming fits. Love is reading the same book about a baby gorilla, over and over again, just to see her baby smile.

"No, honey." Dev turns toward her, reaching for her hand. "I'm trying to say you're an amazing mother. Even if you don't always think so. Our baby loves you so much. *I* love you so much. Your presence makes us both feel so safe and secure. You have to know that."

Maya feels the pressure of tears building behind her eyes. "You have no idea what it means for me to hear that from you."

"It's true. And you know, you don't always have to take care of everyone. You can let us take care of you, too."

Maya laughs. "I guess I have a little bit of a hard time letting go."

"You? No, never." Dev jabs her with his elbow. There's a brightness in his eyes she hasn't seen in weeks.

She stretches her limbs. "I can't believe he's sleeping for seven-hour stretches at night. I feel like a new woman."

Dev wraps his arms around her. "I'm so glad you kept pushing to see the pediatric GI doctor."

When Maya moved from detox to rehab, the absence of

guilt pills in her system cued her into something she had suppressed for months, something she didn't even think she had. Self-trust. She'd been carrying a nagging sense for months that there was something going on with Shaan that they were missing. When she was discharged and the inkling didn't go away, she called Dr. Karp and asked for a referral. After one appointment with NYU's pediatric gastroenterology department and three weeks of reflux medication, Shaan was crying less and sleeping more. He was gaining weight at a steady pace.

"I hate that he was struggling for so long," she whispers.

"But you figured it out and now he isn't," Dev reassures her. "You trusted yourself."

Maya nods. *"Finally."*

"And I should have trusted you," he continues. "I know this doesn't make up for paternity leave but…"

"But what?"

Dev props himself on one elbow. "I'm going to leave Bainbridge. I've already given notice. I told them I can't work in a place that won't honor what it promised. And I've already got three interviews lined up at different companies for next week. But I also want to take time in between for us… Maybe this could somewhat make up for the leave I *should* have taken."

Maya's in shock, and a wave of gratitude washes over her. "You're serious? But…are you sure?"

Dev nods. "I don't want to be an absentee dad. I want to know Shaan and I want to be an active part of our family. I want to help out."

"I don't even know what to say."

"You don't have to say anything." He wraps her in his arms. "I love you, honey."

"I love you, too." Maya kisses him, tasting orange and hot sauce. Their takeout nights are back in business.

Dev pushes his tongue between her lips, and she climbs on

top of him after slipping off her red underwear. He keeps his gaze on hers as he pushes into her. She surrenders to the rhythm of her hips gliding against him, of his hands squeezing hers.

Afterward, they lie side by side, limbs intertwined.

"That was…wow," Dev says, still panting.

Maya traces his collarbones and chest. "Yes, it was."

For so long, she's feared their relationship changing, but she sees now that it's only evolving. It's possible to have different marriages with the same person.

Dev runs his hands up and down Maya's back and she leans into his touch, the stillness of the moment.

Just when her eyes start to flutter, she hears a cry from the baby monitor.

They share a knowing look and pull themselves out from under the covers.

An hour later, Shaan is still tucked into her arms.

"You know you can put him down now," Dev says, smiling as he leans against the doorway to Shaan's room.

Maya nods. "I know…"

She takes in her son's long eyelashes, his lips parting into a smile.

So this is how it can really feel, she thinks. She can just be here, in this moment, without guilt or anxiety or fear suffocating her. She can know that the overwhelming emotions are okay, not a sign that she's doing anything wrong.

She lifts Shaan up. "Hi, buddy!"

He curls his tiny legs upward and emits a high-pitched laugh, one that makes her laugh back.

"I'm so lucky to be your mom," she whispers. "You know that, right?"

Shaan smiles again. Sometimes she swears he can understand her.

"Okay, mister." Dev comes into the room. "I know you love your mom, but I need some time with her, too."

"Let's put him on his play mat and try to scarf down some dinner before bathtime," Maya suggests. She keeps Shaan against her.

Dev walks beside her as they prepare to take on the rest of the day.

Together.

NEW YORK TIMES

Women Rise, Woman Falls

By Vidya Bloom
Published November 14, 2019, 5:00 PM EDT

Elizabeth Anderson had no regrets.

Or so it seemed.

Anderson proudly boasted her career success in building two companies centered on women's wellness. And she always surrounded herself with impressive people—albeit those who may not have had much expertise in her company's products or start-ups in general. The board included Jack Clear, a retired three-star army general, and Toby Rosen, the founder of an internet gambling company.

But power only goes so far.

Last month, news broke that Women Rise, Anderson's popular brand of female supplements, has been shut down—one of two start-ups founded by Anderson that have now been dissolved—after an anonymous tip to the New York Times regarding Anderson's unethical business practices and problematic leadership. When this news broke, a flood of people on social media spoke out about their negative experiences with Anderson, both in professional and private settings. A subsequent company investigation confirmed the allegations, and Women Rise was soon dissolved. In the aftermath of the scandal, many have publicly speculated on Liz Anderson's psychological pathology; in fact, if you search *Liz Anderson* online, you'll likely find her name next to words like *psychopath*, *sociopath*, or *narcissist*.

Now, I'm not a mental health provider, so I will refrain from commenting on any of these rumored diagnoses.

But I am a writer, so what I can do is share a cautionary tale of an ingenious person who lacked—lacks—any and all accountability. (Ever since the news of the shutdown broke, Anderson has gone completely off the grid, and no news outlets have been able to reach her for a statement.)

The following report draws from over fifty interviews with Anderson's current and former friends, colleagues, and associates. Most participants have used their real names; others asked to remain anonymous at the risk of offending the many people in the start-up space who continue to stand by Anderson.

Read on to find out how Liz Anderson went from being a woman who "had it all" to a woman who *lost* it all.

Epilogue

THREE MONTHS LATER

"Let's give a warm welcome to Maya Patel, everyone!" Taylor Rutherford motions to Maya, then to the audience. Alaina, Ryan, Dev, Mom, Dad, and Tarun are sitting in the front row, Shaan cradled in Dev's arms.

Maya keeps her smile intact as a flurry of nerves infiltrates her body. The Spanx she shimmied into hours earlier are squeezing her stomach. Her body may never go back to its pre-pregnancy state, and so be it. Who says it has to?

"It's so great to see you again." Taylor covertly glances at her sky-blue cue cards.

"It's great to be back," Maya says.

"A lot has happened since you were here last time." She gives her an empathetic look. "Let's start with Medini. You released a statement in *Tech Buzz* saying you did, and I quote, 'a company transformation.' Can you tell us a bit more about that?"

In her periphery, Maya catches the steady *blink, blink, blink* of the flashing camera. She's suddenly hyperaware of the sound of her own breath and the heat of the lights on her.

"So much has happened since I was last on this set," Maya says. "Medini raised an incredible funding round. And we're now set to be in half of all Whole Foods stores nationwide by the end of this year!"

She pauses and the audience erupts in cheers and applause.

"And while I'm excited about our wins, I think I've learned the most during our struggles. I've always been aware of the barriers restricting women—especially women of color—not only within my own company and industry, but in the world at large. I couldn't afford to fail because I associated failure with disappointment. The disappointment of everyone who believed in me from the start, including myself.

"I was trying to fit into a workplace structure created by people much different than me. A structure built for men who live to work, and who expect others to do the same. If I want things to be different, I have to set an example. And that includes prioritizing the culture of my company from the inside, instead of just focusing on how it looks on the outside. That starts with the onboarding process and ensuring my employees not only come from a variety of different backgrounds, but that they feel empowered to bring their unique skill sets and experiences to the company. I'm thrilled to say that Medini's team and executive board are now representative of the type of world we—as a company—want to see and be a part of."

Taylor nods, her expression slightly changing, and Maya knows what's coming next. "With your social media platform and frequent press features, many of your fans and followers felt they were on this journey with you. As we—and you—of course know, one of those people was Liz Anderson, someone you were closely connected with for a time. Vidya Bloom recently published an investigative report about Women Rise, called

'Women Rise, Woman Falls,' alleging that the company—and founder—has been carrying out unethical practices for years in the wake of Anderson's second company shutdown. I imagine that in the upcoming months, we'll learn more and more about the dark side of this acclaimed female founder and 'momfluencer.' What are you able to tell us *today*?"

Maya's stomach tightens even though she's prepared for this exact question all week. "I can say this: as founders—specifically female founders—we often feel pressure from every direction to put the needs of our companies first. But it's also our duty as leaders to make sure we aren't inflicting harm, whether it be on our employees or on our consumers. I had to make sure the truth came out in a way that ensured others wouldn't be harmed by Women Rise's practices. I also want to say female founders aren't a monolith, and I hope the actions of one don't reflect on an entire group."

"I see." There's the slightest shift in Taylor's blue eyes, and Maya braces herself for whatever she says next. "I did want to reserve some time at the end here to talk about what happened a few months ago. Back when you went missing."

Maya takes a deep breath and opens her mouth to respond when Taylor abruptly clears her throat. "What did you learn from that time?" she adds.

In journalistic terms, this kind of question would be considered a 'softball,' but to Maya, it's a pure act of kindness.

She gives Taylor a grateful smile. "I learned a lot. I know I've been one to share all of Medini's wins, as well as my own, online. But I've also failed a lot. As the company face and founder, I felt like Medini was an extension of me, and it was where I derived most of my self-worth. Because of this, I lacked boundaries and any semblance of a work-life balance. And the truth is, there was so much—*too* much—going on in my work and personal life leading up to my disappearance. I realized that effecting real change as a leader starts with confronting yourself. And sometimes to rebuild means to dismantle or challenge your internalized biases and beliefs."

Despite the number of times she's rehearsed this response, she still feels submerged in a wave of guilt. It'll take a long time for her to be able to look back on that time and not hate herself. The guilt never stands alone. It's thickened with unworthiness and a failed sense of duty. Among many other things.

But at least she can feel it all now. The guilt, the joy, the regret, the overwhelm, the gratitude. She could never move forward by repressing—or erasing—any of it.

"And look how you've rebuilt!" Taylor exclaims, gesturing to Maya. "I'm sure there's a lot you'll carry forward from this entire experience."

"Definitely. I've begun weekly therapy for postpartum depression and anxiety, and only wish I could have started sooner. I'm also working with an executive coach. I'm still figuring a lot out," she admits.

In her periphery, audience members are nodding.

"Aren't we all?" Taylor says.

"A hundred percent. Mothers, caregivers, we all deserve love and support. It's unfair for any one individual to blame themselves for the shortcomings of entire social systems. We need change on multiple levels for things to truly evolve. The more we can normalize that, the less guilt women will feel." She pauses, then adds, "I won't pretend me sitting here today and saying this all on air will cause some kind of systemic social shift. But if any person watching this feels a little less alone, that will be something."

Though she may never get proper justice for herself, Anita, and the countless other women Liz has targeted for her own gain, Maya can do everything in her power to make women and parents worldwide feel less alone in their struggles. So they never feel like they need some pill or fast-acting "cure" to save them from their guilt.

"Speaking of which..." Taylor smirks. "I believe you have some news to share?"

The giant screen behind them reads *PARENTS IN TECH.* Even though Maya's seen the logo dozens of times, she still can't believe the page is live. Or real. Just three weeks ago, she and Tiffany were brainstorming names for the initiative. And now, here it is on national television.

Maya smiles back. "The past few months, I've been thinking of ways I could help the women who saw themselves in my story and recent journey. To this end, I've joined forces with an incredible group of VCs, founders, and leaders—all parents themselves—to launch an organization geared toward caregivers in the tech industry. It's a place working parents can visit for education and support on everything from workplace rights, to warning signs of discrimination, to parental leave, to resources for finding a therapist, and so on and so forth. Our goal is to help parents all over the world feel a sense of community, to not feel so alone in their struggles, and to hold coparents and workplaces accountable, because this burden shouldn't fall solely on birthing parents... Now, we *do* have an Instagram account," she says, and the audience laughs. "But I promise you won't find some idealized, aspirational standard of motherhood on there. We mainly provide resources and support for people who need them. I want all parents to feel they can be more present at home.

"My long-term goal is to implement more support for parents, not only in tech, but across all industries and in the world at large. To this day, society expects so much from women, without offering them the necessary support to meet such high expectations. Having a baby has reflected my power back to me in more ways than one. My capacity to open up, to get in touch with my emotions, to empathize with others. I want to create a supportive community for parents that empowers them to lean into all their potential, too."

Out of the corner of her eye, a man on the stage's periphery circles a finger, mouthing the word *Wrap.*

Right on cue, Taylor stands up. "Thinking big as always, Maya. We are so grateful for your being here and always love having you on. Maya Patel, everyone!"

She sits back in the plush orange chair and takes it all in. The audience members rising to their feet. Alaina's voice cheering, "That's my best friend!" Her parents clutching each other's hands in the front row. Tarun holding Shaan high in the air as Dev tries to divert their son's attention to the stage.

Her baby boy's big brown eyes lighting up when he sees his mom underneath the bright lights.

Maya doesn't need to remind herself to smile when her life looks like this.

She exits stage left and runs out from behind the stage to hug her friends and family.

"You've got everything?" Dev asks as he hoists the diaper bag on his shoulder.

"Yes," Maya says.

She does.

BBC LONDON

Breaking News: CEO of Canvas Gone Missing

Published May 31, 2020, 5:24 PM GMT

Layla Ahura, founder and CEO of the popular fitness app Canvas, has been reported as missing. Ahura was last seen at her office last week, where she allegedly told coworkers she was leaving early for an exclusive founders dinner at a popular Mediterranean restaurant in Covent Garden. The restaurant has no record of Ahura dining with them that night.

Police are encouraging anyone who has information to please contact the number below.

This is an ongoing investigation.

★ ★ ★ ★ ★

Acknowledgments

Thank you to the advocates and changemakers fighting for mothers and caregivers to be better supported and valued. I am forever grateful for all you do.

To Claire Friedman, the best agent an author could hope for. Thank you for changing my life with your brilliance and incredible vision.

Annie Chagnot, thank you for championing this book to publication and Nicole Luongo, for your enthusiasm from the very beginning. *The Guilt Pill* couldn't have found a better home than the phenomenal Park Row Books. Thank you to Erika Imranyi, Justine Sha, and Brianna Wodabeck! To Taryn Ortolan for your amazing insight. To Sarah Whittaker and Alex Niit for the stunning cover.

Samir, you encouraged me to start all over, write in a new genre, and keep fighting for this book every time I wanted to put it away. Thank you for providing the best tech sensitivity reads ever, watching show after show for research, analyzing plotlines after our kids' bedtimes, and discussing everything from invisible labor to postpartum mental health.

Our boys are the luckiest to have you as their dad.

Laura Dave, thank you for believing in this story from the beginning. Our chats about motherhood, writing, and life mean more than you'll ever know.

To the authors who have provided inspiration, support, and wisdom: Leah Konen, Andi Bartz, Kirthana Ramisetti, Julia Bartz, Stephanie Wrobel, Amy Scher, Sara DiVello, Sue Varma, Pooja Lakshmin, Sahaj Kohli, Roshani Chokshi, Emily Giffin, Allison Winn Scotch, Colleen Oakley, Kimmery Martin, Taylor Jenkins Reid, and so many others.

To Bansari Shah, for reading the earliest drafts of this and being the best hype woman a friend could ask for. To Sarita Subramaniam, for your friendship and feedback on Maya's story.

Tiffany Yates Martin, your editorial expertise is the reason I could shape Maya's journey in the best way possible.

To Sonya Malani Panchal, for your insight into the life of a founder. We are forever Scrumptious Wicks candle fans!

To my incredible family: Mom, Dad, Maansi, and Akshay. Thank you for being both the place where I can return to myself and also learn something new.

Motherhood has given me the courage to truly play with the idea of what-if. I started this novel when I was postpartum with my first son and turned in the final draft right after giving birth to my second son. To Sahil and Sanjay, thank you for making me a mother. You both teach and inspire me every day.